PATRIOT

Seth Sjostrom

wolfprintMedia

wolfprint, LLC
P.O. Box
801 Camas,
WA, 98607

This book is a work of fiction. Names, characters, places, and incidents are products of the author's imagination or are used fictitiously. Any resemblance to actual events or locales or persons living or dead is entirely coincidental.

For information, contact wolfprintMedia, LLC.

Trade Paperback

ISBN-13: 978-1-7350236-8-7

1. Chris Masters (Fictitious character)-Fiction. 2. Thriller- Fiction. 3. Patriot X Series-Fiction I. Title.

First wolfprintMedia edition 2021

For information regarding bulk purchases, please contact wolfprintMedia, LLC at wolfprint@hotmail.com.

United States of America

Acknowledgments

For every man or woman who has served our country in the U.S. military and their families who pine for their safe return after every mission.

For all who stand for the greatest country in the world, with all her flaws striving for peace, liberty, freedom and justice for *all.*

God bless the U.S.A.

for Hayden

PATRIOT

One

"Raider Six, this is Halo. We have a visual on the target, what is your ETA?" the voice crackled through Gunnery Sergeant Chris Masters' earpiece.

Looking through the spray churned by the rigid-hull infiltration boat as it screamed towards the Tunisian shoreline of Le Kram, Masters responded, "Two mikes."

"Solid copy, Raider Six. Update on your situation, we have three fast-moving vehicles heading towards the target location. They do not appear to be official Tunis vehicles," Lieutenant Colonel Scott Lippett reported. "We count at least twelve fighting-age males."

Masters sighed before hitting the transmit button on his radio, "What does that do for our timeline?"

"You'll have ten or fewer mikes to secure the ambassador and exfil before things get a lot hotter."

"Roger that, we'll execute most ricky-tick," Masters acknowledged.

His team knew what the look on his face meant. Their task just became more complicated. "Our window just tightened. Zalinsky, I need you to locate overwatch covering the hotel and the RIB for exfil."

"Copy that, Gunny," Lance Corporal Zalinsky nodded.

"Dobson, when we beach, I need you to hoof it to the south side of the hotel. Create chaos of your liking that will capture the target's attention while deterring new guests arriving to the party," Masters called.

The corporal patted his Milkor M32 grenade launcher in acknowledgment.

"Ramos, Grady…you're with me. Once Dobson delivers his message, we're in. Beeline to the second floor where the ambassador is reported to be held. Quick, in and out, all collapse back to exfil with the ambassador in our possession." Masters scanned his team. Not a single man blinked at their assignment.

The moment the rigid inflatable boat skimmed the first inch of sand, the team launched onto the beach and headed for their appointed positions.

Zalinsky had been scouting the beach for his sentry point for overwatch. Finding a neighboring hotel that looked over the inlet to the inner harbor, the mission location, as well as their RIB, he made a beeline for a side alley. Running alongside the building, he found an access door. Trying the handle and studying the lock, he wasted no time in angling his M4 over the lock and fired.

Swinging the door open, he scrambled up the steps, bypassing each floor of the hotel until he burst onto the roof. Having calculated his preferred angle from the vantage of the shore approach, Zalinksy launched himself prone and scoped his MK 13 lightweight sniper rifle. Starting with his gunnery sergeant, he followed a visual line to the target subject and then to the RIB awaiting their imminent exit. Satisfied with his position, he called, "Overwatch confirmed. Your path is clear, Gunny."

"Copy that," Masters acknowledged.

Dobson sprinted up the beach, finding a strategically, if not aesthetically comfortable spot between two large dumpsters on the street side alley of the target hotel. "Dobson in position, sir."

"Make it rain, Dobbs!" Masters ordered.

Sighting the stubby, six-shot revolver-style grenade launcher at a stand of palm trees on the east side street entrance of the hotel, Dobson squeezed the trigger. Firing two rounds, explosions rocked the area sending palm fronds spinning wildly in the air. Swinging the muzzle to the west side, he eyed the base of a tall statue. Dialing in his sight, he pulled the trigger twice letting lose another pair of incendiaries. “I hope that didn’t have any huge cultural significance,” he muttered as the statute fell.

Reloading the four spent chambers, he slunk into a watch position.

The moment Masters and his team heard the faintest “foomp” of the grenades leaving Dobson’s M32, they leapt over the concrete wall they were concealed behind and sprinted past the hotel pool. Using a tiki bar as a launching point, they scrambled up and launched themselves towards the second-floor balcony.

Without losing a step, Masters slammed the butt of his M12 Assault Rifle onto the feeble handle of the guest room patio door. In the same movement, he flung the door open and strode through. Stepping over the cacophony of luggage and strewn garments, he made his way to the hotel room door.

With a gentle tug, the gunnery sergeant put a cautious eye to the crack. A quick scan of the hallway looked clear. With a nod, Ramos and Grady stepped forward with their rifles at the ready. Masters swung the door wide as Ramos moved through and to the left while Grady stepped right. Masters split between the two and hastened down the hallway, following the muzzle of his weapon.

Pausing at an intersection, Masters pressed himself tight against the wall. Grady filled in close to the right while Ramos eyed their flank. Dobson’s effort had clearly taken hold as the end of the hallway was buzzing. Two guards called through a heavy door, trying to get a sitrep. Their distracted attention allowed for Masters and Grady to easily dispatch them both with their silenced M12 assault rifles.

Moving quick-step down the hallway with Ramos in tow, they leaned against either side of the banquet hall doors. Pressing between them, Ramos quickly adhered a rough circle of det-cord around the double handles. Rolling away from the near instantaneous blast, Ramos followed with a flashbang the moment the doors swayed open.

In an instant, all three Marines were inside the room, their eyes making split-second decisions down the sights of their assault rifles, determining foe from ally. Ramos and Grady worked the left and right halves of the room while Masters worked straight forward. Eyes swung in his direction, followed by gun muzzles. No-sighting the first two, he squared on a gunman who stood over another man who was on his knees. Recognizing the man on the floor as the ambassador, he didn't hesitate as the gunman's finger tensed on his trigger.

All at once, the chaos of gunfire ceased. Masters quickly took in the scene. The only ones left alive were his team and the ambassador. Eyeing a number of bodies on the ground untouched by the recent skirmish, Master's asked, "Your team?'

The ambassador nodded solemnly.

"Halo, this is Raider Six. We have the package," Masters transmitted.

"Good copy, Raider Six. How many for exfil?" Lt. Col. Lippett requested.

"One sir, just the primary."

After a brief pause, "Clear copy. Head to exfil, you are going to have activity on your six. The latest flyover has unknowns east and west of your location making their way to the beach."

"We are en route," Masters confirmed. Turning to his team, he commanded, "Take photos, friendly and otherwise, so that command and the DOD can sort this mess out."

Grady and Ramos nodded and began rolling bodies over to reveal the faces of the fallen.

Masters placed a hand on Ambassador Rogers' shoulder, as much for comfort as to steer him away from the scene, "Ambassador, we're going to get you home."

"Home?" Rogers looked confused. "I can't leave Tunis. This is just what the terrorists want."

"It's my job to ensure you get to live to fight another day, sir. Your team is down and your post is compromised. I'm not one to give in to terrorists either, but sometimes the best tactical approach is to exfil out of a bad situation. This, ambassador, is one of those bad situations," Masters' message was stern.

"Photo album is uploaded, ready to go, Gunny," Ramos declared.

"Let's push on, sounds like we're attracting a crowd," Masters warned.

Grady and Ramos moved out into the hallway, taking the same flanking positions they had taken on their entry. With a hand constantly on the ambassador's shoulder, Masters split between the two and led them down the hallway.

The elevator bell chimed. As the doors opened, Masters spun the ambassador behind him. In the same motion, he hip fired the moment he saw the muzzle of an assault rifle peek through. Grady followed through with hits on two more attackers trying to take aim from the open elevator bay.

Ramos maintained focus on the hallway in front of them. Seeing the stairwell door fling open, he took three well-aimed double tap burst shots, dispatching the combatants barring their outlet.

"Getting crowded in here, our new acquaintances from inside or outside the hotel?" Masters called to Zalinksy and Dobson.

"I am keeping an eye on three non-Tunis tacticals closing in on Dobson's AO, he's got about half a mike. No one has entered the hotel," Zalinsky reported.

"Roger. Keep an eye on Dobbs' flank. Halo reports incoming along the beachfront," Masters said.

Zalinksy swung his scope east and west of the hotel along the sandy shoreline. "Good copy. Not seeing anything yet. Should make exfil exhilarating, though."

"That it will. We're pushing hard. Might be coming out hot," Masters replied.

Continuing their fast walk towards the stairwell, they heard new explosions outside the hotel.

Heeding Zalinsky's report, Dobson was vigilant with his watch on the hotel street front. The gun turret affixed high in the pickup bed brought it into view quickly. Before the truck could brake to a stop, Dobson squeezed the trigger on the Milkor sending a grenade on target splintering the truck and its contents in a concussive blast.

The trailing trucks slammed on their brakes, one diverting left, the other to the right. From his perch behind the steel dumpsters, Dobson lost visual on the insurgents. Rolling out, he sprinted towards the corner of an adjacent building, trying to locate the tactical vehicles and their crew.

A truck careening wildly to the left flashed into view. Dobson was quick to let out a shot. Before the grenade made impact, two gunmen riding in the truck bed released their grips on the roll bar and landed on the ground, guns drawn, locating Dobson.

The blast launched the men forward while Dobson released his grip on the Milkor and raised his M12 delivering two quick shots into each before they could get a solid sight on him.

Spinning, looking for cover, Dobson tried to spy the third truck. As he leaned against a wall, he located the tactical. The gun turret was focused square on him as the feed began to spool. His search for cover as desperate as it was futile, he was surprised when the gunner suddenly lurched forward, spinning the turret wildly off aim sending the bullets peppering the wall to Dobson's right.

The driver launched himself from the cab. Before he could get a hand on the truck bed to replace the fallen gunner, he too was dropped lifeless.

"Time to go, Dobbs. I've got your six. Meet up with the package team at the rear of the hotel," Zalinsky called from his overwatch perch, smoke slowly wafting from the barrel of his sniper rifle.

"Nice shooting, Z!" Dobson called and began his retreat through the alleys, moving towards the beach.

"Don't mention it. I got you, brother!" Zalinsky turned his attention to the rear of the hotel while keeping an expanded eye on the beachfront.

Reaching the door to the stairwell, Masters nodded Ramos forward to take point as he sandwiched behind with Ambassador Rogers in tow. Staff Sergeant Grady took the flank.

Hearing the steel door below clang open and footfalls pound up the steel rungs, Masters pushed the ambassador into the wall and growled, “Close your eyes and cover your ears!” Letting go, with his shoulder pressing into the ambassador, he did the same as Grady dropped a flashbang down the stairs.

Prepared for the mind ringing, they reacted quickly. With a fistful of Ambassador Roger’s jacket, Masters followed Ramos down the stairs. Quickly dispatching the disoriented insurgents, they pushed through to the ground level.

Cautiously pushing the door open, Ramos watched as two gunmen in the alley suddenly slumped to the ground. “Z’s busy,” he mumbled. Glancing down both directions of the alley, he looked back at Masters and nodded.

Spilling out into the alley, the trio hovered around the ambassador as they moved like an amoeba along the outside of the hotel. When they reached the patio, Masters held up a fist to pause his team. Taking in the vast open space they would need to traverse to the boat, Masters weighed his options.

“Halo, this is Raider Six.”

“Copy, Raider Six, go ahead.”

“Any luck in getting air support?” Masters asked hopefully. The gunnery sergeant hoped a helicopter gunship flyover could lay cover for their escape, increasing their odds of keeping the ambassador safe.

"Air support can't engage in Tunisian airspace and they won't enter a hostile space where they cannot engage," Lt. Colonel Lippett reported.

"Copy, Raider Six out."

"Dobbs and I have your back," Zalinksy said from his sniper position. "You get the package out and secure the mission. We'll catch up at the COC."

"I appreciate that Lance Corporal, but getting everyone home is my mission," Masters countered. "Be ready to collapse on our position."

"Roger that."

"How fast are you, Ambassador Rogers?" Masters asked.

"What?" the ambassador wore a twisted expression.

"Never mind," Masters shook his head. Scanning the area, he counted twenty-five seconds before moving forward. As they reached the pool area, he saw a dark streak in his peripheral vision.

"I got you, Gunny!" Zalinksy called as he sprinted to join their flank.

Dobson appeared on the opposite side of the pool, constantly swiveling between the direction he had come and the westerly portion of the beachfront.

"Raider Six, this is Halo. ISR shows you have incoming on either side, less than a mike out."

"Copy, we're on the move," Masters returned. Looking at his men, "It's going to get busy. We have more guests arriving."

An exposed stretch of sand between the hotel pool and the waiting rigid hull boat that would be their escape. Three waves of insurgents came into sight. Shots came from each direction. Using the beach itself to their advantage, Masters, Ramos, and Grady threw grenades towards the groups. Blasts of sand flew into the air, giving the strike team a window of concealment.

"Zalinsky, get ahead and get the motor running. Dobbs, you know what to do," Masters commanded.

The two Marines raced ahead of the ambassador's protection team. Zalinksy leapt into the boat, grabbing the pilot tower, and pulled himself into the driver's seat. Pushing the start button, the twin 630 horsepower engines roared to life.

Dobson slid to a stop just in front of the hull. From his knee, he rotated the Milkor M32 from right to left. Three shots launched in the air, each landing amid the converging insurgent squads. Landing in sequential blasts, bodies, shrapnel, and an explosion of sand burst into the air providing Masters' group cover as they closed in on the boat.

From the pilot seat, Zalinksy aimed his MK 13 at two men that escaped in front of Dobson's grenade shots. Plinking each one, he set his rifle down and slammed the throttle into reverse as Master's manhandled Ambassador Rogers into the craft while Grady and Ramos each gave the grab handles a tug towards the surf.

Free from the sand, the RIB pulled away from the beach while the rest of the team jumped in. Masters and Dobson unloaded their magazines as Grady and Ramos positioned themselves for a follow up barrage. By the time they were ready, Zalinksy had the boat in full forward throttle, jetting away from the shoreline.

"We've got boats coming in," Dobson called. Two fiberglass boats raced at an angle away from the mainland to converge along the RIBs path.

"I see them," Masters nodded. The men sighted their weapons, ready to strike when a pair of Bell Viper helicopters screamed overhead. Each one veered slightly away from the RIB and launched a series of Hydra rockets. In near unison, each threatening boat exploded into a cloud of fiberglass shrapnel.

The helicopters appeared to hit an imaginary wall and pulled one-hundred- and eighty-degree turns mirroring each other at Raider Six's flank.

"Raider Six, you should have smooth sailing. We'll see you at the COC," Lippett's voice called through the team's earpieces.

TWO

After a welcome change of transportation in Malta, Raider Six and Ambassador Rogers watched Naval Air Station Sigonella come into view. The Super Stallion helicopter made its descent towards the tarmac.

Once landed, and the doors were open, Masters ushered his team out while maintaining contact with the ambassador. A few steps beyond the landing zone, the team was met with a crowd of Marine Military Police and a mix of Naval and Marine brass.

Lieutenant Colonel Lippett broke through the crowd and greeted them. "Ambassador Rogers, welcome to Sicily."

"I am most appreciative to be here...Lieutenant Colonel," the beleaguered ambassador admitted as he took in the leaf design on Lippett's uniform. "You have a hell of a team."

"Just doing our job, sir," Masters interjected.

"If doing your job is being shot at while being outnumbered twenty to one, then you and your team did a hell of a job," the ambassador corrected.

"Yes sir. Thank you, sir," Masters conceded.

"We've got the ambassador. We'll check him through medical and get him comfortable. Clean up and we'll debrief in forty," Lippett instructed Masters.

"Yes, sir," Masters acknowledged. "Ambassador." Masters nodded.

Gunnery Sergeant Chris Masters was grateful for the hot shower and opportunity to gather himself after they arrived at Naval Air Station Sigonella. He hardly noticed the adrenaline spike and stress when he was on a mission. The years and intensity of training that he and his team carried with them removed that from his mind when he was in action. The time after the completion of a mission was something entirely different.

When he was younger, he rode the wave of excitement in team celebrations as they hit the town. With his wife and daughter in his life, he had a decidedly different post-mission response. They were always forefront of mind.

Glancing at his watch, he knew he had a few minutes before debrief with Lieutenant Colonel Lippett and his team. Flipping on his laptop, he waited as the screen came to life.

The angelic image of Breanna Masters filled the screen. "Hi, baby!"

"Hi, sweetheart," Chris couldn't hide his grin from seeing his wife.

"Macy…Daddy's on!" Breanna called. "Any chance you can tell me where you are?"

Chris wrinkled his nose, "I can say I am somewhere in Italy."

"Italy!" Breanna scoffed. "You get to visit all the nice places."

Chris laughed as his mind flashed on the scene he left behind in Tunisia. "Yeah, that's one perspective. Next leave, I'll see what we can do for a proper vacation."

"Like you're going to spend leave away from your baby girl, unless you're talking a family trip," Breanna argued.

"Family trip…I want to go to Disney World!" a bubbly six-year-old face framed with vibrant curls burst onto the screen.

"Macy! How's my girl?" Chris beamed.

"Good. Mommy and me have been playing board games," Macy replied.

"Did you win?" Chris asked.

Macy's face fell, "No, Mommy won. But it was still fun."

"That's my girl, fight on!"

"Right. Fight on!" Macy raised a fist in the air. "Did you catch bad guys today?"

Chris struggled for the right words, "I…uh, I *subdued* bad guys today."

Macy's face screwed into a frown, "What's sub…dude?"

"It means bad guys were in the way and Daddy helped get them out of the way," Breanna interjected.

"Right," Chris nodded.

"When are you coming home, Daddy?" Macy asked.

"Yeah, when *are* you coming home?" Breanna demanded.

"Three days."

"For real?" Macy's eyes brightened.

"For real. Lieutenant Colonel Lippett has us in Stone Bay for mandatory evaluations. While not fun for me, it *does* mean I'll be home for a while. With weekends off, too," Chris replied.

"We may not be able to go to Disney World, but there is a Six Flags not too far. Maybe we can go there," Breanna suggested.

"You like roller coasters?" Chris asked.

"I don't know," Macy shrugged with her arms dramatically held in the air. "Are they fast?"

"Fast and hilly," Chris grinned.

"Like when we go in the Jeep in the Blue Tip Mountains?" Macy asked.

Chris laughed, "Blue Ridge Mountains…yes."

Macy clapped excitedly, "Yes!"

"Alrighty. I love you, Bugs!" Chris smiled.

"I love you too, Daddy."

"I can't wait to see you."

"I can't wait to *hug* you!" Macy called.

"Well played. I can't wait to hug you, too," Chris said. "Let me talk to Mommy for a bit."

"Oh alright, bye Daddy. I love you!"

"Love you too, baby girl!"

"Lippett going to follow through on this one?" Breanna cast a stern look at her husband through the video feed.

"No choice. We have semi-annuals we are just shy of overdue on," Chris acknowledged.

"Good. We have lots of making up to do!" Breanna announced, her eyebrows raised.

“Oh,” Chris was taken aback. “Well, I may have to suggest these mandatory evaluations more frequently.”

“I have no doubt you’ll ace the Marine Corps’, question is, are you up to passing mine?” Breanna wrinkled her nose. “It’s quite vigorous.”

Chris rocked back in his position at his wife’s challenge. “I’ll see what I can do. May take a few attempts, but I think I’m up for it.”

“We’ll see. Fight on, baby,” Breanna cooed.

“Fight on, sweetheart. See you in a couple of days,” reluctantly, Chris shut the laptop. With a sigh, he stood, straightened himself in the mirror, and headed for the debrief.

Chris was met by Lieutenant Colonel Lippett outside of the commissary hallway. “It’s not the lair back in Stone Bay, but after speaking with Ambassador Rogers, I thought this might be more comfortable for the preliminary debrief. The brass and DOD have already scheduled a formal review in Camp Lejeune,” Lippett said.

“Alright,” Masters nodded. The sensitivity of certain missions required resolution at bases where the necessary senior personnel weren’t available. Nodding towards a spread of Italian sandwiches and chilled beverages lining the counter, “That for us?”

“Courtesy of the Ambassador. Had the staff pull together something in short notice,” Lippett shared.

“You’ll have to share our appreciation,” Masters offered.

“You can tell him yourself,” Lippett nodded towards the hall.

Masters turned to see Ambassador Rogers treading down the hallway. “Ambassador, I hope you are well.”

“Thanks to you and your team, fit as a fiddle,” the ambassador beamed. His face fell, “I wish the same were true for my staffers and the security team.”

“I do as well, sir,” Masters acknowledged.

Footsteps approaching down the hallway announced the arrival of the remainder of Raider Six. “Gentlemen, we’ll conduct an informal debrief as we have been invited to share your experience with the DOD when we land back in Lejeune,” Lippett announced to the team.

“Ooh, DOD. Such high honor,” Ramos quipped.

“Anytime a terror group is willing to brazenly attack a United States ambassador, it gets a higher level of attention,” the Lieutenant Colonel explained.

“Say, Ambassador Rogers,” Dobson was sincere in his question, “Was there something specific they were after with you or your office, or were they just being a-holes towards a U.S. official?”

The ambassador nodded at the question, "That's a rather astute question. Things in Tunisia had actually seemed like they had cooled off. This was either a brazen attempt to rekindle momentum, or the lull was a just a regrouping and not a sign of real improvement in the region."

"So, a-holes," Zalinsky chimed.

"I suppose. My post would be the highest prize if you wanted to invoke sentiment against the west," Ambassador Rogers declared.

"This was a well-coordinated attack," Grady noted. "Your security was specially trained Marines, our brothers. For a group to get the drop on them…"

Rogers nodded, "That is correct. They caught us at a time of transition and in a compromised location. We walked into a trap. They reacted to protect me and were attacked from both sides."

"They had a team waiting in the room…," Grady continued.

"And reinforcements on the balcony," Rogers conceded. "As good as my team was, they had no chance." The ambassador's head dropped.

"How did they know your schedule and location?" Masters pressed.

"They shouldn't have. My entire detail works on risk protocol. I was offered a meeting with a lieutenant of Ansar al-Sharia. He wanted to broker a deal to bring peace to the region – Algeria, Libya, and Tunisia. It was short notice and it had to be a neutral location. We didn't have time to vet the meeting. It cost my people their lives. *I* cost my people their lives," the ambassador declared.

"What did your security detail say?" Lippett asked.

The ambassador rubbed his chin, "They wanted time to run proper protocols. Get intel to run this guy down, send part of the team to check out the hotel. I… I actually hoped the request was real. I pushed for the meeting."

"Ultimately, the team C.O. is in charge of your safety, their go or no-go is on them," Lippett declared.

"It is," Rogers nodded. "Lt. O'Neil trusted my instinct."

"You were doing your job, sir," Masters stated flatly.

"We got a lotta time to hash all this out, you aren't trained for days like this. Whattaya say we crack into that spread you put out," Zalinksy broker the tension.

"I'd be lying if I said I couldn't use a drink," the ambassador admitted weakly.

"What's your pleasure?" Zalinsky stepped up to man the bar.

Shaking his head, "The stiffest thing you can put in a glass."

"How about some good 'ol American whiskey," Zalinsky popped the top of a bottle and poured several drams of amber liquid into a glass. After that, he began indiscriminately tossing beers to his team.

When everyone had a glass in hand, Dobson raised his glass, "To Lieutenant O'Neil and his team. Our brothers."

"Oorah!" they called in unison.

Ramos stepped up, "Fellas?" With arms raised, he walked into the center of the room. The team instantly fell into place, arm and arm completing a circle with Ramos. "Father, we ask you to elevate the souls of the fallen today. That they may seek your favor in heaven and make a space for all of us when our rightful time comes. That their efforts, their time on earth, and their families carry their spirit in your light. Amen."

The team, including Lippett, downed their beverages in silence. The Lieutenant Colonel quietly leaned into Masters, "Come with me, Gunnery Sergeant."

Masters complied and followed his commanding officer out of the room. "We got some data from the photos the team logged."

Meandering down the halls of Naval Air Station Sigonella, they made their way to the ops room used by their SEAL counterparts. A group of intelligence officers sat behind computer screens while naval and marine personnel swirled about them.

Lippett and Masters snapped to attention as they entered the room of superior brass.

"At ease, gentlemen," Master Chief Petty Officer Jon Samuels welcomed the men into the room.

"Lieutenant Colonel, Gunnery Sergeant," Marine Colonel Mark Jenkins joined alongside the commanding naval officer.

"Excellent work by your team in extracting the ambassador," Jenkins added.

"Thank you, sir," Masters said. "I wish we could have been there sooner."

Spinning to the large screen that dominated the wall, Master Chief Petty Officer Samuels pointed, "The data recognition uncovered some interesting developments. Ms. Statler."

A thin woman stood abruptly and walked excitedly to the front of the room, "Veronica Statler, Intelligence."

As she panned the room, she turned her attention to the faces splashed on the screen. "Several of the faces belonged to members of the radical Islamic group Jund al-Khilafah, a part of the Islamic State rising in the wake of Ansar al-Sharia – Tunisian radicals which isn't of the greatest surprise. But these three men here known members of the *Libyan* Ansar al-Sharia."

"So, we're seeing what? A regional push to unite their efforts?" Colonel Jenkins asked.

Statler twisted her lips as she readied her response, "It would seem, but there are these two here." Drawing a circle around the two pictures in the far bottom right of the screen, she continued, "These two are lieutenants in Barriq Hussein's splinter al-Qaeda group calling themselves the Islamic Light. They profess peaceful intentions though fund other more violent groups to carry out acts on their behalf."

"That might explain why this attack was better coordinated than many historically enacted in this region," Masters blurted.

Heads turned towards the Gunnery Sergeant. "Oh?"

"From the way Ambassador Rogers described the assault on his team and the way the reinforcements converged on our position, including boats in the water converging on our point of contact…that wasn't the effort of a ragtag bunch of uprisers. They had leadership and resources," Masters shared.

"Thank you...," Statler leaned towards Chris.

"Gunnery Sergeant, ma'am."

"Gunnery Sergeant," she repeated. Addressing the room as a whole, she added, "This matches intel we gathered from recent attacks in Syria and Iraq. We'll continue our review, including examining the weapons and ammunition used, and have more to report at the stateside debrief. The Tunisian government has been cooperative and is allowing us to send a forensics team."

"Very well," Colonel Jenkins acknowledged. "Lieutenant Colonel, Gunnery Sergeant, thank you for your time. That will be all."

The room was silent as all eyes followed Masters and Lippett out of the room and the doors were closed.

"So, this is a bigger deal than what we thought?" Chris said to his superior.

Lippett nodded, "Appears so. On paper, we won today. Saved the life of a U.S. ambassador in heroic fashion. In reality, it was a grave loss. Lost good men who were led into an ambush where they were greatly overpowered."

Chris walked in silence as they returned to the team.

"Gentlemen, pack up. Roll out to Virginia Beach in thirty," Lt. Col. Lippett called into the team's barracks.

"Virginia Beach? Aren't you a couple hundred miles off, sir?" Masters inquired.

Lippett froze and faced the team, "Change came in an hour ago. Be there less than a day, back at Camp Lejeune next day."

"Copy that," Masters tossed his neatly folded shirt into his bag. He was well used to the Marine Commande shifting plans on a dime, but he hated sharing those changes with Breanna and Macy.

When he was packed, he headed out to the tarmac. Leaning against the wall he stared out at the C40 Clipper that would transport his team back to the U.S. Pulling his phone free from his pocket, he dialed Breanna.

Her chipper voice quickly came through the speaker. Hitting the video call button, his heart fluttered when he saw his wife's face. "You on your way home, baby?"

Chris rubbed the back of his neck as he replied, "Quick hop to Virginia Beach, a little chat with the brass about our latest effort, and then back home."

Breanna bristled slightly at the news. "Alright, but you *are* still coming home, right?"

"I am. Confirmed with Lippett. Within thirty-six hours I'll have the two prettiest girls in the world wrapped in my arms," Chris promised.

"Got time to say hi to Macy?"

"Yeah, waiting on the crew. Take off in ten."

Swiveling the phone, Breanna panned the camera across the room.

Macy looked up from her book and saw the video on her mom's phone. Launching herself off of the couch, she sent the book flying. "Daddy!"

"Hi, Bugs!"

"Are you coming home?"

"On my way. We've got to take the long way, so it'll be another day or so," Chris replied.

"Alright, but that's soon?" Macy asked.

Chris chuckled, "That's soon."

The door opened next to Chris and his team began spilling out onto the tarmac. Dobson leaned into the phone, "Is that Macy? Wow, you're looking big, kiddo!"

"Hi, Uncle Dobbs!"

"Maybe we can get the families together for a barbecue. Your dad tell you we'll be home soon?" Dobson suggested.

"He did!" Macy nodded.

"Alright, time to hop on the plane. Tell your mama I said hello."

"Hi Dobbs!" Breanna called and briefly swiveled the camera her way before flashing back to Macy.

With a wave to Chris, Dobson ran to join the team.

"I love you guys. I'll be home soon," Chris promised.

"Bye Daddy! I love you too!"

Breanna looked deep into the camera, "I love you, baby. Fly safe!"

With a sigh, Chris hit the "end" button and pushed off of the wall to join his crew.

"That damned libertard, scum-sucking senator and his media outlet sleezebags! They should be charged with treason!" Brigadier General Thomas Mills bellowed as he stormed into the room.

Raider Six was waiting in Naval Air Station Oceana, the home of their navy SEAL team counterparts. They snapped to attention as the Brigadier General breezed in and snatched the television remote from the table amidst the sofas. "At ease!" he snarled.

Turning on the television, he scanned to a news channel. On the screen was Senator Willie Brown of California decrying that the attack on Ambassador Rogers was the direct result of U.S. influence throughout the Middle East, echoing Secretary of State's global agenda.

The reporter went on to admonish the Marine Raider team who "created chaos on the streets of coastal Le Kram". The television flashed from the footage in Tunisia to a sign welcoming visitors to Stone Bay in North Carolina as the reporter sent the segment back to the studio. The anchor posted a photo of a female senator and Secretary of State Janice Green who were building on Senator Brown's sentiment.

Mills seized, "That jackass is putting men and women at risk! Putting you and our embassies at risk."

"Where did the senator get the information on the mission?" Lieutenant Colonel Lippett asked.

The Brigadier General shrugged, "Someone on the intelligence committee, the State Department, whoever wanted him to be the poster boy for their message. Sometimes I think they favor the terrorists over our own men and women in uniform."

"So, it may seem, sir," Lippett nodded. "I am glad our fight is on the battlefield and not in D.C."

Mills looked square at Lippett, "To be sure. Your team ready? The panel is waiting."

"Semper fi, sir."

Brigadier General Mills led the team down the hall to an auditorium. Military police secured the doors and let the men in. On the stage, several high-ranking military officials from the Marines and Navy were sitting behind tables along with a number of Department of Defense officials.

"Raider Team Six, thank you for your service and bringing Ambassador Rogers home," Director of Joint Staff and Lieutenant General Adam Viceroy announced as the team assembled before the panel.

"At ease," the director waved his hand towards the front row seats of the auditorium. "Be seated."

Vice-Admiral of the Navy Jamey Rice leaned towards the group, "From the report, your mission was exemplary. I have no doubt, reasonably accurate. What we are concerned with isn't your actions, but the growing and enhanced threat we are seeing throughout the Middle East."

Behind the panel, the entire wall was lit up in a giant screen fractured into multiple segments. Each segment was a picture of the scene in Tunisia. "The intelligence and Marine forensics teams were able to send some data to us while you were flying back. The details are worrying. From your initial report, the attack on the ambassador was well coordinated and well equipped."

Gunnery Sergeant Chris Masters spoke for the team, "That is correct. The insurgents were highly tactical to subdue the ambassador's protection detail, but also in their response to our rescue effort. They closed in our position and our exfil with the precision of a military command."

"I see. You mentioned how they were equipped. Did you identify any of their arms?" Vice Admiral Rice continued.

"Yes, ma'am. Some of them were armed with weapons you would expect from an al-Qaeda initiative, but some were armed with American military weapons," Masters reported.

"That is what our forensic teams concluded, as well. The question is, where did they get the equipment?" Rice asked.

"There have been supply runs ambushed, materials left behind following skirmishes…," Lt. Col. Lippett started.

Vice Admiral waved him off, "Forgive me, Lieutenant Colonel, my question was rhetorical. Sadly, we know where the arms came from. They were *given* to the enemy by the Secretary of State during the last administration. Much of that discussion is for the DOD to deal with in the Senate and Congress. The point I have for you, your fellow Raider teams, and the Seal teams is, for you to know that when you are in the field, you may be facing the same competent weaponry you yourself are using."

"Yes, ma'am," Lippett acknowledged.

"There are some in power appeasing the Islamic State in hopes to quell further violence throughout the world. The fact is, every time appeasement with the radical outliers in the Islamic faith are met with a greater threat in their advancement. Our theory is Barriq Hussein, leader of the so-called Islamic Light is behind the recent attacks. He is well educated, a charismatic and articulate speaker. The events in Syria, Iraq, and now Tunisia fit into that theory. The weapons provided by the Secretary of State in a clandestine meeting went to Hussein's group. His profession of striving for peace is belied in that military gear scattered across these scenes of terror."

"If you will bear with us, the panel has specific questions about the tactics used in the theater," Brigadier General Mills said to the team.

In usual military fashion, the questions levied on the team were detailed. When the deposition was complete, the team was allowed to stand down until their flight back to Camp Lejeune.

"If what the spook and the Brigadier General fear are true, our dance card is going to get a lot busier over the next few months," Lance Corporal Zalinsky remarked as he pulled beer bottles out of the ice chest and tossed them to his mates.

"Probably why we're spending time at the Weapons Training Battalion one-k range," Grady offered.

"Maybe. We are due. SERE's up next," Masters added.

"Nothing like a little SERE vacation," Ramos grinned.

Dobson shook his head, "You *would* like SERE, Ram!"

"What's not to like? Some remote retreat, getting away from it all for a week," Ramos said.

"Sure. Sleep deprivation, a diet of gruel if you're lucky…," Dobson pressed. Turning to Masters, "Is it true you evaded capture and lived in the woods an entire SERE school?"

Grady strode forward, "*That* is most certainly a myth. He did evade an entire school, but he also snuck back into camp and aided in our escape."

The team spun towards their Gunnery Sergeant.

Lippett walked into the room and nodded towards Zalinksy to hand him a beer. "The brass was pretty pissed about that."

Masters grinned, "What? Survive, Evade, Resist and Escape. It's in the name."

"They didn't exactly like a young upstart showing up and missing out on the Resist part of the training," Lippett cocked his head and took a sip of his beer.

"They made up for it and tossed me in a van and held me for another session completely in the Resistance phase," Masters conceded.

"Until you escaped on Day Three and spent the remainder of the week in the woods again," Lippett reminded.

The team laughed at the exploits of their field team leader.

THREE

Breanna Masters reached for her sunglasses as she accelerated her SUV onto North Carolina Highway 172. Grimacing as she filtered into the heavier than usual morning traffic on the highway that separated the Stone Bay residential area and Camp Lejeune. "Well, Macy, you might be a little late for school this morning."

"That's okay," Macy shrugged. "I don't mind."

Breanna chuckled at her daughter. Pushing hard on the brakes, she saw the reason for the slow down. A construction crew was preparing for a day of work on the Stones Bay Bridge. Men with orange vests were setting out cones along the edge of the bridge. One turned away from the group. With a brief nod, he held his head low and turned his attention to stare out at the New River.

"Do you think Daddy is going to like them?" Breanna asked.

"Matching family shirts for the amusement park? Yeah!" Macy's eyes brightened.

"I'm glad the Base Exchange has some in stock. You can help me pick out the colors and the Cricket decals," Breanna offered.

"Is that why you brought me?"

"Yep, it is a welcome home gift from the both of us," Breanna said. "He's back today."

Macy clapped her hands together, "I can't wait!"

"I know, baby. Me too."

Mahaz Maher set out early. With coveralls, work boots, an orange construction helmet, and vest, he slung a duffel bag over his shoulder and closed the trunk of the second-hand car he had paid cash for a day earlier. Instinctively, he scanned the area as he proceeded toward the bridge.

Walking the entire span, he stopped at the first pillar that rose from the New River. Unzipping the duffel, he pulled a brick of putty out of the bag. Inserting a transmitter with probes into the putty, he located a seam in the bridge. Leaning over the rail, he placed the brick firmly against the concrete.

Moving to midspan, he placed another brick on the north side of the boat channel and duplicated his effort on the south side. As he looked up, he saw the road crew truck pull off the road followed by two passenger cars. The yellow light flashed as men hopped out of the truck. Most carried thermoses as they donned their protective hats.

Mahaz gave a quick wave as he leaned against the rail and looked out at the river.

Several of the crew hoisted tall stacks of cones over their heads and walked along the edge of the bridge. Placing the cones in even spaces, they set them out along the edge of the bridge decking.

"Got here early," a worker called to Mahaz as they passed.

"Yep," Mahaz slurred. "Ready to get started. Need another load?"

"Yeah, that'd be great!" the worker said as he set another cone down.

Leaving his perch along the rail, Mahaz walked back towards the end of the bridge. As he passed the group of foremen walking along the edge, he lowered his head, and with a hand on his helmet, he gave a little nod and stared off towards the river.

Pausing at the pillar closest to shore, he placed one more brick on a seam before moving on. Wrapping around the back of the work truck, he hoisted several cones off of the bed and set them down to adjust his laces as the crew from the passenger cars moved past.

When they cleared the nose of the truck, Mahaz rose. Morning traffic had picked up and with the flashing yellow lights and road crew walking along the bridge, had started piling up. He grinned as he climbed into the driver's seat of his car.

In a break in the flow, he pulled the car out on the highway and headed south. With the bridge in his rearview mirror, he hit a number in his phone contact list. Glancing back up in the mirror, he watched the scene unfold and felt a rumble underneath his tires.

Hit the cellphone once more, the line picked up. "It is done," he said.

"Allahu Akbar!" the voice on the other line called.

"Allahu Akbar!"

"Mahaz, you are a hero of the people of the Islamic Light, the people of Muhamad. We will see in you a few weeks. We have more big plans for you."

"Thank you, sir. It is my honor," Mahaz said. Hanging up the phone, he had to swerve slightly to avoid a car with locked up brakes that careened into his lane. From this point, all he had to do was remain calm and avoid a traffic accident to find his sanctuary.

Breanna kept a close eye on traffic ahead of her, which was appropriately wary of the construction workers.

"It's going to be nice going to the amusement park with Daddy. The three of us. No work," Breanna declared. "We go in three days."

"It's going to be so awesome!" Macy looked out where the New River bent into Stone Bay. "It's going to be…,"

Macy's words were cut off by a giant explosion. Her glee was instantly replaced by shock.

Breanna's first reaction was of a sonic boom, but a second later, the car launched into the air. For her moment of consciousness, the scene was surreal. Cars and bodies of the construction workers launched into the air and seemed to hover for a moment. At the peak of the suspension, Breanna's heart leapt to her throat. She looked over at a terrified, confused Macy. Grabbing her hand and squeezing, Breanna called out, "I love you, Macy!"

As sudden as the blast and the concussion hurtled the occupants of the bridge into the air, it released them, plummeting them into a tangle of metal, concrete and brittle flesh until cars, bridge, and human lives splashed into the tidal water of the New River.

The drivers along North Carolina Highway 172 slammed on the brakes. The chain reaction of sudden stopping led countless cars to ram into the car in front of them. An SUV packed with a family en route to school and work stopped precariously close to the edge of the torn concrete, hovering them close to plunging into the river. Before they could react and appreciate their good fortune, their vehicle was nudging by the trailing passenger car. The SUV slid, dangling for a moment as if it were clinging to the edge for safety before losing its grip and following the vehicles that fell before it. Adding itself and the family it contained to the shrapnel and debris below.

The scene was echoed on the opposite side of the bridge as the line of trailing cars met with the would-be safe vehicle before it, too, was lost to the river below. Vehicle safety systems and passengers with enough wit to fight the shock of the horror furiously dialed 911.

On either side of the bridge, traffic began to back up for miles. Many drivers spun their cars around in a wild retreat while others raced to the bridge to see if they could offer any assistance at all. Most simply stared at where the bridge had stood and the heart-wrenching loss of innocent lives that were concussed, bludgeoned and ultimately resting under the weight of concrete and metal at the bottom of the saltwater inlet.

A small number of vehicles floated, drifting and swirling in the outgoing tidal current of the New River before ultimately giving way to the minute cracks of the seams between sections of sheet metal, filling with water and settling toward the river bottom.

Within minutes, the air filled with sirens, whirling and chopping rotors of helicopters, and the growl of boats at full tilt heading towards the bridge. The rescue and recovery sights and sounds only added to the surreal setting. As rescuers arrived the shouting commands and radios added to the soundtrack.

City, county, state, and military responders blanketed the scene. Trying to ignore the chaos and focus on their desperate search to locate and assist any possible survivors as unlikely as the scene might predict, the rescuers plunged into the water. Sheriff's deputies and local lifeguards dove into the river. Marines from nearby Camp Lejeune dropped into the water from helicopters while drones, planes, and additional choppers filled the air combing the landscape for signs of additional trouble.

The onlookers rejoiced at the few survivors that were miraculously pulled from the water and rubble. Pulled to shore, they were given attention and if stable, whisked away to a nearby hospital. An unfortunate number of lifeless bodies were recovered, piling up along the shore. Fruitless pleas for signs of life were met with silence. The rescuers would abandon the bodies and resume search for another hopeful recovery.

"If memory serves, it's Dobson's turn to buy the first round," Zalinsky announced as the Raider Six team burst into the bar and surrounded the tender.

"Not sure how you'd remember anything after our last outing," Dobson laughed.

Zalinsky wrinkled his nose, "Did we even know what we were drinking? Our Slavic interpreter left after the second round."

"I believe your request was, give us whatever the locals drink," Grady grimaced.

Masters laughed, "The number of patrons slumped over their tables should have been a sign."

"That and the actual sign that read "Not responsible for thefts of passed out patrons!"" Ramos added.

"Is that what the sign said?" Grady asked.

Grinning, Ramos replied with a shrug, "I don't know. Just made that part up."

Dobson, waved over the bartender, "Round of Git-right."

The bartender frowned.

"He means a Two-step!" Grady suggested.

The bartender retained his frown.

"Boiler Maker," Masters said.

The bartender nodded and preceded to fill glasses of beer and set out whiskey shots beside them.

As the team gathered their drinks, they hoisted the shots in the air. "To another successful work trip with my brothers," Zalinsky called.

"And sister," a voice called from behind the men.

The Raider team turned to see Warrant Officer Patty Jacobs saunter up to the bar.

"And sister!" the team chorused.

"One more?" Zalinksy called to the bartender.

Jacobs walked up to Masters, "Lippett asked to see you in the command center, ASAP."

Masters frowned, "He say why?"

Shaking her head, Jacobs replied, "Just to get you ricky-tick."

"Copy," Masters acknowledged. Turning his beer glass upside down, swallowing the remains of the whiskey, and slamming it on the counter, he suggested, "Take my place?"

Jacobs grinned, "I'll do my best, Gunny."

"See you on the hop, boys," Masters called and headed out of the bar.

"Lieutenant Colonel?" Masters called as he found the office Lippett was borrowing.

"Shut the door." Lippett shifted in his seat. His face wore an expression Masters had never seen before on his superior officer.

Masters' stood at attention, his arms crossed behind his back, "Sir?"

"Have a seat," Lippett offered with a motion of his hand.

"I'll stand, if permitted, sir," Masters deferred.

"As you will," Lippett nodded. With a sigh, he cast a glance out of the office window before returning his attention to the Gunnery Sergeant. "There's been an incident. Too early to tell the details, accident or deliberate…in Stone Bay heading into Camp Lejeune…"

Masters body tensed, ready for action. The next words by the Lieutenant Colonel deflated every ounce of power in him.

"Breanna and Macy, they've been identified as victims. I'm so sorry, Chris. They're gone," Lippett said softly, a lump in his throat.

Masters tried to mutter a response. His knees weakened, his mind spun out of control, tears welled in his eyes. Closing them, he tried his best to collect himself, at least enough to hear his commanding officer out.

"When…how?" Masters sputtered.

"The Stone Bay Bridge collapsed. They were crossing at the time. Along with ninety-two other motorists, eleven construction workers," Lippett shared. "I'm sorry, Chris. We'll do whatever we can for you. There's a transport on the tarmac ready to go. I'll get the rest of the team. Give you time. We'll meet you on board."

Lippett rose from the chair. Crossing the desk, he paused in front of Chris. With a solid hand on Masters' shoulder, "I can't imagine what you are going through. We're all family. Bre and Macy are our family right alongside you. I'll see you on deck."

Lippett left the room and closed the door behind him. For a long moment, Chris stared blankly out of the window. His eyes did not take in any detail from what they covered, just light contrasting the rest of the room. In the theater of war, he always maintained vision, focus, ready to make the next move regardless of the chaos and gunfire, death, and bombs exploding around him. At this moment, he had no clarity of thoughts or vision. His insides felt like exploded ordinance, his mind molten.

All at once, the pain and emotion became intensely clear, dropping the Gunnery Sergeant to his knees, his head in his hands as they hit the floor.

Four

Masters had largely turned to numb as he boarded the C-130 transport plane. The Raider Six team froze as their eyes lit on his arrival. Snapping to attention, the crew was as quiet as Masters had ever known them to be.

When the ramp was closed and the engines began to vibrate the plane, the team collapsed around him. Hands on his shoulders, prayers were prayed, sentiment shared. Tears, pain, and anger hung heavy in the air. The team was hurt with the loss of Breanna and Macy, but also for their team leader's anguish.

In the fog of war, each member of the team knew their role, even when missions went bad and losses mounted. This experience was different. There was no control over this situation. No decisive action to take. No words that made the slightest sense. Compelled to pull together, they huddled around their platoon sergeant, their friend, their brother.

Masters accepted the team's support, mainly for their sake. He remained blank and quiet. His body quaked. So much pain and sadness were boiling inside. Violence and outrage were barely held in check. Nothing made sense at that moment. His team swirled around him, appearing like wispy shadows that took shape and then blew away like smoke. Their words came out as sound but were muffled and indecipherable.

Indeed, he felt the love from his team, but he could not requite it. He could just stand there, lost. Overwhelmed.

Fortunately for Masters, and his team who did not know how to console him or reconcile the news themselves, the hop from Virginia Beach to Camp Lejeune was a short one. When they landed, the team gave the Gunnery Sergeant one more pat and then gave him space.

Lieutenant Colonel Lippett walked a few paces from Masters. Like his crew, he did not have the answers or the words. He did, however, have a duty.

Masters didn't mind Lippett's guidance. Chris didn't know what to do or where to go. Home didn't seem right. He instinctively kept checking his phone for a call or message from Breanna. He wanted to call her, though he knew that didn't make sense.

He carried a false hope of a mix up. Some other unfortunate pair wrongly identified as Breanna and Macy, though he wouldn't wish his pain on anyone else. His mind fought the urge to make deals with the devil, forsaking his very soul for his wife and daughter to be at the edge of the airfield waiting for him. He could picture Breanna, her sundress blowing in the breeze. Following her hand to where she clasped Macy's. His sweet girl, her bouncy curls and boisterous grin welcoming him.

"I had…them and the other two military casualties relocated on base. The incident has been officially deemed a terror attack. The bridge collapse was no accident," Lippett shared. "This is going to suck. There are a lot of things over the next few weeks, months…forever that are going to suck…"

Masters nodded, his throat hoarse, "I want to see them." The truth was, he *had* to see them. His brain could not accept the news. It could not accept the finality of what this all meant.

Lippett led Masters down a hall that he was modestly familiar with. He had to make this walk a few times in his career as an operator, never for a civilian, however.

Pushing through a heavy door, they entered a cool room. Two Marine corps medical officers stood at attention alongside two tables. Their faces expressionless.

Lippett took a step back and stood at attention himself.

Masters strode forward. Internally, he was screaming. He begged for the two bodies before him to not be familiar. His stride and his expression were purposeful, emotionless.

Silently, the Medical Examiner took hold of the first zipper and slid it open enough to reveal the face and shoulders. There was Breanna, her hair curly from the water. Cuts and abrasions on her forehead and cheek. But there she was, still beautiful. Silent, but beautiful.

Other than the trauma, she could have looked as she had a thousand times when Chris watched her sleep. He would come home from an operation, when he couldn't sleep he would watch her breathe. Wonder what delights he had missed, what memories they could have shared had he been home.

Looking up at the patient M.E., Masters nodded solemnly. Closing his eyes briefly, he waved off the M.E. prior to revealing the second zippered bag.

"Let's give the Marine a moment," Lippett suggested.

The medical team looked at each other. Nodding, they followed Lippett out of the room.

When the door shut, Masters walked up to Breanna. "I'm sorry I wasn't there for you. I love you, sweetheart."

Masters trembled as a tear slid down his cheek. With the heaviest sigh of his life, he turned to the second table. Closing his eyes, he mustered the necessity of duty and grasped the zipper between his fingers. Sliding it down nearly a foot, he burst into uncontrollable tears, an event he had only experienced one other time in his life, his daughter's birth.

These tears were distinctly different. The others had been from joyful amazement, this…this was inconsolable pain. Through the sting in his eyes, there was Macy. His baby girl. Still sweet, still innocent. Chris drank her in. Lifeless. True to her character and spirit, precious and peaceful, just the same.

"I'm so sorry, Bugs. Daddy was supposed to protect you. I promised I would," Chris sputtered. He was filled, overwhelmed with anger and pain and sadness, each competing for his undivided attention, pleading for his action.

As Chris felt his insides might explode, the doors to the room reopened. Lieutenant Colonel walked softly up. "Gunnery Sergeant…"

Without turning, Chris nodded solemnly. Looking at his wife and daughter once more, he backed off and turned to his commanding officer.

"I've got people for you to talk to, the chaplain, counselor…me…the team," Lippett suggested.

Collecting himself, Chris acknowledged the message. "I've got to…I've got to make calls…the family."

"I get that, Masters…Chris. I really do, I'm not sure you need to be alone with this."

Chris squared up to Lippett. "I'll fight on, sir."

"This is not a fight any of us can be ready to take on," Lippett said.

"*Sir*," Masters glowered defiantly.

Understanding, Lippett backed down and gave Masters his space. "If you need anything…"

Chris nodded and walked on.

Masters fired up his Ford Bronco. Normally, the sound of the throaty exhaust meant he was heading home. His heart would race in the same tenor to see Breanna and Macy like he was a teenager heading out on a first date. The excitement to return home to his family, whether it was a nine-month deployment or the end of a long workday on base, it was always the same for him.

This time, the exhaust note was hollow. The truck was running, but Chris had no idea where he was supposed to point the steering wheel. It felt without purpose. The only thing that made sense to him was his training. Identify the problem, work to a solution. Overcome and fight on.

Masters wanted to lock and load and seek out an enemy. At that moment, the enemy he needed to face down was death, and that was an enemy he could not find to fight.

Instinctively, he turned south on North Carolina Highway 172, as he did every time he was heading home. This time, it wasn't to go home, it was to survey a scene. *The* scene.

Miles from the site, roadblocks were up and manned by county and state police. Federal and defense department crews had replaced the law enforcement outlets in investigating the scene itself. Swinging off the road, Masters guided his SUV down a dirt trail that followed the edge of Ellis Cove, getting him closer to the scene than what he would be allowed on the highway.

The southernmost tip of the peninsula, jutting out into the New River provided Masters a view of the scene. Bright lights lit up the banks on either side of the river as well as the carnage down below. Salvage boats commandeered by investigators worked the waterline while Coast Guard boats kept a perimeter.

From above, workers and forensic teams combed the scene and plotted analyses. Helicopters and drones hovered about, both surveying the area and scanning with an array of specialized cameras.

The entire span of the bridge was completely demolished. Jagged outcroppings cantilevered to either bank were the only lasting remains.

Pacing along the water's edge, Masters made the calls he never wanted to make. He started with his family and then Breanna's. Like him, they swirled the gamut of disbelief, shock, anger, sadness. He allowed them to vent, cry, ask questions, many he did not have the answers to or likely would have refused to answer had he known. Love, heartbreak, and sorrow were shared before he completed the list of necessary calls.

Sliding the phone in his pocket, he stared out at the scene. Shaking his head, he struggled and ultimately failed to understand. He couldn't understand any human being that could carry out an act like this. As an operator, he was no stranger to death and killing, making hard choices. Even in the heat of battle, they were never indiscriminate. Purely innocent life, never mind collateral harm, was never an acceptable target. His team would just as soon take a bullet as opposed to delivering an errant one.

He couldn't fathom any man that would take an innocent life or accept an order to do so. He understood the necessity of taking lives in defense of others, he had to measure that action often. But pure innocents, just living their lives, that made no sense.

He didn't understand a government or organization worth standing on earth who would levy such an order. He didn't understand the twisted interpretations of scripture, false or otherwise, that would condone or glorify such senseless horror. He didn't understand a god, prophet, or bible that would command acts of pain and killing inflicted on innocent women and children as a god any sane man who gives his ear never mind his actions.

The amount of cowardice for a man to slip from the shadows, hide his face, declare his endeavor so worthy to take the lives of innocents.

Masters' eyebrow quivered as his fists clenched. He wanted nothing more than to be standing in front of the worthless, soulless demon who did this. To be face to face with the man who commanded the order. Even stare in the eyes of their so-called god and seek justification for the killing of Breanna and Macy and all of the innocent people who suffered at the hands of his agents.

A footfall behind him caused him to spin.

"Easy, Gunny," Grady held his hands out in front of him. Behind Grady, the entire Raider Six team appeared.

Joining Masters, they stared out at the scene of Stones Bay Bridge. For several long minutes, they stared in silence.

Chris' affect was different than it had been earlier in the day. The visual truths, the time to reconcile and see for himself the damning finality of the events, while no less painful, at least gave him a firm foundation as ugly as it were.

"What are we gonna do about this, brother?" Grady asked.

For the first time that day, Masters' voice did not quiver, "Let's find out who did this and do our jobs."

FIVE

Home was the last place Chris Masters wanted to be. Pulling into the driveway, Breanna's missing SUV was the first heart-sinking sign that she and Macy were gone. Punching his code for the front door and swinging it open, he revealed a dark and empty house. Chris closed his eyes as he walked through.

Shutting the door behind him, he made his way into the kitchen where he dropped his keys on the counter and his go-bag on the floor. As his eyes made their way around the house, his heart twisted and his head spun.

There were times in his career as an operator, the thought of him not going home to them had crossed his mind. Not once did he ever picture in any capacity that Breanna and Macy wouldn't be coming home to him.

Moving into the living room, he gently lifted a photo of the family taken at the beach the previous summer. While Chris was never not on call, they reveled in their time when he could get away without some international emergency pulling him away.

Setting the photo down, he thought that he didn't do that enough, get away and just be a husband, a father. He was always a Marine first. It was the nature of being an operator, but it didn't make him feel any better. Not when his wife and daughter were ripped away from him.

Those words rang through his head again, "ripped away". A picture of him in uniform was on a nearby shelf that Breanna said made her feel closer to him while he was deployed. He closed his eyes, trying to control his feelings. Anger and sadness coursed through him until it reached his shaking hands.

In a furious explosion, Chris swept the shelf clean, pictures and mementos flying across the room. Not satisfied, he grasped the shelf with powerful hands and threw it across the room, splintering it against the far wall. In a rage, he spun around the room, fighting the ghosts that swirled in every direction.

The television was yanked off the wall, the cord ripped, sparking as its connection was severed. A hurricane lantern on the mantle became a missile through the glass doors of the China cabinet. His meaty fists pummeled everything in sight until his knuckles were bruised and bloody.

As his fury reached the shelf with the family photos, his outburst was frozen. Grasping a photo he took of Breanna and Macy along the magnolias last Mother's Day, he froze. Suddenly, his rage was displaced by overwhelming heartbreak. His eyes flooded with tears, his insides ached. Sliding down the cabinet, he landed on the floor, the photo in his hands.

Masters sighed heavily as he had to turn his Bronco around. Leaving home in the direction of the bridge was an engrained habit. With no access from North Carolina Highway 172, he had to maneuver north through Jacksonville. He hadn't slept the night before, yet he didn't feel like he needed sleep. He did need to do what he knew, roll up his sleeves and get to work. Find the problem, work the problem, take the fight to the enemy. There were bad people that needed to be brought to justice. That was the only thing keeping him from crumpling to a pile on the floor.

Pulling through the main gates of Marine Corps Base Camp Lejeune, Masters noticed heightened security around the base. Each car, including his, was scanned and inspected for explosives. The military police officer waved him through.

As he parked and headed for the Raider Command Center, Masters tried to walk deliberately. He did not want to be fawned over, he just wanted to go to work. His hopes were shattered before he could reach the hallway that led to the team rooms.

"Gunnery Sergeant Masters, I am so sorry," Staff Sergeant Johnson called.

Masters just gave a nod and continued on.

"If you need anything…!" Johnson added as Masters slipped through the secure doors of the team rooms.

Walking towards Raider Six's room, he heard the buzzing of conversation. Chris was annoyed when the room fell ghostly silent when he entered. With a glower, he snarled, "This walking on eggshells crap is not helping."

"We just, uh, thought you'd take time off, Gunny," Ramos said.

Masters scanned the room. Ramos and leaned against the counters or propped themselves on the corner of a table. Each had a coffee cup in hand.

Looking each in the eyes, he said, "The last thing I want right now is to be in a house full of memories or with family members wanting to walk memory lane with me. I want to know who killed my family and I want Raider Six called up."

"Understood, sir," Zalinsky.

"You're probably tired of this question, but…," Ramos started.

Looking at the men with mugs in their hands, Masters cracked a feeble smile, "If you really want to help, you can get me a cup of coffee."

Ramos nodded and Zalinsky tossed him a cup.

Dobson and Grady walked in through the door together.

"Boss, I uh, good to see you Gunny," Dobson stuttered.

Grady quietly slapped a reassuring hand on his friend's shoulder and glanced at his knuckles.

"Thanks," Masters grunted to Ramos as he was handed a cup of coffee. "So, what does intel have?"

"Intel is assembling in the Situation Room. I thought you might want to join us," Warrant Officer Jacobs said as she wheeled into the room.

Without hesitation, the men followed Lieutenant Colonel Lippett's XO out of the team room and down the hall. Lippett was sorting through documents on the table as numerous generals and intelligence staffers scurried around the room. Whether on phones, laptops, or shuffling papers, the room was a frenzy.

Lippett paused as he noticed Masters and the team stream into the room. The Lieutenant Colonel collected himself quickly. "Raider Six, Gunny," he acknowledged.

Veronica Statler, ever impeccably attired, addressed the room, "As you already know, there was a horrific attack on American soil yesterday resulting in the deaths of one hundred and five citizens, four of them marines and two family members of Marines.

The attack was not just an attack on American soil, our investigation suggests that the attack was specifically targeting the Camp Lejeune Marine Corps Base and more specifically, the Stone Bay MARSOC headquarters. While the attackers couldn't execute on base proper, they chose a target that would be close to home, too close for some. They would disrupt life for MARSOC operatives, staffers, and family. In that, they succeeded.

The attack appears to be directly related to Raider Six's operation to rescue Ambassador Rogers in Tunisia. Ansar al-Sharia group has already claimed responsibility. Their task in identifying the operational unit to target was made easy by this..."

Directing attention to the large monitor, she pressed the play button. A recorded news broadcast displayed on the screen. A news reporter known to push limited American involvement in the Middle East, including hard left regimes. Speaking to a senator on the Senate Intelligence Committee, they showed clips of the damage left behind in Tunisia and then panned to a stock photo of the Stone Bay sign at the entrance of the community associated with MARSOC.

Masters felt his eyebrow quiver as he watched the men and women on screen share to the world exactly what operation team was in Tunisia and where that team was headquartered.

"This news report preceded the attack on the Stones Bay Bridge by forty-hours. Not a lot of time, but enough to wake a cell or send someone on a plane," Statler shared.

General Watters, the ranking officer of MARSOC slammed his fist, "I'll have that dirtbag censured! Leaking operational intel that got over a hundred people killed!"

"There is some good news with our investigation," Statler continued, her tenor never changing. "We tracked any car that was connected to a database along NC 172 yesterday. A car camera picked up this."

Again, clicking a button, an image of a construction worker walking away from the bridge appeared on the monitor. "After facial recognition analysis, we have Mahaz Maher, a known associate of Barriq Hussein. As in the charismatic leader of the Islamic Light, heavily connected to Al Qaeda and Ansar al-Sharia. Maher is connected to a number of enemy combatant operations throughout the Middle East. He is quick efficient, works alone, and disappears quickly."

"I suppose Maher is long back to whatever rock he crawled out of?" Lieutenant Colonel Lippett asked.

For the first time, the intelligence officer cracked a slight smile, "Actually, we know *exactly* where he is."

Hitting another file, she pulled up a new image. This time of Maher inside a gated compound. "We got this photo of him this morning. He is at the Pakistan embassy in D.C."

Masters stared at the photo, taking in and memorizing every feature of the man that killed Breanna and Macy.

"Initial attempts at dialogue were…strained," Statler reported. "The State Department is in the midst of sensitive negotiations; they aren't willing to push too hard. The Pakistani ambassador claims while the photo has a likeness to Maher, it is not him. The ambassador promises their full support and offers condolences."

"Well, that's a load of crap, now ain't it?" Lance Corporal Zalinksy spat.

Statler nodded, "It's as the Marine eloquently stated. The discussion will continue but with the balance of a Mid-East Treaty in the midst, we are going to have to catch Maher in the dark alley of an Arabic country at some date in the future. I know it isn't what you want to hear, but that is the situation."

The room was quiet as the words were absorbed.

Masters felt like he would explode, but given the audience of the room, he held it all in and managed a blank expression.

"Thank you, Agent Statler. Where do we go from here?" General Watters asked.

"We'll keep eyes on the embassy, try and catch him leaving. We'll nab him, either on American soil or overseas," Statler said.

"You mean to tell me, a terrorist that killed over one hundred American citizens, women and children for Christ's sake, can sit on those grounds and we can't touch him," Ramos fumed.

"That is correct. Embassies are sovereign soil. Assuming Maher sticks to diplomatic travel, we won't be able to touch him in transit, either," Statler confirmed.

"Well, this just gets better and better," Zalinsky growled.

"The entire intelligence community, FBI, CIA, NSA, Armed Forces Joint Intelligence…are all on this. If Maher sneezes outside of diplomatic sanctuary, we'll get him," Statler promised.

"The bigger question is, who sent him?" Lippett asked.

"We are looking into that as well. Following their failed attempt on Ambassador Rogers, it is likely Ansar-al Sharia backed by al Qaeda. We have intel on a lieutenant with connections to Barriq Hussein. The rest is classified and still being investigated," Statler added.

"What the…," Dobson called out. "Blow up screen five."

Statler looked at the bank of monitors flanking the main screen.

"Look who is at our front door," Dobson said.

On the screen was live news footage of the reporter from the earlier clip shown with the senator identifying a MARSOC team operating in Tunisia. Framed offset of his report on the bridge bombing was a sign reading "MARSOC Marine Corps Base".

All eyes of Raider Six swung to where Masters was standing. "Where the hell is Gunny?" Zalinsky asked out loud.

Lieutenant Colonel sighed, “Request the meeting be adjourned?”

General Waters nodded. In an instant, Lippett and the Marine Raider team were spilling out into the hallway. Racing down the hall, they broke for the parking lot and sped through the base after piling into their cars.

The Ford Bronco parked just inside the gate confirmed what the team feared.

Outside the main gate, news reporter Clint Newsom was speaking live into a camera. Two Marine Corps military police officers were rushing to intercede as Gunnery Sergeant Chris Masters strode towards the reporter. Grady raced ahead of the team and slammed on the brakes just as he reached the gate. Jumping out, he ran to be let out himself, his team close behind.

“This isn’t going to be good,” Lippett muttered.

Masters ignored the rolling camera and stepped up to the reporter. The smug newsman was initially excited to taunt a Marine, but seeing the look on Chris’ face, he quickly lost the grin as we washed pale.

“You got my family killed!” Chris growled. Lunging at the reporter, the M.P.s grasped at his arms.

Stunted, Chris was still able to exert some force. Despite two large men holding him back, he was able to hit Newsom with enough impact, the reporter flew backward, tumbling to the ground like a rag doll, landing hard on the ground.

"You got that on tape, right?" Newsom stammered. "I have been assaulted by…"

"Get it on tape!" Masters countered. "This man and Senator Brown, Secretary Green…these people are responsible for the deaths of over a hundred people including my wife and daughter. You want to claim assault, do it."

As the team caught up to the scene, they shut the cameraman down. Grady stepped in front of Masters, "Some other time, Gunny."

An M.P. picked the reporter off of the ground. "It's this type of violent behavior. You and your kind incite terror. *You* did this!" he squeaked as he dusted himself off.

Masters had let his limbs go soft, subconsciously encouraging the M.P.s and Grady to lighten up on their hold. It was enough for Chris to slip through and lay the reporter out with a haymaker. Raider Six gathered around Chris and pushed him back.

"Get him out of here, we'll clean this up," Lieutenant Colonel Lippett commanded.

As the team got Gunnery Sergeant moving back through the gate, Lippett began negotiations with the reporter and his cameraman. "So, you think the father and husband of two people who got killed after you ran a story with classified intel reacting to seeing your pathetic face is a good thing for you and your news channel? Even *your* viewers won't find that real attractive. How about you appeal to your viewers and pull people together following this tragedy? You may disagree with policy and military action, but *no one* asked for this. I know the Mayor of Stone Bay, I can get him to sit down with you, maybe even tour the site. That'll get you better ratings than taking one in the jaw that frankly, you sincerely deserved."

"Why don't you come with me, brother," Grady suggested. He and Dobson walked along either side of him. "We'll get the Bronco later."

Masters relented. He knew he was overheated. A part of him didn't care. He wanted to tear a hole in the world until he put every soul that had a hand in Breanna and Macy's deaths into the ground. He also knew if there was an operation that he could take part in to take on the backers, he didn't want to be left behind because he was in disciplinary action.

Climbing into Grady's Dodge Challenger, he let his Staff Sergeant bring him back to the team's quarters.

"Laid that little fruit loop out," Zalinksy said as the team gathered in their room.

"If this was the wild west, there'd be a trail of bodies," Ramos said.

"But it's not," Grady interjected. "We all want to jack that guy. What's next, the senator? He's got it coming and worse than the slimy reporter. After that, the Secretary of State? Not leaning on the embassy?"

"Come on man, we're just jawing," Zalinsky defended.

"No, Grady's right. We need to let intel do their job. Position us to do ours. I made that harder for them," Masters said. "We defend idiots like that the right to free speech, even when what they say is pathetic and foolish. He didn't blow up that bridge. I'll let the DOJ deal with him and the senator."

"So, what now?" Ramos asked.

"We run through sniper cert like we're supposed to. Hope Statler and her people come up with something for us to act on," Masters said.

The team was put off by their Gunnery Sergeant's calm take on the issue. He was always the first to run into the fight. Grady cast him a glance wondering what was running through his head. He could see in Masters' eyes a different narrative was taking shape.

Lieutenant Colonel Lippett stormed into the room. With a stern glare pointed at Masters, he directed, "My office, now!"

Without hesitation, the Gunnery Sergeant followed his superior officer out of the room and down the hall. Sliding behind his desk, Lippett landed in his chair.

"Sit," Lippett's tone suggested it was a command, not a request.

Masters quietly did as he was told.

The Lieutenant Colonel looked hard at Masters. "Look, I get where you're at, at least as much as anyone can. Giving into the ravings of a-holes like that reporter Newsom is not going to help you, our unit, or those in our command that might get spooled up to take action."

Lippett's demeanor softened, "Take some time off. See family. Go fishing. Do something or go somewhere that will help you get your mind straight, at least enough to ensure you're properly in the game."

"I'm good, sir," Masters defended.

"Are you?" Lippett raised his eyebrows. "You just laid out a news reporter on national television. We are doing all we can to avoid charges being brought against you. I know you are in no position to care right now. I get it. It's understandable. But as someone from the outside, as your commanding officer, as your friend…I am telling you, you are not okay."

"Is this an order, sir?" Masters asked blankly.

Lippett looked down and sighed, "No."

Masters got up from his seat, "I'm going to join the team."

"Very well. Take care of yourself, Gunnery Sergeant."

Masters left the office without another glance at his superior. When he entered his team's room, all attention was on Warrant Officer Patty Jacobs. Like the situation room, several monitors were running. Newscasts and a variety of feeds scrolled across the monitors. Jacobs manned a computer that pulled up specific screens that caught their attention.

The screen in the top left corner showed the scene at the gate. Newsom stood in front of the Stone Bay facility Main Gate outside of Camp Lejeune. Masters strode through the gate, closely tailed by the M.P.s. As the rest of the team gathered around Masters, the broadcast showed him slip free and clock Newsom on the jaw.

The text at the bottom of the screen described an "unknown sailor" at the base. While Newsom's reported comments were derogatory towards his assailant and the military complex that spurred such violent behavior, he was not pressing charges at that time. Investigations into who the attacker was were on-going.

The team couldn't resist a chuckle at their Field Commander's decisive annihilation of the reporter's jaw, even if it may have been in poor judgment.

Warrant Officer Jacobs put a news conference on the main screen while she continued to monitor the MARSOC intelligence feed.

The Secretary of State stood at a podium in the news broadcast. "Citizens of the United States, a terrible tragedy in North Carolina has been felt around our great nation, around the world. An arm of al Qaeda has taken responsibility for the destruction of the Stones Bay Bridge which took the lives of one hundred and five innocents. The State Department, Department of Justice, and Armed Services Joint Intelligence are taking the incident as our top priority. We, and leaders around the world, have denounced the attack. State-sponsored terrorism will not be tolerated. That is why we are moving forward with the Mid East Peace Treaty that we believe will help curb these and other attacks in the future.

While the suspected terrorists remain at large, we are working with the international community to bring them to justice, including members of the aforementioned treaty. We have been given their word that such acts would not and did not come from their hand. They are aligning with us to curb rogue cells who do not want to see the treaty enacted. Our work with partner nations won't bring back those lives we lost but will prevent future attacks."

Stepping down from the podium, rival stations began broadcasting their summaries. On one screen, two congresswomen echoed the Secretary of States remarks on work with partners in the Middle East to build bridges and condemned military and intelligence community actions in response to the attack.

"It's brutish actions like the incident in Tunisia that *invites* conflict," one of the women railed with the other nodding emphatically.

A second screen displayed a senator decrying the treaty wasn't enough and recounted numerous treaties in the past decade which had been broken or flat out ignored by key nations known to have supported or turned a blind eye to terrorist activities.

The Senator gazed directly at the camera, “Denying justice in the hope of an unenforceable treaty is foolish and it is unfair to the American people. It is unfair to the families suffering heartbreak because these monsters came to American soil and we allowed them to carry out this reprehensible act!”

The third screen Warrant Officer Jacobs brought up was the one that drew the greatest ire of Raider Six. Surveillance outside of the Pakistan Embassy showed a man smiling amongst a gathering in the embassy’s courtyard.

“That looks like…,” Ramos started.

“Mahaz Maher,” Warrant Officer Jacobs confirmed.

“They’re not even trying to keep a low profile,” Dobson shook his head. “Look, he’s smiling right into the camera.”

“With the treaty hanging in the balance, Washington is not going to make waves,” Jacobs said.

“I believe the waves have been made, just not by us. You can sign a treaty with a sovereign nation, but not with terrorists,” Grady added.

“There has to be something we can do,” Dobson pleaded.

“You know how this works. We receive orders and we follow them. No orders, no mission,” Jacobs said.

“This sucks!” Zalinsnky spat.

Chris sat in the back of the room, remaining silent. The image of Mahaz Maher etched into his brain. His mind imagined this man setting the charges. He could envision Breanna and Macy driving across the bridge while that smug bastard triggered the blast. Staring back at the scene, he boiled. This man was comfortably at a cocktail party while Chris' family and a hundred others were dead.

Lieutenant Colonel Lippett burst into the room. "Official orders…report for sniper certification at zero-seven hundred. Next week, we're at SERE."

"What about al Qaeda? Al-ansar Shariah? Barriq Hussein and that puke?" Zalinsky exclaimed.

Lippett glanced at the screen frozen on the image of Mahaz Maher, "On that matter, we are most definitely on stand down orders. Even if there was action, we will not draw that billet. Not after Tunisia, not after Gunny decked a reporter on live television."

The Lieutenant Colonel waved off his crew as he observed their reactions to Raider Six's orders. "I'd like nothing more than to go right at the throat of the people who did this and the people who sponsored this. We're Marines. We execute the orders at hand. Right now, those orders are to fine tune our skills so we are ready when called upon."

Raider Six looked at their boss without reacting. "Go home. Spend time with your families. Get some rest. Blow off some steam. I'll see you all tomorrow, zero-six hundred," Lippett ordered.

The team began to disband.

"Staff Sergeant, a word?" Lippett said as he moved toward the door.

"Sir?"

"You're closer to Gunny than anyone else on the team. What's your take on how he's doing, what he's thinking?" Lippett asked.

"We're operators, sir. If it was your family, what would you be thinking?" Grady said flatly.

Lippett nodded, "Yeah, that's what I am afraid of."

SIX

The last thing Chris felt like doing was being around people and in a place where he had to temper his emotions. He had barely held himself in check with his team. Shrugging off the team's urgings for him to join them at their team watering hole, he made a beeline for his Bronco.

Before he could slip safely inside, Grady's voice pulled him short. "Chris!" the Staff Sergeant called.

Chris stood between the frame of the SUV and the open door, staring blankly at his friend.

Grady put a hand on Chris' shoulder, "Hey, I know you don't want to be with the team. I can only imagine how close you must be to exploding. But, I'm not sure bloodying up your knuckles in your drywall is the best idea, either."

"Lippett send you after me?" Chris asked.

"He did," Grady admitted. "I was going to hit you up anyways. Stop by my place, have a beer, a bottle of whiskey, and talk...or don't talk. Just know that you've got people in your corner. Vivian messaged me, too. She'd like to see you."

Chris stared at Grady for a moment. Vivian and Breanna were best friends. Other than calls to family, it was the first time that it registered others had lost someone special as well. Reluctantly, he nodded, "Sure. I'll stop by."

"Great. I'll meet you there," Grady said, heading for his car.

As Chris started up his own vehicle, he was torn. He didn't know what he was supposed to feel anymore. The anger and sadness had drifted apart from one another. Each had its own clarity, no longer muddled together, yet they fought for his attention. He wanted to cry. He wanted to punch things, hunt down every soul responsible for Breanna and Macy's deaths. Closing his eyes for a moment, he took a deep breath. The time would come for action. He had to be patient.

Releasing his sigh, Chris started the Bronco and put the transmission into gear.

The miles to Grady's house were a blur of his friend's tail lights. Chris couldn't recall a turn that he took. Even parked at the curb, he was reluctant to get out. He loved Grady and his family, he just didn't know how he could feel or act human around anyone.

Seeing Grady's wife on the front step, seeing her wipe a tear and force a weak smile at Chris, told him he was there for her as much as for himself. He was there for Breanna.

As Chris got out of his SUV, Vivian bounced with anticipation and unfolded her arms so that she could welcome him with a hug. Her arms around him chased away the anger for that moment, allowing the sadness to overwhelm him.

"Chris, I am so sorry," Vivian breathed through her own tears.

"Me too…me too," Chris squeezed a bit harder.

Grady let the two have their moment. He knew his wife needed that vestigial contact with Breanna through Chris.

Chris cleared his throat and with a final squeeze, pulled away from his friend's wife. "Well, *that* had to happen." He wiped tears away from his face with his fists.

"Come on, buddy. I'm not sure how much Irish is in either one of us, but I think they have the right idea during these times," Grady placed a hand on Chris' shoulder and led him into the house.

Two little faces painted in equal parts Grady and Vivian peered around the corner of the hallway. Instinctively, they searched for their friend that they knew would not be streaking in as she usually did. Chris recognized their young, false hope. Nodding in understanding, he dropped to a knee. “Hey, guys.”

“Hi, Uncle Chris,” they said in cautious unison. Behind him, Vivian nodded, encouraging the kids to come forward. They each leaned into Chris and hugged him. For a brief moment, Chris’ emotions were thawed.

“Why don’t you boys go in the backyard. I’ll put some food together, so it’ll be there if you want it,” Vivian suggested. “Ray and Charlotte, why don’t you two give me a hand.”

“Come on,” Grady led Chris through the house. Pausing at a cabinet on the way to the kitchen, he grabbed a bottle and a pair of glasses.

Stepping out onto the back patio, Grady poured a couple of drams into each glass and handed one to Chris. Setting the bottle down, he raised his glass. “To Breanna and Macy,” the words were difficult for him to say, and he knew harder for Chris to hear.

“Breanna and Macy,” Chris repeated softly. In one motion, he raised his glass to his lips, allowing the amber liquid to run down his throat. Setting the glass down, he didn’t refuse when Grady offered to fill it again.

In their travels, they lost people that they dearly loved. Brothers in the field that they knowingly were put in harm’s way. Tragic just the same, but Breanna and Macy…and all the people on the bridge so unnecessarily ripped away from their world.

Grady was hurting, he still failed to imagine what Chris was going through.

Leaning against the edge of his outdoor table, they sat in silence as they drank their bourbon.

Chris was surprised himself that he was enjoying the quiet company of his friend. Understanding how much his wife and daughter impacted others made him feel a bit selfish for wanting to withdraw. Swirling the liquid in his glass, his mind drifted to the many evenings the families shared. Macy playing with Grady's children, Breanna visiting with Vivian while he and Grady regaled in their exploits of a recent mission.

Life wasn't always easy, but it was good. Finishing his second glass, he set it next to the bottle that sat between them.

"You probably aren't thinking about food, but we should probably get you something to eat. Gotta have your strength. Never know when we'll have an opportunity to take action," Grady suggested.

"You heard the Lieutenant Colonel, we're stood down," Chris said, a sheepish grin spread across his face.

Raising an eyebrow, Grady grunted, "When is Raider Six ever out of the fight?"

"Oorah," Chris nodded, following his friend into the house.

The screen cut to a congressman from Texas, "This is an atrocity from any angle as I can see it. Attack on innocents on American soil is an act of war. Those who carried out the attack, those who helped plan it, order or funded it in any way need to be held accountable in the most severe fashion."

A congresswoman from California took her place at the podium, "While no one can condone attacks on innocent people, you can understand the fear and frustration that drive them. As American politics meddle in foreign governments, as we send drones and missiles into their homeland, as Islamaphobia grows in this country…we have a hand in inviting these unfortunate instances."

"Unfortunate instances…that's what people in our own government call it?" Grady exploded. "Sorry, my friend."

"It's alright," Chris said softly. "I should be going, anyway. Be sure to thank Vivian for the Jambalaya."

Grady paused, looking after Chris. "You sure you're alright?"

"I'm alright. I've got a lot to do tomorrow. Breanna's family is coming to town, they want to help with the funeral service," Chris shrugged.

"Anything we can do? Vivian…or I bet Lippett would let me…," Grady started.

"I appreciate that. Might need another bottle of bourbon with the in-laws, but I'll manage. Work the problem. Always do," Chris said.

"I'm sure that can be arranged," Grady laughed. "Mind if I swing by after work tomorrow?"

"Sure. I'd love the interruption at that point, I'm sure," Chris nodded. He paused at the door. He could see Grady was concerned.

Striding forward, Chris threw an arm around his friend. "I'm good. Thank you for being here for me," he assured.

Grady nodded, "You know I'm here for you, brother."

"I'll fight on," Chris said.

"*We'll* fight on," Grady corrected.

"Yeah," Chris said, turning to leave. "I'll see you tomorrow."

Sliding behind the wheel of the Bronco, Chris didn't notice the feeling of numb that had begun to settle around him. He wasn't aware of the rage and sorrow that seared his soul and was beginning the process of bottling. His consciousness could not grasp the pressure that was so precariously capped within him.

One of the nation's most highly capable operators was becoming an explosive weapon himself.

As Chris drove past streetlights and autonomically paused for stop signs, he was equally unaware of when he would detonate. Like a warhead secured under the wings of a bomber, he passed by homes of countless people unaware of the volatile armament outside their door.

Like the warhead, he was harmless as the Bronco whisked by. His arming switch, at the moment, set to off.

Reaching his house, he entered, tossing his keys on the hall table. Mindlessly, he navigated his way to his bedroom and collapsed. Years of military training, finding sleep when you can, regardless of stimuli to ensure he was ready when called upon had finally kicked in.

Seven

Chris woke to a day that he never imagined. He rolled out of bed as somber and distant as he had ever been. His heart found permanent residence in his gut. He moved because he had to, not because it was his desire to.

Rubbing his face, he pivoted his feet to the floor as he sat up. A brief, habitual glance at the time on his phone precluded a long look at the photo on the bedstand. The glass was marred with fingerprints and dried tears from the countless times that he had studied it over the passing days. This morning was no exception.

Hoisting the picture up, he stared at the smiling faces of Breanna and Macy. The Atlantic Ocean backdrop and the white sand made them look as though they were floating in the sky. The hair gently waving in the breeze as the joy in their faces was captured in the moment. The family enjoyed their favorite place together, doing their favorite thing- being together.

Chris sat the photo down. Getting out of bed, he shuffled mindlessly towards the bathroom. Running the hot water, he ran his hands down his stubbled face. Staring at the mirror, he was taken aback. He had returned haggard from missions, going days without real sleep. He had never seen his face quite like this. His eyes puffy and bruised. He looked as unhappy as he felt.

The steam in the sink began to fill the air. As Chris studied his reflection, a waist-high shape skittered past the bathroom. In the corner of his eye, he caught a figure leaning against the doorway, as Breanna had. He was used to her watching him as he shaved. Spinning, the shadows evaporated, as the hundreds he had spied over the past few days had.

Sighing, he returned to the mirror.

As he glared at himself, his eye twitched. "Why are *you* here, instead of them?" he growled.

Making a fist with his hand, he moved to strike, pulling the punch back just as the static connection could be made with the glass. He had struggled to avoid destroying everything in sight, to avoid breaking down into a puddle on the floor, to avoid running off the same bridge that took Breanna and Macy away from him.

With a deep breath, he knew he had to contain himself, at least for one more afternoon. He had to greet his in-laws, his and Breanna's family friends, his own family and friends, his team. Not for them, but for Breanna and Macy.

Collecting himself, he bathed his face in the hot water and grabbed his razor from the counter.

Chris arrived at the church early. Finding his way to the sanctuary, he saw the flowers and caskets were already arranged at the front of the room. The pastor had been reviewing pages of notes behind the podium. Seeing the look on Chris' face, the pastor offered a quick nod and silently scampered out of the room affording Chris time to himself.

The room itself felt odd. A cacophony of joy, sorrow, hope, despair, light, and confusion swirled about. Chris froze as he looked at the pair of caskets lined up next to one another. He was compelled to move forward, yet held back. There was finality in the scene that he wasn't quite ready to accept. Squeezing his eyes tight, he gathered himself. Breaking through the invisible wall that held him at bay, he made his way to the front of the room.

Opening the first mahogany lid, he was overwhelmed with the image before him. He knew it would exist, he was not prepared to see his wife's face. Not in that way. He swallowed hard as he studied Breanna. Even in death, she was striking, radiant. Chris was overcome with a wash of comfort, confusion, and sadness.

He waited for her to open her eyes. Tell him everything would be okay. She never did.

Chris felt her presence around him. As though she had laced her hand into his, she led him to the second box. Guiding his hand, the lid was opened. A sight that should never be seen by a parent's eyes confronted Chris as though a sledgehammer crashed into his skull. The most beautiful, innocent picture of life, lying perfectly still. Looking peaceful in slumber as she had so many nights Chris sat by her bed and studied her as she slept. Watching each breath as her chest heaved. This moment, her chest was still. The stillness brought Chris to his knees.

His hands on the coffin, he tried to be strong for her presence, but he was lost. Through a river of tears, he screamed for God. He pleaded, he cursed, he demanded. He was lost.

Breanna was his rock. She was his anchor to earth. Through all of the horrible things he had seen, through all of the horrible things he had done, her outreached hand kept him grounded. Kept him within arm's reach of God's path, kept him touched by the light. Without her, he wasn't sure how far into the darkness he would fall. The pain and rage that bristled inside him knew how far he *wanted* to descend into darkness. Unleash his fury on the world in his fullest might, be damned the consequence. Be damned losing sight of the light.

He felt a touch on his back. A calming touch. Whirling around, fully expecting to see the pastor, or *someone*, his tearful eyes found nothing. "Oh, God!" he cried. He knew the touch. He knew the message. Breanna.

With a deep breath, he gathered himself. For her. For *them.* His wife and his baby girl.

As he rose, he worked to recap the emotions that blew their precarious capture. He wiped away the streams from his face to see the pastor standing in the doorway. Determining Chris was together enough, he stepped aside, allowing Breanna's parents to enter the sanctuary. Trailed by Breanna's sister and her family. They offered a quiet nod and moved to the front of the room.

Chris looked at them, unsure of what to do. What to say. With a slight bow of his head, he shuffled away and allowed them their time. The pastor welcomed him. With a light hand on his shoulder, he led him into the atrium.

"Chris, there are no words right now that will make any sense. God's plan is unfathomable. I married you and Breanna. I Christened Macy. I see the love, the hurt, the pain, the anger. I watched you. You know God sent her to you. He doesn't control you or your actions, but he lays out a path. He can't make you decide to take it. But I promise you, Breanna and Macy are at the end of it. Waiting for you," the pastor said. "I'm here if you need me. Otherwise, I will leave you to your thoughts."

Chris watched as the kind man walked away. He didn't have much time to consider the words or much else, as a wave of bodies poured through the door. Leading the charge was his mother and father who collapsed on him in a warm, long embrace.

As much as Chris witnessed as he faded in and out of the reality of the moment, the service was beautiful. Sadness and tears were largely replaced with love and memories, drawing from the joy of Breanna and Macy's lives as opposed to the pain of their losses.

The service migrated to the second auditorium where murals of photos and memories decorated the room. Guests lined up at multiple buffet tables as family and friends connected, many for the first time since Chris and Breanna's wedding.

Chris' parents and sister huddled around him, lauding warm support. Friends and his teammates one by one gave him a hug or a pat on the shoulder. Some prayed with him. All rejoiced in the love that they shared for Breanna and Macy.

Breanna's family approached. Her father shook his hand while her sister and nieces hugged him. As they parted, Breanna's mother approached. She looked every part the mess that Chris felt inside. She strode towards him with a familiar haze of sorrow shaken with anger watered down with a kiss of restraint.

Her eyebrows twitched as she fought for the words she wanted to convey. At first, her lips quivered without sound until the dam that held them broke wide open in a tearful burst of anger, "I know you loved Breanna…and Macy. I know how much they loved you." Her voice quaked, the confused look in her eyes turned to clear and undeniable outrage, "This is yours. This is your death. You and your hero's arrogance. They targeted you. They wanted to hurt you and they took my baby girl."

Chris stood still and moved while his father-in-law tried to console and pull his wife away.

"They *did* hurt me. More than they ever could have on any battlefield," Chris whispered softly.

As the families parted, Raider Six gathered around Chris. Lance Corporal Ramos led the team in prayer as their heads bowed together and their arms wrapped around one another.

When the church was cleared and the last family member had left, Chris was again left alone in the sanctuary. His thoughts were muddled, but he approached the caskets with a different air in his heart.

A part of him did not want to leave. Another part of him wanted to run out and begin kicking in doors. As he neared the coffins, he felt a flickering moment of peace. He wanted that moment shared with Breanna and Macy. He loved them both with all of his heart, which left him wondering what remained in the cavity of his chest.

His wife and daughter were so still. They seemed as though they still had life in them, though Chris knew the contrary. Leaning in, he placed kisses to each on the forehead. "I love you two forever. Make room for me, if I'm ever allowed to join you," he whispered.

"That was a nice service," Grady said as he walked alongside his friend. The waves lapped yards away, the setting sun dazzling off the water.

"Yeah," Chris grunted, his hands in his pockets as they wandered.

"A lot of love in that room. Your family touched a lot of lives," Grady said. "A lot of people love you, brother."

Chris cast a quick glance at his friend but returned his gaze to the unblemished sand in front of him.

Grady and Chris walked in silence for what seemed like miles. As they neared the end of the beach where the Atlantic washed into the New Topsail Inlet. Turning to his friend, Grady said, "Man, whatever you need to do, you know the team is with you. You know that, right? *Whatever.*"

"What I have to do, I have to do alone," Chris was blunt in his reply.

"Can I ask what that is?"

“No, and I wouldn’t place the burden of hearing those words on you,” Chris offered a defiant look.

Grady stood still, absorbing the comment, and then nodded in understanding, “What do I say?”

“Tell them the truth, the last time you saw me was after the funeral…and I wasn’t much in the mood for talking.”

Grady stared at his friend for a long moment. “Alright, I hear you, brother,” he relented. He didn’t like it, but he understood. “Clear copy.”

Chris studied Grady, appreciating his steadfastness and discretion. Turning his attention to the ocean, he allowed the waves and haunting power and beauty of the Atlantic to remove his mind from the world.

EIGHT

Chris pried off his tie and tossed his suit jacket onto his dresser. Rolling up his shirt sleeves, he maneuvered through the house making a pile on the bed. Opening his gun safe, he pulled a box from the bottom shelf. Tossing the lid inside, he pulled out a wad of bills. Grabbing his personal concealed carry weapon and several boxes of ammunition, he added those to the assortment of items he had already tossed on the bed.

Next to the safe, he grabbed his tactical "go bag". Pre-stuffed with critical gear, he augmented the pack with the sundry he had wielded around the room. Whirling around the room to see what else he might be missing, he spied his black Belleville boots and threw them next to his tactical pack.

With a sigh, he looked around the house, not for gear, but as what he knew might be his last look. Stuffing everything but the boots into his bag, he spun and sat on the edge of the bed. Picking up the photo he had studied more in the past 72 hours than he had the entirety of its existence, he abruptly brought the frame down against the bedstand, cracking it in a shower of glass and wood fragments. The photo freed from its detention, Chris grabbed it. Holding it up, he sat calmly for a brief moment. Taking in his first visual sight of Breanna and Macy since he closed their caskets at the funeral.

Folding the picture in half and in half again, he stuffed it in his shirt pocket.

Without another glance around the house, Chris grabbed his gear and stormed out towards his Bronco.

Driving through the gates of the base, Chris gave a wave to the MPs that were used to seeing him arrive at all hours of the day. Pulling up to his team's building, he strode through as he always had. Inserting his phone into the secure cubby outside the team room, he pushed his way through and to the gear cage. Inserting his code, he grabbed a big duffel and hoisted it on the counter in the center of the room.

Working quickly, he selected his chosen items and stuffed them into the bag. Leaving the cage with the duffel over his shoulder, he made his way to his locker. Pulling his night ops gear from their hangers, he crammed them in the bag as well.

"Chris, what are you doing here?" a voice called over his shoulder.

Hoping for a clean visit, though not expecting it, Chris wasn't surprised. The Raider building had almost constant action.

Looking up, he eyed at Warrant Officer Patty Jacobs. "Grabbing a few things before I go on leave. Lippett suggested I do so."

"He ordered you to take leave," Jacobs pried.

"Pretty much," Chris grinned.

Jacobs studied the Gunnery Sergeant, "I'm glad you're taking some time. Where you headed?"

Chris shrugged, "See family, maybe do some fishing. I don't know. Just as soon be operating, to tell the truth."

"I get that," Jacobs nodded. Placing a hand on Chris' shoulder as he quickly zipped the duffel. "Take care of yourself, Chris. I'm so sorry."

"Thanks. I'll collect myself and be back soon," he said without a lot of conviction.

"Yeah," Jacobs nodded.

Without another word, Chris slid the duffel over his shoulder and left the building.

Warrant Officer Jacobs watched the Raider Six operator leave the building. Following her intuition, she dialed Lieutenant Colonel Lippett, informing him that Chris had been by.

A few moments after she hung up with Lippett, she heard a phone ringing from the lobby. Following the sound, she spied the phone in the secure cubby. Picking it up, she saw Lippett was calling the Gunnery Sergeant.

She started for the door to chase after Chris, but seeing the taillights of his Bronco speeding away, Jacobs looked around and pocketed it after hitting the "decline" button. Her own phone ringing, she opened the call.

"Is he still there? He's not picking up," Lieutenant Colonel Lippett called into the phone.

"That's not surprising as he left with the phone still in his secure cubby. What would you like me to do?" the Warrant Officer asked.

A pause on the other end suggested Lippett was mulling the situation.

"I'm sure he'll realize he left it and come back for it. The Gunnery Sergeant had a lot on his mind today," Lippett said.

"Yes sir," Jacobs understood the message and closed the call. Slipping the phone back into the cubby, she paused, contemplating Chris Masters' state. She had worked with operators for a long time. They were human, but they were trained to rarely miss a detail, regardless of duress. Still, what the

Gunnery Sergeant has faced was clearly in a category that no amount of training could surmount.

Under different circumstances, the six-hour drive to Washington D.C. would have been almost pleasant. Chris guided the Bronco through lightly trafficked highways making the run in the dark of night. Wheeling the SUV into the heart of the sprawling greater capitol region, Chris used the Marine Barracks at Quantico as his reference point, driving until he found a series of hotels.

Raider Six often settled in questionable establishments while on their missions. At times, the seedier the better, these selections afforded a locale where eyebrows weren't raised and questions weren't asked. Pulling alongside a curb, he felt he found the right location.

The sidewalk outside of the hotel was active despite the early morning hour. This was the period of time when during the rare breaks provided in boot camp, his superiors would warn nothing good happened. A warning at the time for young soldiers to cap their playtime and stay out of trouble. For Chris, this was the perfect time to slip into the hotel and not be bothered.

Slipping past the earnest solicitors at the front door, Chris found an empty desk with a bell on it. He hated ringing it at that hour. Through the crack in a door behind the desk, he could see a man slumped asleep in a chair. Grabbing a pencil from the desk, he hurled it through the opening, smacking the man on the chest. With a snort, the man shook his head, looking around for what woke him.

Chris smiled through the crack.

Disgruntled, the man heaved himself and pushed through the door. "What do you want? Room by the hour?"

Rolling his eyes, Chris responded, "Two nights. Something near the stairs? I like stairs. Back alleys are even better."

The man looked irritated through his sleepy eyes, "Room without a view. Right by the ice maker, but you're in luck, it doesn't work."

"Sounds perfect," Chris nodded. Pulling a wad of bills out, he slapped them on the counter.

The man raised an eyebrow and nodded towards the front door, "Need a key for one of the ladies?"

"No. That won't be necessary," Chris said, snatching the key.

Eyeing the number on the fob, he disappeared up the steps and found the room number. Pushing through the door, he flicked on a dull, amber light. Looking around the room, it was as charming as he had expected. Ages of aroma built from the humid bodies that enjoyed the room before him. He didn't even want to contemplate the horrid tales that bed could tell.

Setting his gear on the bed, he walked to the window. With a flick of his hand, he spied through the gauze drapery and appreciated the fire escape that led to the back alley. "This'll do."

Pushing the bed away from the wall, Chris drew his combat knife, and pulling up the delightfully stained sheet, he cut a wide slit in the mattress. Sorting through his gear, he selected a handful of critical items that he did not trust to the fifty-year-old lock on the room door and stuffed the mattress. Sliding it back to the wall, he did the same with his tactical pack, stuffing the pillows before stowing the remainder of the bags at the foot of the bed.

Checking his watch, Chris calculated he had two hours until sunrise. Weaving back through the peddlers at the front door, he emerged on the street. He didn't like the idea of using his personal vehicle for reconnaissance, but he knew it likely wouldn't matter once he initiated his mission.

Wheeling the Bronco through the quiet streets, he sought a location near the embassy. Driving along the increasingly high rent office buildings and hotels, he found a comparatively modest location. Pulling the narrow SUV into an alley, he parked between a pair of garbage dumpsters. Eyeing the space available, he estimated it wasn't trash pick-up day.

Slinging a long bag from the backseat over his shoulder, he took advantage of the nearby garbage bins. Rifling through a bag of trash, Chris sifted through the contents. Collecting discarded key cards, he grabbed a handful and walked casually to a side entrance. Trying the first card, he slid it through the entry panel only to be greeted by a red light. One by one, he tried the cards until he found one attached to a room that had not yet been checked out. As soon as the green light flashed, Chris swung open the door and slipped into the hallway.

A quick glance down the corridor, he found the placard for the stairwell. Floor by floor, Chris ascended until he met with the final landing. The door was both locked and armed with an alarm. Glancing up, he spied an old camera with a frayed cord dangling from the ceiling. Nudging the camera slightly, it captured the frame, but not the door itself.

With his combat knife, Chris popped the cover to the emergency lever on the door. Finding the wires to the tiny Pietro speaker, he disconnected it from the alarm. Grateful for the old technology that did not link the door to the rest of the hotel's security system, Chris was free to burst through the door and onto the rooftop.

Finding his bearings, he moved directly to the edge of the roof and knelt. Unzipping the long bag he had carried, he produced his compact sniper rifle. Leaning against the low-slung wall of the rooftop, Chris dialed in the scope. His heart picked up a beat as he spied his objective. In the narrow field of view, he could see the Pakistani embassy.

A part of him, a large part of him, wanted to tear down there in the remaining low light and complete the mission. His years of training told him that preparation and intel were keys to a successful mission, not that it was always accurate or plans didn't implode. His internal C.O. demanded that he stand down.

What really held Chris back was ensuring his objective was still there. Being captured with an incomplete mission was not an option. It would tear him apart knowing he was in custody or dead while Breanna and Macy's killer was still free.

Activity at the embassy was appropriately subdued. Chris noted guards at the entry, upstairs balcony, and a pair on patrol that would intersect at a point near the rear of the building as they made their way around the fence line.

Settling into surveillance, Chris' mind was constantly designing scenarios and calculating probability. Security detail habits, building ingress points and grounds infiltration, and cover all fed his mental blueprints.

As sunlight began cresting over the Washington D.C. skyline, activity around the embassy began to blossom to life. Staffers bustled about ensuring the dignitaries' needs were met. Preparations for visitors were next as the business office opened up. Key officials began to arrive from the posh Virginia homes, their gleaming luxury vehicles lined up on one side of the drive.

Chris covered the objective end of his scope with a glare shield to avoid unwanted attention from lens flash. His eye twitched as the well-attired men walked casually into the building to start their days as though life was normal. To Chris, life was anything but normal. He did not know who, if any of these men had anything to do with the Breanna and Macy's deaths, but each one of them was harboring the killer.

Through unblinking focus, Chris knew that he could dispatch any one of them at any moment. He could obliterate the entire embassy if he wanted to. A part of him did. With a deep breath, Chris allowed his cerebral function to overtake his emotions. He had an objective to carry out. If he failed, he would be letting his wife and daughter down.

A man walked out onto a third-floor balcony as a server laid out his breakfast on a small table. Fine linens draped over the table while settings of juice, coffee, and a full breakfast were put in place. Oblivious to the world, the man stretched as he took in the low morning sun. Leaning against the rail of the balcony, he stared out at the D.C. landscape, a content smile crossing his face.

Chris' finger pulsed, gently sliding along the trigger. In one quick moment, that smile would be washed off of the man's face. Gunnery Sergeant Masters glowered as he studied Mahaz Maher, the monster who needlessly stole the lives of Breanna and Macy along with others in the Stone Bay.

As Chris watched Maher glibly enjoy his breakfast as he was joined by a female companion. The fact that this man could smile across the table at the woman Chris determined was noticeably younger while Chris would never get to look at the faces of his wife and daughter set Chris to a boil. The tension on the trigger found its limit.

Images of Macy running into Chris' arms as he arrived home from a mission, and Breanna wrapping her arms around him as leaned against their porch flashed in his mind. Each image vanished into a haze as he looked away in disgust. He wanted nothing more than Maher dead on that balcony.

As he observed the man, Chris determined he was a merciless order taker, not a tactical order giver. The Marine snapped his attention to Maher, his finger instinctively wrapped around the trigger once more. A 7.62 round to the head was too good for this piece of garbage. With a wicked grin, Chris began crafting a far more unpleasant end for his family's killer. Higher risk, much higher reward.

Biting his lip, Chris went from surveillance to planning. One thing he was sure of, now that he positively identified his target and the room he was staying in, Maher had carried out his last attack. Reluctantly, Chris packed up his gear and headed down the hotel stairs towards the lobby.

Climbing into his Bronco, he roared away before the cleaning crew began making their trips to the dumpsters he used as a parking spot. Driving away was as difficult for Chris as walking away from the funeral home. He fought the urge to finish his objective at that moment, knowing he had a significantly more appropriate end to Maher's remaining time on earth in store for the terrorist.

Nine

Staff Sergeant Grady had barely pushed his way through the Stone Bay Raider Team building when a man in a Marine Corps windbreaker stepped in front of him. The man was unusually stoic, which itself was a Marine trademark.

"Staff Sergeant," the man announced with a glance at Grady's stripes. "Perhaps you could help me locate Lieutenant Colonel Lippett."

"Perhaps I could, if I knew what this was about," Grady squared himself in front of the man.

Pulling a badge from his jacket pocket, he spat, "Chief Warrant Officer Buchannan, CID."

Grady winced slightly at the designation of the United States Marine Corps Criminal Investigation Division. Many

Marines viewed CID the same way a police officer might internal affairs.

"Well, Chief Warrant Officer, I know who you are now, I still don't know the purpose of your inquiry," Grady countered.

Buchannan raised an eyebrow, "Staff Sergeant, I question your rank to question me other than to comply with my request."

Acknowledging the superior rank, Grady acquiesced. "Right this way."

Placing his cell phone in the acrylic bin leading into the team rooms, Grady slid one out for the CID agent and tilted his head towards the bin.

Rolling his eyes, Buchannan placed his cellphone in the drawer.

Sliding his badge over the sensor, Grady opened the door and led the investigator down the team corridors. Rounding the hall, he moved to Lippett's office. Rapping against the doorframe, he announced himself, "Lieutenant Colonel, CID Agent Buchannan is here to see you."

Lippett rustled papers on the desk, freeing his paper calendar. "I don't recall having a meeting with a CID investigator. What is this about?"

"Well, sir…," Grady started.

"You don't have a standing meeting and I did not respond to the junior officer's request for the intent to my meeting,"

Buchannan peeled around the corner and stood in front of Lippett's desk. Turning towards Grady, he snapped, "Staff Sergeant…you're dismissed."

Grady stood agape, shooting a questioning glance at Lippett. The Lieutenant Colonel simply offered an acknowledging head nod, confirming that the Staff Sergeant should retreat to the team room.

Grady relented and rolled out of the room. As he exited his commander's office, he slowed his pace.

"Chief Warrant Officer Buchannan, as you can imagine with an unannounced visit, I am terribly short on time. Let's get right to the point," Lippett was curt in his statement.

"The entire Marine Corps is saddened by the attack that occurred just outside of the base. Upon a routine follow up with one of the marines in your command personally affected by the incident, we found him unavailable with whereabouts unknown," Buchannan stated.

Lippett sighed, "Cutting through the crap, you are talking about Gunnery Sergeant Masters. His wife and daughter were killed in a terrorist attack, not an 'incident'. He was understandably impacted by his loss and I sent him on leave."

"Where did Gunnery Sergeant Masters go?"

Lippett looked cross, "I don't know and I don't care. Neither should the Marine Corps. He is a fine man. An exceptional Marine. He needs to sort his losses and emotions and when ready, he will return to the team."

"We would like to follow up with Masters regarding the incident," Buchannan said. Tossing a file on the desk, he added, "We, the CID, the United States Marine Corps is officially recalling him."

Picking up the folder, the Lieutenant Colonel flipped through the documents. "No."

Buchannan shook himself, "Excuse me, sir?"

"These documents were signed by you. I respect the office of the CID, but you are well junior to my station. Request denied. My Marine gets the time to collect himself and return to duty," Lippett stated flatly.

Buchannan raised an eyebrow, "You are sure you wish for escalation of this matter? I will return by end of the day with satisfactory signatures but you implicate yourself in anything your Gunnery Sergeant may involve himself in by doing so."

Lippett scoffed, "What is Gunny going to do? Attack a country on his own?"

The Lieutenant Colonel rose from his office chair and pushed the folder into the CID investigator's chest, "Get appropriately authorized documents and I will gladly comply. Until then, I am not recalling my Marine."

Hearing the office chair slide out from Lippett's desk, Grady rolled away from the wall and scampered down the hallway. Retrieving his cell phone, he darted out of the building around the side. Dialing Chris' phone, he was met with the notorious "caller unavailable" tone. Chris was either way off the grid or he had purposely disabled his phone. Knowing his friend, Grady was sure it was the latter.

He didn't like the idea of Masters off on his own, grieving or otherwise, but he knew his Gunny Sergeant had to manage his own way. Grady just wished he could be there with him.

Not desiring another run-in with Buchannan, Grady made his way to the vehicle gate of the team barracks as Lance Corporal Ramos was driving his pickup through. Grady flashed his identification at the guard and hopping on the side steps of the truck, hitched a ride into the compound.

Wheeling the pickup to the rear entrance of the Raider team building Ramos parked and cocked his head at Grady. "Avoiding the same suit I saw on my way in?"

Nodding, Grady admitted, "I am. Asking a bunch of questions about Gunny I'm not too keen on answering."

"I hear you," Ramos studied the Staff Sergeant. "Lighting up Lippett?"

"He was. It was a short run as the C.O. had no stomach for answering a CID on a witch hunt without provocation," Grady said.

"Gunny's gonna have to do his thing. Wish it was a team effort," Ramos said. "Having a terrorist on American soil and having our hands tied. It's not right."

"Technically Pakistani soil."

"Yeah, a lot of wars started over similar technicalities," Ramos countered.

Grady grinned, "I'm ready the moment Halo greenlights us."

"We all are," Ramos clapped his hand on Grady's shoulder. "We all are."

Chris Masters sat in his Bronco looking out at the Potomac river as he studied a sketch he penciled into his notebook matched to the documents that he took from the Raider offices in Stone Bay. He marked everything he could recall from his surveillance through the sniper scope. Each sentry with directional arrows indicating their repeated routes, each camera placement, and the location of Mahaz Maher were detailed.

Masters ran scenarios through his head covering entry points, potential guard movements, room, and building access. Mental walkthroughs of each with projected outcomes, probability of success, and egress options were carefully constructed.

When Chris found one that held promise, he closed his eyes and ran through the op from start to finish. He tried to account for every variable, house staff, guests, unseen security detail, speed of outside response. He was calm through each phase of the operation until he reached the room where Mahaz Maher was staying. The gunnery sergeant's heart would race. He stared down the terrorist. Rage, pain and hurt searing his soul.

Even in the safety of his Bronco, parked in a lot overlooking the Potomac, Chris had no idea how this was going to end. No amount of run-throughs could prepare him for one aspect of the operation – how we would respond when he faced the terrorist that took Breanna and Macy from him.

The anger at Maher gave way to an overwhelming wash of sadness. He missed his wife and daughter, the pain and loss were unbearable. Opening his eyes, he watched the water of the river flow by. Collecting himself, he had a long night ahead of him. Starting the Bronco, he headed back towards the seedy motel.

TEN

United States Marine Corps Criminal Investigator Phillip Buchannan flashed his identification and waited to be buzzed in. Tapping a folder impatiently against his hand, Buchannan rocked on his heels as he waited.

Lieutenant Colonel Lippett took his time before ultimately sending a junior Raider team member to escort the investigator in. As the Marine operator held the door, he nodded silently towards the bins against the wall. Reluctantly, Buchannan fished his phone out of his pocket and laid it in a bin.

Approaching the office, the Raider stated, "Wait here, sir." Spinning on his heels, the operator left to rejoin his team duties.

Once more, Buchannan waited, rapping the folder against his palm. “Buchannan,” Lippett called.

The investigator wheeled into the office, folder held in the air. “Official orders to recall Gunnery Sergeant Christopher Masters,” Buchannan tossed the folder onto the desk.

Lippett leaned against the desk, hands folded over the unopened document. With concerned eyes, he stared at the investigator, “Do you have a family, Warrant Officer Buchannan?”

Buchannan frowned, “Like a mother, father, brothers and sisters, sir?”

“Like wife and kids.”

“No, sir. I hardly see how…,” Buchannan started.

“Spent any time in combat?”

Buchannan shrugged. “I’ve been trained, sir.”

“Have you spent any time in combat? Away from friends, unable to call Mom on Mother’s Day, Christmas, or wish your girlfriend a happy birthday?” Lippett pressed.

Buchannan became cross, “Sir, I don’t see how any of this has to do with the orders signed by Brigadier General Golliday.”

“They have to do with decorum and concern for the well-being of our Marines who leave their families behind. They knowingly risk themselves, happily, for our command and country. What they do not sign up for is the risk of their families targeted because of the work that they do. Gunnery Sergeant

Masters is grieving and he should be allowed to do so," Lippett snapped.

"Sir, that is precisely why we have orders to have the gunnery sergeant recalled. He is a highly capable operator in a great emotional distress with access to the suspected killer of his family on foreign sovereignty," Buchannan countered.

"Orders are orders. I'll recall Gunnery Sergeant Masters," Lippett relented.

Chief Warrant Officer Buchannan stood in front of the desk.

The Lieutenant Colonel looked up and sighed, "He is not going to magically appear. You can go now."

Buchannan produced a card from his jacket pocket, "When Gunnery Sergeant Masters reports."

"You'll be one of the first to know," Lippett sighed, tossing the card inside the orders folder and shoved the packet into a desk drawer.

As the investigator left the office, Lippett leaned back thoughtfully. He had to admit to himself, he wasn't sure what his gunnery sergeant was going to do, but he certainly knew what he was capable of.

ELEVEN

Gunnery Sergeant Chris Masters sat in his dingy hotel room. The bed had become a pre-mission workbench. He diligently inspected each weapon, carefully loaded each magazine to capacity. He wouldn't be laden for this operation. He elected speed and stealth as the preferred tactic.

A night assault, Chris was adorned in tactical black from head to toe. His finishing touches were smearing black face paint on his forehead and cheeks.

The gunnery sergeant was strangely calm, almost numb. He had entered his usual pre-mission status, suppressing anxiety, excitement, concern… at this point in an operation, it was all about executing the plan, awareness, and making adjustments when the plan inevitably unearths unforeseen variables or hits the fan entirely.

Completing his mental checklist, he paused. Picking up the folded photo of Breanna and Macy, he stared at it in the weak, yellow light offered from the hotel lamp. His eyes traced their shapes, etching them in his mind. Their smiles sang at him through the still photo. Their eyes, through the lens of his camera, peered into his soul. He imagined they saw what he was feeling – an empty, completely dark space with the two of them holding hands while a single, soft light showered down on them.

Chris was lost without them. All he wanted was to bring their killer to justice and join them. Meet them there in that dark space, grab their hands and walk into the waiting light together. Without an ounce of emotion, Chris knew both of those objectives could be well met this night.

Folding the photo, Chris placed it in the breast pocket of his tactical shirt. Placing his assault gear in the bag, he slipped out of the hotel room and crept down the stairwell to the back alley. Reaching his Bronco, parked strategically beyond the reach of streetlamps, he stowed his gear and fired up the SUV, launching it towards the Pakistan embassy.

Arriving at a discrete location he had scoped out on his earlier recon, he was less than two blocks away from the embassy. Without hesitation, he strapped on his gear and launched into his operation. Slipping through the Washington, D.C. streets, he remained in the shadows. Using trees and buildings retarding the angles and reach of lights, he reached the tall, iron fence of the embassy.

From his surveillance, he stood in an obscure spot that was shadowed by years of vegetation growth since the lights and cameras had been installed years prior. Using thermite bands around two adjacent iron bars, he shrouded the scene with a floor mat from the Bronco to dampen the luminous work of the thermite.

Masters knew the top of the fence line was monitored via a laser sensing system, the bottom was not. The thermite did its job quickly, allowing Chris to remove just enough of the iron fence to shimmy through.

Following the path he constructed from his surveillance, he made his way to the stone wall that surrounded the rear of the embassy building. From there, he had to manage an expansive tile patio that was completely exposed before reaching the building itself.

True to the pattern he viewed in the early morning hours, two guards intersected directly above him. This time they paused to exchange words before carrying on their patrol. Chris considered this variable. Eliminating two guards at this point would leave him subject only to camera angles prior to penetrating the embassy.

Chris tossed his keys at the foot of the patio steps, both guards ceased talking and snapped on flashlights. Beams shone throughout the lawn of the embassy. The light picked up the glint of metal, encouraging the guards to investigate. As the guards neared the last step, Chris sprung into action.

Launching himself out of his crouched position, the Marine executed a lightning-quick punch to the throat of the first guard, causing him to stumble back, choking and wheezing, unable to get a breath or expel a sound. Chris was able to concentrate on the second guard. Before the guard was able to react, Chris spun the guard with a palm to his shoulder and wrapped his forearm around his throat before he could call out in alarm.

Applying pressure, Chris used his free hand to leverage the hold until he felt the guard's body go limp in his grasp. Tossing him into the shadow of the wall on the lawn, Christ leapt towards the first guard who began running towards the side of the embassy building, while still grasping his throat.

The gunnery sergeant snatched his keys from the lawn and sprinted towards the guard. Launching himself in the air, Chris wrapped his arms around the man and lurched his body backward, preventing either of them from breaching the sidewall of the embassy where Chris knew they would be in view of the patrol and cameras in the front.

Rolling into the deeper shadows against the base of the building, Chris squeezed the man's throat until he, too, succumbed to unconsciousness. The clock was on before the guards would recover and the embassy would come to life collapsing on his position.

Eyeing the balcony he spied during surveillance, he pulled the grapple from his pack as he sprinted to position. In one motion, Chris hurled the hook to the railing of the balcony and leapt onto its trailing rope. Hand over hand, he ascended until he could reach the terrace rail and launching his body onto the balcony.

Not a single moment or movement wasted since the inception of the operation, Gunnery Sergeant Masters pressed on. Slamming his shoulder into the French doors of the balcony, they burst open. Moving swiftly through the stately suite, he moved with purpose to a door he calculated to be the bedroom. His entry alerted the occupants as they scrambled out of bed. As most people did, in Chris' experience they flattened themselves to the walls opposite the door.

As his assault weapon-mounted tactical light swept the room and glinted on two pairs of eyes, he warned in a hushed tone, "If you make a sound, I will shoot you."

He trained his light on each of the occupants, ensuring that they understood. Eyeing the young woman, her lips quivering, he pressed a finger to his lips and shook his head. Motioning for her to duck down behind the bed, she complied and pulled the covers over her.

Chris focused his attention on the male.

"I do not fear death," Mahaz Maher sneered.

"I know, the bad guys always say that, but I know deep down, you really do," Masters chided. "All cowards do."

As the man began to open his mouth again, Chris strode forward and slammed the butt of his weapon into Maher's face.

With his left hand pinning the terrorist to the wall by his throat, Chris spun the gun, pointing the muzzle at his face. Aiming point-blank, his fingers danced along the grip, finding their way to the trigger. The veins on his forearm tensed. His eyes burned as he stared his wife and daughter's killer in the eyes. Every cell in his body wanted to complete that action.

Beyond this useless soul, was someone who ordered his attack. Chris did not believe it was the Pakistanis. He didn't understand why they were protecting him, but it didn't make sense for them to instigate this action. Maher or the people behind him wielded some undo influence for the Pakistan embassy to grant him asylum.

Chris realized at that very moment, he had come to pull the trigger. He plotted the entire mission with the objective of erasing Maher from this earth. He succumbed to a much better, far more fitting plan.

"You can't be here! This is sovereign territory!" Maher spat as he recovered from the punch.

"So was the bridge you blew up, but that didn't stop you!" Chris snarled, once more fighting the urge to pull the trigger. He had to look away from Maher to allow his finger to lighten.

"Kill me, there will only be another warrior to take my place!" Maher croaked.

The words gave Chris pause. He knew the terrorist was correct. Reluctantly, Chris snapped back into action. Taping the terrorist's mouth, foregoing any gentleness. Pulling plastic zip ties from his pocket, he bound Maher's hands.

Thrusting the terrorist forward toward the balcony, Chris scanned the rear of the complex. No alarms had been sounded, no security scrambled. Taking the opportunity, though knowing his time was running out, the gunnery sergeant moved quickly. Reaching the rail of the balcony, Chris reeled the grapple he used to enter and stuffed it back into his pocket.

With a hand on Maher's collar and another around the waist band of his silk pajama pants, Chris hurled the terrorist over the side and onto the flower bed in a bone crunching heap. The sound of the impact was not insignificant, but not alarming either. Flipping over the rail himself, Chris glided his hands down the iron spindles until they met with the floor of the terrace. Letting go, he landed next to the squirming Mahaz Maher.

Hoisting Mahez up, he forced the terrorist to sprint alongside of him, all the while, Chris maintained a strong grip on the man's collar. As they made their way across the lawn and to the iron fence line, voices and lights began to come to life around the embassy. The telltale bobbing of flashlights began to comb the grounds at the rear of the building and room by room, embassy lights were turned on.

Without wasting a moment, Chris shoved the terrorist to the ground in front of the missing bars. Once more with a grip on Maher's collar and waistband, the Marine hurled his family's killer through the opening and dove through himself. Snatching his floor mat and grabbing the terrorist's bound hands in his other hand, Chris kept moving. Following the same shadowy path in exfil that he used to enter the compound.

Reaching the Bronco, Chris opened the rear window. Ramming Maher to the ground, Chris landed with his knees on his back. With a second zip tie shackle, Chris twisted and tied the terrorist like a bound calf at a rodeo. Hoisting Maher in the air, Chris tossed him in the back of the SUV and slammed the window shut. Tossing his assault rifle in the seat next to him, the Bronco roared to life and Chris made a beeline for his next destination.

Checking his hand-drawn route he penned on a tourist map, by-passing the first location he had circled- the Pentagon, he brought the Bronco skidding to a stop outside the entrance of another stately building. His arrival quickly garnered the attention of armed guards. Their assault weapons raised towards Chris and his SUV.

In the light crimson glow of the just budding morning sun light as it chased the dark, Chris' arrival must have been a bewildering scene. Without a word, the gunnery sergeant made his way to the rear of his vehicle, each move increasing the odds that the anxious guards might fire on him.

Reaching in the SUV, Masters grabbed two fistfuls of the terrorist. Hoisting Mahaz Maher over his shoulder, Chris made his way towards the gates of the building. The bewilderment of the guards only heightened seeing their silent visitor with another man over his shoulders. Reaching the perimeter gate, Masters flipped Maher over his shoulders and landed him on the concrete at the feet of the guards.

Without a word, Chris spun and began making his retreat. The guards called for Chris to halt as he slipped away into the red and black shadows of the rising sun. The jurisdiction of the Israeli embassy stopped at the gate. The guards would likely have been in their right to shoot Chris, but as he had hoped, his, though odd actions, were not aggressive towards them and what they stood to protect. With a roar of the Bronco's engine, Chris sped away into the growing red cast of the rising sun.

Chris mulled his decision on where he chose to dump the terrorist. Not taking Maher's life with his own hands, he wanted to ensure Breanna and Macy's killer was treated with the irreverence the demon deserved. He also knew the strong U.S. ally was adept at extracting information using means that U.S. intelligence was unwilling to perform. The right U.S. intel figures would get the information, eventually. Chris hoped, providing he wasn't incarcerated or dead himself, he would get the answers he needed. Who ordered the attack on Stone Bay?

Twelve

Raider Six sat in the team room, watching the news reel play over and over. The street cameras captured the man clad in black dump the bound man on the doorstep of the Israeli embassy. It didn't take reporters long to learn the man delivered to the Israeli Mossad was suspected terrorist Mahaz Maher.

Even without the Bronco showed in some of the photos, the team had no doubt who the man in black was. Most could barely stifle a grin, even as Lieutenant Colonel Lippett, closely followed at his heels by Chief Warrant Officer Buchannan. Warrant Officer Patty Jacobs and Intelligence Agent Veronica Statler filtered in behind the two men.

Lippett looked serious, but not overly agitated, quite juxtaposed to the animated CID Officer Buchannan. "By now, you all know some serious accusations have been made towards one of our team members. He had already been recalled, but our efforts to reach him have failed so far. No one can be sure where he is or what actions he may or may have not been involved with. Chief Warrant Officer Buchannan has some questions for you and I expect your full respect and participation. Warrant Officer Jacobs will be the team envoy in this matter and Intelligence Officer Statler is serving her own department in their investigation of the reported incident," the Lieutenant Colonel instructed.

"We'll need your phone data, team and facility logs, and any other information that may trace the whereabouts of Gunnery Sergeant Masters over the past seventy-two hours," Buchannan spat.

"You have signed orders for all that? Pretty sure we go out there and risk our lives to ensure certain rights are protected," Zalinsky countered to the CID investigator.

"You have something to hide, Lance Corporal?" Buchannan asked.

"I have a country and a constitution to protect. Pretty sure operators and cake eaters swear the same oath," Zalinsky fired back.

Knowing the exchange was only going to get worse from that point, Lippett interjected, "The Justice Department, State Department and Department of Defense have all issued signed orders to get to the bottom of what happened in D.C. last night."

Corporal Dobson scoffed, "Imagine if they all took the same interest and acted so quick to catch the terrorist who bombed the Stones Bay Bridge?"

"Them guys in D.C. dine with dignitaries hosting terrorists at their embassies, not us door kickers who are sent to do their bidding," Lance Corporal Ramos added.

"That's enough. I expect you'll say what you're required to and otherwise act like the Marines you are," Lippett said. Spinning to look Buchannan in the face, he offered a slanted grin, "Good luck."

One by one, Buchannan sequestered the Raider team into a room and interviewed them regarding their contact with Gunnery Sergeant Chris Masters. Marine to Marine, their messages were consistent.

"When is the last time you saw Gunnery Sergeant Masters?"

Grady squared his gaze directly into the eyes of the investigator, "The evening of his bride's and daughter's funeral."

"When was your last contact with Gunnery Sergeant Masters?"

"I believe I gave him a hug just after his wife and daughter were buried," Zalinsky glared.

"Is the man in this photo Gunnery Sergeant Chris Masters?"

Ramos scoffed, "Doesn't look like it to me. But then again, I can't see his face, his build is muddled by his attire and the known terrorist draped over his shoulders. Where were *you* last night, Chief Warrant Officer Buchannan?"

"Gunnery Sergeant Masters owns an old Ford Bronco, does he not? Is this his Bronco in the surveillance photo taken in front of the Israeli embassy?"

"From this infrared photo, I can't make out the color, I don't see a plate, it's blurry, can't see the VIN, there are no definitive blemishes or aftermarket equipment that I can identify to suggest the vehicle in question belongs to Gunnery Sergeant Masters," Grady returned fire at the investigator. "You're wasting your time. You came on a witch hunt. It's unfortunate that a terrorist attacked citizens of our country and innocent people died. It's unfortunate that the terrorist found asylum within the borders of our country on an acre of sovereign dirt belonging to a country claiming to be our friend. It is unfortunate that one of our teammates is suffering inconsolable pain."

"Staff Sergeant, it is your sworn testimony that none of this footage might be your gunnery sergeant? That less than three days after the death of his family, a highly-skilled Marine operative only a few hours' drive from where the suspect was identified, didn't do this? Come on," Buchannan pressed.

"Based on what I know about this international piece of scum, there is no shortage of people and nations that would like to take him down. Someone did. We may never know who had the guts to do it. Maybe the Pakistanis themselves through a moment of introspection decided to do the right thing," Grady countered. "If it were an accomplished Marine, why go through the trouble of attacking a sovereign entity without collateral damage and deliver the killer to a foreign intelligence agency? Anyone of us could've dealt with Mahaz Maher from two kilometers away without stepping foot on sovereign ground."

Buchannan looked blankly at the Staff Sergeant.

"It is more likely that some other nation, perhaps the Israelis themselves, took advantage of the situation for their own gain," Grady concluded.

"That'll be all, Staff Sergeant," Buchannan grumbled, rubbing his face.

Grady wasted no time in sliding out of his chair and exiting the room. Leaving Buchannan to his impossible case, the staff sergeant returned to his team.

THIRTEEN

The swirls in the water were a sign that the dam had worked. Deeper under the surface, the sleek, torpedo-shaped vessel confirmed it. It was trapped.

Gunnery Sergeant Chris Masters raised his arms in the air, steadied above his target, and plunged the gig down. Gingerly lifting out of the water, he was pleased to see the brook trout stuck to the three-pronged stick that he had crafted.

He was going to have some excellent protein to go with his dandelion and ramp salad. Even better, he was pleased he didn't have to get completely soaked to retrieve his meal.

Using the handle end of the spear, he stuck it in the muddy bank as he moved the rocks used to create a crude dam funneling the trout into his temporary dead end. Snatching his lunch, he made for his encampment, nestled deep in the Blue Ridge Mountains along the Tellico River.

If it weren't for the solitude, he wouldn't half mind his living situation. Even in the western reaches of North Carolina, his peripheral vision haunted him with fleeting ghosts of Breanna and Macy. Even though months had ticked by, he couldn't help but turn as his heart skipped a beat and confirm what he already knew. They were waiting for him in heaven, were he fortunate enough to join them.

Chris had escaped Washington, D.C. before the roadblocks were put in place. He traced a route that he determined wouldn't be a priority and he had guessed right. He was curious if the Pakistani embassy would try and keep the capture of Maher quiet, as it was both embarrassing and an international incident under their watch. After all the flaunting and verbal window dressing on the terrorist being misidentified, he was plucked from their sovereign compound.

Swapping vehicles with a young man who was thrilled to get a classic Bronco in exchange for his hand-me-down economy car. Chris drove several hours before abandoning it in a wrecking lot on the outskirts of the Blue Ridge Mountains. He immediately disappeared away from civilized roads and trails with what gear he could carry on his back.

Despite the ghosts that would follow him regardless of where he fled, he had made a surprisingly comfortable home for himself. His years of military survival training served him well for his life off of the grid. His shelter was barely visible from almost every angle. It was water and airtight except for major storms. Chris' elevated bed and storage made those hard nights bearable.

A sand and activated charcoal filter system fed by the Tellico River, kept fresh water flowing. Boar, deer, and fish along with an array of edible flora kept him well fed. His rugged location saw nary a hiker or hunter. A smokeless fire he learned from SEREs school kept him from being spied from nearby ridges.

Only when he was lazy or feisty and used his M-4 or sniper for hunting, could anyone possibly have known he existed there. His small cache of arms and ammo was kept buried outside of the homestead's immediate radius. Otherwise, he was always armed with a side-arm and a shotgun or assault rifle.

The only piece of identifiable item he had was the photo of Breanna and Macy that remained in his breast pocket at all times. Life along the Tellico River was almost pleasant.

As Chris approached the camp, he froze. At first, he thought it was instinct, an intuition picked up from years on the battlefield. His sub-conscious became conscious. Movement always betrays concealment. Shadows that move in a fashion unlike the vegetation's natural sways. Shapes that are uniquely human. Shapes the Marine's eyes hadn't seen for months.

Without moving his head, he began to locate the figures now that he was aware. He was surrounded.

In a sudden burst, Chris sprinted towards the dense tree line of the nearest ridge. He didn't need to look to know that the figures had turned assailants chasing after him. Darting in and out of the trees that he had become innately familiar with over the past dozen weeks, he had a slight advantage over his pursuers. He also knew that if they had enough manpower, it was only a matter of time that their shared energy would wear him down.

The gunnery sergeant's only hope was that by heading into more and more rugged terrain, he would outlast their search. He also knew the odds of that actually happening were less than slim as reinforcements would be called in.

A helicopter suddenly roared overhead, swooping down from the trees of the previous peak. Chris' plan of using a river for a speedy getaway was abandoned as the chopper would easily be able to follow the waterway.

Hearing the now careless footfalls and snapping of branches behind him, his best chance was taking a risk his assailants wouldn't. Continuing up the ridge, he launched himself off the face of a cliff as the hillside gave way to a steep ravine. Leaping towards a tall pine he had eyed on one of his many hikes,

Chris allowed his weight to bend the tree low enough that he could let go and land feet first on the rocky slope. Sliding like he was riding an earthen wave, he descended the slope until he reached a rock outcropping above the Tellico River.

Launching himself off of the rockface, he flipped in the air, hitting the water feet-first. Using the flow from the current to drive him away from the few chasers who dared follow him, Chris angled towards the opposite bank. The moment his feet hit the shallows, he hopped up and high stepped out of the water and up the nearby embankment.

Scrambling up the river shore, he glanced over his shoulder at his pursuers on the other bank. Turning towards the next ridge where he could disappear in the canopy of the trees and avoid being trailed by the helicopter, he was stopped by half a dozen assault rifle muzzles aimed at him. He knew there were at least that many on the other shoreline.

Parting in the middle, their gun sights never wavering, a man in a tailored suit appeared, an odd contrast to the tactical clothing worn by the rest of the assailants, never mind the environment.

"Gunnery Sergeant Masters, stand down," the man smiled calmly, a hand waving in front of him. "You're among friends."

"Friends don't normally show up at my home unannounced and stick guns in my face," Chris glowered.

"We tried to call," the man offered a smug grin. "You're not exactly easy to get a hold of."

"I kind of like it that way," Chris growled. "You found me. I assume you are here to take me in? You got me."

"Take you in? We're *inviting* you to come with us, not apprehending you," the man scoffed cheerily.

Chris raised a suspicious brow, "What is it you want from me?"

The man smiled, "I think we can help one another."

"Who says I need help?" Chris countered.

The man cocked his head, his tone a bit more serious, "If we can find you, so can others. Your clock is ticking, Gunny. We can help you slip into the shadows for as long as you like."

"Suggesting I need such a thing, what are you looking for in return?" Chris asked, wary of what he had walked into.

The man grinned, "I am looking for you to do what you have always done… seek and employ justice on a worldly scale."

"So, you want me to become a mercenary," Chris frowned.

"Mercenary is such a definitive word with a negative connotation," the man wrinkled his nose.

Chris squinted his eyes, "Are you CIA?"

The man laughed and waved the suggestion off, "No. Like you, we are merely concerned citizens who prefer to pursue and enforce liberty in ways the government cannot or is too afraid to. We like to remain under the radar."

Chris sighed in disgust, "You're a mercenary. No, thank you."

"As I said, we are not mercenaries. They get paid to play. We're patriots who don't like politics binding the hands of free governments to the detriment of their citizens. Failure to do the right thing due to optics. I believe you are familiar with the injustice, the pain of politics failing to do what is right and necessary," the man pressed.

Chris shook his hands, "Play with words all you want, I'm not a gun for hire."

"I'm not here to *hire* you. I'm here to give you a path to respect your great loss by living your life. By doing what you can to make this world a better place in honor of your family's absence. Like what you did with Mahaz Maher. I thought you might appreciate our shared stance."

Chris looked stunned, conflicted by the information he had just received.

"It really wasn't that difficult to put together. The files you pulled before you left on leave, going AWOL at that exact time, your very public outspoken frustration. Your skillset. You have been among the State Department's most wanted since you left your post. Interesting choice to dump Maher with the Israelis as opposed to killing him yourself. The entire incident at the embassy dispatched a few bruises, but no casualties. Exactly the smart move we liked. Instead of a rabid manhunt directed at you, a killer, you get the result you wanted without the unneeded attention. Unfortunately, you are still very much a target of the intelligence community. We can help you with that problem," the man confided.

"I'm not interested."

"You should be," the man in the suit snapped. "That antimilitary reporter who leaked your unit's information got your family killed. They have uncovered new data that certain people would like kept private. Information that shows their actions have been very detrimental to our country, to families much like yours."

Glancing at the man's squadron, "Your team seems highly capable. Why me?"

"The reporter is being protected by CAIR and a certain few congresswomen. You've proven yourself to be quite good at quiet extractions. That and I couldn't think of anyone with more incentive to see this through than you."

"*And* the reporter and her duly democratically voted friends appear to be connected to Barriq Hussein, the radical leader who gave the order for the attack in North Carolina. Together, they broadcast a very moving false narrative interview with Hussein two years ago," the man said, straightening his suit jacket. "You want the man *behind* Mahaz Maher. So do we."

Chris' shoulders relaxed for the first time. "Alright. Fine. Let's talk."

FOURTEEN

The helicopter flew low to the ground in a pattern avoiding metropolitan areas and major freeways, a technique Chris was familiar with as Raider and Seal team pilots would do the same to avoid radar detection.

With the mic'd headphones on, they could talk, but the ride was mostly devoid of communication outside of wary looks from Chris and smug smiles from the man in the suit.

Keeping an eye on the terrain and direction, he estimated they were somewhere near Kentucky when the helicopter descended to land. As the aircraft touched down, the doors were opened and they were greeted by two men armed with assault rifles. Chris tensed, wondering if he had been lured into a trap nonetheless.

The man in the suit offered a calm smile and waved his hand in front of him, suggesting Chris should proceed to the farmhouse field they had landed in. Not seeing other viable options, Chris complied.

The man walked alongside the gunnery sergeant. Climbing up the steps, they were again met by two armed men who held the doors open for them.

The farmhouse was well appointed with a surprising number of people milling about. Most ignored Chris and the man in the suit aside from peripheral glances. Chris' trained eyes took in as much as he could, identifying pieces of potential intel, count of obviously armed personnel, points of egress should it become necessary.

The man paused outside of what appeared to be the kitchen and spoke to an attendant, "How about you plate up a couple of steaks, I believe we interrupted our guest's lunch."

The attendant nodded and disappeared into the bowels of the executive galley.

"Nice looking fish, by the way," the man smiled at Chris. "Did you actually gig that thing?"

Chris looked at the man, feeling somewhat annoyed by banter given that he still had no idea what situation he was involved in. Nodding, he said, "I did. Made a little dam to channel fish into, easier to pin them with the gig that way."

"Smart. Resourceful," the man nodded approvingly. Stopped outside of a set of French doors, he proclaimed, "Here we are, come on in. We can clear the air and speak freely in here."

Chris entered a room that he assumed was once a master suite, now converted to a conference room. Monitors lined one wall while computers dotted the long table that dominated the room.

"Our remote command center. Temporary home to bring a recruit that we can abandon if conversations don't go well," the man in the suit conferred. Nodding to a wet bar, he offered, "Can I pour you a drink? Being in Kentucky, we have stocked some world-class bourbon. The echelon of them all, some Pappy Van Winkle. Perhaps a glass of red wine, we have some exquisite Chilean reds that would go great with our steaks."

Chris studied the man for a moment and replied evenly, "Water would be fine, thank you."

The man paused, looking at Chris, "Keep your senses sharp in the event you need to fight your way out and flee. Prudent. I'd probably have done the same. Let me say this, right now. You can leave at any time. I don't give you long before the FBI, NSA or CID eventually capture you, but you are free to leave. You are here on your own free will."

"Until I hear you out, in which case I become a liability," Chris countered.

“And then we’d have to kill you,” the man nodded. “Either way, you might as well be comfortable. Neither will be affected by enjoying a glass of spirits.”

Chris shrugged in acknowledgment, “Sure, a glass of Pappy would be great. I’ve always wanted to try it.”

With a chuckle, the man poured two robust glasses of bourbon. Carting them to the table, he sat next to Chris. Handing the gunnery sergeant, a glass, he held his own out in front of him. Reluctantly, Chris clinked his glass against the man’s.

“Jonas Carter,” the man in the suit declared as he settled back in his chair and sipped his bourbon whisky. He held the glass of amber liquid in the air and studied it. “The 20 year has always been my favorite. It’s not as exclusive as the 23 or the Rye, but… it is exceptional. It’s buttery, a touch of cinnamon and cherry… this is the good stuff. Never had this when I was on deployment.”

“Deployed?”

“Army Green Beret Brigadier General,” Jonas Carter nodded. “Served my country the traditional way for thirty-one years before a particularly nasty incident on the border of Iran. My unit was left to manage on our own since we had crossed into sovereign territory. Fortunately, a different group was nearby and pulled us out. I was shot up pretty bad, probably would have died. I was given a second lease on life and have made the most of it.”

"Who? Who was there to pull you out and patch you up?" Chris demanded. He realized they were at the precipice of the conversation.

Jonas didn't flinch at the question, "They simply call themselves 'The Cadre'. A group of people that love democracy, freedom and liberty for people around the globe, including the United States."

"The Cadre," Chris scoffed. "Like some James Bond film? A bunch of rich elitists employing soldiers for their bidding?"

"I thought the same at first," Jonas admitted. "I was in a position that I needed their help, so I listened. The keywords I have already uttered… democracy, freedom, liberty. That is *everything* they stand for. Yes, some are quite wealthy. Leaders of major corporations and even some countries. It is what they stand for that encouraged me to complete missions and now, recruit fellow operators like you."

"I've got to hand it to your HR department, they have quite the package, work for you or get shot. You must have quite the acceptance rate."

"You'd be surprised," Jonas smiled. "Actually, it is less about finding a competent operator, we can get those. There are plenty that will work for a paycheck. But *that*, is not all that we are after. That would be mercenaries. We are after true patriots. Operators that love their country, that are motivated to do what needs to be done to protect her and her fellow democracies around the world."

"You assume I am properly motivated?"

"You *are* a patriot. We know that to be true. Your motivation is a bit more than country." Jonas put down his glass and clicked on a computer terminal near him. "This man, as I shared earlier, ordered the attack that killed your family. We are going to take the perceived to be 'untouchable' Barriq Hussein down. We thought you might like to join us."

Chris stared at the image of Hussein on the screen. Jonas made a great sales pitch. Chris was itching to complete the objective he elected not to levy on Mahaz Maher. He was wary as the doors opened and a gentleman in chef's garb burst in carrying two plates, setting one in front of each man.

"Gracias, Paco," Jonas said as he stared at the perfectly prepared steak. Turning to Chris, he grinned, "Paco is from Brazil. He makes the best steaks you have ever tasted." With a nod, he picked up his knife and fork and easily cut through a piece.

After a moment's hesitation, Chris followed suit. He had to admit, the meat was tender and juicy. It likely was the tastiest steak he had ever enjoyed, then again, he had gone months eating unseasoned fish, grubs, foraged plants, and the occasional wild boar or deer.

Chris felt unusually numb with his circumstances. His existence in the Blue Ridge Mountains, the capture-job offer from Jonas, and his don't call them mercenaries mercenaries... even the capture of Mahaz Maher was less cathartic than he had hoped it would be. Everything in his life without Breanna and Macy was hollow.

Taking down Barriq Hussein, the head of the terrorist cell that ordered the bombing that killed his family and so many others worldwide, piqued Chris' interest in a way he hadn't felt in months. As he enjoyed another bite, Jonas clicked a button on the terminal and one of the monitors cued a newsfeed.

Splitting the screen, Jonas captured opposing media outlet perspectives. The one on the right leaned towards heralding the mysterious capture of Mahaz Maher as a hero. An analyst was breaking down evidence garnered from various video clips of a man in black and an old Bronco.

Dubbing the assailant 'Patriot X,' the analyst shared his theory that the mystery captor was likely military, possibly a Navy Seal, Army Ranger, or Marine. The anchor asked if this Patriot X was even an American. The analyst paused reflectively and responded, "I can't be one hundred percent confident, but the style of entry, the way he moves, and I say 'he' because of the masculine frame. Look at the weapons, these are derivations of common issue for American special operators. I would say SOCOM, either Seal or Marine. Whoever he is, I'd say he did America…the world a favor. Mahaz Maher was an evil, sadistic monster."

"So, this Patriot X, may just be a shadowy American hero," the anchor suggested.

"Maybe," the analyst nodded. "Maybe."

The screen on the left painted a very different picture of the events. "This vigilante broke, how many… countless international rules and violated them. No jury. No warrant. No oversight," the guest on the news panel exclaimed.

"This is certainly an unprecedented case. A clear breach of international law. Some have dubbed the culprit Patriot X. What do *you* make of that?" the anchor asked.

"X as in ex? Look, this is no folk hero. This is someone who attacked a sovereign government. An ally of the United States," the analyst fumed.

"Tensions are high with Pakistan," the broadcaster nodded.

The analyst slammed his fists on the table, "This was an act of war. How do you suppose relations might be between our sovereign governments?"

Turning to his other panel members, a senator and a congresswoman, the anchor asked, "He's right, this act was a blatant violation of international law and very possibly an act of war perpetrated on the American continent though on sovereign soil."

"Well, Don," the senator straightened in her seat and looked cross at the camera. "This act was greater than an American incident. This was an act on the world stage. I think if the United States alone was going to investigate the incident alone, it would be viewed as invalid by the rest of the world, perhaps protecting our own."

"Excuse me, Senator Waters, sorry to cut in. This was certainly not sanctioned by Congress and not by our president. The world must unite to resolve this. I have put forth legislation to create an international task force, invite investigators from Pakistan and Russia to assist or at least observe the investigation," the congresswoman stated, giving the camera a proud glance.

"So, you are advocating for investigators and members of the Pakistani and Russian intelligence community to come to the United States and aid in the investigation?" the anchor asked.

"This is an international incident, it deserves an international response," the congresswoman shared.

"Representative Sanders, it is unprecedented, but the betterment of world order does lend itself towards your bill. I hope it passes," Senator Waters declared.

The anchor nodded at his guests, "Even if it means combing through our military records and intelligence, you'd invite other countries in to assist."

Representative Sanders nodded, "Why not? We are part of the international community. Why aren't our doors are open? Like our borders should be, by the way."

"That is a segment we will invite you to be on the in the future," the anchor laughed. Turning to the analyst, he asked, "Any insight into who this…vigilante might be?"

"As Mr. Harris has suggested, this was a military assault. Look, we all know who perpetrated this heinous assault. Gunnery Sergeant Chris Masters had the ability, opportunity, and clear motive to throw his career and his life away, all while risking setting off a war and putting additional lives in danger," the analyst on the left spat.

"There is no proof of that allegation and it is irresponsible, and dangerous to blurt out the name of a military hero, or anyone, for that matter," the analyst Harris countered.

"Masters was vocal about his disapproval over the State Department's refusal to enter the embassy or demand Maher's release. He threatened a reporter on live television. His Bronco was seen near the embassy at the same time of the attack…"

"*A* Bronco was seen. The FBI themselves admit they have no identifiable proof that the Bronco seen in that video belonged to Gunnery Sergeant Masters. Any husband or father would be enraged by the government's lack of action on this attack on American soil. And honestly, if I was him and had to deal with irresponsible voices like that, or you, for that matter, I'd probably punch them in the face too," Harris defended. "Let's just say it was, and I am not suggesting that was the case, Gunnery Sergeant Masters…or whoever was Patriot X is a hero."

As Jonas finished his steak, he clicked off the monitors and leaned back in his chair. "Well, you know how to make an impact."

"The only impact I want to make is impossible," Chris snapped.

"There is no way to bring your family back," Jonas said. "But there is a way to bring their killers and everyone involved to justice. That is what we want to do with you. Side by side."

Chris placed his fork down, "When do we start?"

Fifteen

Forgoing the helicopter for more nondescript ground transportation, Jonas and a small team caravanned away from the farmhouse towards the eastern hill country of Kentucky. Snaking through windy and desolate roads, they swung off the pavement and onto a narrow dirt road that burrowed further into the brush.

The driver gunned the engine up the slope until they met with the base of a hill. A large gate swung open and the vehicles launched into an opening carved into the hillside. Swinging the SUV around to face the entrance, they parked.

"Welcome to Facility Twenty-three," Jonas called as he climbed out of the truck. He watched Chris take in the setting and gather his bearings. "It used to be known as Hells Mines, an old mining town, long forgotten. I know it seems a bit movie cliché, but the caverns conceal the vehicles, heat signatures, and most of our electronics at the site. Don't worry, much of our housing is outside among the canopy in our rather nicely rebuilt ghost town."

Chris' head swiveled, following the string of amber lights that led deeper into the cavern and further from the natural light spilling in from the entrance. "Seems like a lot to secure."

Jonas smiled, "We use advanced technology and sensors. Being this remote, there is ample time to neutralize, defend, or exfil. We like farms, mines, old industrial sites… they tend to have a lot of open ground we can use as a natural defense. Come on, I'll introduce you to some of the team. Our situation and mission prep rooms are all in the belly of the mine."

The gunnery sergeant followed the man through the dimly lit halls. Pausing at a heavy door, a facial recognition scanner swept his face and a latch was released. Once inside, the room lights gradually grew brighter. "Kind of like decompression for your eyes," Jonas declared as he moved into another room.

A wall of monitors covering different vantages of the grounds from the road in, the mine itself, and even an aerial view of the mountain was displayed on screen. A pair of men watched the screens, pausing to offer Jonas a quick nod of acknowledgment.

"Here we are," Jonas pushed into another room deeper within the mine.

A pair of men and a woman were pouring over documents on a table and referencing images on a screen. Looking up, Chris determined starkly different reactions from each.

Jonas introduced them, "This is Drake Fallon. Drake is former Australian SAS 2nd Commando Regiment, you two have a lot in common."

The man looked at Chris from his peripheral vision, not taking his eyes off his work. "Welcome to hell," he muttered.

A man next to him took a stride forward and held his hand out, "Cole Porter."

"Cole was an intelligence officer in D.C. and a former Ranger sniper. We stumbled on one of their operations. Lucky for him, we decided to recruit him," Jonas said plainly. Turning to the woman next to the men, he added, "This is Cara, though the team calls her Dragonfly. Army pilot, well, former."

"They thought my flying was 'too aggressive, but these boys don't seem to mind," Cara grinned.

Cole raised a disapproving eyebrow.

"Any infil in which the objective is reached and exfil where we don't get blown out of the sky is a good one, I say," Fallon grumbled.

"If you'll excuse me, we have a situation brewing and I need to report. Cole, would you show Chris around and bring him up to speed?" Jonas asked, met with an assured nod from Porter.

Fallon looked for the first time, "Up to speed… you aren't suggesting including him on the op?"

"That is what we recruited him for," Jonas nodded.

"Can't bring an FNG on that kind of op," Drake spat, referring to Chris.

"Gunny can handle himself," Jonas assured, his voice not wavering.

"Not a matter of handling himself, it's a matter of trust at your six," Drake argued.

Jonas paused and looked serious, "You question our recruiting? If we bring someone to the table, there's a reason. You don't need to trust each other yet. You need to trust me."

"Yes, *sir*," Fallon snapped. "But does FNG trust you?"

All eyes naturally lit on Chris.

"Probably not. Not yet. But we very much have the same goals for this mission. That focused directive is enough trust to get the job done," Jonas responded.

"It's not *your* six in the field," Fallon countered.

"It very well may be. Now, if you'll manage the op and prep Gunny as you have been directed, I'd like to get to the mission room so that I may finish putting this op together," Jonas declared and disappeared through the next door.

Cole shouldered past Fallon, "Don't mind Drake. He always spreads his tail feathers when a new operative joins the team."

"Something about staying alive is important to me," Fallon quipped.

"Staying alive is only half of the battle. Making an impact while alive is the *real* objective," Cara added. "To increase the odds of completing the objective and returning in one piece, how about you let Porter get the FNG properly acquainted and outfitted."

"Could always use a minesweeper, I guess," Fallon grumbled.

"And I thought all Australians were friendly," Chris muttered.

"That's Canadians," Cole quipped.

"Right," Chris nodded.

"Let's give them some space to absorb the orders from Jonas." Cole nodded for Chris to follow, "That is the team room. Sometimes the room is shared between a couple of teams. The room beyond that where Jonas disappeared is the mission room. That is where the brass and intel prep us for our missions and monitor world events."

"This is called Facility Twenty-Three…how many facilities are there?" Chris asked as Cole led him towards the entrance of the mines and past the motor pool.

Shaking his head, he admitted, "I don't know. I've been to three of them. One in Nevada, this one, and one in Europe. I know there is one in Israel and a couple strewn throughout the Middle East and Asia from other operators passing through."

"What do you know about this group?"

Cole cast Chris a glance. "They came along and pulled me out of a bad situation. They seem to have good intentions. Treat us operators well. They aren't just American, there are people from several nations involved. The missions are legit, support liberty, go after bonafide bad guys that governments are for one reason or another unable or unwilling to go after."

"That's part of the problem. Who is 'they'? Who decides what missions and who is bad? Who pays the bills?" Chris asked.

"You ask a lot of questions," Cole laughed. "Look, they're all good questions and most will be answered in time. Confidence comes down to working with them for a while and building trust. I mean, are there any words I can say right now that will give peace of mind? Other than, right now, their target is the man that ordered the attack in North Carolina that took your wife and daughter."

Chris froze in his tracks. His eyes winced slightly as he looked at Cole. Relenting, he shook his head, "I suppose not."

As they continued, Cole pointed out shacks sprinkled along a walking trail that snaked through the forest canopy. "These are the barracks. They aren't much, but they work. There is a workout area at the edge of the housing. Includes weights, obstacle course, just about anything you would find on a military base on deployment. Chow hall is right in the center of it all. We have an indoor shooting range that can handle anything up to an assault rifle in the belly of the mine. If you need to dial in a sniper, there is a trail that leads to a platform between the hills."

"It seems better than some of my deployments," Chris admitted. "So, what's the deal with Fallon?"

"Drake? He's a bit of a hotshot and a hothead. He's a top-tier operative. Likes to call the shots. Not gonna lie, a bit more enjoyable to be around on a mission than in between," Cole admitted as they headed back towards the mine.

"What's the end game with all this?" Chris asked.

Cole grinned, "You mean, is there a retirement plan? I don't know. I mean, at some point, my body's going to wear out. I assume I'll progress like Jonas and run a team."

"And after that?"

"After that? I'm not sure I figure I'd last that long. It's not like a normal life is waiting at the end of all this. By the time we end up here, normal life is in ashes," Cole shrugged.

"Comforting," Chris muttered. "I just want Hussein's head on a platter and his organization dismantled."

"We'll get him," Cole assured.

Nodding silently, Chris allowed Cole to lead him back into the underground facility.

SIXTEEN

Jonas pointed two fingers at Chris and Cole as they entered the mine shaft that comprised Facility 23. Waving them towards the team mission prep room, he wore a look Chris was quite familiar with. Lieutenant Colonel Lippett wore the same expression before he was about to spin Raider Team Six up for a mission.

Cara and Drake reeled around the corner and fell in line behind Jonas. Jonas acted as a commanding officer would, taking control of the room and rolled out the information to his team. Jonas looked positively excited as he spoke. "We have caught a major piece of evidence. This reporter, who I believe Chris might have a few feelings about, well…this footage won't likely improve his disposition," Jonas clicked on a large monitor for the team to see.

Video footage showed reporter Clint Newsom meeting with Barriq Hussein. The two walked along the streets of Istanbul. Pausing after serious discussion, Newsom glanced around and then produced something from his pocket and hands it to Hussein.

Jonas stopped the video and zoomed in on the item in exchange. "That is a zip drive. On it, is data on U.S. and allied troops. All in exchange for exclusive footage of traveling with Hussein as Newsom documents the false narrative of 'humanitarian' good works in a number of countries. Hussein is painted as kind and giving, progressively driving for change. Strangely, each country was riddled with unrest and subversives not long after his visit."

Chris bristled at the sight of Newsom and Hussein together. His muscles tensed. He remained stoic in his presence in the midst of the team. He was a patriot. He loved his country. But he wasn't there for all of that. The vision of his hands around the throat of Hussein fueled him.

"We're going after Hussein?" Fallon danced in his seat.

"This exchange between Hussein and Newsom has information that has already been used in terrorist attacks in multiple cities. It isn't just the U.S. at risk with this information, it can impact all of western civilization. Whether Newsom knew what he was doing or not, we'll find out if we can bring him in.

We have an operative that has a twenty on the location, we fly out in three hours," Jonas replied.

"Assignments?" Cara asked.

"You, Angel, and I will hold the Tactical Operations Center with you ready to fly. Drake, Cole, and Chris will rendezvous with our asset and determine if a takedown is viable. If it is, we'll execute. Take the head of the snake and if we can, the American traitor along with him," Jonas replied.

Chris regretted that they were two hours to wheels up. He was ready to go right then.

"What's the geo?" Cara asked.

"Turkey. The asset is in Istanbul waiting on our arrival," Jonas declared. "Pack your bags, grab your gear. Cole, if you'll show Chris to the armory."

Cole nodded, "Let's go."

Pushing his way through the team doors, he led Chris further into the depths of the mine. Just before what was clearly the armory, they turned into a cage that opened via another facial scan.

"Have to talk to H.R. about my access," Chris muttered.

They entered a room that would have been the envy of any requisitions officer in the Marines. Nearly every make and caliber of weapon Chris had ever seen was on display. Each classified by country and military branch that used a particular weapon.

"You an LMG or AR guy?" Cole asked.

"Assault Rifle…light sniper," Chris replied.

"Nice. You'll be an asset. Fallon is a tight quarters breacher. I'm a sniper's nest, spray with a shotgun if close kind of guy. Cara, she's all light machine gun. Whether bolted to an aircraft or pressed against her shoulder. Then again, she grins pretty big with a rocket launcher, too," Cole shared.

"Sound like a fun bunch."

Cole paused as he began kitting a Barrett M82 sniper rifle. "You aren't really into this whole team thing, are you?"

"I have a team… had a team that took orders from the U.S. government," Chris replied.

"And yet you went AWOL to remove a bad guy that was hiding beyond the reach of the government. This team is no different. You'll see. We all had reservations before going dark. You'll come around. These are good people," Cole assured.

"Are they?" Chris pressed as he disassembled two nearby carbines and used parts from each to create a weapon to his specs.

After a brief pause, Cole shrugged, a sheepish grin sweeping his face, "We'll see."

SEVENTEEN

The flight from Kentucky to Istanbul was quiet. Some operators slept, others poured over documents, presumably regarding the mission. Chris woke from dozing off himself. Seeing Jonas Carter and Cole Porter standing over a dimly lit table, a map and several photos of Istanbul and the surrounding region spread out, the gunnery sergeant joined them.

"Our operator in Istanbul sent some new footage. After Newsom had filmed the meeting with Hussein charming the crowd with a speech on regional unity, he captured a pro-Kurdish militant leader meeting with General Razi Naib," Jonas shared.

"Hussein's right hand," Chris acknowledged.

"Hussein gives the orders, Naib decides how they were carried out," Jonas nodded.

"How could someone like Newsom betray his country like this?" Cole asked.

Jonas shrugged, "Likely he is so caught up in his ideologue B.S. that he doesn't realize the connection. Buys the Kool Aid that Hussein spouts. America is an imperialistic monster that is not inherently bad but needs to be put in its place."

"The same crowd that burns American flags on college campuses. They work harder to bring our country down than help struggling nations rise up," Cole reasoned.

"He likely graduated one of those schools, yes," Jonas nodded.

They both turned to Chris who was silent. "Incompetent or intentionally traitorous, he needs to be dealt with," the gunnery sergeant finally muttered.

"Our surveillance has followed the thread. Hussein is careful. His smiling media and public interactions are never intertwined with one another. Even Naib is portrayed as a purveyor of peace, not the leader of terrorism we know him to be," Jonas said.

Chris' eyes twitched as he envisioned Hussein, Naib, and Newsom in the same space. The three people who had a hand in Breanna and Macy's deaths.

"It's like a shell game, trying to keep track of who has the data," Cole said.

Chris frowned, "Wouldn't there be copies at this point?"

Jonas shook his head, "The encryption drive can allow for reading, but not copying. That's a bit of solace in this. If we retrieve that drive, the damage from the information included on it stops."

"Is your ground team able to keep tabs on all three?" Chris asked.

"All four, and the data…no," Jonas admitted. "Our man is glued to the data."

"So…," Chris mused.

"He's on Olan Yado, the Kurdish leader and the data."

"Hussein, Naib, and Newsom?" Chris pressed.

"In the wind, for now," Jonas admitted.

Chris snapped his head away before returning his hate-filled gaze on the photos spread on the table.

"We'll get them," Jonas assured. "Whether it is this mission or the next."

A red light flashed. "We'll be landing soon," Jonas said. "Let's get the rest of the team ready to move."

The moment the plane rolled to a stop, the team was off the plane and into a series of civilian vehicles heading for their rendezvous with their operative in Istanbul. Turkey's most vital city overflowed with activity. The volume of traffic made it fairly easy to slip in unnoticed, but that meant it was easy for unsavory types as well.

The cars stopped several blocks from one another with the team members taking different routes arriving at a derelict warehouse that appeared to be used for storing metal salvage. Weaving through the stacks of broken down equipment and machinery destined for dismantling, they gathered in an upper floor office.

"Team, this is Aban Kinza, one of our Middle East operators. He has been tracking the data since it arrived in Turkey," Jonas announced.

Kinza cast the team a glance and then dove into his review, "The data was passed off this afternoon. I first picked up the reporter Newsom three days ago. He arrived via commercial airline and stayed at a hotel in Atokay, a high-end district near the marinas. The next day he met with Barriq Hussein very publicly and they toured Istanbul. Yesterday, General Naib arrived by car from the south, likely through Syria. That is when I detailed the exchange. Naib then met with Olan Yado at the village of Izmir."

"That's three hundred miles down the coast. Why are we back here?" Jonas asked.

"While Hussein, Newsom, and Naib have maintained a high-profile downtown, Yado and a sizable contingent of the Kurdish brotherhood have assembled very close to here," Kinza reported.

"I thought the Kurds were largely seeking peace in the region," Fallon asked.

"Most are," Kinza nodded. "There is a fringe element that resorts to violence to get their voices heard. They are an impatient minority."

Jonas shuffled, not liking the complication that the operation was seeming to develop. "Where is the data? *That* is the mission."

"I am unsure. It was in General Naib's possession when he met with Yado. It is unclear what happened," Kinza admitted.

"Why are we here, specifically?" Chris pointed at his feet. "It seems like the best course would be to go after Hussein, Newsom, and Naib."

“There is a covert CIA-Turkish outpost at the southern edge of town. The existence of the outpost was on the data. Yado’s men have been moving in. I believe that is their target,” Kinza replied.

“I have to assume Hussein or Naib have the data,” Chris scowled. “Isn’t that the mission, Jonas?”

Jonas studied both men for a moment prior to responding, “The mission is the data. But it is also about the damage that the data can cause. The imminent threat is the outpost. Mount up and follow Kinza’s lead, Cara and I will try and keep tabs on Hussein and the data.”

Chris sighed but relented to the mission. Every bit of his fiber wanted to confront the men who had his wife and little girl’s blood on their hands. His missional instinct also kicked in. People were in jeopardy. It was his job to see that those people were saved. “Don’t let those bastards get away,” he growled.

Jonas’ nod in return was the sincerest gesture the man had made since they met.

“We got this, if you could use the FNG with you,” Fallon snarled.

“If my sources are correct, we’re going to need all the firepower we can get,” Kinza pushed.

“I have zero concern with Gunny on my six,” Cole replied.

"Fine. Kinza, you're with me," Fallon grumbled.

Jonas pulled out a case. Unlatching the locks, he opened it. Pulling out an earpiece, he handed it to Chris. "Your eyes and ears for ops."

Chris accepted the earpiece with curiosity. As he powered the tiny headphone up and placed it in his ear, a cheery voice chimed, "Welcome to the team, Gunnery Sergeant Chris Masters. I am 'Angel'. I will feed you any assistance I can on your missions…satellite and drone surveillance, maps, blueprints, and operational updates."

"Hello Angel," Chris replied, his voice a bit unsure.

"Your route is clear though there is a rather large contingent of vehicles filled with fighting age males heading towards the outpost," the voice in his ear said. His eyes told him that the rest of the team received a similar report.

Pressing the earpiece, he asked, "What is their ETA relative to ours?"

"They'll have a five-minute head start if you move out now," Angel said.

He didn't have to share the news. The team was already heading out of the room towards their vehicles. "We'll be able to catch them at their flank," Chris said.

"Or be sandwiched as reinforcements arrive," Fallon countered.

"Glass half full, eh, Drake?" Chris scoffed.

"Just a realist who is not excited to work with an operator hell-bent on revenge," Fallon declared as they separated for different vehicles.

Cole took the wheel as they followed Kinza and Fallon through the streets of Istanbul towards the southern outpost. Had it been any other time of day, traffic in Istanbul would have been insane. The benefit of late evening hours allowed the team to navigate the streets with relative ease. Chris wasn't sure if the same voice was in Cole's ear, but he was receiving satellite-aided instruction from someone as he whizzed the SUV along at high speed, confidently running red lights and shifting down side streets to navigate the most expedient route.

The Japanese-sourced diesel lacked the speed and growl of an American V-8, but it worked hard as Cole flogged it relentlessly through the crowded city. As they reached the southern edge of town, they met up with Fallon and Kinza. The pair of vehicles darted off the main roads and began to wind their way towards the covert outpost.

"Has the CIA been warned that an attack is coming?" Chris asked.

"They have, but the one thing our group lacks is an open communication channel. By the time Jonas and the back office found someone to listen to them, well, let's just say they aren't ready," Cole replied.

"Why not evacuate?" Chris pressed.

"Depends on how valuable the information in the outpost is. Must be something they are willing to hunker down and fight for," Cole shrugged.

"Reinforcements?"

"En route, they'll arrive just in time to clean up the mess," Cole said, his voice grim. "Well, lock and load."

Cole brought the SUV to a stop behind Fallon's. In an instant all four men were out of their vehicles, weapons ready. Following Kinza, they made their way towards a dark and seedy block of south Istanbul.

As expected, a team of Yado's men were already infiltrating the building. Security measures slowed them down, but they eventually made entry.

Fallon halted the group, "We know more men are coming. The last thing we need is to be inside in full firefight mode with a second team up our tails. Cole, find a high point, you've got overwatch. Kinza and I will go straight towards the breach. FNG, you see if there is a rear entry that you can counter infiltrate. If not, keep your comms on. We'll either pull you inside or you can deliver ground support against the second wave. Clear?"

Chris didn't particularly like taking orders from Fallon, though his strategy was sound. Nodding, they separated to man their particular roles. Gunfire began to ring from inside the building, making each man hasten their already urgent paces.

Cole identified a location with clear vantage and made his way through the building and up to the roof. Finding a corner that had sightlines on both the outpost and the road incoming from the south, he radioed his position as he settled into place, his eye through the scope downrange.

Chris navigated his way around the outpost building. The location was well scouted with dank, dark alleys and an overall unpleasantness of standing puddles and strewn garbage conjuring a pungent smell. The building was solid with few entry points. Windows and doors were sparse and nearly all but the front entrance were filled in with brick and concrete. With little access in, he assumed the team inside had devised explosive charges to provide a quick escape if needed. Blowing them from the outside was possible, though dangerous.

Circling the remainder of the building, he settled into a location partially protected by the corner of the outpost and low concrete wall that bordered the sidewalk. The location provided a similar view as Cole's but from the ground level and obstruction of parked cars and traffic. Calling in his position, Fallon had him hold.

Drake Fallon and Aban Kinza did not have to move too quietly as the barrage of gunfire from within the building concealed their footfalls. Fallon sighted on a single sentry in the main hall on the first floor and quickly took him out with a double-burst shot. Despite the gunplay on the stairs, Fallon and Kinza swept the first floor thoroughly before moving to the stairs.

The insurgents sent by Yado were perched at the base of the stairs, their muzzles pointed towards the third floor while they traded volleys with the outpost team. Fallon and Kinza hesitated momentarily, wondering if they could subdue the squad without killing them, as one spun in their direction and began firing, the decision had been made.

In several successive shots, Fallon on the left and Kinza on the right, they dispatched the remaining members until they met in the middle and no fighter was left standing.

As the gunfire died down, Fallon called, "We're friendlies! We eliminated the initial threat, but there are more on the way!"

"Identify yourselves!" a voice called from above in crisp English but with a Turkish accent.

"The only proper way for us to identify ourselves is that we just took out half a dozen men that had intent to kill you," Fallon replied. Both he and Kinza held their weapons away from their bodies.

"Yeah, we were told 'someone' might be coming. We have resources on their way," an American voice called as a man descended the steps. "Jonathan Blackmon."

"I'm Drake, this is my associate Kinza."

"There more of you?" Blackmon asked.

"We have a sniper perched nearby and a man on the street," Fallon declared.

Blackmon studied the men as several other outpost personnel peered down the steps. "You mind telling me what is going on?"

"An American reporter got a hold of data that disclosed key intelligence outposts, mostly from American ally nations. He's sympathetic to the Islamic Light," Fallon shared.

"And we were part of that data set…"

"Easy soft target to begin their campaign," Fallon nodded.

"I suppose we should be grateful, but I am not accustomed to having unnamed gunmen in my outpost, friendly or not," Blackmon stated.

"Understood," Fallon agreed. "You may not have much of a choice. Our intel has two more groups coming, separated about fifteen minutes apart."

A man behind Blackmon confirmed, "We have the same on satellite. Four vehicles in each, no way to tell how many heads."

"Well, it is clear this location is burned. Continue exit protocol, leaving nothing that can fall into enemy hands. Most of the staff here is admin. My friend Emine here, Turkish OKK maroon beret, and I are all the muscle we've got," Blackmon admitted.

"Then you did well to survive this far, let my team assist until your official help arrives," Fallon urged.

"And then?"

"And then we slip into the night like we were never here. You and Emine get to be the heroes, a triumphant collaboration between Turkish Special Forces and U.S. Central Intelligence…unless you want to explain…" Fallon started.

"No, no. I understand discretion," Blackmon consented.

"Then let's get ready, we have less than five minutes before the next wave hits," Fallon said.

It didn't take long for Chris' earpiece to spring to life. "Chris, you have four civilian vehicles with an undetermined number of occupants caravanning towards your position, two mikes out," a woman's voice declared.

"Copy that, Angel. I have a solid sightline," Chris replied.

From his sniper perch, Cole saw the vehicles first. He followed them through his scope until they reached a chokepoint he had identified on their path towards the outpost. Framing the driver of the lead vehicle with the reticle, he squeezed his finger.

The driver slumped. The vehicle's wheel spun wildly and with the momentum from traveling at speed and no one to hit the brakes, the small pickup careened towards a parked car, hitting with such force the impact sent the vehicle on its side, sliding to a stop in the middle of the road. The three insurgent vehicles following locked up their brakes to avoid slamming into the lead truck.

Cole dispatched the first occupant to get out of their vehicle, causing the others to duck and exit more cautiously. He watched as Chris shot the fuel tank of the turned over pickup. The man nearby winced, expecting the vehicle to explode. With a grin, he spun and fired his weapon towards Chris. As he did, the truck and the gunman burst into flames.

"It's not the bullet, it's the nearby ignition source, dummy," Cole scoffed. "Nice job, Chris."

A man from the trail vehicle pulled a long tube from under a canvas tarp in his truck. As Cole hit another gunman, the man slung the tube over his shoulder and using the trajectory from Cole's sniper shots, triangulated his position.

Chris saw the man with the tube aim it towards Cole's perch. Calling into his radio, he screamed, "RPG! Cole, get out of there, I'll draw fire!"

Chris sprung from his position, ignoring the two men with assault rifles closest to him. Firing wildly towards the insurgent with the RPG, he caught his attention for just a moment before returning his aim on Cole's position. Chris clipped him in the shoulder just as he fired. Diving into an alley, Chris used the concrete wall of the building to shield him from a barrage of bullets that came his way. He didn't divert the RPG assault for very long, he hoped it was enough to give Cole a chance.

As Cole landed his third shot, Chris' call came in. He didn't hesitate, he didn't try to sight on the insurgent with the RPG. He moved instinctively towards his pre-planned fallback position. Rolling away from the wall, he landed on his feet and sprinted to his right. Springing over the edge, he leapt across a narrow alley, rolling as he tucked his rifle against his body, landing on an adjacent roof as the corner of the building he was at burst into an explosion of rubble.

Running the expanse of the lower rooftop he had landed on, Cole made his way to the small stairwell portico which would give him just enough height to resume overwatch. Quickly setting up on the smaller roof, he found gunmen closing in on Chris' precarious spot in the alley. Moving his scope to the man Chris had the worst vantage of, he fired, dropping him as he watched Chris eliminate the other. An instinctive look up towards the roof, Chris acknowledged his appreciation before rolling out of the alley and continuing his counterassault.

Each time Chris rolled and ducked under new cover, he took a mental snapshot of each insurgent's position. Using a parked vehicle as a shield, he pressed his back to the grill as he used the rear windshield of the next car as a mirror. He saw two gunmen on either side of his cover advancing. Spinning up, he shot two bursts, dropping one man. Momentarily ducking back behind the grill, he rolled the opposite way, this time diving low to the ground dropping the second.

"Chris, I count six more men, including your friend with the RPG trying to relocate another shot at Cole. Two behind the van immediately at your six, three in a line protecting the RPG," Angel called.

Chris darted out from the vehicle he was backed to and sprang towards the next alley. As he did, he fired over his shoulder, taking another gunman out. Hearing the crack of the sniper rifle, he hoped Cole had done the same with the other side of the van.

"Down to four," Angel confirmed.

The building Chris used for cover had windows on either side of the corner. Chris squatted, peering through the dust coated glass. He had a clear line on the man with the RPG. The men in front scanned the street and sidewalk as he readied for another shot on Cole.

Seeing the telltale readying of shoulders and steadying of the weapon, Chris knew the grenadier was ready to launch another volley. With a careful aim, Chris fired multiple bursts just as the grenadier's shoulder flinched. Shattering the first set of windows and then the second, the third burst sailed unimpeded into the man with the RPG. Each round finding its way just as he pulled the trigger. Instead of aiming towards Cole, the slumping man's shot fired into the ground in front of the truck.

The old Soviet rocket exploded immediately, launching the remaining combatants into the air. From the safety of his position and Cole from his perch, they surveyed the street. Following the blast, there were no signs of movement, no additional gunfire.

"Chris, I do not detect any additional threats, but proceed with caution," Angel said into his earpiece. "The third and final wave we have been tracking is ten mikes on delivery."

Moving through the scene, Chris cataloged the insurgents. First checking them for vitals and second snapping a photo of their faces for intelligence referencing. "All clear," Chris called.

Fallon, Kinza, and Blackmon appeared in front of the outpost just as Chris completed his walk-through.

"Looks like you didn't need our help after all," Fallon declared. Glancing at the overturned truck fully engulfed in flames, the corner of a building shattered in a pile of rubble on the sidewalk, and several destroyed vehicles showered in shrapnel from the errant RPG, he added, "Not too much trouble for you, I see."

"Quiet evening in southern Istanbul," Chris quipped.

"With full support, we should be able to suppress the next wave with a bit less destruction," Fallon said.

Into his earpiece, Chris called, "Angel, what is the ETA for the trailing group?"

"They seem to be diverting."

"Turning around and heading back home?"

"No, they just turned off the highway and are heading east from your position," Angel replied.

Fallon was receiving a similar report through his earpiece, "Flanking… trying to find a different attack point?"

"Not the direction they are heading, they bypassed any routes that would take them to you."

"What's out that way?" Chris asked.

Kinza thought for a moment and then his face fell. "Muslim school in the suburbs. Anti-sharia, anti-violence being used in the name of Islam."

"They're going to go after kids?" Chris asked.

"Yado wants to save face after failing to get to the outpost. He'll take on a defenseless target that has been vocally oppositional to insurgents," Fallon scratched his chin.

"Let's mount up," Chris said.

"Our mission is the data. It's not going to be on Yado's men. The outpost has been defended, our mission here is done," Fallon said.

"We have to do *something*," Kinza pleaded.

"It's not our mission," Fallon was firm.

"Protecting the innocent, the undefended…that's *my* mission," Chris countered. Looking at Kinza, he shook his assault rifle, "I'm in."

Fallon looked cross, "I am commanding you to stand down."

Chris looked incredulous at Fallon and just laughed, "Yeah." Tapping Kinza on the shoulder, he began walking towards their vehicle, "Let's go."

The ride was a quiet one. Chris and Kinza focused on navigating towards the school.

"Angel is offline," Chris reported.

"Not her mission," Kinza said quietly.

Nodding, Chris understood. They were on their own without overwatch. He knew from previous transmissions; this was another four-vehicle force with anywhere from two to four combatants per vehicle. What he didn't know was how vicious Yado's men would be taking a school of unarmed Muslim boys.

Kinza stopped their SUV a few blocks from the school. They could hear men shouting, but no gunfire. Making their way on foot, assault weapons safety free, they approached the school. At each entrance, two men were stationed. They counted four other men that were stringing lines around the perimeter of the school with two others kneeling next to several canisters.

"They're going to firebomb the school. They are stringing the perimeter with det-cord and thermite, the canisters are likely a mix of explosive materials with thermite," Kinza guessed.

"Thermite? That's pretty brutal for a bunch of kids," Chris gasped.

"A curtain of 4,000-degree flames prevents escape and makes for dramatic video," Kinza replied.

"Let's not let that happen," Chris said, angling himself and readying his assault rifle. "I'll take out the gunmen, you take out the pyrotechnics crew."

Launching himself towards the school, Chris began shooting while he was in full stride. Taking out a pair of guards at the main entrance and didn't hesitate before racing towards the next set of doors. Hearing the gunfire, the next team was ready for him, weapons drawn and pointing in his direction. Launching himself into a full slide, he fired as a volley of bullets narrowly soared overhead. Sliding dangerously and directly towards the gunmen provided Chris with clear shots, dropping both before they could correct their aim with him at ground level.

Bracing his feet, he launched himself upright and sprinted towards the remaining set of doors that were guarded. The gunmen used effective cover, forcing Chris to find cover of his own. Diving towards a tractor parked between the school and soccer field, Chris used the steel wheels to protect him from the spray of bullets lobbied his direction.

Flattening himself to the ground, Chris used the tiny area between the edge of the mammoth tires and the ground to use as a small gun port. He was able to just peek down sights and aim the barrel towards the rear entrance. As one guard poked their head up, Chris fired off a shot. The man flung back. Reading the reaction, he clipped him in the shoulder.

The second gunman hailed a barrage of automatic weapon fire towards Chris while the first man recovered. With their mutual angles and solid cover, Chris knew the gun battle could wage for a while before either side was successful. He knew he had to help Kinza and the kids. His urgency was expanded as he heard an explosion from within the school.

Cautiously, Chris raised a hand to the instrument panel of the tractor. Turning the wheel so the front tires faced the school, he flipped the ignition and put the tractor into gear. Allowing the machine to flow past him, he hopped on the trailer hitch at the rear. Holding on to the tractor with one hand, he shouldered the assault rifle with his other. The men downrange parried back and forth unsure of how to deal with this new threat.

Taking advantage of the indecision, Chris levied a final shot into the man with the injured shoulder. Leaping free of the tractor, Chris ran in a sweeping arch until the second gunman was in sight and fired. The tractor rolled on, crashing through the rear entrance of the building, allowing smoke to billow out.

Kinza didn't hesitate, as Chris encountered the insurgents with guns at the ready, the Iraqi army vet targeted the men stringing the thermite line first. Caught by surprise, they had little time to react and draw their own weapons. Dispatching a pair, he turned, spinning to face the men at the canisters. One drew his weapon and sent a volley of bullets towards Kinza. Rolling, he sent his own shots downrange. Hitting one man, he also ruptured one of the canisters. The second man snatched a canister and flung it high in the air, landing it on the school roof.

The man reached for a second canister. Kinza followed through with several rounds to the chest, dropping the man while igniting the rest of the canisters as he was unable to release a second throw.

A brilliant flash lit from the top of the school building. The thermite charge from the first canister came to life burrowing a hole through the roof, dropping the canister into the center of the school erupting into a ball of fire.

The second line crew ignited their det-cord thermite string and pulled their guns to face Kinza. As they wheeled away from the school, one man fell immediately, the second got a shot off before being hit by Kinza.

Kinza winced, looking at the stream of blood running down his chest. He couldn't lift his left hand. Wheeling around, he tried to spy any other threats before dropping to a knee. Ripping a pocket open on his tactical pants, he pulled out a packet of dressing. Tearing at the packet with his teeth, he pressed against the wound as he continued to surveil the scene.

Chris, once confident the combatants were no longer a threat, followed the tractor which came to a stop against an interior wall of the school. Switching off the ignition, he flipped on the tactical light attached to his assault rifle and began searching the school halls as the building began to fill with smoke. The fire alarms blared, the power abruptly shorted plunging the school into a dark, chaotic scene.

Moving quickly from room to room, Chris located classrooms of frightened students and instructors. It took effort to convince them he wasn't a threat, finally getting them to funnel through the hall the way he had entered to make their escape.

The firebomb had melted through the ceiling of the offices and was rapidly spreading throughout the building. Entering a large central room, Chris figured to be the school mosque, he found the remaining students and staff. They stared at Chris from their prayer positions, afraid to move and untrusting of the westerner as their school burned. From behind Chris, a hobbled Kinza appeared. Behind him, several Turkish officers who urged the students to flee. Forming a broken chain, the officers guided the students and teachers through the hallways until they had reached the safety of the soccer field.

The entire school was fully engulfed in flames. Turkish officials moved in to care for the children and school workers as Turkish police began investigating the fallen insurgents.

The Turkish intelligence officer from the CIA outpost strode through the haze of smoke and flashing emergency lights. "I tried to mobilize help as fast as I could. I can see without you two, it would have been tragically too late. My country is indebted to you," Emine said.

"Just doing what is right," Chris said. "My friend, here, might need some medical attention, though."

Kinza shook him off, "Through and through. I stopped the bleeding for now and will get properly patched up at HQ. What we would benefit from is a quiet exit." The Iraqi special operative glanced at the Turkish officials who were taking interest in the foreigners amidst the school chaos.

Emine nodded, "I can manage that. Follow me."

The Turkish intelligence officer used his powerful credentials to navigate Chris and Aban Kinza through the growing police presence at the school. Kinza used his relationship with his handler, his version of "Angel" to secure transportation for the pair to their European base, a commune near Campoverde in Italy the team had nicknamed Camp Green.

The location provided excellent access throughout Europe, the Middle East, and Northern Africa. Protected estates and private helicopters being common in the region provided cover to their coming and going and if needed, roads connected most of Europe.

"You gonna be okay?" Chris asked. He had seen wounds like Kinza's many times. He knew with proper care, the operator would be fine. He also knew first-hand how miserable the journey to receive care could be.

Kinza nodded, "Just a flesh wound. Have had worse."

The former Iraqi special forces fighter studied Chris. "Thank you for helping save the school."

"Why did you agree to come with me?"

"Innocent children and people caught in a political crossfire. Doing my duty," Chris shrugged.

Kinza paused, his expression serious, "A Muslim terrorist killed your family."

Chris returned a perplexed look, "Are all Muslims the same? I didn't think all Muslim people had a hand in my family's death. A radical Muslim lowlife took orders from a rogue Muslim General who is propped up by a radical Muslim elite."

"Not everyone sees the difference. No, not all Muslims are the same," Kinza admitted. "My teachings of Islam forbid the taking of innocent lives and demand such lives be protected."

"Right is right, wrong is wrong. Regardless of your religion, what country you were born in, or what flag you represent," Chris replied.

"Those lines can get blurred," Kinza pressed.

"They can. That is what concerns me about a rogue military group that decides behind some anonymous backroom what is right and wrong, aiming our bullets at their discretion," Chris countered.

Kinza nodded, "It is a delicate situation. They will not be happy with our insubordination. They will see our actions as a grave mistake."

"Good thing I don't work for them," Chris said. "The only mistake I may have made was to follow Drake on the outpost mission as opposed to holding to the data and more importantly, the men behind the data. That is my mission."

"Barriq Hussein and General Razi Naib," Kinza nodded.

"And that rat reporter. They are the reasons I am here, not some private war machine led by people no one voted for," Chris added.

Kinza nodded, "The veil is discomforting to you. You will be welcomed into it in time. They do good work. Protecting the outpost, we saved lives and in turn, many more."

"Yeah," Chris nodded reluctantly. He hoped that Jonas and Cara were successful in pinning down the head of the snake while they were chasing the tail. If it wasn't for Kinza's injuries, Chris would not have left Istanbul.

EIGHTEEN

General Naib's entourage made him easy to find in downtown Istanbul. Nicknamed the "Peace Broker", a moniker pushed by Barriq Hussein, he was a powerful regional figure. Few, and mostly only in the intelligence community, knew how deeply he was involved in arming, training, and directing terror cells. He kept an arm's length from most work and further insulated Hussein from being connected.

Clint Newsom stood nervously by. His eyes darted around the streets. Like the rodent he personified, he stayed alive by being skittish and alert. His demeanor belied the arrogance he displayed on camera and in his field reporting. Even as he was addressed by Naib, he snapped into character. His chest out, his affect confident and direct.

Jonas and Cara studied the reporter and general from across the street. Selecting a little cafe where they could sip on Turkish coffee and observe without notice, they settled in. Naib was exchanging pleasantries with the reporter and others as a luxury SUV sped up to the curb.

Apparently bidding farewell, Newsom begin to walk away from the crowd and Naib started towards the SUV before being pulled into a conversation with another man that had accompanied him.

"Looks like time to divide and conquer," Jonas said softly. "You take the reporter, I've got the general."

"Copy that," Cara acknowledged. Sliding out her chair, she spun and smiled, "Thank you for the coffee."

Jonas nodded and tossed a few bills onto the table. He mulled his tactical approach to separate the general from his detail. Eying the luxury SUV that was clearly there for him, he called into his comms. "Late model Range Rovers have excellent security systems, don't they?"

Angel's voice chimed in his ear, "They do. I'm zooming in on the VIN as we speak. There is a great little traffic camera at the next intersection. Most appreciated."

Jonas waited. He squirmed a bit as Naib and the man shook hands and he again started for the SUV. When the voice called to him again, he was on the move. "The vehicle is disabled.

It will likely require a tow before they figure out they had a glitch in the system."

"Nice job, glitch," Jonas commended. Rounding a corner, he found a parked taxi. The driver had just stepped into a diner.

With a glance around the street, Jonas strode to the driver's door, from his jacket, he pulled a shim and deftly unlocked the car. Tossing the shim aside, he went to quick work on the ignition. Bringing the small diesel car to life, he wheeled onto the street. At the intersection, as he waited at a red light, he could see the hood on the Range Rover pop up and several of Naib's men pouring over the engine bay. Naib himself seemed irritated. Pushing up his sleeve, he examined his watch.

Jonas spied another taxi as one of Naib's men raised his hand to hail. Jumping the light, Jonas cut off the oncoming taxi and sped to a stop behind the Range Rover. Ignoring the horn from the other irate driver, Naib's man opened the door. He and the general climbed in while his remaining men stayed with the Range Rover.

Adopting his best colloquial accent, Jonas grinned, "Where to, gentlemen?"

Naib spat an address as he scowled into his phone, typing madly. He was clearly in a hurry. Hitting the gas, Jonas pulled the taxi away from the curb. Jonas used his inattention on the road to his advantage. Slamming on the brakes, both passengers lurched forward, hitting their faces on the seatbacks in front of them.

Calling in Arabic, Jonas scolded, "Seatbelts, gentlemen." Spinning the car into an alleyway, he slammed on the brakes, pinning the passenger side doors against a dumpster. Rolling out of the driver's seat, he had his gun drawn and foot on the rear door before Naib's man could react.

Rapping the glass with the butt of his handgun, Jonas ordered the man to place his hands on either side of the driver's seat headrest. Securing them in place with zip ties, Jonas opened the door, ignoring the torrent of threats from Naib who was slowly reaching into his own jacket. Jonas glared and focused the muzzle on the general.

"I wouldn't," Jonas shook his head. Reaching in, he grabbed General Naib by the collar and drug him out of the car, shoving the man he had tied to the driver's seat out of the way.

Putting up a fight, the general tried to break away. Jonas brought a crushing blow with the back of the pistol and with a kick to the back of his legs, dropping the general to the ground. With a quick search, Jonas relieved Naib of his pistol, tossing it into the dumpster. Next, he began a thorough search for the data drive.

Not finding it on the general, Jonas searched his man. Neither had the device on them. With another set of zip ties,

Jonas bound the two men together. With a grin, Jonas snapped a photo of the very irate general and his man.

"It's moments like this that make me really love my job. Thanks, boys!" Jonas crooned before disappearing down the alley.

Cara kept an eye on Clint Newsom as he strode through the crowds of Istanbul. His profile in the digital dossier she reviewed illustrated the reporter as being extremely arrogant and cocky. His nervousness as he departed General Ravi Naib suggested something in their meeting rattled him. She hoped that it was an indication that he might have the data drive in his possession.

Cara was a capable operative on the ground, though her forte was as a pilot. She was quick, decisive, and cunning. She would use her wiles to isolate the reporter. Ducking into the lobby of his hotel, Cara was both encouraged and disappointed that Newsom stopped at the hotel bar first.

On one hand, it was an indicator that he was not carrying anything that he wanted to stash right away in the safety of his room. It could also be that just by reaching the hotel, the reporter had a false sense of security. Either way, Cara was going to find out if Newsom was carrying the data.

Pushing through the hotel doors, she tousled her hair and undid a button on her blouse. Eschewing her normal tactical flight gear so that she could blend in on the streets of Istanbul was an advantage she was going to play.

Seeing Newsom order a drink from the bartender, Cara slid into the seat beside him. Initially, she avoided eye contact, seemingly intent on ordering her own beverage. Offering a sultry smile, she eyed the bartender as he delivered Newsom his drink. “I’ll have whatever he’s having.”

The bartender nodded and scampered away to pour her glass.

Newsom cocked his head, “You like Cosmos?”

Cara offered a wicked grin, “Not gonna lie, I’m typically a Kentucky bourbon rollin’ alongside a beer girl, but I’m ready to celebrate.”

“You’re American,” Newsom acknowledged. “A long way from home.”

“Business trip. A tiring, yet very successful business trip,” Cara shared as her pink drink was slid in front of her.

“Oh, what kind of business are you in?” the reporter pressed, taking a sip of his own Cosmopolitan.

“Acquisitions, mostly. Nothing too exciting, but I do get to travel the world,” Cara was coy in her reply. “How about you?” Suddenly her eyes widened, “Oh my. You’re that reporter. You tackle all those international social justice issues. I'm having a drink with a gal dern hero."

Newsom couldn't help but gush at the comment. "The real heroes are the people I report on. The ones trying to make a difference."

"Wow. You're doing your part, just the same," Cara cooed. Settling back in her seat, flashing the reporter her biggest smile, ensuring that her unbuttoned blouse was in full effect, something dawned on her. Something that was not in the dossier. Eyeing the drink, recognizing what and who Newsom's gaze lit on during their conversation, she realized she would need to change tactic. Newsom was not her type, and more importantly, she not his.

Undaunted, she pressed, "I'm not sure how this works. If one of the companies we are working with is…" Cara darted her gaze around the room before falling into a hoarse whisper, "…making questionable deals for a Republican U.S. senator, would that be something you would be interested in."

Newsom nearly fell out of his chair with the opportunity. Leaning forward, he grinned, "Absolutely. Tell me about it."

Cara shifted in her seat, "Not here. Can we talk somewhere private?"

"Sure," Newsom nodded. With a smile to the bartender, he waved at their two drinks to have them put on his hotel tab. "We can talk in my room if you are comfortable with that."

Cara did her best to look meek and unsure before nodding, "Yes. I suppose that would be fine."

She had to suppress a grin as she followed the reporter to the elevator.

"This business of yours, is it based here in Turkey?" Newsom asked.

"All over Europe and the Middle East," Cara replied.

"I see," Newsom nodded, inserting his key into the slot, releasing his hotel room door.

The moment the door was closed, Cara delivered a vicious kick to the back of the reporter's legs, dropping him to his knees. Leaping to one knee herself, she wrapped her arms around Newsom. Her forearm wrapped around his throat while her other hand grasped his wrist and pulled with all of her might.

Newsom tapped at her, kicking his feet against the floor as he gasped for breath. Cara didn't relent until his body went limp. Checking for a pulse, she found it faint. Shrugging to herself, she admitted, she was good either way, though the mission was to keep him alive if possible.

Starting with the reporter, she rifled through every pocket and fold of the reporter's clothing. Taking care as she hunted, noting the reporter had wet himself. Searching for something as small as the data drive, it could be worn on a necklace or taped anywhere. Cara's search was thorough.

Before she could move on to the rest of the room, she was interrupted by a knock on the door. She hesitated, glancing at Newsom's naked body lying in the middle of the floor. Deciding to take advantage of the scenario, she unbuttoned her blouse fully and removed her bra.

Opening the door just enough to reveal her full form and a glimpse of Newsom's bare limbs, she offered a smile to the attendant.

"I'm sorry, ma'am. We received a complaint of noise from the guests in the room below you," the attendant replied.

Producing her most wicked grin, Cara licked her lips, "We may have gotten a little carried away." Wriggling so that her blouse blew open a bit further, she promised, "We'll do our best to keep it down."

"Tha…thank you, ma'am," the attendant stuttered. "Sorry to disturb you."

Cara shut the door, refastened her blouse, and made hasty work of thoroughly searching Newsom's room for the data drive. With a sigh, she straightened herself up and after one final scan ensuring she didn't miss a vent, picture frame, or lamp base that could conceal a device, made her reluctant exit.

Nineteen

The entire team had found their way back to Camp Green in the Brescia province of Italy. Chris Masters helped Aban Kinza manage his wounds while in transport. Once on the ground and in the safety of the compound, a medical team was quick to give him aid.

Chris paced the grounds, waiting for information from the rest of the team. If they had found the data, but more importantly, if they had captured or killed Clint Newsom and General Razi Naib. Parts of him regretted not going after them himself, but he was grateful that he was in a position to help Kinza rescue the children and staff of the Muslim school.

It was Cole Porter who found him. The former intelligence officer flashed Chris a broad smile. "Glad to see you made it back in one piece."

"You too," Chris said. He couldn't help but to look past Cole and the pleasantries, eager to hear about Naib and Newsom.

"I only got pieces of it, but by reports, you and Kinza saved two hundred and twenty-three children and nineteen adults," Cole reported.

Chris nodded slightly, "I'm glad we were in a position to help."

"Gonna catch hell for that. Fallon and the brass don't like breaching the mission parameters," Cole said.

Chris merely offered a shrug.

"Speaking of which, the entire team is assembled in the conference room for debrief," Cole shared.

Chris perked up. He would finally get some answers on what happened in Istanbul from the surveillance team. "Lead the way."

Winding their way through the serene grounds of well named Campoverde, rich in green foliage, they made their way to the main building and into the situation room. Chris had barely entered the room when several pairs of heated eyes landed on him.

"I told you bringing an FNG into a mission was a bad idea. He breached protocol, disobeyed orders, left the team, and endangered the very existence of this organization!" Fallon spat. He strode toward Chris until he was squared up directly in front of him. Clearly still heated from Chris' decision to leave with Kinza.

Jonas stood with his arms crossed, his typical cool demeanor not wavering. "Protocols exist for a reason. Team safety is paramount. As a dark organization, we exist because of anonymity. We need to be ghosts. We accomplish that by adhering to the specific objective at hand."

The team leader looked directly at Chris, "As a Raider, these principles aren't lost on you. Orders must be followed." He paused as though his statement were a question.

"The objective is not lost on me at all. There was no superior present in Turkey to give me orders…or in this room," Chris replied evenly.

The words stoked Drake Fallon's temper, a meaty finger poking Chris in the chest as he glared, "As the senior operative on that team, it was *my* orders that needed to be followed for the results of the mission and the safety of the team."

Chris glared back, "I'm not a member of your team."

A finger still digging into Chris' chest, Fallon turned to Jonas, his other hand gesturing towards Chris.

"Transitioning is a process," Jonas didn't waver. "What you and Kinza did was bold, brave, and impressive. It was also reckless, dangerous and Drake is right, threatens everything. We can't answer every call, but we can execute those we are called to operate. I understand you are on the outside looking in, but we have a common goal. I hope that will build our bond as opposed to separating us."

"Speaking of which, where is General Naib and Newsom?" Chris was torn between wanting to hear they were both dead and buried or tied up in the basement of the compound.

Jonas and Cara shared their experiences and failure to uncover the data drive. Chris' entire body twitched as he listened to their stories. Hearing that both men were apprehended. Hearing that both men were still alive.

Unable to control his emotion, he burst, "You left them alive! Not in custody, not with bullets in their heads… alive to harm more innocent people! You came back two bullets heavy…"

"There is nothing I would have liked more than to deliver General Naib at your feet. There is a greater play here. We want the link to Barriq Hussein, Naib is that link. He thought himself untouchable. Well, he just got touched," Jonas said.

"And he knows we are after him!" Chris growled.

"He and his man won't say anything about the incident. They are way too prideful to admit that incident ever happened. Yes, he will be more wary. For the first time in his campaign of terror, he is going to have to second guess himself and his environment," Jonas replied.

"And Newsom?"

"Based on the piss running down his leg, I wouldn't be surprised if he gets out of the game completely. The cocky S.O.B. has run around unfettered for years. I think his righteousness fell a peg or three," Cara grinned.

Jonas relaxed his arms, "If Cara killed Newsom in Istanbul, it would have appeared as though a reporter was silenced because he was on the right track with his reporting. If we can complete the loop, we'll be able to dump enough evidence to hang him as a traitor and more importantly, expose the trough of lies that he has spread for years. You want to stop terror on innocents, exposing the false narrative is the most effective way to do that."

Cara looked at Chris and promised, "He'll get his."

Chris sighed. After shouldering Fallon out of the way, he paced the room for a moment. Much of what Jonas said resonated. He didn't like hearing it, but the man was right.

Turning back to the group, Chris asked, "So, now what?"

"We have eyes on Naib and Newsom. The general will attempt to return to business as usual, the best that he can. Newsom is not an operator. He will be scared and as such, he will run for help," Jonas declared.

"Help from where?" Cole asked.

"From *whom* is the more operative question," Jonas said. "Someone leaked that data. My guess is, that is where he will go for help."

Nodding to Cara, she flicked on one of the large monitors that blanketed an interior wall. The team looked on as the monitors displayed a news report of the firefight south of Istanbul.

"The operation at the intelligence outpost was successfully kept under wraps. The assault on the school… not so much," Jonas said as they continued watching.

The images on the screen showed the fire crews working on the flames and the crowd of students, teachers, and parents. The Turkish and CIA intelligence had remained off screen, security footage captured Chris and Aban Kinza. The images were not crisp, but it was possible to identify them if you knew them or had prior footage to match. That is precisely what one outlet did, comparing the shots of Chris at the embassy with the footage in Istanbul.

"Could this be Patriot X?" the reporter asked. "This connection raises further questions whether this mysterious warrior is an American operative who also works abroad or is a foreign operative who brashly assaulted a sovereign entity within U.S. borders."

Turning to his guest, the man labeled as former Department of Defense analyst, "I continue to attest the actions taken, the style of movement, how he handles his weapon and techniques used, this is either American military, former military or at the very least, American military trained…"

Jonas paused the feed and faced the room.

Fallon was beside himself, "That is why we stick to the mission. We need to control the situation!"

Jonas waved his hand in the air, "Drake is absolutely right. Footage like this, the possibility for identification… could be a death blow to our entire operation. That said, our benefactors see a potential positive angle with this."

Continued coverage showed politicians arguing in favor and against the actions taken by the rogue soldier. Both were critical of unsanctioned action, but some found the assault on the embassy and the rescue of the Muslim school to be positive, branding Patriot X as heroic.

Others argued heroism in these actions was imperialist taken without global guidance and therefore unjust, even criminal. "Vigilante justice on a world stage cannot be tolerated!"

"Protestors turned angry mob, burning down churches, mosques, government buildings are okay, but a few actors righting what few would refute to be wrongs is unjust?" the other politician defended.

"We don't know who this Patriot X is, what their intent is. Anytime you have one person or a small group deciding on their own to violate sovereign territory or to determine who lives and dies, it threatens society," the politician on the left screen declared.

"So far, what we have seen, *if* this is the same person, a terrorist was brought to justice… justice left to the world court, not his own actions and rescuing a school full of children from what appeared to be a terror attack. Sounds pretty heroic to me," the politician on the right argued.

Another screen showed a similar debate among religious leaders from multiple faiths. Most regaled the school rescue, though a few hardline Imams decried the event as a political hoax to strengthen the growing division of Islamic philosophies.

Christian, Jewish, and Islamic leaders stood firm on the blessing of protection afforded the children at the school. Caring for the innocent was a consistent virtue of most faiths. As each was represented in a panel, they shared a message of peace and unity despite their disparate teachings.

"There are members of our organization that see this as an opportunity for greater influence, behind the scenes, that is. We will always be a black site operation. Despite the recent notoriety, anonymity and as Drake said, ghostlike is still our lifeblood," Jonas said.

Drake Fallon glared at Chris. The Marine didn't flinch.

"We will continue to track both General Naib and Newsom. In the meantime, we don't have much time to reorganize. We have a situation with a downed operative. We need to spin up. Kinza, you need to sit this one out, try and heal up. Chris, you would be an asset. We'll be in hostile territory with sophisticated communication. Use call signs. Chris, we'll use 'Gunny' for you," Jonas declared.

The team nodded.

"Airborne in sixty. Collect your things. I hope you slept on the plane," Jonas added.

Cole and Chris burst out of the room together. "You good?" Cole asked.

Chris looked at him and nodded. "I'm fine."

"I know you wanted to get a hold of the people responsible for your family. This gets us the people behind *them*," Cole emphasized.

"I get it. It's the right play," Chris acknowledged. "What do you know about this operative?"

“Not much. From another team. Call sign “Jackal”. Works mostly the Mid-East and Eastern Europe,” Cole said.

“What’s your call sign?” Chris asked.

“2K.”

“As in…,” Chris started.

“As in my consistent kill zone.”

Chris grinned in appreciation, “Good name.”

“Gotta earn the good ones,” Cole smiled back.

“I earned Gunny, I guess. Not sure it is deserved anymore. There is a Raider team down a man. Not gonna lie, that hurts me a close second to losing Breanna and Macy,” Chris admitted.

The two men stopped in the hallway. Cole looked at Chris, “You are still working for your country. I get it. We all struggled with what led us here. We all had oaths. We are carrying them out. Just not in the way we thought we would. I look at it like this, if by doing the work we do, we make their jobs easier, a little bit safer, we’re still helping them out.”

Chris didn’t look so sure.

“Your team knows you. They know how you operate. Are you going to tell me that as soon as that bastard hit the switch on that bridge, your team didn’t know what you *had* to do? Especially once politics got in the way?” Cole pressed.

“I can’t help but to feel it is a selfish act against the greater good,” Chris admitted.

“You brought justice for hundreds of people and their families. You just saved hundreds of kids in Istanbul and an outpost that restrictions would have prevented help from reaching. No. I sleep fine at night,” Cole said.

Slapping Chris on the shoulder, “When we bring down that entire house of cards that terror cell is built on and those that support them, you will have done your country… the world a great benefit.”

TWENTY

The flight from northern Italy to Baghdad, Iraq felt short. Most of the team caught sleep, already weary from the mission in Turkey. Chris was able to force himself to sleep, knowing it might be his last opportunity in some time.

An hour before their arrival, Fallon woke the crew and began detailing their assignments. "We have split intel. Looking at Cole and then Cara, he directed, "2K and Dragonfly, you're with me. Chief, that's Jonas, and Angel will man the comms and provide us with any updates. FNG, I mean, *Gunny*, you will track down a contact of ours, Anya Oshevsky, call sign 'Duchess'. If she has a lead, report in and wait for team instruction, which will come from either me or Chief. Are we clear?"

"We're clear," Chris nodded. He knew the play. He had done it himself when a non-team guy was added to his mission. Send them off on some side boondoggle well away from your six.

"It's kind of the wild west out there, you'll have to be careful," Cara warned.

Chris nodded, "I know the area."

"Good, we're preparing to touch down. Godspeed, everyone!" Fallon said in earnest.

"Oorah!" Chris muttered.

"Hooyah!" Cara, the former Army pilot, winked.

Gear slung over their backs, Fallon's team and Chris were met with vehicles on the airport runway. The team was provided with gleaming black Landcruisers. Chris was provided with a dusty, decades-old Toyota FJ SUV.

At first glance, it would appear that Fallon was hazing him with inferior equipment, but Chris knew what the selection meant. Modern, especially glistening new SUVs were led by occupation and international teams making them common targets for attacks from rebels and terrorists. A dusty, tan pre-war FJ would blend into the environment and suggest the occupant had little of value and was themselves unimportant. The perfect vehicle for treading into the largely anarchist Salahuddin province of western Iraq.

Pulled apart by competing tribes, political parties against themselves as well as within, close to the upheaved borders of Syria, the entire area was a dangerous mess – a free for all much like the old west depicted in a young America.

Chris nodded farewell to the team, fired up the FJ, and followed the map on his phone that Angel had provided for him.

"Gunny, this is Angel. I'll be on your comms throughout your mission. I'll guide you the best I can as you travel through Iraq," a voice called in his ear.

"Angel, it's good to hear you again," Chris said.

"Sorry I couldn't follow you to the end in Turkey. We have protocols to follow. Try and stay on mission this trip, what do you say?"

"No promises," Chris called back.

Shifting the old Toyota into gear, he sped along the Iraqi highway. Having served multiple tours in the Middle East and a number of Raider missions throughout Iraq, this was familiar territory. He was, however, used to being surrounded by his team or platoon. Moving through the countryside solo was a new and somewhat unnerving experience.

Outside of Baghdad, aside from rough roads, the drive was almost pleasant. Windows down, he rolled through the desert. The only thing missing was the ability to listen to his playlist on his road trip.

He knew enough from his previous ventures to remain vigilant. Bandits were renown throughout the unpopulated areas and the route crossed through multiple self-proclaimed territories from different political and religious sects, each claiming the region as their own.

Circumventing a checkpoint he eyed on the horizon, Angel walked him through a reroute and tweaked the display on his GPS. Avoiding major delays, he pulled into the outskirts of the rebuilt settlement of Sinjab. Liberated, embattled, liberated again, multiple forces battled for power over the little town.

Ultimately, Sinjab became a delicate no man's land where no one had specific control though certain individuals through weapons, food, healthcare, or hedonistic wares held some degree of power.

Chris parked the SUV on the outskirts of town, out of the fray, nose pointed for a getaway if needed. Walking through the dusty streets of Sinjab, Chris thought the scene must have been reminiscent of Dodge City in the wild west. People of all walks of life sought something in the western Iraqi outpost. Some were there to reclaim their homes lost during the war, some gathered to plot their group's resurgence in the region, others were there to profit from the desperate people who wandered in.

Following the directions outlined in the mission briefing, he passed a hookah house, several mosques, and a restaurant. Finding himself in front of the busiest location in town, a hotel that was also used as a casino and tavern. Chris eyed several young women dressed provocatively in front of the building, suggesting the hotel was being used as a brothel as well.

Stepping through the entrance, he side-stepped a brawl between three men that spilled out into the street. The remaining guests in the lobby that was filled with revelers dotting the variety of gaming tables barely took note of the skirmish. In the center of the room, Chris found the bar. A large, haggard man leaned against the counter and glared at Chris.

"Room, game, or drink?" the bartender asked.

"I'm looking for someone," Chris declared.

The bartender raised an eyebrow and spat, "I'm not a matchmaker."

"They call her the duchess," Chris said. As the words tumbled out, those within hearing distance froze and snapped their heads in his direction.

The bartender glanced around nervously. "The two men by the door to the right. They'll let you in if she wants to see you. They'll kill you if she doesn't."

Chris shrugged with a sideways grin, "Fifty-fifty, I've played worse odds."

"The odds always seem to play out in the house's favor," the bartender warned and went back to his work.

Chris made his way through the tables and stood in front of the men at the door the bartender suggested. They instantly moved tighter together, blocking the door. Chris studied them momentarily. They were both large men. Armed with Russian Makarov handguns and Spetsnaz steel blades at their sides.

"I need to see the duchess," Chris said.

Without another word, the men snapped into action, lunging towards Chris. Side stepping the first man, Chris struck quickly at the second guard's throat. Instinctively, the guard put his hands in front of him and gasped for breath.

The first man grasped Chris from behind, wrapping a large forearm around his throat and squeezed. As the second guard recovered, he moved in for a haymaker. Chris used his attacker to run up his chest with his feet, launching in the air over the first guard's head, slipping free from the chokehold. With a powerful kick, Chris pushed the guards together against the door.

With a second kick to the knee bringing one guard to the ground, Chris grabbed the Spetsnaz blade from the man's sheath as he fell.

Just as the first guard's meaty head shrunk in front of him, revealing the second guard readying for an attack, Chris struck out with the point of the knife pushing into the man's throat, stopping just at the point of penetration.

The door to the room opened and a man peered over the guard's shoulder, "Anya will see you now."

Stepping over the downed guard, Chris spun the knife in his hand and pressed it flat against the second guard's chest. "Your friend might want that back. Nice blade."

Chris followed the man who was similarly imposing, though carried an air of professionalism as opposed to bar bouncer persona. Going up a flight of stairs, they arrived at an office overlooking the hotel main lobby below. The room was dimly lit with streaks of pink and blue LED lighting providing most of the illumination.

The furniture was posh and modern, a stark contrast to the simple, mismatched décor of the rest of the hotel. Standing at the window observing the scene below, an elegantly dressed woman waved her hand as the men entered. In a flash, the room cleared. A man and woman in dark clothing rose from a plush sofa, following the man who led Chris to the office trailed by two more men outfitted like the guards but of Middle Eastern descent.

As she heard the footsteps descend the stairs and pile out of the backroom, she spoke as she remained watching her guards recover from their entanglement with Chris. “So, you’re the guy Jonas sent me.”

“I’m the guy,” Chris acknowledged.

The woman spun to face Chris.

Her blonde hair spilled over her shoulders, exposed except for the straps of her elegant dress. Her attire as much out of place in Sinjab as her office furniture. “My men are direct from Ukranian Alpha Group, inherited from a former Soviet Spetsnaz in that area. I’m not going to lie, I am a bit disappointed with the ease in which you dispatched them.”

Chris shrugged, “Guard duty is always a challenging task for someone who is used to being the infiltrator.”

“Perhaps. Perhaps the lavish lifestyle in Sinjab is softening them,” Anya suggested with a sardonic grin.

Chris glanced around the room, “Quite the space you have here.”

“Modeled after the VIP room of a favorite old haunt. Recalls a time when life was a bit more… civilized.”

“You work for… Jonas’ group?” Chris realized he had no idea what the organization he was working for was called. He was mission-focused on bringing resolution to Breanna and Macy's deaths. The nomenclature was an insignificant factor.

Anya laughed, "Work for them? No. I work with them...they work with me from time to time when our interests coincide. Occasionally, we owe each other favors."

"Is that why I am here? To reconcile a favor?" Chris asked.

"Not just. The information my lost operative has might be of use to Jonas on a case that I understand is very important to you. I'm sorry for your loss, by the way," the woman looked directly at Chris. She carried a confounding air of sultry, devious with just a hint of genuine concern. The way she moved and talked, she oozed confidence and sensuality.

"You know about me?"

"Gunnery Sergeant Chris Masters... or former Gunnery Sergeant by now. It is my business to know operators around the world. Your missions have periodically caught my attention," she admitted.

"And you?"

Anya grinned. "I am Anya Oshevsky. Some have taken to call me 'Duchess'. Not all who have done so have walked away."

"How did you come to your current position?" Chris pressed.

"My family held very high posts in a contested region between Russia and Ukraine. The tug of war upset the balance of power forcing my family to… relocate. We had political, military, and commercial influence. I took the family business underground and have done well for myself since," Anya shared.

"And your family?"

"Some have been arrested, some murdered or martyred. Some operate underground as I do," Anya said, her voice falling flat. "Now, if you don't mind, we have rather pressing matters not benefitted from flipping through my family scrapbook."

"I am here to work," Chris nodded.

Anya eyed the shooter for a long moment before she spoke, "I have an important asset, Matthias Lanikov, who has gone missing. Matthias has been tracing the steps of General Ravi Naib, trying to put out the fires that Naib has been starting. I'm afraid he had finally stepped in the wrong steaming pile and has gotten himself captured."

Anya paused, flashing a momentary look of genuine concern. She then returned to her sultry, objective focused persona, "Matthias has gathered tremendous information on General Naib that can be crucial to halting his widespread virus of radicalization and violence. Matthias holds a wealth of information about others, myself included, that Naib and his puppet master Barriq Hussein would kill to get."

"And you need me to get him back," Chris interjected.

"I do," Anya nodded. "It won't be easy. I sent another operative. She is... highly skilled. She has disappeared as well. I fear the worst."

Chris studied Anya, despite her forward demeanor, when she spoke of specific people, there was a soft kindness that resonated ever so briefly in her eyes. "Who is the operator?"

"Her name is Cait McBride. Irish Republican Army trained, or at least a dissident splinter of it. She had a... reckoning that brought her to us. A bit rough around the edges, but fiercely dependable," Anya said. "She was sent to infiltrate and locate, retrieve Matthias if possible. That was a week ago. We have not had communication for five days."

"Could just be holed up or gone dark to maintain cover," Chris suggested.

Anya grinned and shook her head, "Not Cait. She is more of a blast her way in than sneak through the shadows kind of operative. Something went wrong, I am sure of it."

"And you have an idea where they might be?" Chris asked.

"There is a settlement south of Baaj called 'The End'. Aptly named at the end of the road in the middle of nowhere. It was originally a camp for Iraqis who wanted to avoid the war, live in a tiny hovel of peace. Unfortunately for them, it was an excellent staging outpost for groups prepping activity along the Syrian border," Anya shared. "It is now a free-for-all marketplace for ISIS supporters that makes Sinjab seem like Eden."

"How well are the supporters fortified?" Chris asked.

"There is one road in and out. The settlement ebbs and flows about two hundred strong, all supporters," Anya declared. "What kind of team do we need to put together?"

Chris chewed his lip and responded, "A team against a group like that would be a blood bath. If Lanikov or McBride are still alive, they would need to be shuffled out or eliminated in the chaos. A team would increase the likelihood of chaos. I'll have to go in alone."

"Jonas said you had become a lone wolf."

"It's not about preference, it's tactical. Going in strong, there is no way to be quiet. No way to avoid eliciting a major response. Slipping in, identifying if either are still alive, and devising an extraction is the only way," Chris said. Pausing, he frowned, "I'm going to need a few crates of guns. The more powerful the better, ideally with novel calibers."

Anya cocked her in curiosity.

"A fortified outpost in the middle of the desert surrounded by harsh terrain, a single road in poses a bit of a problem. I can get in myself… HALO drop, ruck it, whatever, but I'll need a vehicle inside to get your people out, especially if they are injured," Chris said.

"You're going in as a gun runner, sent by me, that's rather on the nose," Anya grinned. "The rare caliber gives you leverage."

"If I go in with everything they need, they can just kill me and take everything they want. If I go in with a sexy new weapon with ammunition they can't supply themselves, they'll either still kill me or welcome me in," Chris admitted.

"It's a bit suicidal, don't you think?" Anya asked, her eyebrows raised.

Chris shrugged, "Fifty-fifty. What were your odds with McBride?"

Anya looked away and then nodded. "I'll have an armored vehicle packed with assault rifles ready to go by first light. AK 79s with GP 40 grenade launchers. They use an experimental 6x9 millimeter caliber rounds, splitting the NATO standards. Nicknamed *Lyutik Zolotistyy*… 'Goldilocks'."

"Leave a few loaded mags and shells in the passenger seat. My new friends will likely want a demonstration," Chris said.

"I wish you luck, former Gunnery Sergeant Chris Masters," Anya said. With an alluring smile, she added, "I hope to see you again."

Chris took a step to leave, he noted the juxtaposition of the powerful woman's character. She was clearly intelligent, well-spoken, and a bit conniving. Her crisp professional stoicism was marbled with veins of wanton sensuality and provocateur. Laced behind those veils was a depth of kindness and human compassion that she appeared to try and hide as her most shameful traits. Chris thought, perhaps in her line of work, they were.

"It is my hope you'll see all three of us again," Chris said and exited the room feeling her eyes follow him until the office door closed behind him.

Twenty One

Chris woke to find an armored Mercedes G-series SUV parked outside the room Anya arranged for him. A quick inspection showed his request had been met. Four cases of experimental AKs and two with grenade launcher capabilities. In the passenger seat, a half dozen loaded six-by-nine magazines and a metal case containing three explosive shells.

A large man approached, studied Chris for a moment, and then silently handed him the keys to the SUV. Turning without a word, the man retreated towards Anya's casino and tavern.

Tossing his own gear into the Mercedes, Chris fired up the powerful vehicle and pulled away, leaving the streets of Sinjab behind. Turning on his earpiece, he called, "Angel…are you there?"

In moments, a crisp voice greeted him, "Always. Good to hear your voice, Gunny. What is your sitrep?"

"I am en route to infiltrate a trader settlement called 'The End', just south of Baaj, I'm about forty clicks out," Chris called.

"Copy that. Our intel suggests that marketplace is heavily supported by insurgents," Angel said.

"So I've been told," Chris said. "Mission is to identify two missing assets, discern their condition, and extract them if possible."

"Do you need additional support?"

"Negative. Not for infil. I don't suppose you provide air support for extraction?" Chris asked.

To his surprise, Angel's response was prompt and unwavering, "What kind?"

"There are a series of checkpoints on the only access road in and out of 'The End'. I have a hunch, they may be a problem for exfil," Chris stated.

"Understood. We could have a gunship to your location with a three-hour lead time, crew transport with six," Angel replied.

Chris was stunned at the response. "Copy that, Angel. When I make my plans for exfil, I'll be sure to give you a call."

"I'll be with you all the way," Angel said. "You are correct. I am seeing three checkpoints on your route. The connector road to forty-seven, an arterial road to Wardiya, and entering Baaj all have checkpoints with at least half a dozen fighting age males posted at each."

"I guess I'll have to be especially charming today," Chris muttered. "Know any good jokes in Arabic?"

"Anya should have you cleared for the roadblocks on fort-seven and the road to Wardiya. The one heading into Baaj you'll need to use your best smile," Angel said.

"I'll see what I can do," Chris said as he turned the SUV south.

He hated dead-end roads with limited arteries. They were one giant death funnel. In combat areas they were just too easy to set up an ambush, pen someone in or sit in a lawn chair and wait for a vehicle to go by and set off an improvised explosive device.

Pre-empted checkpoints or not, Chris knew things on the ground changed quickly. His biggest concern was exfil, if he was able to find Matthias Lanikov and Cait McBride alive. Once an alarm was raised, he wouldn't make it a mile on that road without all hell unleashing on the single path in and out of The End.

Angel was right, Chris sailed through the first two checkpoints. As he made his way toward Baaj, it was apparent he would face his first real obstacle. A dozen armed men milled about as three assault rifles pointed at the driver's side window of the Mercedes SUV.

A quick swivel of his head, it was clear Chris did not fit in with the others at the checkpoint. The only Anglo, he was immediately identified as a threat as three assault rifles turned into twelve. With his hands up, he got out of the SUV as a pair of men spun him against the vehicle, a gun muzzle pressed against the base of his skull.

"Easy boys, easy. I'm a trader. Not a troublemaker," Chris called, hoping someone in the group spoke English. "Guns…I sell guns!"

He was spun to face the checkpoint guards. "You look American. That spells trouble to me," one man spat as he strode up to Chris.

"American? I am the nationality of whatever country the check clears in, my friend," Chris smiled. "Today, I am Russian. I am bringing the latest tech. I am bringing you an advantage over…well, whoever it is you are fighting at this moment."

The man Chris was speaking to didn't look impressed. "New tech, huh? We don't need tech, we need firepower."

“That is the type of tech I am talking about. Increased caliber, explosive compatible, stuff even the Americans don’t have,” Chris nodded.

“Let’s see this ‘stuff’,” the man said, nodding to one of the men to open the back of the Mercedes.

Seeing the cases of Russian armaments, the man shrugged, “AKs, great. We can use them.”

“Not just AKs, the *latest* AKs. Six-nine cal. Check it out. Better knock than the NATO five-five-six, more compatible than the seven-six-two. Your enemies literally won’t know what hit them,” Chris said. Nudging towards a crate to the right with his shoulders as two guards continued to hold him, “Got more goodies in there.”

The guard who spoke English consented for the crate to be opened.

“Experimental explosive rounds. Standalone with a GP launcher or connectible to the barrel of the AK. The ultimate in fully engaged combat,” Chris marketed.

The English-speaking guard rubbed his chin, a wicked grin spreading across his face, “So we take all of them and shoot you in the head. Another American insect who can’t come back to bite us.”

Chris chewed his lip and nodded, "You could, I can even see why you might want to, but…" Chris wrinkled his brow, "I haven't survived as an entrepreneur in the Iraqi countryside by being stupid. You can have all the guns, but if you want the ammunition to make them work… you're going to need me alive."

The man thought about Chris' words for a moment. After a rattle of Arabic to his compatriots, the man looked at Chris, "Alright. You can go through. We'll be watching you."

"Wouldn't expect anything less," Chris said. "When I come back through, I'll give you your own setup… on the house!"

Climbing back into the SUV, Chris didn't hesitate to fire up the engine and start forward towards the gate as it was reluctantly raised for him to pass.

"Guns that are useless without your safe passage, smart," Angel called into Chris' ear.

"That got me through stage one. We'll see what I can get away with the rest of this trip. I'll have eyes on me constantly," Chris muttered.

Passing through Baaj, which had clearly seen its challenges in the chaos of war, was nothing like entering The End. Nestled, literally at the end of the roadway, the settlement reminded Chris of a Hollywood set. Ramshackle buildings were laid out in a rough circle with a marketplace in the center. Trucks, vans, and even wagons that been pulled in by donkeys were laden with guns, ammunition, clothing, drugs, food, and more.

The lawlessness of the town almost made Chris chuckle. In some respects, it would make his job easier amidst the pandemonium. On the other hand, anyone in the town at any time could elect to kill him. Parking the Mercedes near the entrance of The End, he observed. Men sat at tables playing games under the shelter of a makeshift tavern. Several firepits were roasting goats over a spit. A fight broke out over an argument near one of the vendors which ended abruptly as the merchant shot the man.

Chris sighed. He was in for one helluva mission.

"Angel, I am at the location," Chris called into his comm.

"Copy that, Gunny. Godspeed, I'll be on standby," Angel replied.

The moment Chris climbed out of the armored SUV, he garnered the attention of the settlement. The large American stood out among the primarily Arabic population. Merchants eyed him as they continued to prepare their wares. The Ur and Dama games paused as players and spectators watched the newcomer exit the Mercedes. With no additional occupants joining Chris and an armed contingent making their way to greet him, the settlement returned to their chores and tournaments while keeping a wary eye.

Four men with AK47s approached Chris as two more moved in from his flank. A man with a toothy grin offered an insincere welcome. "Halla Wallah! Come, we will guide you through what you Anglos call 'The End'," the man gestured with his hands for Chris to follow. The half dozen assault weapons trained in his direction left him feeling as though he didn't have a choice in the matter.

While he had hoped to get his bearings and scope out the settlement quietly and on his own, being led directly to what he assumed to be the insurgency cadre in the town helped him bypass scrutiny and if Lanikov and McBride were still alive and held captive, their most likely locations.

Entering a simple building, Chris noted a pair of guards at each entrance. Passing rooms buzzing with activity, most holding caches of weapons and ammunition being sorted and bundled, the group could outfit a small army. Each man he passed paused and glared at him. Returning to their work only after the armed contingent paraded him past.

One interior room had a guard stationed at a closed door. At the end of the hallway, a final door led to a man behind a desk, a wide display of military weapons from around the world neatly arranged on the wall behind him. "Halla Wallah, welcome to 'The End'. We don't get many…," the man eyed Chris for a moment before nodding to himself, "Americans here. At least not with the ability to stand on their own two feet."

Chris frowned at the frank introduction, "A pleasure…?"

Laughing, the man concluded, "You're not military, at least not any longer. Not mercenary, at least not formally backed. In either case, you wouldn't have come alone. Perhaps a disgruntled version of either of those possibilities, with skills to profit from my country's despair."

"My family died and my government did nothing. I was stuck here, so I figured I would make myself useful and take care of myself," Chris replied, choking at his own partial truth.

"I see. Well, The End welcomes entrepreneurs," the man said. "There are few rules to abide by, though following them is only negotiable if you are willing to accept a bullet…or bullets as a consequence."

After a pause for effect, the man continued, "The war is outside of this town. Your business or pleasure, is your concern. Falling into debt has dire consequences, so spend wisely. All trades are final, rescinding them is fatal, so trade wisely."

"You and your welcoming committee are in charge, I take it?" Chris asked.

The man waved Chris' notion off, "Oh, there is no one in charge in The End. We welcome you as your particular wares are of interest. Clever, the way you arrived with part one of a two part shipment. Likely the reason you survived the checkpoint."

"Can't be too careful," Chris shrugged with a grin.

"No, I suppose not," the man agreed. "Perhaps you can arrange a demonstration of your offerings. If we like what we see, you may not only survive, but stand to profit nicely."

"Of course, my products speak for themselves," Chris acknowledged.

"Let's hope they don't disappoint, for your sake," the man glared.

"Look, it's been a long drive, Mister....," Chris started.

"Al Wadi," the man behind the desk stated.

"...Mr. Al Wadi. How about I get a bite to eat, maybe quench my thirst and we'll find a secure location for a demonstration?"

"Very well. My men will escort you out. Satisfy your cravings. When you are ready, let one of my men at the door know. Until then, stay out of trouble. The End is very unforgiving," Al Wadi warned.

"Yeah, I've noticed," Chris nodded. Turning to the armed men that brought him in, "Boys..."

The men glanced at Al Wadi and then led Chris back the way that he came. The closed door in the hallway was still manned by an armed man. With rooms overflowing with weapons and ammunition without guards, Chris couldn't help but to wonder what was special about that one room.

With what might actually be a stay of execution, Chris used the opportunity to explore the small town of The End. On the one hand, there were not a lot of places to hold prisoners, on the other hand, there was very little way of maneuvering through the town without being seen.

Chris determined that if he couldn't maintain quiet discretion, and in fact that would only foster more suspicion, he would instead play the role of the gregarious, overconfident American. Acting as though he had nothing to hide would have to be his best cover.

The settlement, with its simple circle of buildings wrapped around a central marketplace, Chris decided to use the central marketplace to his advantage to study the buildings along the perimeter, who came and left when. See if there was a pattern. He knew at some point, he would need to see what was behind the mysterious door guarded by Al Wadi's men.

Following the scents of the market, *Kebabs*, *Gauss,* and *Quzi*, most traditionally made with lamb or goat seemed to be the menu of the day. A large rack of meat cooked the day before was being smoked behind the vendor's booth. Chris assumed they were making jerky for preservation.

Pulling up a seat offering the widest view of The End, with Al Wadi's building in clear sight, Chris ordered *gauss*, a sandwich wrap similar to a Gyro. To complete the appearance of his presence as a businessman and not an operative, he ordered a Farida Lager. The merchant slid the bottle in front of Chris. Playing the liquid in the light, he found the Baghdad beer pale with scarcely any foam in the head.

Taking a sip, Chris found it neither offensive nor particularly pleasing. As the heat of day poured over him, he could see how the light lager would be welcomed.

Drinking the beer while he waited for his wrap, it provided him the advantage of leaning back and from behind his sunglasses, scour the town, cataloging the activity. Al Wadi's location received by far the most traffic. Some travelers leaving with large cases after making a visit.

One building caught Chris's attention. A large, empty cage stood in front of a low-slung shelter. Next to the shelter was a workout area where several men lifted weights, pummeled a heavy bag, or strained under a pull-up bar.

Next to the workout area was a goat pen, a handful of horses milling about an adjacent pen. A shop with clothes ranging from traditional Iraqi garb, military surplus, and some western wear sprinkled throughout. Another merchant sorted through bins of used parts, returning to a vehicle with a raised hood.

Beyond the town, foot and horse trails snaked beyond the end of the road into the desert and hills of western Iraq.

Chris took another sip of the lager as his sandwich was delivered to him. From behind his sunglasses, he could see that the entire time he sat at the bar, there were never less than three pairs of eyes trained on him at any time.

A glint of light from atop Al Wadi's building caught Chris' attention. As he took a bite of his *gauss*, he studied the area he saw the flash. Without reacting, he recognized the telltale signs of a sniper roost. While presumably a fixture of Al Wadi's regular security, he had little doubt that the scope was keeping the infidel American in sight.

Chris was comfortable that his weapons proposition piqued Al Wadi's interest or he would already be dead. The thought was just reassuring enough to allow him to remain relaxed despite the sniper scope that would be trained on him throughout his visit to The End. It also meant that any investigation would need to take place after sundown. He hadn't intended to stay that long, but he realized that would indeed be the case. He would need to earn his vendor status or he would not survive until nightfall.

Using the hottest part of the day to his advantage, Chris hoped the rogues of The End might be more sluggish in the event he needed to at least attempt a hasty escape. Signaling to the guards at Al Wadi's shop that he was set for his demonstration, he walked to the Mercedes Anya provided for him and slung the experimental Russian assault rifle and attachable grenade launcher over his shoulder.

Al Wadi and an armed entourage flowed out of the building and into the heat of the day. Led to a clearing overlooking a shallow valley backdropped by a craggy hill, Chris was shown a variety of targets, including a military truck that had rolled down into the ravine.

Crossing his arms, Al Wadi nodded to Chris, "Show me why your new weapons are superior and why you might have some value to us."

Chris nodded. Slamming a magazine into the modified AK, he sighted a target fifty yards away and popped off several shots in succession. Glancing at one of the gun runner's men and then back to Al Wadi, Chris nudged his head, "May I?"

The gunman looked confused, even more so when Al Wadi relented, instructing his man to give up his standard AK to Chris.

Ensuring a round was chambered, Chris fired a similar number of shots into the same target. Raising his eyebrows, he uttered optimistically, "Eh?"

Al Wadi squinted, scarcely noticing a difference in the shots fifty yards away.

Recognizing the insurgent's lack of impression, Chris raised the experimental AK once more and squeezed off three shots into a 25-yard target. Switching to the traditional AK, taking his time with each shot, he fired three more times.

Tossing the AK back to the gunman, Chris leaned back and grinned. "Well, what do you think now?"

Al Wadi stepped towards the target, smoothing his fingers against the holes Chris had made. One had a chip out of the edge, slightly expanding the hole, the others were clean. His mouth agape, he spun back towards Chris, "You shot clean through with the standard rounds."

"Well, yeah, I kinda nicked that one. The diameter of the ammo is... impactful. As you can see, the NATO five-five-six round is small enough to go through the gap made by the six-nine," Chris pointed at the target.

"Your aim is as impressive as the weapon," Al Wadi approved.

Chris simply nodded, "I've dabbled in past employment. Now if you really want to start the party, snap this on and..."

The former Raider team leader connected the attachment and loaded a round. Pulling the secondary trigger, a pleasing *foomp* echoed momentarily throughout the ravine before the military truck below burst into an explosive blast, rock and bits of shrapnel raining around the men.

"Double break grenade, when a sensor detects the descent following the peak of the arch, it splinters into two shells landing within six yards of the other increasing the radius and making it well, a whole lot more terrifying," Chris grinned.

Al Wadi returned a broad smile, "Yes, Mr..."

"Sheppard. Chris Sheppard."

Putting a hand on Chris' shoulder, the gun supplier conceded, "I think we can make a deal. How many of these can you supply?"

"I have several cases with me. I can double that on a subsequent visit."

"When can you get the ammunition for your current stock?" Al Wadi pressed.

"I have a stash a day and a half drive away," Chris replied.

Nodding, Al Wadi urged. "You be my guest tonight. We'll talk terms."

Chris didn't flinch as the man's hands clapped him on the shoulder. He just grinned, hoping he wouldn't stay for the entire night.

Twenty Two

Chris stretched, pleasantly surprised by how comfortable the armored Mercedes was to sleep in. Finding a shady spot and occasionally running the air conditioner, he grabbed a couple of hours of rest not knowing how long his night could turn out. He wanted to be primed.

As the sun began to slip from the sky, the activity within the modest confines of The End markedly increased. More unsavory types arrived, most gathered around the bar while many browsed the merchants who took advantage of sales during the cooler temperature hours.

Towards the end of town, just past the big cage, a crowd formed amoebically from the bar. A barker stood on a step ladder, calling for bids. Curious, Chris wandered to the edge of the spectators, with an eye on the rest of town to see if the attention provided him an opening.

Unfortunately, security at Al Wadi's did not change and the merchants held enough attention to keep numerous eyes in that portion of the settlement. Relenting, Chris observed as the men who took center stage began trading shots at the targets downrange. Unloading their magazines, one was declared the winner by two shots. The crowd roared at the results as money changed hands.

The barker set up the next pairing as a wide range of weapons took their spot in various contests. As the evening wore, Al Wadi even strolled up, standing beside Chris, he stood silently until the barker called for the next event.

Al Wadi strode forward, handing a large stack of bills in front of the barker. With an outstretched finger, he targeted Chris and a man who stepped in behind Al Wadi with a Dragunov sniper rifle. It was clearly custom, a gun the shooter was well familiar with.

Chris was handed an Iraqi Tabuk sniper rifle that had clearly seen decades of use and abuse. Knowing he was not going to have much say in the issue, he did his best to quickly dial the weapon to his personal preferences. Having no idea how it was going to shoot and track, he reluctantly followed the confident Al Wadi-selected shooter.

On the far ridge was a series of targets. Without a word, Al Wadi's man took out the first target. Chris stepped forward, judged the wind, distance and topography, and in a single breath, squeezed the trigger. Never taking his eyes away from downrange, he watched as a dust cloud rose low and to the left.

With a sigh, Chris ignored the loud cheers of the crowd and reset his sights. Following the sniper's shot and shattered target, Chris fired, taking out his own. Moving along the ridge, the two men successively took out their pairs of targets until the final pair remained. Knowing there was no redemption in store for him, Chris had an idea.

As Al Wadi's shooter lined up his shot, Chris quickly flicked up his rifle. Before his opponent could fire, Chris pulled his trigger hitting his opposing target's narrow post, toppling it before the target could be hit. With a second round held in his fingers, Chris quickly chambered it and took out his own target.

The crowd roared in mixed excitement, some cheering Chris' antics, others denouncing the tactic. Al Wadi chewed his lip before smiling and nodding. "Very well. You have each taken out the same number of targets. We must get to resolution," with a long pause, Al Wadi pointed above the ridge in the fading evening light. "The first shooter to drop a buzzard wins."

Chris and his opponent studied the birds circling over some unseen carcass in the distance. Similar in size to the targets but in constant motion, they would present a considerable challenge. Each man tried to locate and time a shot, tracking the birds in their flight, trying to shoot into their pattern. Chris paused his targeting and instead held his sight steady. He waited, staring at the sky through the sight until the outside edge was tinged with a dark shape. Squeezing the trigger, he watched through the sight as the bird dropped.

Once again, the crowd erupted into a roar, this time louder than before. Al Wadi shot his man a disapproving look and dismissed him, Chris presumed back to his post atop the depot building. As the man walked through the crowd, he glowered at Chris. Without the stunt, he would have clearly been the victor.

Al Wadi, obviously disappointed and a pocketful of Iraqi *dinars*, faced Chris. "Clever... and good shooting, if a bit unfair."

Chris shrugged, "Almost as unfair as handing someone a badly sighted sniper rifle and expecting him to compete against a sniper with a personally dialed Dragunov."

"It was clearly a test of a shooter and not of weapons," Al Wadi admitted.

"The good news is you will easily earn back your *dinars* once you sell the weapons following our deal," Chris said.

"Ah yes, our deal. What are your suggested terms?"

"When I leave here tomorrow, I will give you the weapons. Upon my return with the ammunition, I get market price for traditional AKs. That will allow you considerable room for mark up," Chris suggested.

Al Wadi studied Chris for a moment. "A bit of trust."

"I need to earn it," Chris said robustly.

"Very well. We have a deal," Al Wadi said. "Enjoy the remainder of your evening. The End gets… very entertaining as night takes hold."

Chris watched as the leader of the insurgent armory walked away from the crowd. As Al Wadi disappeared into his building, Chris took the opportunity to slip away and perform some sleuthing. A scan of the market revealed that the security detail for the gun depot remained strong while many merchants packed up for the day. Food and drink vendors remained vigilant, hoping the sporting crowd would require their services into the evening.

The battle with Al Wadi's sniper must have been the premier contest as the shooting events disbanded. The spectators flocked to the bar and the food vendors.

A new bout of activity caught Chris' eye. Near the large cage, the men who had been working out earlier in the day began to spill out of the nearby building and assembled next to the cage. They danced and stretched, helping Chris understand what the next evening activity would entail. The same barker that proctored the shooting contests strode to a small platform on the outside of the cage. Standing up, he raised a megaphone and called to the crowd, announcing a pair of contestants.

The crowd whooped and craned their necks as they stood with a beer in hand or gnawed on a kebab. Two men were corralled into the ring. From Chris' viewpoint, they seemed to be jostled and cajoled as opposed to entering on their free will.

The barker encouraged bets to be placed as the men moved about the cage. With a fist full of bills, the barker signaled for the contest to begin. Circling one another, the pair jockeyed for position before launching into a fury of punches and kicks.

With so much attention on the fight, Chris had hoped he would see some sign of the Anya's operative Cait. If she didn't make her presence known by sundown, she was most likely captured or dead. Chris had no way of knowing if either Cait McBride or Matthias Lanikov were locked in the back room of the armory and the risk was very high to ascertain for sure.

Chris grabbed a drink from the bar and wandered at the edge of the spectators, slowly distancing himself as he used shadows to his advantage. Ducking in and out of the buildings, avoiding the watchful eye of the repositioned sniper and guards of Al Wadi's building, Chris tried to locate a clue that his mission objectives were still viable.

Each crude building was empty of people, just crates of wares, basic bedding, and personal items, none of which belonged to Lanikov or McBride. He had worked his way adjacent to the armory. Eager to find some way in, he wrapped himself in the darkened space between the windowless buildings.

Peering around the rear of the armory, Chris froze as a voice shouted at him in Arabic. Chris didn't understand the words, but he understood the tone. If he started a fight at that moment, there was no chance that he would be able to locate either of his objectives, the mission would be blown.

Taking a quick swig of the liquid in his glass, he splashed a healthy portion of the rest on his chest, the scent of alcohol and the licorice flavor of anise mixed with fermented grapeseed hovered in the air. Drinking the remaining splash of Arak, he leaned against the wall and undid his fly.

The man approaching spat more Arabic, this time less threatening and more annoyed. The guard waited as Chris forced a stream of urine. He had scarcely any to offer with so much sweat leaving his body throughout the day. Humming a tune, he zipped up, trying to appear oblivious to the gun-toting man impatiently waiting for him. When he was done, a hand clamped on his shoulder, an AK rammed into his ribs, and a stream of Arabic as he was manhandled out of the alley.

Standing dead center in the alley, his assault rifle pointed towards Chris, the guard sent his message, cutting through the language barrier. Mumbling and nodding, Chris sauntered away, ensuring his steps appeared clumsy and imprecise.

While he looked ahead, his mind was on the building behind him. He had to see inside that room. Either Lanikov and McBride were in there or they were food for the vultures somewhere outside of the settlement.

Slipping back into the crowd, Chris wiped the spilled Arak off his shirt. The barker announced another match. By the reaction of the crowd, the fight they were most interested in was about to take place. In the center of the cage, a man bristled at the barker's announcement as he eyed the cage entrance warily.

A woman dressed in a risqué, certainly for Iraq, leather gladiator outfit was marched out of the building and into the ring. Her hands shackled together, she spun as the door slammed shut. Glaring at her handlers, she shoved her arms through a slot in the cage and one of the men who led her out unlocked her bindings with a key.

The moment the woman was freed, the crowd let out their loudest roar of the night. Spinning, she faced her opponent. Her shoulder length crimson hair whipped in an arch as she lunged forward. The man she faced loomed over a foot taller and more than twice her weight. Rushing headlong, he tried to use his size to overwhelm her. Sliding, she slipped completely underneath the man, instantly popping up on the other side readying for his next attack.

Head down, the man rammed forward for another bull rush, keeping his body lower this time. Leaping into the air, the woman reached up. Grabbing the roof of the cage, she lifted her legs around her attacker. Spinning quickly, she faced the man wrapping her legs around his neck.

Maintaining her grip on the bars of the cage with her hands, she squeezed with her legs, pressing into the man's windpipe. The staggering man's weight too much for her to wield, she let go with her hands, while maintaining pressure with her legs around his throat. Riding the man as he wobbled around the ring, his face turning from red to purple, his hands flailing at her while she slapped his arms away.

By the time the purple had turned definitively blue, the man dropped to his knees and started to fall backward. Leaping away to avoid being pinned under the man's weight, the woman pounced, slamming her heel into his throat before he could regain any of the oxygen he so badly needed.

As the man succumbed to limp unconsciousness, the woman reluctantly removed her heel from his throat. Other than supreme confidence, the woman refused to emit any emotion with her easy win. The crowd, however, erupted into an uproar.

The barker called out the victory and beamed at the wad of bills he retained in his pocket.

The bout over, the woman waited impatiently at the door. A guard nodded towards the hole in the cage. Embittered, she thrust her hands through as shackles were again wrapped around her wrists.

As the cage door opened, the woman shouldered into the first guard, nudging him towards the second. Slipping past, she darted through the crowd. As more guards warily descended, she made an abrupt turn towards the bar. A path cleared as she made a beeline, the man closest to her gaze vacated his seat and she slid onto the stool.

The bartender looked at the woman and then at the guards. Receiving a nod from the guards who encircled her, the bartender relented to her glare and poured a glass of Arak. With her shackled hands, she lifted the cup with both hands and slammed it to her lips. Downing the liquid in a single gulp, she slammed the glass down on the bar and stared at the bartender.

With only a nervous moment of hesitation, he filled the glass as a wicked grin swept across the woman's face. This time, she sipped the Arak, still using both hands to bring the glass to her lips.

Watching the antics in relative silence, the crowd again erupted into a victorious cheer as the brazen woman got her way. Chris' hunch deepened as the woman swallowed her third glass of Arak. The guards having enough, they approached, eager to pull her back into whatever hole they kept her in between fights.

Grasping her arm, a guard tried to yank her off the stool. Spinning, she spit a mouthful of Arak in the guard's face and kicked him away. Leaping up on the bar, she danced away from a flurry of grasping arms. The guards clamored to surround her. Dropping onto her back, she used her feet to flip the bottle of liquor the bartender had been pouring in the air. Catching it as she hopped to her feet, she took a hearty pull of the liquid. Spinning, she spat in a circle, fueling a blast of flames from lit tiki torches set in front of the bartender's station, buying her some space as men ducked out of the way.

Running along the bar, she leapt off and over the crowd. Running through the market square, she slid into the legs of an oncoming guard, knocking him to the ground. She reached for his gun, but he was quick to grab her leg and pull her back. Rolling towards him, the change in momentum caught the guard out of synch. Wrapping her shackles around him, she rolled over his shoulders and pulled back, choking him.

Another guard approached only to be met with a kick to the sternum. Using the guard held in her grasp, she deflected another oncoming attack, the attempted punch landing on the fellow guard instead.

Guards poured from all over The End, collapsing on her position. The fight moved in and out of the shadows. Chris watched as the sniper, who had apparently been cleared to end the episode, tried to get a bead on the girl.

Jostling towards a spotlight, Chris reacted. Slipping through the crowd, he leapt in the air, grasping a guard by the neck and spinning him brutally to the ground. In a mad dash, he launched himself towards the woman and her captive, landing them to the ground just as a bullet from the Dragunov pierced the ground where they had been standing.

Chris drove his knee into the back of the guard the woman was holding at bay, crumpling him to the ground. With an arm around the woman, he spun her further into the shadows as he repelled another attacker with a blow to the sternum.

The guards finished with the subordinate disruption began firing their AKs in their direction. Pulling her below a wall as bullets and shrapnel whizzed by, they landed in a heap.

"Cait, I presume?" Chris asked, his face inches from hers.

"Maybe. Who the hell 'er you?" the woman spat, her Irish accent undeniable.

"I was sent to help you…"

"Help? I had them right where I wanted them," Cait snapped as she wiped blood from her lip. "They are moving Lanikov tonight. This was my only chance to get him."

"Not sure about your handle on the situation. You had to know bullets were going to start flying," Chris said as gunfire continued to chip away at their modest protection.

"I had to try something. I thought, why not get them in a lather and use the chaos to get Lanikov?"

"Alright, they are in a lather. Now what?" Chris asked.

"I need a gun," Cait said.

"You need a gun… you needed a better plan," Chris retorted.

"Well, we're here now. Are you going to help a lady out, Yank?" Cait growled.

With a sigh, Chris produced a sidearm from his waistband and handed it to her. Unholstering the one from his drop leg, he relented to the situation.

"We have half a dozen collapsing from the bar, another half dozen from the armory, where I presume Lanikov is?"

"Yes," Cait said, as she steadied her gun with her shackled hands and fired into the semicircle of guards descending on their position, knocking one to the ground.

"And my dear friend, the sniper," Chris muttered.

"I heard about that. Nice job, he's kind of a grade A d-bag but a helluva shot," Cait said, trying to line another guard up in her sights. The spectators that had been cheering her, produced arms and were joining the guards, descending towards them as well.

"This is not good. Not a good plan, Cait," Chris scolded.

"Aside from kicking some loser's arse, I've been stuck in a hole for the past week," Cait defended. "It's all I've been able to put together."

Chris scowled, "Somehow I imagine some bullheaded plan got you captured and put in that hole in the first place."

"Well, I'm not all talk like you. We need to get a move on," Cait urged.

"Buy me two minutes. Here's an extra mag," Chris said.

The moment Cait opened fire, Chris dove into the shadows. Racing between bullets, he slid to the back of the Mercedes. Opening the hatch, he grabbed a grenade launcher and stuffed as many shells into his pockets as he could. Seeing Cait was in trouble, he slid to a knee, chambered a shell, and sent one between the crowd and the girl.

The double shot exploded in a line, knocking the guards closest to Cait to the ground while sending the rest running for cover. "Come on!" he called, sprinting towards the armory.

As they approached, powerful lights illuminated the entire area in front of the weapons depot. Chris could feel the sniper's muzzle bearing down on him. Knocking Cait to the ground, he rolled the opposite way. Landing on his back, he steadied his sidearm in front of him. Snapping off several shots, he jumped to his feet, racing towards the building, taking himself out of the sight of the sniper and into the waiting gun barrels of the door guards.

Two shots screamed from behind him and the guards dropped. Cait sprinted behind him. "Thanks," he panted.

"No problem, Yank."

"We have to get into Lanikov," Chris said as he pressed his back into the relative safety of the depot's outer wall.

"We'll never get through the front door. I was scoping for another entrance when I got caught… and then I blew up a building as a distraction. It didn't work. Seemed like it only pissed them off more," Cait shared.

Chris chuckled, "So, that was your handiwork over there, I was curious."

"They were going to kill me on the spot, but the guy in charge of the entertainment thought I might be valuable as part of his sideshow," Cait said. "Point is, the only soft spot is the roof. They put this settlement together quickly, mostly with spare materials. The roofs of most of these buildings are wood and patchwork sheets of tin."

"If we can't get in through the door, we come in through the ceiling," Chris nodded. "I like it."

Eying the roof of Al Wadi's depot, he declared, "I'm going to need a distraction."

"Oh, I can do distractions," Cait grinned.

"Here," Chris handed Cait the grenade launcher and the shells he had crammed into his pockets.

From the other side of the wall, they could hear the footfalls of the guards closing in on their position.

"Let her rip," Chris called as he found a way up to the roof. Scrambling to a pile of wood scrap, he grabbed a pair of two-by-fours. Using a board with nails sticking through either end, Chris slammed his boot to drive the nails from one board into the other, adhering them together. He didn't take time to admire the wobbly, elongated apparatus he created. It was crude but was going to have to do.

In the marketplace, Cait's barrage started, blasts scattering the guards into multiple directions. The spotlights swung wildly, trying to locate her position.

Sprinting towards the building, Chris rammed the bottom board into the ground. Leaning the other end against the wall, he scrambled hand over hand up the board. Reaching as high as he could, he was just able to reach the top of the roof with his fingers. Curling them to grip tighter, he wriggled until his entire hands and then forearms were on top of the roof.

Peering over the edge, he saw the sniper spin from his position overlooking the square. A grin crossing his face, he tossed the rifle down and drew his sidearm as fast as he could. Chris launched himself completely onto the roof and rolled away from the bullets landing where he had just been.

Drawing his own gun, he took several wild shots to give the sniper pause. Landing on his feet, both men squared off, guns at their sides. As the sniper's shoulder twitched, Chris snapped his gun up, firing as he moved, pelting the sniper with poorly aimed shots, it was enough to throw the sniper off. Bullets pierced Chris' side and ripped at his bicep, but failed to land a serious shot.

Each man bleeding, yet undeterred, readied for another volley. An explosion, closer than the others, lit up the marketplace, rocking the building. Both men ducked from the blast and shrapnel, diving to the roof's surface. Losing grip on his gun, the sniper drew a long, curved blade from a sheath at his hip.

"Well, I don't have one of those, but I see where this is going," Chris muttered.

The sniper lunged forward, thrusting the blade in a smooth arch towards Chris' throat. Scrambling, Chris did not have enough time to swap mags. Rolling out of the way, he dove towards the Dragunov rifle the sniper tossed aside. Chris grabbed it with both hands, parrying just in time to dodge a blow from the sword, grateful for the steel barrel stopping the blade.

Rising to his feet, he deflected another arching swing. As the blade passed, Chris spun the rifle so that he was holding the muzzle. Before the sniper could counter, Chris twisted his hips into a home run swing, connecting with the sniper's chin, staggering him backward.

The sniper tried to steady himself, Chris spun the weapon so his finger could find the trigger. Pulling, he knew he had a fifty percent chance that a round was chambered as the sniper charged with the sword high for another attack. The pin hit the explosive charge, sending a bullet downrange, hitting the sniper square in the chest, knocking him clear off his feet and onto his back. The sword clattered to the rooftop, inches from teetering over the edge.

Chris tossed the rifle down and dove, grasping the sword blade with his hand. "I can use this!" he exclaimed. "Thanks!"

Aware of the gunfire exchanging in the marketplace square, he knew Cait had to be running out of ammunition and time. Dropping to his knees over what he estimated to be the room where Lanikov was assumed to be held, Chris began chopping at the wood sheet, trying to cut between the support beams.

As soon as he created a crisscross cut in the wood, he leapt to his feet and began pummeling the wood with the heel of his boot. The roof splintered, a hole beginning to take shape. Leaping in the air and driving into the spot with his full force, Chris broke through the roof and fell into the room below.

Landing in a squat position, he swapped his mag and scanned the room. In the far outside corner, a man huddled with his head protected. "Lanikov?" Chris called in a hoarse whisper.

The man lifted his head, bewildered.

"I was sent by Anya. I'm getting you out of here," Chris assured.

As he helped the man up and leaned against the doorway, he listened for guards checking on their prisoner.

"Let's go," Chris urged. Maneuvering the man under the hole in the roof he created, they both stared at the hole. "I'll lift you up and you can crawl..."

The man waved him off, "I'm...I'm too weak."

Chris chewed his lip for a moment. "Can you stand here?"

The man nodded weakly.

"Good," Chris exclaimed and launched himself at the man, pushing his feet off of Lankikov's hip and then his shoulder. He reached the roof and pulled himself through. Flipping himself around, he reached down as far as he could, spreading the sole of his boots against the roof to create added friction.

The man picked himself after toppling from the force of Chris' escape.

"Come on, all you have to do is jump with your hands high in the air, I'll do the rest!" Chris urged.

Complying the man took a few steps and leapt as high as he could, though not nearly as high as Chris had hoped. Swiping, Chris was just able to grab Lanikov's fingers. Gripping hard, Chris gave a yank, leading their palms to meet. With a hearty, steady pull, Chris dragged the man onto the roof. Helping him to his feet, he asked. "You good?"

The man offered an unsure nod in reply.

"Almost out of here, stay close, no matter what," Chris commanded. Into his earpiece, he called,
"Angel. I have Lanikov, McBride is laying down cover. We are heading for exfil."

"Strong copy, Gunny."

"It is a hot extraction. Getting out of here is going to be a challenge, there is no way with this kind of heat we'll make it through Baaj," Chris continued.

"Copy that. Stand by," Angel said, her voice calm and business-like. A moment later her voice rang again, "We'll clear a path at Baaj. You just need to make it there."

"Copy. Raider…err…out," Chris stammered. With a glance towards Lanikov, he urged, "Let's go."

Leading the beleaguered man to the edge of the roof, he found the board. "Soft grip, bend at the knees as you land."

Chris hopped over the edge, grabbing the boards halfway through his descent, and slid to the ground. His head swiveling, ready for an onslaught, he paused to catch Lanikov. Leading him to the corner of the building, he held him back with his arm as he peered out towards the continued battle between Cait and the rest of The End inhabitants.

Cait had the grenade launcher over her shoulder and presided over a half dozen assault rifles she had collected from guards that she had taken out. She would pop up randomly and unload a magazine towards the insurgents. Spraying in an arching pattern, it reminded Chris of a sprinkler. She would run through an AK in one direction to pick up another and spray back the other way.

In the chaos of gunfire, he didn't know how to get her attention. As she reached for the next AK, Chris fired near her, shattering the concrete inches away. Spinning, she frowned, assault rifle muzzle pointed in his direction.

Waving wildly hoping she wouldn't shoot him, Chris beckoned Cait to follow him and rally with Lanikov. Even from that distance, he could see her eyebrow dance as she located who was shooting from behind her. Relenting, she gave a quick nod and hunching over, jogged to him as he laid down cover fire.

The entire encampment was closing in on them. As Chris and Cait reached Lanikov, they didn't hesitate. With a fistful of Lanikov's shirt, without breaking stride, they ran towards the edge of town where Chris' Mercedes was waiting.

Chris and Cait fired wildly over their shoulders as they ran. Reaching the Mercedes, Chris pulled Lanikov into a slide, skidding them to the front of the armored vehicle.

Cait dropped to a knee, leveling the grenade launcher for one more concussive shot. Taking aim, ignoring the bullets impregnating the ground within inches of her, she pulled the trigger. The familiar *foomp* was a sweet sound. She didn't stop to enjoy the well-placed shot that clipped the corner of Al Wadi's building exploding in a blast of shrapnel that for a valuable moment, paused the guards.

Spinning, she sprinted the rest of the way to the SUV that Chris already had in gear and ready to go. Running into the open door, she was scarcely inside before Chris floored the accelerator, launching the armored SUV forward as a barrage of bullets sprayed the vehicle.

"Angel, we are on the move," Chris called into his earpiece.

"Copy that, Gunny, we are tracking you on satellite and drone camera," Angel replied, her voice as calm and reassuring as ever.

Chris hoped her confidence was warranted as they rocketed towards the checkpoint town. In the rearview mirror, he could see headlights trying to close in behind him. Despite the weight of the armor, the Mercedes' powerful engine kept them out of harm's way. Chris knew, however, that any obstacle would allow the angry fleet of vehicles chasing them to catch up.

As Baaj came in to view, a flash streaked from above followed by several other flashes lighting up the night sky. A series of blasts littered the roadway heading into Baaj. Metal and concrete scraps flew through the air as Chris trusted the armor to keep them safe. Driving through what stood only moments before as a roadblock, they cleared the town.

The headlights behind them struggled to maintain pace but persisted. Chris coaxed whatever he could from the SUV's engine. Knowing there were additional checkpoints ahead, Chris veered off the roadway, rolling through a ravine, leaping the Mercedes completely in the air off of all four wheels.

Landing with a jolt, Chris flipped on the massive array of powerful off-road lights and streaked the SUV across the desert. Avoiding the remaining checkpoints and traveling over rough terrain that he hoped the German vehicle could navigate better than the insurgent counterparts.

In his rearview mirror, he could see his pursuers attempt the same feat, landing much harder in catastrophic fashion.

"Gunny, I see you have left the roadway. You had three insurgent vehicles on your six. All three appear to be stopped," Angel broke into Chris' ear.

"So, about this 'Gunny' thing," Chris bristled. "I don't deserve the title. I left my team. I am no longer a Marine."

"Do you really think this is the time to discuss this?" Angel asked.

"I've got windshield time. We seemed to have slipped the insurgents for the moment," Chris replied.

Angel went silent for several moments before returning to his ear, "Jonas says to call you 'X'. You were the start of Patriot X. Your callsign is X."

"Copy that, Angel," Chris acknowledged. "Not what I would've chosen, but it will do."

"Nice to see you have your priorities straight, worryin' about your nickname and all," Cait quipped from the passenger seat. With a fight not imminent, she addressed her more serious wounds and helped Lanikov with his.

"Being a Marine is an honor. It's an honor I no longer deserve."

"You *are* a patriot, aren't you?" Cait pressed.

"Am…was…I don't know, anymore," he stared through the windshield carting a path to the paved highway that would take them back to Baghdad.

"Losing people you care about tends to muddy the waters a bit, don't it? On one hand, it fuels you, burns a passion right in your stomach. On the other, a sense of country tends to matter less when the ones you love's blood is emptied onto the floor in front of you," Cait said.

"Sounds like you have some experience."

"I do, as I sense do you," Cait nodded. Turning towards the backseat, she extended her arms, "Here, lean your shoulder towards me." Cait helped Lanikov bandage his arm that had either taken a bullet or shrapnel.

Eyeing Chris, she raised a concerned eyebrow, "You're nicked up a bit. Why don't you let me take the wheel and you can do some patchwork yourself."

Chris glanced at his blood-soaked clothes, "I've had worse."

"I bet. Still, if we get into another fight and your heads woozy for loss of blood, it'd be a mistake to not tend to it," Cait said, her voice a mix of sarcasm and concern.

"Fine, would you just see what you can do while I keep the accelerator down?" Chris relented.

Scowling, Cait leaned over, inspecting Chris' hip. With a cloth rag, she dabbed at the wettest portion of his pants. "Think I found your problem."

Tugging at the fabric with one hand, she sliced a section open with a knife. "Lift up a bit," Cait ordered.

Complying, Chris lifted his seat in the air, allowing Cait to wrap several layers of gauze and tape around his leg, just beneath his hip. Leaning further over, her back against the dashboard, she unbuttoned his shirt. Gingerly tugging at his sleeve as he lifted his right hand off of the wheel. Chris' eyes caught hers for a moment before returning to the desert landscape before him.

With a pack of bleed-stop material, Cait fashioned a rectangle and framed the material with tape. Gliding her fingers over the edge, she traced the tape over Chris' ribcage. "You sure that's a through and through?"

Chris shrugged, "No. I'll deal with it in Baghdad or…" He suddenly realized he didn't know what to call his new situation. He also didn't know how much Cait knew or didn't know about the operation as she was one of Anya's operatives, not Jonas'.

"Or your super top-secret mercenary group?" Cait teased. "We all are part of something unofficial…me, you, Lanikov, Anya…"

"And what are you a part of?" Chris asked.

"Freelance. The people who pulled me into this life kinda lost their way. By the time I pulled myself out from them, I was who I am. Not exactly easy to return to normal life. Besides, I'm good at what I do," Cait grinned.

"I see that," Chris said, pulling the SUV onto the highway leading to Baghdad. "IRA?"

"IRA splinter group. They appealed to me at a time when… I was angry and needed focus for that anger," Cait admitted.

"Why'd you leave?"

"Wrong is wrong. Regardless of what flag it's for. I lost my affection for their inattention to detail," Cait said.

"Inattention to detail as in collateral damage," Chris read between the words.

Cait looked away for a moment and nodded. "How about you, cowboy? What's a nice Marine like you doing running merc errands in Iraq?"

Chris sighed deeply and muttered, "A story for another day."

Cait shot Chris a perturbed look and cast her own weary gaze on the blacktop the big Mercedes was gobbling up at a rapid pace. Folding her arms in front of her, she shut down. Remaining closed off was more her style as well, she understood.

Her eyes fluttered with weariness, fighting off sleep. Her time in The End was not kind to her.

Even as the lights of Baghdad began to glow into view and the rearview mirror was clear of insurgent pursuers, a flash lit up the night sky. The heavy Mercedes lurched in the air, landing hard on its side before skidding to a stop on the opposite edge of the highway.

Lulled into the malaise of a long drive and the end in sight, Chris shook himself and snapped into action. Crawling through the back seat, "Stay down!" he ordered Lanikov.

"I can shoot," the Ukrainian operative said.

"You may need to. Here," Chris handed him one of the experimental weapons and a full mag. "You are mission critical, I am not. This rig can take some abuse. Hang tight and show your muzzle only if you absolutely have to."

Opening the rear hatch, he slipped through. Wriggling into his Crye Precision 2.0 armored vest and carrying his own assault rifle with traditional ammunition. He wasn't surprised when Cait appeared beside him.

"Think there might be baddies around here?" Cait asked.

"A lot of IEDs require manual detonation so they take their enemies instead of friendlies. On this highway, it was most likely a manual trigger. They're out here somewhere," Chris said sighting through his illuminated reticle, searching for a target.

"Stay here," he hissed.

Low jogging across the roadway, he slid into the ditch, his finger on the trigger. Spinning, he sighted the opposite direction. Carefully cresting the ditch that ran alongside the patch of road, he spied a low berm that mirrored the ditch. Perched on one knee, his rifle in firing position, he scanned the desert scape.

It was his ears that alerted him first, not his eyes. Two pairs of footfalls crunched just past the berm. Hearing no other movement, he took to his feet, sprinting to the apex and with hop, landing feet first, sliding down the other side of the berm directly at the sounds he heard. In the dim light, he saw two fighting age males scrambling away from the scene, pivoting to face him with AK47s drawn. Firing as he slid, Chris dropped both men as their misplaced shots scattered at his feet.

Hopping into a single knee position, he hastily scanned the area, looking for more insurgents. Up on the ridge, he found the threat he hoped wasn't there. A half-dozen men were waiting for their compatriots, erupting in gunfire as the scene below them unfolded.

Chris scrambled, up and over the berm, rolling towards the roadside ditch before pushing his boots into the dirt to arrest his slide. A volley of bullets soared over his head as Cait peered out from behind the turned over Mercedes.

"Angel, we have a situation," Chris called through his earpiece as he targeted an insurgent on the hill. Squeezing the trigger, he hit low, scattering shrapnel at the gunman, causing him to roll out of the way. The other insurgents sighted on his muzzle flash, forcing him down into the ditch, his back against the dirt wall.

"What's your sitrep, X?"

"We're about ten mikes from Baghdad, got hit with an IED. Our wheels are in the air and under heavy fire from a nearby ridge," Chris called.

"Copy that. We can have a helo in your direction in fifteen."

"Understood. We'll hold out," Chris said.

"Sit tight, help is on the way," Angel replied.

"Copy Angel. We're going to engage as we can."

Cait moved from one side of the armored SUV to the other, taking shots up the modest slope. Chris jogged several yards down the ditch. Finding a rock on the other side, he positioned himself low, at the point where the rock met the ground. In the natural curve, Chris pushed his muzzle through and sighted downrange. As muzzles flashed in response to Cait's attack on them, Chris squeezed the trigger twice. The shadow upslope collapsed forward. He saw a neighboring shadow drop. Cait had hit her man as well.

Facing another barrage of fire, bits of shattered rock raining on top of him, Chris crawled flat against the boulder. Spinning right, he fired off several shots, sighting on a target he had pinpointed the previous volley. Perfectly aimed, he was dismayed when he heard the horrifying click. His magazine was emptied.

Retreating back behind the boulder, Chris unholstered his sidearm. Holding it in front of his chest, muzzle in the air, he breathed calmly. Listening to the shots from Cait and the shots from above him, triangulating in his mind his next target. Popping straight up, he squeezed off several pulls of the trigger, dropping another insurgent. Collapsing down behind the safety of his rock, the area around him was peppered with return fire.

The sound of sliding feet alerted him to an insurgent coming towards him. He could hear Cait firing from the Mercedes as gunfire rained down from the above.

With a deep breath, Chris had a fifty-fifty guess. Rolling hard left he fired into the air. Closing his eyes as he laid prone on his belly, he could feel the muzzle pointing at his head from the other direction. He could hear Cait in a firefight with the remaining two shooters. He guessed wrong. His time was up.

Chris didn't expect to hear the shot. As he lay with his head down, his nose breathing in the Iraqi dirt, he waited to be overcome in darkness. Instead, he looked up to see Lanikov kneeling beside him, "You're okay."

"I thought I told you to stay in the car," Chris gasped, relieved his fight was still on. Renewed, he steadied a clean shot as the gunmen above concentrated on Cait. As he dropped one, Lanikov dropped the other. Suddenly, the concussive night fell silent. Chris, Cait, and Lanikov studied the ridge for movement.

No shadow, no muzzle flash met their eyes. Regrouping at the overturned Mercedes, they inspected one another, ensuring themselves they all made it through unscathed. A beam of light and the clatter of rotors reawakened the night as a helicopter descended from above them, landing a dozen yards away. Several soldiers hopped out, one corralling the trio, escorting them to the chopper.

"They'll secure the scene as a ground team arrives and maintain possession of the vehicle," the soldier shouted over the rotors.

With a hand on Chris' back, he urged him into the belly of the helicopter. Cait and Lanikov crawled aboard ahead of him. As soon as he was in, the aircraft lifted and pivoted for the awaiting city of Baghdad.

Twenty Three

Anya Oshevsky's demeanor didn't change as the beleaguered trio entered the room. She eyed each member in silence. Starting with Lanikov, she surveyed his weariness and obvious wounds. Weeks of torture, abuse, and lack of most human needs were blatantly apparent.

With Cait, she cast a glance of appreciation. She sent the operative into a lion's den and Cait looked every bit the effects of it. Cuts, bruises, swelling visible throughout her body revealed by the ridiculous skimpy outfit her captors made her wear.

As her gaze moved to Chris, a look of curiosity almost pierced the veil of emotionless Anya wore. Wearing the familiar patchwork of bleed-stop bandaging, he had clearly accepted his share of punishment during the conflict. Yet, there he stood, looking as though he was ready for his next assignment, which was a good thing.

Anya sat cross-legged on the couch in the VIP booth of the Baghdad discotheque, shut down for the day. Amidst the stench of stale beer, sweat, and cigarette smoke, she wore an odd air of elegance and grace. She reminded Chris of a beautiful viper, moving with sinewy movements, captivating to watch but could strike with deadly ferocity at any moment.

"I'm pleased to see you all made it back in mostly one piece," Anya purred. "I have a medical team in back ready to treat anything you need, including…bullet wounds." She eyed each patch of blood-soaked gauze.

"Here's the thing. Matthias has a target on his back with the information he holds in that noggin of his. There are five international organizations gunning for him. He won't make it out of Iraq alive unless we go ahead and exercise what he knows, rendering the information useless," Anya declared.

The look of Matthias' face was one of sheer terror. "Anya, you aren't saying…"

"Matthias, you know I am," Anya cast him a stern look.

Despite his weariness, Chris bristled with interest. Cait flopped on a nearby sofa, her weary body overlooking the concern of what human contact the material had soaked in over the years.

"Matthias was on his way to meet with a black site contingent in Syria. On a mission in Afghanistan, he captured evidence of Barriq Hussein funding a massive, multinational program to destabilize countries throughout the Middle East and southern Europe," Anya said.

"If he has this evidence, why not share it in on an underground platform? Feed it to people like Jonas," Chris asked.

"Unfortunately, my dear brother Matthias, lost the physical evidence. It has been relocated to Aleppo," Anya said.

"Aleppo?" Chris's mouth fell.

"Right? Who in their right mind would travel there right now? Five different insurgencies, every neighboring country with military units, even the big bad United States and Russia circling that pile of rubble," Anya replied. A grin crossing her lips, "Kind of brilliant, really."

Chris's shoulders slumped as he assessed Lanikov, apparently Anya's brother, who was in no shape for combat. Cait was not fairing much better.

Shooting up straight, the Irish woman surprised Chris, "I'm in. A chance to knock off so many of those evil bastards in one place sounds like fun."

Chris cocked his head, "We're going to need a sophisticated army to penetrate Aleppo. Even then, the odds of getting out alive are nearly zero."

"Matthias' evidence would hang Hussein and General Naib," Anya said.

"I'm in," Chris snapped.

Anya's grin turned a shade of evil at his sudden turn. She hit the right button.

"Still, we are going to need a team," Chris said.

"What do you suggest? It will take time for me to gather operators," Anya said.

"Jonas."

Anya twisted her head away, musing the implications of combining efforts. They passed assignments back and forth, loaned each other operators and equipment, but never worked together before.

"You get cleaned up, dig out whatever metal shards and lead you're wearing, patch up your holes...," Anya said. "I'll put my thoughts together on working with Jonas' team."

Despite needing two bullet holes patched up, a swipe from a sword blade, and countless pieces of shrapnel extracted from his body, Chris was the first to emerge from the medical bays installed in the Ukrainian run, Baghdad nightclub.

"You okay?" Anya asked, her voice displaying an uncharacteristic amount of concern.

Chris took the kind tone to be pragmatic. "I'm mission-ready. Five-by-five and ready to go."

Anya cocked her head at the reply. "Good. This place may not seem like much, but we employ a crack field medicine team."

"Thank you for the touch up," Chris replied coolly. "How are Cait and Lanikov?"

"Cait seems to be made of rubber. She clearly took a beating. There wasn't much on her that wasn't bruised, cut, or worse. Still, outside of a hydrating glucose drip, she seems to be okay. Her ribs are being taped to help mend a couple of fractures," Anya replied.

"And… your brother?"

Anya offered a grin, "Matthias will be okay. I am afraid he will not be 'mission-ready' as you say. We'll ship him to some safe black site and tap him into a communications team to extract his knowledge and translate it into the Syrian mission."

"I am glad to have found him alive," Chris said.

Anya pursed her lips, "He wouldn't have made it much longer. They tried beating, shocking, depriving information out of him. It wouldn't work. We are trained to die and allow all others around us to die before expelling proprietary information."

"We?"

"I wasn't always a mafia queen. I was an operator like you. Like you, I had a moment where I felt it best to… go into business for myself," Anya said.

Chris offered a simple nod. "The mission?"

Anya sighed and looked out across the neon bathed nightclub. "You're right. We need a team. Jonas can likely spin up faster than I can put one together and Aleppo is rather time-sensitive."

"What do you know about them?" Chris asked.

"*Them*?" Anya repeated thoughtfully. "I've rarely met a group quite so good at remaining so far off the radar. I guarantee, before you and your 'Patriot X' infamy, none of their ops or operatives have ever been aired on television and social media. I have worked with the pinnacle of covert operations. None have remained as elusive as the one Jonas is involved with. I know Jonas. I know his team is well outfitted, trained, and are ghostlike in covering their tracks. I know there are multiple 'Jonases' out there. At least five different teams by my count. Each multinational. Each operating on largely western ideals, though have engaged in crises across Africa and lesser developed Asia for humanitarian reasons."

Chris was thoughtful for a moment. "I don't even know what to call them."

Anya grinned. "I call them the Cabal. They don't like names. Names threaten anonymity. What do they call you? Everyone has callsigns. Outside of their inner sanctum, I have never heard a name other than yours and Jonas'."

"They wanted to call me Gunny," Chris said.

"But being a good Marine, that didn't sit well with you," Anya said, knowingly.

Chris cocked his head slightly, "Right. Now they call me 'X'."

"X," Anya repeated. "The enigmatic Patriot X. The only moniker they didn't find a way to bury."

Chris frowned.

"Like I said, names, even nicknames threaten anonymity. It is an associative term that allows people to string places and events together, ultimately leading to people. In black ops, that is a bad thing," Anya said.

"Then why allow Patriot X?"

"Marketing. You entered an embassy and extracted an A-hole for justice. No one does that. No one pierces that blanket of sovereignty, at least no one outside of loser terrorists. You did. And you disappeared into nothingness. That instills a new sense of fear in world governments that a legit team is not willing to put up with their bullshit," Anya said. Taking a sip of her drink, she smiled, "I'm not gonna lie, I find that… attractive."

The black market boss' expression turned seductive. Gone was her icy, unmovable stone, replaced with desirous respect for the former Raider team leader.

The amorous moment was broken as Cait burst into the room. "I haven't had so many clumsy hands on me since that bastard in Dublin."

Anya's business-only demeanor immediately returned, "Clumsy or not, I assume effective?"

"I'm ready to kick arse of the bastards who killed my family," Cait snapped.

Anya couldn't resist a soft chuckle, "Then I guess you and Mr. X here, are both mission ready. Let's get Jonas on the phone."

Jonas called Anya back after a half an hour. "Alright, we're sending a team, wheels up in an hour. But, you need to synch us to the comms you are running on Lanikov's data."

"Fair enough. We'll provide you with a secure link. Rendezvous in Kilis, Turkey in seven hours. I'll send the coordinates," Anya replied, hanging up the phone. Turning to Cait and Chris, she said, "We have an armament in the basement. Petro here will let you in. And Cait, for God's sake, put some clothes on, dear."

Cait and Chris followed Anya's man to an elevator door. Operational only through a coded keypad, the metal doors sprang open. Flipping on the slow, sequential fluorescent lights, the basement was an impressive warehouse of military gear. The scent of gun oil permeated the air in a way that was obtrusive, but yet, not altogether unpleasant.

"Anya says to help yourself," the man said and retreated into the elevator.

As the doors closed, Chris and Cait walked along the shelves. Like children in the toy aisle of a department store, they ran their fingers along the items that caught their interest. Almost overwhelmed by the choices, they languished to devise the ultimate option for the mission in Syria. Working their way around the room, their shoulders collided as they both reached for an Israeli Carmel 5.56. Their fingers settling on top of one another for a moment.

Turning, they looked at each other. Cait shrugged with a grin, "It's highly customizable to adapt to a challenging mission such as this."

"High fire rate with three settings, could be useful depending on what we find ourselves faced with," Chris offered.

In stereo, they blurted, "Standard NATO five-five-six!"

"We can grab ammo along the way," Chris said.

"Each kill is a potential source," Cait whispered, her lips close enough to Chris he could feel her breath.

After an uncomfortable, heated pause, Chris pulled the gun off of the shelf and handed it to Cait. The weapon serving to put distance between their bodies.

"I was torn between that and the Colt R4…," Chris shrugged.

"Look, she has two," Cait into the shelf and pulled a second assault rifle down, handing it to Chris.

"Check out Anya's accessory shelf?" Chris suggested.

"Oh yeah," Cait beamed, streaking past him and down the aisle.

Assembling their assault rifles to their specific preferences, interchanging sights, stocks, and barrels, they pilfered the well supplied armory. Returning to the elevator, tactical bags laden, Chris and Cait slid in behind the closing doors.

Cait's freckled cheeks and bright eyes smiled as she looked up at Chris, "Well, that was fun."

Chris flashed a rare smile in return. “It was. You have excellent taste in outfitting a weapon.”

Cait gushed, “You know how to flatter a girl, Mr. X.”

The energetic banter suddenly hit Chris as wrong, filling him with guilt for allowing the playfulness to take away from his focus on the mission. Deeper down, he knew his feelings had nothing to do with the mission, but enjoying a moment while Breanna and Macy were gone didn’t sit well with him. At all.

“This mission… anyone who goes might not be coming back,” Chris warned, his tone serious.

Cait looked at him questioning, “How is that different than any other mission?”

“There’s going into a hornet’s nest. This is squeezing through half a dozen nests where the hornets are already pissed off,” Chris said.

“I’ve lived most of my adult life getting shot at from all angles,” Cait looked away for a moment and then back at Chris as the elevator doors opened. “Just another day in the life of Cait McBride.”

Pushing past, she marched towards Anya. “Let’s get this show on the road, sister.”

"I like your enthusiasm, Ms. McBride. I wish I could do more for you than provide you with toys, but I'm afraid we have our own troubles to contend with in Baghdad," Anya said.

Chris' head snapped in her direction. Anya waved him off, "Nothing we can't handle, but I will need my personnel."

"Understood. We've got this," Chris nodded.

"I'll keep my pilot in some safe spot not far from your position in Syria for exfil," Anya promised.

Nudging his tactical kit towards the door, Chris urged, "Let's go meet up with Jonas."

TWENTY FOUR

The flight into Kilis, Turkey was long. Chris did his best to allow the constant drone of rotors to provide white noise to aid sleep, at least the kind of sleep he had learned to accept as a Marine.

As customary, he had himself awakened an hour outside of the landing zone, giving him time to acclimate and prepare his mind and body. He studied Cait, slumped in the corner of the helicopter. She almost looked peaceful. Chris didn't know her full story, but the physical scars on her body were backed by the emotional scars seen he when peered through her eyes.

The Irish woman was tough as nails, but there was a childlike spirit under all of that brokenness. He didn't realize he had been staring, but Cait awoke and her eyes opened and met with his.

"Rise and shine, we're about forty minutes out," Chris called across the cabin.

With a deep stretch, Cait replied, "I'm not sure which is worse, sleeping awkwardly or not getting any sleep at all."

"As someone who has slept in caves, under a truck, and standing up trapped in a stairwell, I can attest any amount or quality of sleep once on the battlefield is useful," Chris said.

"Had to sleep with one eye open in The End. A shackled girl locked in with a bunch of brutes. What could possibly go wrong?" Cait replied.

"How did you handle that? It must have been awful," Chris said.

"The first night a man tried to take advantage of me, I wrapped him in a leglock and crushed his windpipe. I dumped him in the middle of the floor as he gasped and choked to death. I made sure everyone in there was awake to witness it. Then one by one, I kicked every one of their pathetic heaps in the ring," Cait said.

Chris smiled gently, "You sure can take care of yourself."

"No choice," Cait said, pulling her pack close as she continued to wake fully.

The moment the landing skids touched the tarmac alongside the sleek, high-tech assault helicopter Jonas' team flew, they were greeted by an armed envoy.

"They are assembled inside," one of the operatives called over the decelerating blades.

Chris and Cait toted their packs and followed the men.

Jonas' team had taken over a hangar in a private airport in the Turkish border town. The operation center was still being set up as the pair was announced.

Jonas looked up from the documents spread out on a table, "Chris!" With a hand in the air, he strode over to welcome them. "Ms. Cait McBride. I have heard a lot about you. Never thought we would be working an op together."

"Wasn't sure you guys really existed. You accel at being ghosts wherever you work. Even when people knew something went down, there was no tie to anyone," Cait said in appreciation.

"I'm glad we don't have a reputation to be preceded, then," Jonas said. Turning to Chris, he held out his hand, "It sounds like your op for Anya went well."

"As most ops go, it wasn't without some setbacks and improvisation, but the objectives were met, I'm happy to say," Chris said.

"I gotta say, I wasn't thinking Anya would call in her chip so soon," Jonas said, glancing at the operation center being put into place.

Chris nodded, "If we can work together to bring down Hussein and General Naib, I am happy to work with them."

"Good," Jonas said. "The team is getting geared up, we'll synch in this room in fifteen."

"Copy that," Chris nodded. Holding his hand out for Cait to go first, they followed the sounds of weapons checks.

Entering a room of benches, each team member worked over their gear in their own manner. All eyes snapped up as they entered the room. Chris and Cait received a variety of looks from the operators.

Starting with those who offered the friendliest welcomes, Chris introduced Cait to Cole Porter and Aban Kinza.

Both men jumped to their feet.

Porter reached out his hand, "Pleasure Ms. McBride. I've read your bio, you are a welcome asset."

"A friend of 'X' is a friend of mine," Aban Kinza said.

"This is 2K and Gazi," Chris introduced the men with their codenames.

"2K?" Cait raised an eyebrow as she accepted Porter's welcome.

"Sniper," Porter grinned.

"À propos then," Cait nodded. Turning to Aban Kinza, "Gazi, that's Arabic for Muslim warrior…"

Kinza beamed, "It is. You speak Arabic?"

Cait wrinkled her nose, "A few dialects. Not because I wanted to, it comes with the job."

"I understand. I must say, I welcome the way you say it," Kinza smiled.

"Nice to have another female on board, and not just one whispering sweet things in the team's ears," Cara joined the group.

"This is Dragonfly. Ace pilot and when called upon, a vivacious heavy gunner," Porter shared. "And that curmudgeon over there is Beast. What he lacks in manners, he more than makes up for in battlefield prowess," Cole shared pointing at Drake Fallon. Fallon looked up from his work and cast the group a blank glance.

"You met Jonas," Chris added. "From here on, he'll go by Chief."

"And somewhere in a bunker safely under bedrock is Angel. You'll hear us speak with her in comms. She runs oversight through satellite, ISR, and anything else with a camera on it. She'll also relay directives as missions take shape. She'll protect our butts and find us a clean exfil when the mission is complete," Porter shared.

"I can understand why you call her Angel," Cait replied.

"If we're all done hugging it out, we've got a mission to prepare for," Drake said. He had his combat attire on and his kit ready.

"Don't mind Beast, he ate too many sprinkles off of a yogurt shop floor as a kid," Porter quipped.

Chris looked at Cait, "Let's suit up."

Grabbing his gear, he set off to put on his tactical gear.

The sixty-five-mile trip to Aleppo was a short one in the two helicopters, landing just outside of the ravaged city. They had to hike the remainder of the way to their target. The pair of helicopters lifted off within seconds of the crew piling out. They would wait for exfil in Kilis, away from the risk of attack.

Angel would provide overwatch from satellite feeds but ISR or Intelligence, Surveillance, and Reconnaissance drones normally used would be unavailable due to air restrictions over the tormented city.

It didn't take long before the team was hunkering next to cover with their weapons drawn. Gunfire sporadically erupted as the team moved closer. "Let's try to avoid contact as much as we can until we hit the bank Naib is using," Fallon said as they pressed on.

"While not a live shot, I count ten, armed, fighting age males patrolling nearby buildings, an additional five at the bank itself," Angel shared over their earpieces. "That was about twenty minutes ago."

"Copy that, Angel. We're encountering gunfire from outside the city and sounds like more the further we move. We're doing our best to stay out of it," Fallon reported.

"I'd say where we have reports, but it's basically the entire city," Angel said.

Chris placed a hand on Fallon's shoulder and warned the group to duck down as a technical vehicle with a mounted machine gun drove past, clearly headed for a fight. The team held for a moment to ensure additional vehicles weren't in tow.

With no further threats, they rose from their cover and hurried across the street. Moving from shadow to shadow, they avoided obvious skirmishes. The setting sun behind the city offered long, full shadows providing them reasonable concealment as they moved.

With the bank in view, they surveilled the immediate area. About to slice a path through the broken streets and rubble, Fallon shouted, “Down!”

A split-second later, the woosh of a rocket soared over their heads, exploding into a building directly behind them. Concrete and debris rained down over their heads as they fought for protective cover.

“Is everyone okay?” Fallon asked.

Each team member accounted for, Porter observed, “Here’s the good news, I don’t think that rocket was meant for us.”

From his concealment, he pointed out a group of insurgents picking themselves out of the worst of it, trying to find someone to fire on.

“Question now, is who sent it?” Fallon asked.

“Could be Russian, US, Syrian…,” Porter mused.

“Either way, we are in the crossfire,” Chris said.

“After that rocket attack, the insurgents are going to fire on anything that moves across that street,” Cait added.

Fallon moved from his position and moved a few barriers closer to the group that just got targeted. Counting only three survivors, he tossed a grenade in their general direction. "Move, now!"

Darting across the street, with only a single gun from the insurgents shooting wildly towards them. Sliding into the concrete doorway of the bank, they fell into position. Chris, Cait, and Kinza kneeled, training their scopes in opposite directions while Fallon and Porter worked on setting a breach charge around the heavy door.

"We have some very confused Russians wondering who gave them an assist," Chris declared, studying his side of the Aleppo marketplace.

"The insurgents retreated, pulling their wounded out of the rubble," Kinza said.

"We have another group, tough to identify, coming our way. They sure remind me of General Naib's kind of guys," Cait called.

"Likely took cover when the Russians and insurgent group started going at it," Chris said.

"They see us and don't look happy," Cait said, her finger on the trigger of her assault rifle.

As a bullet flew overhead and into the door that Fallon and Porter had just rigged, "Take them out," Fallon urged.

The team slid behind cover and began firing on the approaching gunmen. Chris made sure that the Russians didn't have an angle on him, either, in the event they elected to chime in. Squeezing off a few shots down range, more bullets flew overhead.

"I'm going to take this fight inside, time to blow the door," Fallon declared.

Hitting the trigger, the entire frame of the door gave way, blasting into the interior of the bank. "Let's go," Fallon urged, firing over his shoulder as he wrapped into the bank entrance. Providing cover for those on his side of the door as they slipped in.

Chris maintained fire downrange as the rest of the team moved inside.

"I've got you, X," Porter called laying down a barrage of gunfire.

Chris slipped from his cover and lunged into the relative safety of the bank.

"Gazi, maintain watch on this location. Lay some claymores to give you some time in the event, well… when the door is breached," Fallon ordered.

"Copy that, Beast," Kinza nodded. Kneeling on one side of the door, he pulled the tiny tripod legs out from the small, rectangular mine and repeated the exercise on the other side before retreating to a spot on the stairs that could watch the door but also have an escape route.

The rest of the team split into two, Porter following Fallon and Cait following Chris. It didn't take long for Naib's men to come out of hiding. Popping out of doors in the first-floor hallway, they forced Fallon and Porter to seek cover. Pulling a flash bang from his vest, Fallon lobbed it down the hallway. As soon as the flash resolved, he and Porter advanced, making quick work of the men in the hallway.

Chris cautioned for Cait to pause as he pressed against the wall at the first intersection of their hallway. Both teams worked their way to the rear of the bank where the vault was supposed to be with the Lanikov's documents.

A shadow in the shape of an AK47 weaved back and forth against the wall. Chris estimated from the shadow, where its owner might be. Giving Cait the ready signal, he positioned his assault rifle and blind-shot several rounds with his left hand while the rest of him remained wrapped around the corner.

Screams of pain declared Chris the victor even as rounds peppered the wall he used for cover. Cait, meanwhile, rolled to the other side of the hall. Doing so, she sighted on two more members of the cell, firing and hitting one of them. As she readied another shot, Chris had dropped to the floor and peered down the hall with his forehead and rifle muzzle barely revealing themselves, giving him a clean shot at the third gunman.

Cait didn't hesitate, "Moving!" she whispered hoarsely as she sprinted down the hall to the next area of cover. Chris scrambled to his feet in pursuit. Using opposing offices for cover, they dove away from a new hailstorm of bullets further down the hall.

Chris tried to peer around the corner, but the flow of bullets was consistent. Realizing they were likely up against a machine gunner, he looked around for another solution. Spying the drop ceiling of the offices, he climbed from desk to file cabinet. Pushing up against the perforated ceiling tile, he moved a panel out of the way. Raising himself gently with the modest metal girder to support the weight of his muscular frame.

Making his way over the metal grid to the more supportive wall, he carefully slid a panel from the other side of the hall while Cait continued to take shots from her cover.

At the end of a hall, using a pair of overturned desks as a makeshift berm, lie a mounted machine gun turret laying waste to their end of the hall. Taking a moment to breathe, he sighted the gunner through the ACOG scope and squeezed the trigger, abruptly ending the machine gun barrage. Before the gunner could be replaced, Chris and Cait dropped the next two men in line for the gun.

Dropping through the ceiling, Chris advanced with Cait quickly on his flank. Instantly dropping another pair of gunmen peering around the corner, taking hasty shots, they reached their portion of the insertion. “Might as well make use of that gun,” Chris nodded towards the mounted machine gun.

Cait grinned, “I thought you’d never ask.”

Drake Fallon and Cole Porter met mirrored obstacles on their path to the vault. Launching themselves away from the firing line of their own machine gun turret, they spun and faced each other in office doorways on opposite sides of the hall.

Pulling grenades from their vests, they timed their throws, aimed directly at the base of the machine gun. The blasts sent a cacophony of metal, glass, and wood throughout the room. Those closest to the gunner were killed in the blast. Three remained. Two wearily trying to regain their focus, their muzzles waving in the air. Each was dispatched quickly by Porter and Fallon. The third sat against a wall, futilely tugging a long piece of desk that transformed into an airborne dagger during the explosion. Almost out of pity, Fallon mercied the man with a shot to the forehead.

Pushing through, they found Chris examining the vault, wrapping det-cord around it. Seeing Cait manning the mounted turret, Porter mumbled, “Yeah, ours isn’t real useful anymore.”

Chris called over his shoulder as he worked, “Afraid a grenade would have collapsed the building, chose a different solution.”

“I see that,” Fallon nodded.

“Nearly did, too. See that entire section of concrete? The weight of the building is pressing on it. Those cracks and fissures mean this place is a time bomb,” Chris said. “A little concerned what blowing this vault open will do.”

Porter and Fallon studied the vault and mutually assessed the remaining structure of the bank. “We don’t need to blow the entire vault. Just a corner. A directed charge at this seam here and if needed, this corner, it should open right up,” Porter suggested. “I think you’re right. This place doesn’t have much left to hold it together.”

“Let’s get to work. We don’t have much time either,” Fallon said.

As his words filled the air, the concussive sound of a claymore rang from the lobby. Soon after, a second blast followed with a wave of shooting.

“Sounds like Kinza will be joining us,” Chris said.

Stepping aside so that Porter could take over the vault opening duties to his updated specification, Chris joined Fallon in guarding the grenade ravaged room from unwanted visitors while Cait held a steady sentry with the machine gun.

It didn't take long for the gunfight to head in their direction. Cait readied on the trigger as her eyes stared down the steel gunsight of the turret gun. She breathed as a man with an assault rifle appeared in her view. Wide eyed, the man flailed to the ground as she let loose with a barrage of bullets slicing down the hallway.

The insurgents trailing the gunmen were mowed down in waves until the visual message of their fallen comrades halted their assault.

"I'm glad you recognized me," Kinza gasped as he scrambled to his feet and launched himself over the barricade.

"I didn't at first, I was going to end with you," Cait grinned.

"Great," Kinza muttered meekly, training his eye back down the hallway. "More coming!"

Chris glanced at Fallon, "I'm going to advance down."

Leaving his post, he moved to the lobby. Pausing as he ensured the entrance was empty, he circled to the other hallway. Just as the insurgents were about to emulate Fallon's method, perhaps taking the building with it, Chris lined up a shot. Hitting the man before he could pull the pin, the grenade landed on the floor and rolled along the hallway.

The insurgent team was trapped between his attack and Cait's gunner position; the group chose to deal with Chris first. Chris was able to drop another before he was outgunned and out of position.

Cait could hear the shots from around the corner of the hallway. "Here, take over the gun!" she called to Kinza, leaping to her feet and over the barrier. Sprinting down the hallway, her assault rifle at the ready, she slid low as she reached the corner. Seeing the grenade, she scooted further away from Naib's men and from her prone position, began taking them out.

Chris did his best to back away, but knew there were too many. Firing a shot at the first two, he was surprised when the remaining two also fell. Cait's smiling face and smoking muzzle of her assault rifle came into view.

With a relieved sigh, he said, "I am *so* glad to see you."

"What were you thinkin'? The heavy gun was doing its job," Cait remanded.

Before he could answer, Fallon called from down the hall, "We're through! It's here, we've got it!"

"Patriot Team, the situation outside your position is getting worse. Four vehicles, our intel has identified full of General Naib's men are heading towards your position while other shooters are intent on squaring off in downtown Aleppo," Angel called over their comms.

"Is there a back door?" Fallon asked.

"Negative, Beast. Your Area of Operation is the center of attention," Angel replied.

Fallon looked at the team, "Look like we're going to have to fight our way out of here."

Looking at the aerial display on his cellphone, he added, "Looks like this group here, identified as anti-democratic socialists, have the weakest location. We should be able to cut through to the LZ for extract."

"If we're going to be putting bullets in anyone, shouldn't it be Naib's people? Besides their deservin' it, they'll be able to report back who is gunning for him and Hussein?" Cait asked.

"I'm not gonna lie, that would be ideal. But the best, most expedient plan is for us to cut through the socialist group," Fallon said. "Been fighting commies for years, nothing new for me here."

Hearing the vehicles Angel mentioned screech to a halt outside of the bank building, Fallon worked the group to the rear of the building. "Still got extra det-cord?"

Porter nodded, patting his pack.

"Let's make a door!" Fallon instructed.

Porter began adhering the chord to the wall. He had enough to punch through a full size door. "This building might not hold. She's pretty weak."

"As long as it holds long enough where we stand, so much the better if it falls," Fallon shrugged. "Light it up."

Complying, Porter let loose on the charge as the team ducked and covered. As the wall blew out into an exit for the team, the bank's structure began to fail. Ceiling tiles dropped and support beams lost their integrity as the balance of components shifted.

Pressing forward, the crew pushed to make their escape amidst the chaos of dust and debris. Chris prepared himself for blinded movement towards the exit. As he strode forward, he could feel the rush of heavy materials fall inches behind his heels.

In a few steps, he escaped into the alley of Porter's newly formed doorway. He dropped to a knee and scanned his side of the door to ensure it was free of insurgents. In the corner of his eyes, he could see Porter doing the same on the other side.

Fallon pulled Kinza along with him and assessed the situation, preparing for a hasty retreat to exfil. Nodding for Kinza to take his place, Chris eyed the doorway looking for Cait. When she didn't immediately present Chris slipped back into the crumbling building.

"Cait!"

"I'm…stuck!" a raspy voice barely made it through the noise of the deteriorating building and ever-present violence of the city.

"I'll get you out of there. Are you pinned?" Chris called.

"No, just trapped. I think most of the second floor slid in front of me and well, the rest of the building fell behind me. I hear Naib's men trying to pick their way through!" Cait called back.

"Hang tight!"

"What else am I going to do?" Cait bristled.

With Porter and Kinza not moving their eyes from their watch positions, the team convened as Chris shared Cait's situation.

"Naib's men are combing through the building as we speak, more are likely on their way never mind every other faction in this state that has interest. Our window is closing. We need to head for exfil," Fallon proclaimed.

"What the hell are you talking about, Fallon? I'm not leaving a man behind," Chris spat.

"Noble. It pains me too, it does. But the die has been cast. She is already dead and if we stay another minute, we are too," Fallon defended.

"Death is part of the job, leaving a teammate to die is not," Chris growled.

"The mission is priority. We need to get the drives out of Aleppo. The team is second and well, she isn't even part of the team," Fallon snapped, his eyes cold.

Chris thrust his hand out, grabbing a fist full of Fallon's vest, slamming him into the wall. "I'm not leaving without her. I wouldn't leave without any of you if were still breathing."

Fallon was unmoved, "I hate it, but by the time you reach her, she won't be breathing and neither will you."

"I'll take my chances," Chris said, letting go of Fallon. "Go."

"I'll stay with you, Chris," Porter stepped up. Kinza strode forward as if to echo the sentiment.

"No. You guys get to exfil," Chris demanded as Fallon was already making his way down the alley.

Porter tried to speak, but understood the look in Chris' eyes. "Good luck," he said. Tugging Kinza along, they disappeared towards the route Fallon had taken.

"What's going on? The thermal from satellite shows you guys have split up," Angel's voice crackled over the comms.

"We have a teammate trapped, I'm going to try and get her out. The rest of the team has the objective and is heading towards exfil," Chris said as he examined the rubble between him and Cait.

"Can you get her out?" Angel asked.

"I don't know. Most of the building is caved in and Naib's soldiers are working their way through the other end."

"I'm sorry X, exfil sounds like the right move."

"I may have left my post, but my oath still stands. X out," Chris said. Digging his earpiece out, he tossed it into the rubble.

Studying the remnants of the second floor that became a sloped wall blocking Cait, he followed the line until he reached the section where the floor met the exterior wall. "Cait! You still good?"

"I wouldn't say good, but I'm breathing!" Cait called back.

"What's it look like at the northern wall?"

"It's a bloody mess in here, which frickin' way is north?" Cait spat.

"If you are facing my voice, north will be to your left," Chris said.

"Copy that," Cait said. Moving through the debris, she used the tactical light on her assault rifle to track the rubble to the wall Chris wanted her to inspect.

"The space is a bit bigger here. The floor above seems to have sloped towards the back and center," Cait replied.

"Good."

"Good?"

"I think," Chris shrugged, his tone of voice not convincing. "But I have a plan… just back away from the wall and cover your eyes and ears."

"Not sure I like the sounds of that," Cait said. Complying, she knelt next to a desk.

Chris slipped around the corner of the building. He could see activity building in front and knew it was only a matter of time before the scene would be hot. Digging the remaining unused det-cord from his pack, Chris stepped a few paces from the corner of the building. Wasting no time, he rolled against the side of the building and triggered the cord.

The explosion triggered more debris and instability in the building, but the wall remained intact. Slipping through the small hole, Chris crawled through the debris. Seeing Cait's tactical light bobbing through the thick dusty air, gave him a sense of relief.

"Did you think more explosions was a good idea?" Cait grumbled.

"It worked, mostly. Come on, before the rest of this place comes down," Chris tugged her free hand and led her to the hole he created. "I determined, well, hoped really that with the weight of the floor above you sagging…"

"Can your construction story wait? We've got company," Cait said. Pivoting, the muzzle of her assault rifle passed his shoulder and flashed twice.

"Here they come, come on," Chris said, taking a step towards the narrow path Fallon, Porter, and Kinza had taken.

"Those are Naib's men," Cait said. Instead of following Chris, she strode towards the front of the building. As another soldier turned the corner, he glanced down at his fallen comrades. By the time he looked up to see Cait's gun, he was dead himself.

"Cait, this could be our only window out," Chris urged, moving to her side.

"One of these men may have executed my family," Cait's eyebrow furrowed and twitched.

"You really want to do this?" Chris asked.

He didn't need a response. The look in her eyes said it all.

"Alright," Chris conceded. Patting the magazines he still had left in his vest. Taking lead, he pushed through the alley, Cait by his side as they split the target zone.

A trio of soldiers appeared, all three dropped before they could levy a shot.

Reaching the front corner of the building, several trucks pulled up with men jumping out to join the search of the bank building. "They're like roaches, coming from everywhere," he gasped, assessing his next move. He didn't have a chance to think long as Cait was clenching grenade pin after grenade pin with her teeth. Spitting the metal pin out, she lobbed a succession of incendiary grenades moving from the trucks, lining the entire path to the entrance of the bank.

Snapping into action, Chris spun around the corner as they began picking off soldiers that weren't affected by the blasts. Gunfire seemed to come from everywhere. Back to back, they rotated their way through the chaos, making their way through Naib's men. The closer they got to the bank, Chris realized they were quickly becoming surrounded by soldiers.

Pulling Cait down behind the concrete steps of the bank, he looked her in the eyes, "There's no way out of the bank. We can't go in there."

Cait flustered, "We'll take them all out!"

"We've won more than our share of gunfights, all it takes is one win on their side, Cait," Chris said, his voice stern. "We've sent a message to Naib. We have information that can take him down and every part of his organization. Let's live to see that happen."

"Fine," Cait sulked as she saw a man targeting them with an RPG.

Standing straight up, directly in his line, Cait unholstered her sidearm and snapped it up. In one fluid motion, she pulled the trigger without the aid of her sights and placed a shot into his forehead.

Sprinting, she dodged bullets that peppered along her path, jumping into a slide where the man she had just shot had fallen, she snatched the RPG and leveled it towards the front of the building.

Chris' eyes went wide, "Oh, shi….!" Launching himself away from the bank, he flattened himself to the ground behind a truck's wheel as whatever was left standing in the bank collapsed in a fiery blast.

Helicopters, drones, and more vehicles could be heard making their way towards the site. Dodging shooters and taking out others, Chris sprinted across the square, tackling Cait as a helicopter flew overhead, spraying the area with bullets. Dragging her away as drones swooped in releasing small payload missiles, the square lit up in the night sky.

"Naib?" Cait gasped.

"Probably Russian or Syrian by way of Russia…or the U.S. It doesn't matter. Whoever, they have had enough of tonight's fighting. We need to get out of here!" Chris urged.

Not accepting hesitation, Chris clenched Cait's vest with his fingers and pulled her into the shadows.

Twenty Five

Chris wheeled the stolen vehicle onto the tarmac in Kilis, Turkey. He was surprised to see the helicopter still there. Getting out of the vehicle, the second one he and Cait had to abscond with, one to get from Aleppo to the Turkish border. The second after crossing the well-guarded border on foot.

"Chopper is still here, at least one of them," Cait said.

"I didn't expect Jonas' team's. I didn't expect either, actually," Chris confirmed.

"Let's find the pilot and get the hell out of here," Cait pleaded.

Chris looked towards the nearby hangar, "I think Nikolai is as eager as we are."

The pilot strode towards the helicopter, his flight gear already donned. "Not sure if I expected to actually have passengers."

"Wasn't sure if you were going to be here," Chris admitted.

"That makes two of us," Nikolai grinned. "Anya instructed me to wait. She had misplaced faith that you might show, and here you are. Nearly missed your window though."

"Nearly missed a lot of things on this trip. I hate to say these words, but I'm eager to get back to Baghdad," Chris said.

The pilot cocked his head, "Anya's not in Baghdad, she's in Morocco."

"She gets around," Chris replied.

"She goes where the business goes," Nikolai replied.

"Then off to Morocco we go. Last I checked, no one was trying to kill us there," Chris said.

"I'm sure we'll fix that," Cait murmured.

The eight-hour flight to Morocco was a time for Chris and Cait to receive some much-needed sleep. Waking up in helicopter seats only made their many injuries that much more pronounced.

Chris, a few years Cait's senior, felt it the most. As he climbed out, he instinctively stretched like a cat, trying to pull as many kinks out as he could. As many times as he had ridden a helicopter, he couldn't help but to hunch as he passed under the rotors.

"Welcome to Morocco," Nikolai beamed, giving Chris and Cait a brief salute.

A limousine awaited them on the tarmac. Their tattered, dirty attire was in stark contrast to the luxurious vehicle they climbed into.

Not arguing the comfort and ample amenities of the limo, Chris and Cait settled in for their ride to whatever situation Anya found herself in.

Chris flipped the toggle for the bar, searching for a water. "Want something?"

"That thing got whiskey in it?" Cait asked. "A good Powers or Slane would hit the spot."

Chris cocked his head as he inspected the labels. "I've got Eagle Rare, Maker's Mark and Jameson."

"You have to ask?" Cait said, her tone never more Irish.

"Eagle Rare should do nicely," Chris said.

"If you don't pour the Jameson, good for over three hundred years, Irish whiskey, I'll dot you in your nose," Cait threatened.

Chris, already with the Jameson in hand, "I figured as much. I gotta tell you, the Eagle Rare is a better choice."

"Blasphemy from an American redneck," Cait said.

"Rocks or straight up?"

"Ice gets in the way of the drinkin'," Cait acted offended.

Chris nodded and poured a glass. Cait accepted the glass of Jameson poured in the fine Polish crystal. "Slainte!"

Chris, after guzzling a bottle of water, poured a pair of fingers of Eagle Rare for himself. Raising the glass, he clinked it with Cait's, "To a successful mission, cheers!"

Cait met her glass with his. Downing the entire cup, she held it out for him to refill.

As Chris gingerly sipped his, he set it down and poured another couple of drams for Cait.

"Why do I need to be served by a fit American with skinny fingers? Pretend you're twice as big and then pour me a drink," Cait drawled.

Chris complied and handed her the glass.

"Slainte!" she raised the glass in the air. This time, she savored the liquid. Leaning back, Cait welcomed the warming whiskey as it slid down her throat. "My lord, the number of times we nearly died."

Chris looked over at her, "But we didn't."

"It's just that easy for a Marine, isn't it? Stuff hits the fan, as long as mission complete and all accounted for are coming home, it's all okay?" Cait asked.

"We do our job. Protect our brothers. Come home to our families," Chris acknowledged. The word family set his heart aflame. He looked out the window and drained the Eagle Rare in his glass.

"I'm sorry. My family's been gone so long, I didn't mean…," Cait started.

Chris shook her off, his eyes not leaving the passing countryside. "It's okay."

Cait stared at him. Reaching across his body, she refilled his glass. "It's not. It never really will be, but you'll callous just enough to live on."

"That why you suicide every mission? Going after Naib's men at the bank was bull and you know it," Chris said, his hands grasping the crystal glass Cait handed him.

Cait paused, glancing out her own window before responding, "After those bastards razed my family… yes. My most luscious fantasy is dyin' to avenge my family."

Chris took a deep pull of his drink. "Now *that*, I understand."

Cait raised her glass, "Two kamikazes hell bent on our appropriate ends."

Chris sighed deep before taking another drink, "I suppose."

The pair sat in silence for miles before Cait whispered, "Thank you. You've saved me more times than any one person ever had. Even when it didn't make a lick of sense."

Chris didn't answer right away. He sipped his drink and stared out of his window. "Thinking you're worth keeping alive."

"That makes one of us that thinks that," Cait spat, downing the remainder of her beverage. "If there's any more in that bottle, I'd take the rest."

Chris turned and looked at Cait for a long moment. He knew in no world should the woman next to him own the bottle of whiskey saddled in the pantry next to him. Looking into her eyes, the pain was searing. With a deep breath, he grabbed the bottle and handed it to her.

Grasping the bottle, she stared at it for a long moment. Glancing at the glass in her other hand, she abruptly cast it over her shoulder in the rear of the luxury vehicle. "Thank you," she stated simply before succumbing in to her own world of questionable dulled solitude.

Chris couldn't argue. A part of him wanted to indulge as deeply himself. Forget the world as it stood. Find a place, even if false, where he belonged. Where the pain of losing Breanna and Macy didn't exist.

With restraint, he sipped on the meager volume of alcohol he allowed himself and allowed the visions of his wife and daughter to pass through his mind with every mile they passed until they reached Morocco. Cait had slipped into blissful unconsciousness. Chris admired her. She felt no pain, either physical or emotional. A state he longed to find but refused to go until his time was called. The fact was, he *wanted* to feel the pain. The moment he ceased to hurt, was the moment that he knew he would lose them.

He didn't attempt to wake Cait until they reached the subterranean garage of the luxury hotel their driver delivered them to. With a hand on her shoulder, he nudged, "Cait…Cait…we're in Morocco. Come on, it's time to go."

Cait's freckled face came to life with her bright green eyes flickering, adjusting to the light of the world, wincing at the headache that fought for control over her brain and body. "We're where?"

"Morocco. Anya's place," Chris stated.

"Right," Cait straightened up, shaking off her malaise. "Right. Let's go."

"Here," Chris handed the Irish operative a bottle of water.

Grabbing one for himself, he thanked the driver.

Scrambling out of his seat, the driver relented to Chris and Cait already having exited the vehicle and scurrying away not having any luggage.

"This is certainly a step up," Chris said, taking in the luxurious hotel.

An attendant approached them. Pausing for a moment, the man cast the pair a disapproving glance before nodding in understanding. "You are the expected guests of Ms. Oshevsky. Of course! Right this way, right this way," the man said, spinning and shuffling into the hotel lobby.

With an apologetic nod to the distinguished man behind the desk, he turned abruptly towards a bank of elevators. Slipping a key into a lock, he pressed an innocuous button among the numbered ones.

Standing in front of the doors with his arms crossed, he stepped aside as they reached the top floor and the doors opened. "Here you are," the man waved his arm horizontally from his hip to the room.

Pulling the key, he resumed his posture as the doors closed.

"He's an odd duck," Cait quipped.

"Cait and Chris! So good to see you both!" a burly, thickly accented voice sang out.

"Petro! It's good to be seen!" Cait smiled back.

"Ms. Oshevsky's waiting for you. Follow me," Petro said, waving for them to follow him.

Framed by massive bay windows, Anya sat behind a grand desk, nestled in a massive, plush chair. Chris stifled a chuckle. No matter where Anya was, whether the slums, a war-torn capitol, or a wealthy district in Morocco, she exuded a regal presence. She commanded whatever room or situation she was in.

A warm smile crossed her lips, "You two are a sight for sore eyes, even if your actual sight is a bit tattered." Her eyes observed both operatives, assessing their condition.

"You survived. I expected you to return with Jonas' team, at least you, Chris," Anya announced.

"I had to take a detour they weren't willing to take," Chris said evenly.

Anya's smile broadened, "I'm not sure they are used to such discord from their teams. I guarantee they didn't expect it from a Marine."

"My decisions are my own," Chris said.

"I see that. I rather like that about you," Anya said. "And how is my favorite rogue?"

Cait rolled her eyes but seemed to relish the term just a bit, "I'd be dead if it were not for Chris going off script. Even better, we got to take a few more of Naib's men out."

"Always a good day when one can do that," Anya said approvingly. "Speaking of which, I have some news on that front. We found the cell that took out the train that your mother and sister were on."

Chris could see a vein on Cait's neck make an appearance as Anya shared her information.

"It was indeed one of Naib's cells. The attack took place the weekend after Barriq Hussein held one of his 'peace rallies' in Paris. The train your family was on originated from Paris on its way to Dublin. Your mother and sister boarded while in route and the bomb that derailed the train went off at its peak capacity just prior to the Channel crossing," Anya shared. "That cell is based out of Algeria."

"Algeria is friendly to the west," Chris frowned.

"Exactly. That friendliness and free society stuff doesn't sit well with many interests from the Middle East. Hussein's influence isn't all that strong where peace reigns," Anya said. "We have intel to suggest that cell is rallying for another attack in Libya. The attempted peace with Egypt, Libya, and Tunisia isn't sitting well with the terror types. They are plotting to disrupt that peace by attacking a border installation."

"These are the people who killed my family?" Cait danced with energy.

"They are," Anya nodded.

"I'll kill them all," Cait scowled.

"The trick will be to show some constraint. A rogue Irish operative taking out a group of apparent peaceful Algerians would only further their cause. We need them to begin the attack. You need to save the day before they are successful," Anya said.

Cait looked up at Chris who nodded, assuring she had his support.

"You are going to need a team, a plan," Chris said.

"I thought you might say that," a voice boomed from behind them. Jonas rounded the doorway and entered the room.

"You have a unique habit of disobeying orders and somehow making something good come out of it," Jonas smiled. "It's good to see you in one piece, both of you."

"I wouldn't be if Chris followed Drake Fallon's order," Cait snapped.

"No. No, you wouldn't. It sounds as though Fallon made the right call… for the mission and the team. All that ends well passes muster with me," Jonas replied. "Our interests align on this. Hussein and Naib destabilizing an already tenuous region while giving Algeria a black eye is bad for every democracy. Taking out the cell that harmed your family and furthers the trail to Naib and Hussein sounds like everyone wins."

Chris cast a glance towards Anya.

She grinned as though she swallowed the proverbial canary. Wrinkling her nose, she admitted, "Algeria is my gateway from Europe and the Middle East to Africa. I'd like things to stay tidy there."

"The team?" Chris asked, looking at Jonas.

"They arrive tomorrow morning. We head out immediately after," Jonas replied.

"Fallon's going to be alright with this?" Chris asked.

"No," Jonas shook his head. "But I've got point. This mission has some sensitivity to it. My higher ups suggested I be hands on."

"Copy that," Chris nodded.

Cait looked sullen.

"Ms. McBride, your loss would've been felt. You may not be a team member, but we are on the same side and you have proven to be a formidable operative. Fallon made a tough call on the battlefield. The impact of the mission was greater than any one of us," Jonas said. "I am personally relieved that Chris was successful."

"I'll be sure to have you pen my eulogy when the time comes," Cait replied.

"Why don't you get cleaned up? I can have my staff call up a meal. The restaurant at the hotel is a five-star. We can mission plan or even better, just relax," Anya suggested.

"I'm not gonna lie. I could eat," Chris admitted.

"I was going to ask if those flowers were edible," Cait quipped at the enormous bouquet in the hallway leading into the office.

"We'll take care of that," Anya promised. "Petro will show you to your rooms."

With a wave of her hand, the robust Russian appeared and gently swung his arm for them to proceed out of the office.

Twenty Six

The dinner that Anya called up was a veritable feast. Mechoui lamb, Tangine hare, lamb and chicken along with a variety of couscous platters dotted the table. Specialty teas were offered in steaming pots, hand poured into cups as servers wandered the table.

As the dishes were presented, a belly dancer maneuvered her shapely body around the room as music played by a band who stood in the doorway. As one plate of food was finished, another took its place until the room called it quits.

Anya sat at the head of the table. She smiled as the dancer sauntered away, accompanied by the musicians. Servers replaced the Moroccan tea settings with chilled glasses as Russian vodka was poured.

"I hope your appetites were satiated, for food at least. Chris and Cait looked absolutely famished when they arrived," Anya said, her legs tossed over an arm of her chair as she held her glass in the air. "To the safe recovery of our dear Cait and the daring rescue of gallant gunnery... former gunnery sergeant... Chris."

The table cheered, each clinking their glasses together.

"I'll never miss directly serving my country, but I will say, serving from the shadows is certainly a helluva lot more fun!" Jonas raised his glass in the air as they were quickly refilled.

The room fell silent, flickering candles sprayed warm light over the table. The ambiance was enchanting if almost discombobulating. Chris sat deep in his chair as the protein and carbohydrates his body was starved for made their way through his system.

Cait sat silently as Anya and Jonas traded stories. Chris would occasionally chime in. Largely, his mind reeled, absorbing the banter, still trying to determine who in this new life of his that he could trust.

As gregarious and talkative as Jonas and Anya could be, they were careful in the words they chose and the stories they disclosed. Chris had been in enough covert assignments with intelligence officers to pick up on that. Share, share a lot even, in each string of words, pieces of truth marred by misdirection.

Moving from Anya's vodka to bourbon, he excused himself and found the wide balcony that overlooked much of Morocco. The night air in the Mediterranean city was cool and pleasant compared to the heat of the day. His weary body relished leaning against the railing and just being still.

Halfway through his drink, he became lost in his thoughts. Downtime, when he was exhausted from a mission and had a moment of peace, he was flooded with images of Breanna and Macy. In his dreamlike state, he watched them walk toward the balcony, toward him, hand-in-hand. Macy walked with her trademark bounce, her curls bobbing as she stepped. Breanna wore a stoic smile, one that Chris had fallen in love with the moment he saw it. There was power in that smile that made him melt.

His heart clenched as they neared the railing of the balcony. Forty stories in the air didn't compute in his brain, he was desperate to see them. When they were a step away, his thoughts were disrupted.

"Are you okay out here?" the Irish voice sang through his ears. It took him a moment for it all to make sense as Breanna and Macy vanished, Cait's face came into view. "I hope I'm not interrupting, I felt like a third wheel in there," Cait quipped.

Chris didn't respond right away. He looked out past the balcony, confused, heartbroken when his wife and daughter were not still suspended alongside the balcony.

"Chris, are you alright?" Cait repeated.

"What….uhm," Chris shook his head. "Yeah, yeah. I'm fine. Just tired, I guess."

"I know that look. It's the same look I get when I see my Mum, and Sienna, my sister. Or Wilhelm and Ryan, my brothers," Cait said. "It's okay. It's part of the process. I am so sorry to interrupt."

"No. It's okay," Chris stared out at the city. "I'm not sure what's worse, that the pain lingers or that the edges start to numb."

"Both. It will always sting, but the drive to bring justice on their behalf, the edges *have* to numb. You have to be able to push forward. For your sake and for theirs," Cait said.

"Are you worried at all? When we bring down the house of cards that stripped us of our families, what will we have left?" Chris asked.

"I figure that'll be a good problem to have. Until then, there are bullets in my magazine for each one of 'em bastards," Cait cursed. "But yeah, I've thought about that."

"What do we do?" Chris asked, his voice hoarse.

"We live. *For* them," Cait's twinkling green eyes inches from his.

"Then why do we dive into the fire, ready to die?" Chris asked.

"Because it's the fastest way to return to those we love," Cait replied in a breathy whisper. "But just 'cause we're okay with dyin' don't mean it's okay we just let it happen. We'll fight to the bitter end, even if it takes longer than we might like."

Chris stared into her freckle enhanced eyes. Her breath soft on his lips. His heart on fire, though not for this moment.

"There you kids are," Anya's voice sang over the balcony. Jonas followed, lighting a cigar as he stepped out.'

"Chris?" he offered.

Shaking his head, Chris declined.

"I always like the night before a mission. There are the butterflies and racing thoughts of overplanning, but then there is the calm before the storm. The time to enjoy an evening, in the event it may be your last," Jonas declared.

"Never met an Irishman who didn't relish going to battle with the prodding of a solid hangover. Just what the enemy wants, a cranky redhead with an assault rifle in her hand," Cait quipped, taking a step away from Chris.

Anya flipped a switch and a firepit came to life between a pair of sofas. Taking a seat, she patted the open spot next to her and looked up at Chris, her bright blue eyes glistening against the flames, "Sit."

Chris hesitated before relenting, moving towards the sofa. Cait bristled slightly as Jonas leaned against the rail, enjoying his cigar. "I'm disappointed a renaissance man such as yourself didn't offer the lady a cigar," she said, moving alongside them.

Jonas grinned, "Forgive me." Taking a cigar out of his breast pocket, he lit it alongside his own and handed it to Cait.

Taking the stogie she took a long drag and breathed deep into the Moroccan night.

Anya glanced above the flames at Jonas and Cait at the rail. She always appreciated Cait's unconventional bar brawling nature. Every once in a while, a glimmer of femininity would appear, like when they first stepped out on the balcony, but would quickly be replaced with a fury ready to fight. Even if that fight was merely a norm or ideal that needed a kick in the sack.

"Quite the young fighter," Anya praised as she settled into the couch and focused on Chris.

"She is. There's so much pain bottled up in there," Chris nodded.

"I think you've become a father figure to her," Anya twisted in her seat.

Chris shrugged, "Just two warriors who've been through the grinder together."

"Perhaps," Anya cocked her head a bit. "Why'd you break mission?"

Chris stared at Anya for a long moment, "Because I had a teammate still alive on the other side of that wall."

"But what if that moment ended your mission to avenge your wife and daughter," Anya pressed, genuinely intrigued by his responses.

"I'll do the right thing. When my time comes, it comes," Chris said.

Anya looked impressed over her vodka glass, "You *were* a good Marine, weren't you?"

"I was a Marine," Chris said, his voice flat.

Anya scrambled, flashing a rare moment of being flappable. Her eyes squinted slightly, "You don't fail to impress."

Chris studied the posture of the gun runner as the firepit flames cast an ethereal light over the sultry woman. She wasn't without charm or persuasion; he would give her that. "I'm not here to impress. I'm here to get my job done."

"But you divert from your job, your goal for others," Anya pressed. "That is twice you strayed from your mission to help our dear Cait."

Chris' eyes moved from Anya and her alluring presence to Cait, freeing her lungs of cigar smoke into the air over the balcony. She bantered with Jonas. More comfortable with her bar room persona than her own natural self. Somewhere in between was a young woman shielding herself from a world that let her down, significantly.

"She carries so much pain with her. I would hope that if I was gone and someone saw Breanna or Macy in such a state that they would step up to help them through it in whatever way they can. For me, it's taking out terrorists. Mine, Breanna's, Macy's, or Cait's. You can throw yours out there, I'd take them out if I could too," Chris said, his eyes shifting back to Anya's.

For a few moments, they sat in silence, taking in the night, the words they just shared.

Anya moved subtly in such a way that her blouse opened a fraction more, revealing her skin gleaming in the firelight. Chris refused to show he took notice and leaned back against the couch and stared out at the night sky.

The entire balcony had fallen into contemplative silence before Cait pulled away from the balcony. "More typically the last to leave the bar, but I think I'll get some sleep before I put my family's killers into the ground tomorrow."

"I'm not getting any younger," Jonas admitted, bidding the group good night.

"What about you, soldier? A nightcap?" Anya cooed from her side of the couch, facing Chris more fully.

Taking in a deep breath, "A long day after a series of long days with other people's lives in my hands. I'd better call it too."

"A rain check, then," Anya proposed.

"Perhaps," Chris nodded. "Thank you for everything you have done for us. Goodnight, Anya."

Her eyes followed Chris as he rose from the sofa and walked past the firepit, disappearing into the bowels of the hotel.

Swirling the clear liquid in her glass to the light of the firepit flames, Anya tossed it back, slamming the vodka down her throat. "Boy scouts!" she muttered to herself.

Twenty Seven

Jonas, Chris, and Cait boarded a helicopter in Tangier, Morocco. Flying around the northern tip of Africa, carefully avoiding challenged air space, they made the long flight to Egypt. Settling on the north shore in a deserted spit of land along the Mediterranean Sea, they met with the rest of Jonas's team.

Outfitted with gear before they left Morocco, courtesy of Anya, they were mission ready the moment their feet hit the sand. A series of SUVs waited for them.

Fallon hopped out and greeted Jonas. Casting Chris a disapproving look and an indifferent gaze towards Cait, he motioned for Porter and Kinza to join them.

Spreading a map across the hood of one of the vehicles, he used loaded magazines as paperweights to hold it in place. "We are here, just north of Salum, in Egypt. Angel is tracking Naib's men moving in from Musaid on the Libyan side of the border. The border crossings are separated by a gap between the Libyan Gateway Emsaes and the Egyptian Gateway Salloum," Fallon waited for everyone to take in the geographic reference points.

Porter snickered from over Fallon's shoulder, "That section of the border there looks like a giant…"

"Porter!" Fallon snapped. "Can we focus?"

"No, he's right. That is a big 'ol chunk of manhood engraved on the map," Cara nodded. "Not a healthy one, though."

Jonas stifled a laugh at the inappropriate though accurate observation.

"If you children are done, I'd like to review the mission so that we can all walk away in one piece," Fallon snapped.

"All of us, or just your chosen ones?" Chris quipped.

Fallon glared at Chris, "If we can help it, *all* of us. In combat, choices need to be made. The sanctity of the mission and the team depends on us working together and following orders, if you can handle that."

"If the orders don't include leaving a team member behind, then, yes. I can handle that," Chris squared up to Fallon.

For a long moment, the two stared at each other, neither flinching.

"Gentlemen, the mission," Jonas prodded.

Fallon snapped right back into presentation mode, "The question is, do they attack both at the same time, or sequentially?"

Chris took a step closer, studying the map, ignoring Porter's observation, he replied, "They're going to attack sequential. There's no way they could take on both without one side seeing them coming. They start on the Libyan side and fire towards Egypt and mount their own retaliation. They conger up their own conflict."

Without looking up, Fallon nodded. "That's how I read it, too."

"So, what's the play? Jonas said last night, we wanted Naib's group to make their move," Chris asked.

"Yes, we need to catch them in the act. We are going to pose as a film crew for a BBC car show. They'll clearly halt us at the border, go through a thorough inspection. Our equipment truck will be trailing, hopefully arriving just in time to equip us," Fallon said as a semi-truck pulled up, its air brakes announcing the big vehicle's arrival.

"Cait, can you play the part of a show producer? Your accent and mine should be sufficient if we can keep the Americans quiet," Fallon suggested.

Cait nodded.

"Very well. Chris, Cole, you two get to be the show personalities. Jonas and Kinza will be in the tuck," Fallon instructed. "Boys, your show costars should be unloaded."

Behind the truck, the driver parked the latest Ferrari and Lamborghini. With a wave, the driver headed for the helicopter with Cara at the controls.

Porter grinned from ear to ear, "Best…mission…ever!"

As he nearly raced towards the gleaming red sports cars, he called over his shoulder, "Lambo or Ferrari?"

Chris merely shrugged.

Porter stood in front of both Italian cars, admiring both.

"Exfil?" Chris asked.

"Once Naib's men start firing, things are going to get out of hand quickly. We'll want to eliminate them quickly without either the Libyan or Egyptian guards firing on us or each other," Jonas began. "We'll need to be quick and precise. Our team back at home has calls ready to both governments timed moments before the attack. They'll drive stand down orders."

"And if they're unsuccessful?" Chris pressed.

"Let's just hope they are," Jonas said. "We get out as quick and quiet and in one piece that we can."

"There'll be casualties on both sides," Chris warned.

"It's our job to prevent that," Jonas replied.

The sound of a twelve-cylinder starting up caught their attention. With a light overwork of a clutch and gas pedal, the massive tires of a Lamborghini chirped.

"I guess we're ready to roll," Chris said, heading for the Ferrari. Jonas and Kinza headed for the tractor trailer while Cait, Fallon, and Kinza climbed into the pair of SUVs.

Chris slid into the tight quarters of the Ferrari. Once in, he was surprised with the comfort of the thin magnesium seats. It took him a moment to acclimate to the myriad of switches and controls of the Italian sports car, especially the laden steering wheel. Finding the start button, he pressed the brake pedal and fired the gleaming red car up.

With an instant rev, the engine came to life. "Alright, here we go," Chris muttered to himself. Finding first gear with the paddle shifters, Chris let the parking brake go and launched the red car forward. Zipping up alongside Fallon's SUV, he sat behind the taillights of Porter's Lamborghini. With a spin of the tires and an irreverent rush of tire smoke, Porter took off.

With a grin, Chris momentarily forgot the risk impending on their mission and took off in pursuit. Clicking through the sequential gears, Chris caught up with Porter as he rounded the somewhat phallic northwest Egyptian border with Libya. At the apex of the curve, Porter held the brake for a moment before letting off and hitting the gas. Chris poured onto the accelerator at the high point of the curve, rocketing the Ferrari past its country counterpart.

The boyish antics continued the entire way to the border crossing with Porter owning the straights and Chris overtaking on the curves. Each man was disappointed when they hit the taillights of the border traffic, winding their massive engines down to a stop.

As if Jonas saw the scenario playing out the way it did, it fit the story they were trying to sell to the Egyptian border guards. Neither driver had their papers, as they were forced to climb out of their vehicles. Pointing at the cameras throughout the vehicles and showing off the sports cars to a growing crowd for the narrative, Chris and Porter played off the attention as show stars.

Lagging behind, the SUVs led by Fallon and Cait with their accents at least derivative of the UK, arrived in a fervor. Waving press documents and personal papers at the guards, they approached as though the last thing they wanted was delay.

While the pair argued with the guards, unveiling reams of documents that fluttered in the air as Fallon seemed to lose his grip. The irate guards joined in a mad dash to collect the papers that scattered across the lanes.

"Well, he sure can put on a show," Chris whispered to Porter.

Acting as though they were headed for the rest area, they took turns leaning against the building, staring off towards the Libyan border. Using their phones in the air as though they were trying to improve their coverage, they took photos across the mirrored port and zoomed in to see if they could catch a glimpse of Naib's men.

Angel's voice told them what they needed to know. "Naib's caravan is three clicks out."

Jonas and Kinza arrived in the semi behind the line of cars. Jonas pulled off to the side to allow cars to get into the queue. Mainly, he wanted to maintain access to the cargo compartment unfettered.

"One click," Angel's voice called.

Porter cast Chris a look, "Time to get to work."

Nodding, he followed Porter as he weaved his way between the vehicles awaiting their turn to cross the border. Meeting with Jonas and Kinza, they saw Cait and Fallon slip away from the guards. An explosion rocked the station as gunfire erupted. The Egyptian guards scurried in a frenzy to assess the attack and face their foe.

A few assembled with rifles and took shots at guards at the opposing border station. Kinza tossed weapons to the team from the truck. As soon as their hands gripped an assault rifle, they didn't hesitate to grab a vest loaded with magazines and headed to the front of the conflict.

"How are we going to tell who is who?" Chris asked.

"Check your phone, X," Angel called into his ear. "I have marked each combatant with a thermal tracker, they should be lit up."

"Here, put your phone in this Picatinny holder on top of your barrel," Porter said. As they looked through the phone's screen downrange, they could see the reddish-orange silhouettes mixed in with whitish-grey ones.

"Red is bad," Angel said.

"Got it," Chris said. Sliding to a stop in the ditch that ran alongside the roadway, he shuffled on his belly until his scope and muzzle just crested the top. Taking in a deep breath, he targeted an enemy combatant, slid the phone out of the way, and used the scope to drop Naib's soldier in a single shot.

Porter lie prone next to him as Cait and Fallon assumed the same position on the opposite side of the road. As they were able to quickly eliminate the front line of the insurgents, both pairs advanced as Jonas and Kinza took a spot on either side in their absence.

Chris sprinted along the gully, leaping over the barrier, face to face with a confused Libyan border guard. The guard began to lift his weapon, wide-eyed. He became even more confused when Chris waved him out of the way. The guard shifted just enough for Chris to take a shot, dropping one of Naib's men directly behind the guard.

The guard seemed to understand that Chris was there to help. Finding cover, his weapon drawn, the guard let Chris pass without issue. Porter ran alongside and the two fell in to step together, each taking a ninety-degree view in front of them. Relying on the phone and no scope at close range, they worked through the site, looking for the reddish figures to appear on the screen.

Chris paused. Porter sensing it, stopped himself, never taking his eyes off of his own kill zone. Chris could see a thin orange shape framing one side of a pillar. Lining up his shot, he squeezed the trigger. Reeling, the shape pulled away from the pillar revealing a full silhouette. Firing again, Chris hit his shot, taking the gunman out of play.

Hearing Porter fire followed by the unmistakable, if gut-wrenching crunch of flesh and bone, he knew his team member took out someone high atop the Libyan guard building, toppling to the concrete ground below.

As they entered the heart of the Libyan border station, they encountered a new problem, Libyan guards were firing on anyone not in their uniform. Slipping into the shadows, they proceeded with more caution, knowing each moment meant more attack could be carried out on the Egyptian border and more return retaliation would ensue, with them caught in the crossfire.

Tapping Porter, he held up the 'quiet sign'. Freezing, a pair of Libyan guards entered their hallway, inching their way along, poking their muzzles into every nook. With a rhythmic nod, matching the gait of the guards, Chris struck. With his palm, he lashed out at one of the guards, driving the muzzle away from his head as a bullet went off. Porter lunged his shoulder into the second guard, driving him back into the wall, grabbing the guard's gun as he flailed.

Both guards disarmed, Chris and Porter tried to convey they were friendlies. Using his phone, Porter highlighted a thermal mass. Chris snapped his assault rifle and dropped the mass.

Horrified and confused as they were kept alive, the guards followed to the body. They were more horrified to see the man Chris shot was in a Libyan uniform. With his muzzle, Porter flipped the dead man's hat away, to better reveal his face. "One of yours?" Porter asked.

The guards talked rapidly between themselves, it was clear they didn't know the man. Widening the scene, they could count half a dozen such masses on the screen. As a shot rang from the other side of the building, the number dropped to five.

Handing their weapons back to them, Chris and Porter trusted they wouldn't be shot in the back and resumed their search. A pat on his shoulder from one of the guards who followed them closely, pointed. Swiveling, Chris swung his gun over. The camera picked up a shape on the thermal. With his naked eye, Chris shot, chipping a pillar. The figure moved, further revealing himself.

"That's one!" Porter called as he used his phone to confirm.

Chris lined up his shot and hit his target.

"Four more," Porter counted.

A shot rang from directly behind them. Spinning, they saw Cait standing over a body. "Three," she grinned. "That one was sneakin' up on you."

Three successive shots later, Fallon called over their earpieces, "Zero. Caught a trio on the roof setting up some sort of rig. Looked like a suicide rocket. It would fire to the Egypt station and then detonate explosives here."

"Angel confirm," Jonas' voice called.

“Copy that, Chief,” Angel said. “Confirmed. No additional marked targets.”

“That’s our cue, get to exfil,” Jonas called.

“Uhm, that might be difficult,” Porter said as the Libyan guards turned their weapons on them. Laying his weapon down, his hands in the air, “Uh, fellas, we’re friends, remember?”

Chris pointed his muzzle to the ground but tried to maintain possession. “I get it, you want to sort things out,” he said, having no idea whether or not they spoke English.

At least for this pair, it didn’t matter. Cait stuck with such speed and ferocity. With the butt of her assault rifle, she hammered down on the back of the skull of one and then spun, reversing her grip on the weapon, swinging it like a baseball bat, clocked the other in the jaw.

Without a wasted second, they sprinted. Shouts for them to halt and gunfire sprang at them. As they ran, Angel called through their earpieces, “Good news and bad news team. Both the Egyptian and Libyan embassies received the message and are standing down their guards towards one another and are sending joint teams for an investigation which will highlight Naib’s team. The bad news is, they want to hold you for questioning.”

Streaking back the way they came, they worked to avoid capture as well as being shot when they refused to stop. “I have an idea, but it's going to be a bit awkward. I recommend you call shot gun!" Chris called.

"Aw, crap," Jonas groaned, realizing what Chris meant. "Shotgun."

"See you at the cars," Chris grinned. Sliding into the ditch, they sprinted back into Egyptian land, trying to avoid the chaos and confusion from the attack. Without breaking stride, he launched himself over the low-slung hood of the Ferrari and started the engine. Cait arrived first with Jonas in tow.

"Get in!" Chris called as the exhaust note caught the attention of the guards. Cait rolled her eyes and let Jonas in before squeezing into his lap and slamming the door shut.

Porter brought the Lamborghini to life as Fallon and Kinza arrived. The two men stared at the remaining seat. "Just get in!" Porter urged as guards raced towards them.

Chris already had the car in gear and spinning the tires, brought the Ferrari in a tight arch around the traffic that snarled as the border locked down. Weaving his way through the tight spaces, never softening his foot on the gas, Chris jetted away from the border.

After considerable wrangling and endless grumbling, Porter gave chase. Guards climbed into their military trucks and started pursuit. Breaking through the last of the jumble of cars that took up the expanse of the roadway, Chris was able to wind through the gears. He could see in his rearview, though substantially behind, the red gleam of the Lamborghini was able to keep pace.

Porter chuckled as he peered through his rearview at the futile chase from the military trucks. His enjoyment was short lived as the jumble of limbs in the passenger seat inadvertently struck the mirror, freeing it from its mooring.

“Don’t make me stop this car!” Porter teased.

“We will never speak of this…ever,” Fallon growled, as he was under Kinza, sitting atop his lap.

Chris brought the Ferrari to a sliding halt several miles from the border. A helicopter was waiting for them. Cara sat at the ready with a mounted gun.

“Well, that looked cozy,” Cara called as the team scrambled out of the Ferrari.

“I didn’t mind,” Jonas shrugged.

“Don’t be getting any ideas I enjoyed it, big fella,” Cait growled.

The Lamborghini slid in next to the Ferrari, kicking up sand at it came to a stop. Porter jumped out, followed by Fallon and Kinza rolling out of their seat onto the ground in a ball.

Cara burst into laughter. In her earpiece, she called, "Please tell me you got that on satellite, Angel."

"Recorded in the event we ever need to blackmail either of them," Angel's voice called back.

"Let's go. Dragonfly, as always, good to see you," Jonas said, leading the team into the bay of the helicopter.

Twenty Eight

The team met in a board room inside Anya's grand hotel in Tangier, Morocco. Showered and assessed for injuries, they gathered around a long *thuya* wood table. Anya pushed her way through the double doors, striding with the regal confidence she consistently oozed, tossing a nod to her men for them to wait outside.

She paused, assessing the room while letting eyes fall on her as her presence was acknowledged. Finally offering a smile, she strode forward with confidence and took a spot at the head of the table.

"Giving a quick count of heads, it looks like you all made it," Anya said. "That is good."

"We are grateful for your assistance with supplies," Jonas said.

"All for a good cause. A good, mutual cause," Anya said. "It seems like the mission was a success."

"Was it?" Chris asked. "We allowed the Egyptian border station to get attacked, two men were killed, three more injured with guards at either post injured during the siege."

"It was a risk," Jonas admitted.

"But you have to look at the results," Anya said, her voice calm. Snapping on a monitor, the thermal footage captured by Angel was matched with surveillance coming out of General Naib's camp. "Those pieces of footage along with Lanikov's evidence will put the world on notice. They were specifically trying to antagonize nations that Hussein claims to be friendly with."

"It's proof he is an instigator, wanting nothing more than to maintain instability in the region," Chris understood.

"Not just maintain it, ignite it. Not just in the Middle East and Africa, throughout Europe, Asia and if he can pull it off, the west," Jonas added.

"So, yes. Your effort yesterday was a success," Anya concluded.

"There is more work to be done. The mission that brought you're here is finally upon us," Jonas said. "The data retrieved from Lanikov is more than breadcrumbs. It has bank accounts, transactions, travel data, and even surveillance photos. It is enough to bring the whole cell down."

Chris felt his eyebrow quiver in anticipation.

"Then let's go get them!" Porter said eagerly.

"We're putting the plans together as we speak. I need to get the team to Camp Green right away," Jonas said. Turning to Chris, he added, "We're going to get justice for your family."

The words barely registered for Chris. For the first time in weeks, he wasn't numb. The burning in his stomach to get his hands on General Naib, Hussein and anyone who had a hand in the death of his wife and daughter returned. It was painful and beautiful at the same time. The searing ache made him feel closer to Breanna and Macy.

Cait shifted in her seat.

"Ms. McBride, you have been a tremendous asset," Jonas said. "Anya, we appreciate your support."

"I'm grateful your new operative was able to bring Matthias back. Hussein is an evil plague. For someone who lives in the space I do, that should tell you something. Bring him down, Jonas," Anya stated.

The team pushed away from the table. As they collected themselves and began to filter out through the double doors, Chris eyed Cait. Chris knew her soul had been darkened by Hussein and his regime of terror the same as his.

Calling after the team leader, he stopped him short of exiting, "What about Cait?"

Jonas turned, glimpsing the spirited woman over his shoulder, "She's proven to be a solid operative. We are about to enter into missions of high sensitivity. I'm afraid it is team only from here on."

"She has as much to stake as any of us," Chris pleaded.

Jonas looked squarely at Chris, "You two have personal stakes in bringing down Hussein. The team has world democracy at stake."

"She's capable. I can tell you firsthand, when missions go awry, and they will, that drive can pull a team through," Chris said.

"Look, there's no way an outsider is coming to Camp Green," Jonas said. With a long sigh, he contemplated, "If she so chooses, I'll find a spot in the mission for her. She can join up with us in the field."

Chris smiled, appreciative, "Thank you."

Jonas shared kisses on her cheeks with Anya and exited after the team.

"I don't need anyone fightin' my battles for me," Cait snapped.

"It's *our* battle," Chris said. "We have different reasons for fighting it, but it's the same fight."

"Well, thank you, just the same," Cait said, looking up at Chris' eyes.

"We'll let you know the when and where," Chris promised.

Anya wrapped around the pair, cutting off Chris' exit out of the board room. Leaning in close, she pressed towards his lips and whispered, "When the business with Hussein is over, you should come back and talk. There is a lot we can do together."

"I'll weigh my career choices once Hussein is buried," Chris said.

Anya grinned a wicked grin, "I wasn't just talking business."

"Yeah," Chris nodded, his face not offering any emotion. "Thanks for everything, Anya."

"Take care, Gunny," Anya called.

"Gunny's dead," Chris corrected.

"Right. The mysterious Patriot X."

Twenty Nine

The team wasted no time after arriving at Camp Green to assemble in the briefing room. A wall of screens was filled with images. Digital lines spread throughout, linking documents, photos, and map locations.

Headshots of Barriq Hussein and General Ravi Naib dotted the matrix. Towards the end of the line, the familiar face of reporter Clint Newsom started to appear. A few frames further, a new face implicated in connection to the cell caught Chris' eye. Secretary of State Janice Green was the final connection, linked to Newsom.

A long line drew from Green to Hussein, the insurgents in Ansar al-sharia and Ambassador Rogers. Seeing an official so high in the U.S. government involved even indirectly with the terror cell made Chris bristle. Seeing Mahaz Maher's face in the midst of the images did not improve his mood.

Jonas caught Chris' gaze. "Hard to believe, isn't it? A trusted public official is somehow involved in all this. While you've been busy trying to right the wrongs, she's been denigrating your assault on the embassy and lobbying for Maher's release," he informed.

"Nice to know our public officials have our best interests at heart," Chris fumed.

"You are on the precipice of bringing it all down," Jonas said with a nod. "Come on, let's run through how we are either going to capture General Naib and see that he pays for his crimes or we put a bullet in his head."

"Sounds like a mission worth planning," Chris agreed, joining Jonas and the team around the table.

"Here is what our intelligence has gathered," Jonas leaned over the table littered with maps and pictures complementing the screens. "General Naib is staging an attack in Irbid, Jordan. No big surprise, Barriq Hussein was recently there holding a rally. Currently, he is holed up in an Afghanistan bunker. We want to target him while he is on the move to his mission base outside of Amman, Jordan."

"We know his travel route or where that base is?" Fallon asked.

Jonas looked up at Fallon and then panned the rest of the team, "No, we don't. Intel has picked up Naib's scouts and deliveries into Amman. The activity has been within a fifteen-mile radius of the city, on the southeast quadrant towards Irbid. They will continue to isolate the exact location while we assemble."

"We've worked with less," Fallon nodded.

"Our plan will be to separate General Naib from his men so we can attempt to take him alive. If the mission breaks down, the objective will change to terminate and send home a photograph. No one left standing," Jonas said.

"From the moment of Naib's takedown, we'll be on the clock to capture Hussein. There is a team trailing him. I have requested they act in support and await our arrival before they take action. Chris, I know you will want to be there when he is taken down. It adds risk, but the support team is under orders to take him out only if things go sideways before he can go underground," Jonas shared. "The moment Naib is dead or in our possession, we move to Hussein. He is currently at a Nobel Peace rally. They are having a dinner in his honor."

Porter let out a grin, "Can we take him down while he is on stage, in front of everyone? Can we?"

"That would be a bonus," Jonas admitted.

Chris could hardly contain himself. The people responsible for Breanna and Macy's deaths were finally about to receive justice. Chris stared at the monitor on the wall showing Hussein smiling amongst a panel of dignitaries as he made a speech about the West's need to push for peace and suppress their imperialistic desires to change and control the Arab world.

Another screen showed the Secretary of State Janice Green at a press conference. Chris couldn't tell what she was announcing.

His eyes followed the trail of evidence. Hussein's reign of terror started long before the bombing in Stone Bay and had affected so many people around the world. Chris' eyes couldn't help landing on the destroyed North Carolina bridge.

THIRTY

The team dispersed from the meeting room in Camp Green to their quarters to prepare for the flight to Jordan and their mission.

Chris was restless. Wandering the verdant grounds, his mind strayed from the focus it usually adhered to prior to a mission. He was more ready for this mission than any in his time in the Corps, yet there was a fog muddying his thoughts. He couldn't figure out what was gnawing at him.

Pausing, he watched a pair of dragonflies chase each other from fountain to fountain, zig-zagging their way through flowers and bushes.

"In a world with so much beauty and peace, there is so much corruption and violence," Jonas' voice boomed from behind Chris.

The former Marine Gunnery Sergeant didn't show the slightest surprise. He just kept staring at the scenery.

"Didn't figure I'd sneak up on you," Jonas admitted. "You ready for this?"

Chris paused before he spoke, "I am."

"But?"

"I'm not sure," Chris said.

Jonas took in a deep breath as he stood beside Chris. "When you are fighting to take down the people that harmed your loved ones, there is a fear that once you complete that mission, you close the final door on them. Until then, you get to carry them around with you for a little while longer."

The two stood in silence for several long minutes.

"The fight will still be there, it just changes. You won't be gunning to put down the people that killed your family. You'll fight to ensure their lives have a legacy. That your time as a Marine meant something. You're a patriot. You're a husband and a father. That hasn't changed. It never will," Jonas said. With a large hand clamping down on Chris' shoulder, he added, "Let's give them peace. Then we'll worry about their legacy."

As Jonas walked away, Chris' gaze remained fixed on the dragonflies. "Thanks, Jonas."

Kneeling to pray for the first time since Breanna and Macy's funeral, Chris was alerted by a knock on his door just as he said "Amen."

Porter stood in the doorway. His affect was in stark contrast to his usual jovial self. "There is a press conference taking place right now that we thought you'd want to see."

"Care to tell me what it's about?" Chris asked.

Porter wrinkled his nose. "Jonas is still gathering information… probably best you just see it for yourself."

Chris nodded and followed Porter in silence. Not known for his patience, Chris' mind reeled. Wondering if there had been another attack or their mission to Jordan was being scrubbed.

Following Porter into the situation room, he saw Jonas wearing a similar expression as all eyes turned to Chris as he entered. The team was dressed for the mission and appeared ready to go.

Jonas stood in front of the room and flashed Chris an apologetic glance as he began. "This news conference was just aired. It took place from the White House Press Briefing Room. I'll let Secretary of State Janice Green speak for herself."

Moving the feed to the beginning of the conference, Jonas turned on the volume.

The United States Secretary of State welcomed the reporter pool, a wide and energetic smile spread across her lips. "Thank you all for coming on short notice. This an unprecedented carriage of justice and multinational participation.

A few months ago, the Pakistani embassy outside of Washington D.C. was infiltrated. Violating multiple sanctions of sovereignty and worldwide civility, a man was forcefully removed from the embassy compound. Without a warrant, without due process, the man was abducted, bound, and delivered to the Israeli embassy.

Working for months with delegates from Israel and Pakistan, we have secured a release of this individual back into Pakistani custody. There are conspiracy theories that link this man to horrific crimes, but these theories are without legal merit. The United States, the United Nations, and world order demand that we conduct ourselves with decorum and policy and principle. Vigilantism will not be tolerated, most particularly on an embassy's sovereign soil.

My team and the Secret Service are working with Israeli and Pakistani agents to secure the safe transfer of the individual. Pakistan has assured, that if their citizen is indeed legally linked to any crimes, that justice will be carried out.

Here, in the U.S., we adhere to due process. Thank you."

The situation room sat stunned at the news. Most faces fell to disbelief at what they just watched. All but one. Chris' eyes were fixed in a glare. One that any operative could recognize.

"They are releasing Mahaz Maher," Cara shook her head in disbelief.

"Why would Israel release him? I mean, Chris, you chose their embassy for a reason," Porter asked.

"It means Israel got what they needed from him. They're done with him," Fallon stated.

"Why? Why would the Secretary of State want him so badly that she is willing to go through so much trouble and deal with a country that has links to terrorism?" Porter asked.

"Political favor, some backroom deal? We'll find out," Jonas said.

"What happens to Maher?" Cara asked.

"It depends on how valuable he is any more to his cell. They'll execute him because he is burned. They'll bury him in a hole somewhere until he is useful again. Build a statue in his honor," Jonas quipped.

Fallon looked terse, "They'll immediately put him back in action with his fingerprints on an attack. Show the world, especially the west, how they got one over on the United States."

"What happened to not dealing with terrorists?" Cara asked.

"What happened to politicians serving their citizens?" Porter added.

"I can't let the exchange happen," Chris spoke for the first time. Halting the conversation.

"Chris…," Jonas started. "I can't imagine what you are feeling, but this deal is out there. Worldwide involving a close ally. This is too hot, even for us. Any action taken on that stage, no matter how warranted, will be viewed as terrorism. Everything we are doing, you are doing… the ability to take down Naib and Hussein, they are the ones who ordered the attack on Stone Bay… will be lost."

"I'm not asking and I'm not asking for your help," Chris said.

"Secretary Green will have the Secret Service, Marines, hell, maybe your Raider Team, ensuring the security of the exchange. Never mind the Israelis and the Mossad, though they might just let you walk in," Jonas said. "We have ID'd Maher. We'll tag him. I promise you, we will help you find him after the exchange. After we bring down Naib and Hussein."

Chris didn't like the answer. He was prepared to rip through an army to not allow Maher free, but he relented. He knew Jonas was right. Even with all of their resources, the odds of a successful mission with all of the scrutiny and power of the U.S. and Israeli military bearing down, they had no choice.

Fallon turned to Chris, "Let this fuel you. We have two tough missions coming up. Use this to hone your focus razor sharp. We'll help you finish this. All of it."

Chris was taken aback. The words were among the first from Fallon directed his way that weren't derogatory or demeaning. Nodding, he replied, "Let's get General Naib."

Thirty One

Cait leaned against a post holding up a ragged canopy, the only shade within sight on the dirt tarmac of the makeshift airport. With the city of Amman, Jordan visible at the horizon, the site was positioned between the metropolitan area and the Syrian border.

As the team piled out of the helicopter, she eyed the crew, her eyes landing on Chris. "Took you long enough. My Irish skin isn't cut out for sitting in the desert all day," she quipped.

"Glad you're here, Cait," Chis said.

"And miss the fun of takin' down a demon like General Naib? I wouldn't miss it for anything," she grinned.

"Anya's helicopter just dumped you and took off?" Chris asked.

"The Duchess has pull in many regions. The Jordanians in particular don't like her," Cait shrugged.

Jonas looked at his watch as the rest of the team stood behind him.

"What's the play, let them attack and clean up the mess?" Cait asked.

"Not this time. We're taking him down the first chance we've got. There are three intercepts – Amman, Irbid, or in transit. Amman is heavily protected by Jordanian forces. We don't know if Naib will travel with the convoy. That leaves Irbid. East of Irbid in Ar-Ramtha. Naib is planning a missile attack on Daraa, Syria. They'll be using U.S. and Israeli ordinances. As one of the few nations in this region to sign official treaties with Israel, this will cause untold turmoil," Jonas said. "We need to locate and capture Naib and take out his operation in Ar-Ramtha. Thirty mikes into our mission, our intelligence team will alert the Jordanian government. Let them be the heroes to have stopped the terror attack and preserve the border with Syria."

"We have a lot of ground to cover, does intel have an idea where the attack will be staged?" Fallon asked.

Angel's voice entered the conversation via their earpieces, "Naib's lead team has secured a sight just outside of Ar-Ramtha.

The Jordan University of Science and Technology has a research site there. Our satellite thermals detect what could be missile banks transported in overnight. We have been tracking his envoys to that location all morning."

"He's breaking them up as opposed to a major convoy, smart," Fallon said.

"We'd have little chance of targeting him en route. The Ar-Ramtha site is our only option," Cara added.

"We'll have to wait until the last arrival. That will be Naib. By the time he does show, they'll be ready to fire, we'll need to strike quick," Jonas said.

"Porter, you'll be overwatch. Cait, as I understand you have considerable knowledge of explosives, you'll be with Fallon on the missiles. Kinza, you need to take out their comms, both internal and external. Find a fallback to be secondary overwatch. Chris, you're with me. We'll be going after General Naib," Jonas directed.

No one flinched among the team. All standing at the ready. Taking that as an indicator, Jonas added, "Let's mount up."

Nodding to Cara, they followed her to the helicopter. Climbing in, they instinctively sat next to their mission partner. Fallon reviewed with Cait what supplies they brought to aid their objective.

Jonas sat next to Chris, who stared out of the helicopter window. The team leader let the former Gunnery Sergeant to his own thoughts as they closed in on the far western edge of Ar-Ramtha. Landing the helicopter outside of a vehicle depot.

"Angel has located a fleet of university vehicles. These are what we'll use to get to the objective. They are frequently used to bring research students that direction and won't generate much attention," Jonas said.

Selecting a pair of vans, they transferred their gear and piled into the vehicles. Dressed in colloquial *Shemaghs* wrapped around their heads, their trip through Ar-Ramtha was without incident. Parking the vans at a location not far from Naib's site that was consistent with satellite surveillance photos, they exited quickly.

Wasting no time, they began their short treks to their given assignments. Porter separated first. In a near run, he knew he had to get into position before the rest of the team could. Moving to the edge of the Jordan-Syria border, he was able to use a series of six-hundred-meter hills to find a high point for overwatch.

Letting the team know he was in position; he unzipped the case for his Mk22 MRAD Barrett sniper rifle. Methodically swinging the scope through the objective theater, he relayed what he observed, "I've got eyes on four separate missile launch stations, all lined up within one hundred meters of the other, four-man teams each with a pair of overwatch observing the field. Comms center is the university outpost. A temporary antenna is erected tripod style with wires strung through the southwest window, no guards. The command center looks to be the building itself, which is, let's just say, teeming with guards. I count a half dozen armed security detail outside and enough vehicles to more than double that count."

"Copy that, 2K," Jonas called.

"X-ray, command echoes 2K's count. With thermal, we can identify four more enemy combatants. Our intel shows the complex has a subterranean level. Based on our thermals, I would bet you will find the primary objective there," Angel shared into their earpieces.

"Clear copy, Angel. All teams proceed," Jonas said.

Aban Kinza knew his task was the pivotal piece. If communications were left unfettered, the team wouldn't stand a chance versus a timely response from the widespread team of Naib's cell. Moving cautiously through the open space, he had two areas he needed to avoid in order to prevent detection – the missile site overwatch pairs and the six guards rotating around the command center.

A shallow ravine ran alongside the dirt road leading to the command center affording Kinza some degree of concealment as he kept low while he moved. Porter's voice hastened through his earpiece, "Gazi, hold!"

Kinza froze in place, flattening himself to the bottom of the ravine, hoping the gear on his back didn't rise above the surface.

Porter reported, "You are clear of the missile crew overwatch, you have one bogey from the command center with eyes on. He's turning…he's heading to the front of the CC. Go now, go now!"

Staying low, Kinza scrambled towards the communication tower. Maneuvering his pack with the Spread Spectrum Jammer, he slithered to within range. With a signal analyzer, he found a spot that was within ideal range. Pushing the communication jammer forward, he dug into the sand at the bottom of the ravine and dusted the pack with more sand to provide a level of concealment.

Whispering into his own comm, he declared, "Jammer is in place. Moving to secondary overwatch."

"Copy that, Gazi," Jonas called. "Teams, ready to engage."

Kinza retreated to a soft bend in the dirt drive. Keeping low in the ravine, he used his low position as his observational position. From that vantage, he could monitor the road inbound, the southernmost missile sites, and the front entrance to the

General Naib's command center. "Gazi is at secondary overwatch."

"All teams go," Jonas called softly into his radio with a nod to Chris.

Waiting was the hardest part for Cait. She and Fallon split the overwatch teams, with Fallon taking the northernmost pairs while she focused on the southern pair.

With the word go, she pulled the trigger on the guard that she had locked on, tracking his movements. Of the four overwatch guards that she was assigned, he was posted in the northernmost position. That was the only reason his life was taken moments before the next three. Cait watched just long enough to see the telltale shudder of the guard's body. Without a blink, she rotated her sight to the next guard who spun in surprise, dropping him before he could understand his partner's fate.

In a sprint, Cait moved to the second overwatch site. Leaping over a low-slung bush, she fired at a guard who turned her direction. By the time she landed, she slung a tactical knife with her left hand and finished off the final overwatch in her assignment with a bullet to the chest just as he tried to raise his weapon in response.

Kicking the body to the side, she assumed their overwatch position, but with an entirely different intent. She used her assault rifle scope to surveil the scene. Each missile site was manned by two men, one who worked the targeting system, the other the ordinance launch.

Drake Fallon slunk closer to his objectives than Cait had. When Jonas called 'go', he launched. Springing from a shallow bush for concealment, Fallon's arm was wrapped around the first guard. With a smooth draw of his arm, the guard's throat was slit. In the same movement, he had propelled himself towards the second guard, kicking away his weapon. The impact knocked the guard to the ground.

Falling heavy on the guard's throat, he plunged his ka-bar into his throat. In a flash, he was on one knee targeting the second pair of guards. Lining them up, he squeezed the trigger twice. Through his scope, he watched one man fall followed by the second. "Northern overwatch dispatched," he called into his earpiece.

"Copy that, Beast. You are clear to neutralize the site crews," Angel declared over the airwaves.

Fallon looked across at Cait, who was waiting for his response as though she was annoyed that he had taken too long. With a nod, they moved towards one another and split the missile sites below them, each peeling off again to their north and south objectives. This time, they were cleared to fire. Their silenced assault rifles would muffle their assault somewhat, but not enough to avoid detection from the nearby sites or even alert the command center guards.

Moving swiftly, they approached and easily took out the central missile sites. Attracting attention from the outermost launch crews, they each had a two on one fight on their hands. Finding cover to avoid the oncoming fire, the missile crews called into radios only to look at each other in confusion and frustration.

Cait took advantage of her crew's confusion and moved aggressively towards their position, firing as she did. Dropping the first who instinctively peered towards the command center when he realized their comms were down. The second had taken the offensive and exchanged shots downrange with Cait.

Sliding with her back against a boulder, she watched the dirt splash up into the air from her right. Rolling left, she landed on her belly, her elbows propping her up into a firing position. No-scoping, she fired, moving her aim as the bullets flew until she saw the man drop.

Fallon raced forward, sliding into the first launch station, firing as he moved low to the ground, taking out the first missile team. Like Cait, he faced an alert second team. One ignored him and prepared to launch the missile. Ignoring the AK47 rounds rattling towards him, Fallon dropped the man at the missile controls. Rolling out of the spray of gunfire, he took cover against the missile terminal. Before he could counter the attack, Porter's voice sounded in his ear, "Missile crew cleared, Beast."

Relieved, Fallon called, "Copy that, 2k."

With a motion of his hand, he alerted Cait to move onto the next phase of their assault.

Jonas turned towards to Chris to see if he was ready, but the former Marine was already moving towards the objective. Their path to the command center was the most open of the assault roles. The vehicles providing the most cover. They knew with the numbers they had to contend with, this would not be a quiet part of the operation.

Both Chris and Jonas wrapped around the SUVs parked in front, trying to take angles that would corral Naib's men to avoid multiple shooting angles. Moving foot over foot, their assault rifle optics downrange, they closed in.

The first guard to spy them targeted Jonas. As the gunman's eyes widened, Jonas fired. Quickly acquiring a second target, he continued pressing forward, intent on putting the terror cell on their heels.

Chris pushed in from the opposite side, he had precalculated his first three targets allowing him to move with speed. Placing shots above their presumed Kevlar or ceramic vests so that he didn't encounter unpleasant surprises from recovered targets.

He scarcely watched the first guard react before he was on to the next gunman. Pushing into the man, he held his limp body for a moment of cover as he tracked his third moving target. Catching the third guard in the base of the skull as he darted for cover, Chris let go of the man he was holding, landing him in a heap at his feet.

Dropping, he crouched by the steps of the command center as bullets whizzed over his head, inches from ending his day short. Wide-eyed, he wheeled, swinging his sight in front of him. As he saw the man fixing his aim, trying to hone his shot, he suddenly rocked as multiple shots him in the chest and a final one in the head even as he was falling.

Chris caught Jonas' eye, who shrugged an apology, "Took me a sec to locate the third. I think Kinza delivered the headshot."

"Better late than never," Chris muttered. "And that was the easy part."

Lining up at the command center door, they readied for entry. By now, Naib's men would be alerted and ready. The wily general would likely have security measures in place for his location.

"Odds the door is boobied?" Chris asked.

"Claymore pulls, at least," Jonas nodded. "Let's blow it."

Jonas began pulling breaching cord out of his pack and made a rough rectangle and moved back as Chris jumped over the side of the porch. Pressing the detonator, the door shattered inward in a storm of sharp wood and metal bits.

"Chief, hold!" Kinza called through the earpiece. Through the smoke and dust, he could just make out an armed figure peering through the debris, ready to fight whoever blew the door. With a squeeze of the trigger, the figure fell. "Clear. You're on your own until exfil. We'll watch for reinforcements."

"Copy that," Jonas called. Casting a glance at Chris, who responded with a quick nod, they rolled through either side of the doorway, each taking a pie shaped sweep of the first room in the command center.

Each side had a hallway with a wooden desk blocking the doorway. Jonas took a guess that at least one of Naib's men was hiding in wait behind the wooden barrier. Shaking his head in disbelief, he fired a series of shots through the desk. Tossing a flashbang further into the room, he leapt over the desk, finding a man gasping behind the barrier.

Jonas lined a mercy shot at the man's forehead, "It's wood. Bullets pass through wood." Squeezing the trigger, he scanned the room, seeing two men scurrying into the hall beyond, holding their ears. As one, in his disorientation from the flashbang, ran into the door jamb on the way through, Jonas took the opportunity to take him out.

Chris stood at an angle to the desk barrier, his assault rifle pointed just above. His patience paid off as an unfortunate peer over the barrier cleared Chris' path forward. Pressing his back to the doorway, he tossed his flashbang towards the next hallway, driving the two guards occupying that space towards him. Easy targets for burst shots apiece, Chris pushed forward.

The hallways merged and Chris and Jonas stood shoulder to shoulder, staring at a single door. "Subterranean level," Chris acknowledged.

As they began their approach, a small, low hatch on the door slid open and a barrel protruded. Grabbing Jonas by the shoulder, Chris yanked him to the ground and then pushed their boots against the floor to back around the corner as bullets peppered the hallway, penetrating the thin walls of the building.

"Sounds like a Russian Kord," Chris said.

"That's not good," Jonas said. "I was wondering how we were going to breach. I think they gave us our answer."

Chris nodded, pulling a scalable offensive hand grenade from his tactical vest, he stacked a trio of incendiaries together. Receiving a nod from Jonas, Chris lobbed the device down the hall and the two covered themselves.

The over-pressurized grenade easily destroyed the door at the end of the hallway and instantly ended the barrage from the Kord heavy machine gun. Shielding themselves from the falling bits of building as the entire structure was rendered unstable, they shook off the debris, gathered themselves, and pressed forward.

Proceeding forward in a crouched position, moving foot over foot, their thermal scopes highlighting anything with warm blood Chris and Jonas carefully made their way to the shattered doorway. Beyond a toppled mounted gun, gunner and spotter scattered down the steep stairwell.

Shouts and the sound of foot traffic below told them everything they needed to know, Jonas cast a glance at Chris, "We have a whole team down there."

Nodding, Chris motioned for him to take his right flank while he trained his visual pie-shaped sweep to the left. As the lower floor began to take shape in Chris' view, he assessed their odds of making it to the bottom and surviving an onslaught from Naib's men below.

Past the stairwell, four feet from the final step, Chris spied a pair of concrete buttresses that provided structural support for the subterranean space. He wasn't thrilled with his odds, but he signaled Jonas to be ready. The team leader watched Chris in horror as he realized what the former Marine's plan was.

Without waiting for discussion, or for the men below to continue to settle into position, Chris launched himself. His left leg tucked and extended his right leg, he slid down the steps like a runner in baseball trying to avoid a tag. As he neared the bottom, he began firing in the direction of the lower hall. The surprised terror cell gunmen adjusted their aim to the lower figure as Chris slid by and pressed himself between the concrete base of the buttresses.

Jonas pressed his back to the stairwell wall and descended. Taking careful aim as all attention swung towards Chris, he was able to knock out two men on the left. Spinning across the stairs, he slammed his back on the opposite wall, able to sight another gunman.

Chris recovered from his slide. The gunmen whirled from Chris to Jonas giving him an opportunity to fire cleanly, eliminating another man on the left. As Jonas continued to work the opposite side, he called, "I got this Chris, go…go!"

Understanding that Jonas saw an opening, Chris slipped from his cover and raced down the hall. The thermal scope remained clear as he maneuvered down the hallway, searching for General Naib's location. Suddenly a red shape burst into his scope followed by a second. Dropping to his knee, he fired two burst shots, one into each shape.

Approaching, he saw that they were securing either side of a door. He had found the general.

Cautiously pushing against the heavy door as he slowly turned the handle, he was surprised it wasn't locked. By the time he realized why, it was too late. Naib had two men on either side waiting for him with a third directly in front of him. Each pointing an assault rifle at his head. Before he could react, the man in front fired, missing Chris' ceramic flak jacket and burrowing expanding hot steel into his side.

Chris dropped to all fours, his mind racing. He wasn't thinking about being shot. He wasn't worried about being shot again. He was trying to figure out how he could recover enough to get a shot off before they finished their job.

General Naib calmly strode forward. Nodding to one of his men to secure the door, while another cleared Chris of his weapons. Carrying a series of explosives, the man on security detail disappeared into the hallway.

Chris understood, Naib's team was getting thin. In the event whoever was coming to rescue Chris was successful making it that far, they would blow the entire building and everyone in it.

Standing directly over the slumped former Marine, the terror cell leader cast a short nod. A man grabbed either side of Chris and pulled him to his feet. Naib stared at Chris' face and into his eyes. A curious smile crossing his lips.

"Who are you? I would like to know who I am sending to hell," Naib questioned, pacing in a tight square in front of Chris.

Chris remained silent.

"You are part of this group causing so many problems for us, yes? This... Patriot X?"

Chris returned a stare before releasing a grin, "I *am* Patriot X. Every father, brother, sister who has lost someone at the hands of your cowardice is Patriot X."

"You attack my men and I. You defy Geneva Convention treaties..."

"Geneva? We aren't soldiers restricted to military code or country politics. Our sole purpose is to chase down pathetic cowards that hide behind innocent people and civil society," Chris laughed.

Naib shrugged with a nonchalant wave, "I am just a soldier. I carry out orders."

"Orders to kill innocent women and children? What soldier would knowingly comply with those orders?" Chris spat.

"I know of no such acts. We protect the peaceful motivations of Barriq Hussein, the revered bringer of peace."

"That is why he had you give the order to destroy a bridge in North Carolina killing civilians?" Chris pressed.

Naib grinned, "Living so close to a military installation carrying out atrocities against my people. No doubt connected to your military… like you. Like your family. They are not innocent. They are complicit."

Chris' eyebrow twitched with Naib's declaration. His last images of Breanna and Macy flew through his mind. The rage he had suppressed for so many months came flooding back. In a sudden surge, he struck.

The guards released their grips ever so slightly with his weakened stance as he strung the conversation with Naib out. Twisting both of his arms, he stepped backward, pulling the guards together in front of him. In the same motion, he unholstered one of the men's sidearms. Before they could spin back towards him, he delivered a shot into each of them.

As the guards fell to the ground, Chris and Naib squared off in the space they vacated. Both men squeezed the trigger without hesitation., each man hitting the other. Naib fell to the ground, holding a hand just above his clavicle. Chris rocked backward before dropping to a knee, coughing to get air back into his lungs as he recovered from a point blank shot to his armored vest.

Instead of recovering his weapon for another shot, Naib grabbed his radio and called the order, "*Tabda*! *Tabda*!"

He waited expectantly as Chris struggled to stand. Naib's face fell to one of complete disappointment as the door swung open and Jonas pushed through, a series of detonators dangling from his clenched fist.

Relenting to his situation, Naib tossed the radio down. "You are enviable foes. Your capture of Maher from the embassy, that was you, wasn't it?" the general looked at Chris. Chris nodded. "So un-American of you, ignoring so many international rules. You should kill me, but you won't. You want me to stand trial in some ridiculous world court. Torture me, see what secrets you can pull out of me."

Chris stared at Naib in silence.

"Allah rewards those who live out his message," Naib assured as he choked on the blood that welled in his throat.

"You don't carry his message," Chris snapped.

"I'll be a hero to my people. Like Maher, I'll only be more empowered," Naib sneered.

"Yeah, I'm not going to take that chance this time," Chris said. In a blur, he brought the handgun up.

Naib's eyes widened as Chris delivered a bullet to his forehead.

Without the slightest hint of human remorse, Chris snapped a photo of the slain general for confirmation and turned to Jonas.

"Let's get out of here," Chris said, accepting Jonas' aid as his own wound was taking its toll.

Jonas and Chris scrambled out of the failing command center structure. Jonas wrapped his arm around Chris as he picked a careful path through the rubble and strained beams.

As they made their way out of the building and along the driveway, they found Fallon and Cait moving quickly to merge with their position. Cait wore a wide grin across her face as she held up a transmitter and pressed a button.

The remote detonator set off the first explosion. The first missile launcher erupted into a violent explosion over her shoulder in the distance. As the initial blast had just begun to dissipate, the next site erupted followed by the remaining pair in a sequential line. Each concussive detonation added to a wild scene of fire, shrapnel, and debris.

Fallon's head snapped as he did a double take at Cait's handiwork. With a shake of his head, he cast a disapproving glance.

Cait's grin only grew wider as she shrugged, "What? You said ensure their inoperability. They're inoperable."

As their group made their way from the scene, Angel's voice crackled over the radio, "We have a convoy headed your way. Looks like the Jordanian military and police. We've tried to contact their government but have not been successful yet."

"That… is not my fault," Cait defended.

A trail of dust began to rise at the horizon. "Copy that, Angel. I have eyes on the convoy. They appear to have slowed in reaction to the missile site explosions," Porter called from his perch.

"Heh," Cait scoffed, clearly proud of herself.

"Dragonfly…," Jonas began.

"Already in the air, Chief. Five clicks out," Cara replied.

"2K, any ideas from overwatch?" Jonas asked.

Porter eyed the convoy through his scope, "I can delay their arrival, Chief."

"Remember, they are allies," Jonas warned.

Releasing a breath, Porter squeezed the trigger, sending a .50 cal round into the engine block of the lead vehicle. Chambering another round, he impregnated the vehicle with another impact. Adding one more shot, the truck slid to a stop, halting the vehicles in line behind it.

"Made them think twice about continuing, but it won't stop them for long," Porter said. "Bullets sent downrange into a vehicle rarely disable it, but most drivers tend to think twice about their path."

"Good work, move to exfil," Jonas said.

Kinza rolled out of his spot and sprinted away from the convoy towards the team, "Time to go, boss!"

The team headed for an open area of ground behind the command center, putting more distance between them and the Jordanian military and police vehicles which again advanced towards their location.

The sound of rotors screamed overhead as a helicopter flew in at high speed scarcely a hundred yards in the air.

"Looks like a warzone down there," Cara called as she brought the helicopter in for a landing.

"Thank you," Cait beamed, rising proudly on her heels.

"Coming in hot, looks like you've got company knocking on your door," Cara said, hovering just off the ground.

"Copy that," Jonas called helping Chris reach the helo and spun to ensure the rest of his team boarded without incident.

Porter sprinted from the opposite direction, tossing his gear aboard. As his belly hit the floor of the chopper, Cara pulled back on the stick and launched into the air. Snapping the lever, she pushed the helicopter spinning away from the scene at high speed.

"Dragonfly, the Jordanian Airforce has granted you a window, but I wouldn't dawdle," Angel called into their radios.

"Angel, when have you ever known me to dawdle?" Cara grinned.

"Copy that, Dragonfly. Fly home safely," Angel replied, a chuckle in her voice.

Thirty Two

The team doctor at Camp Green cleaned and stitched Chris' wounds, taping several layers of post-surgical dressing to his side.

"Tore up your external oblique pretty good but missed your liver and kidney. Overall, quite lucky," the physician said.

"Thanks Doc!" Chris said, wincing as he sat up and tried to pull a shirt over his shoulders. "The staples and stitches will hold?"

"If you rest and let your body heal… sure," the doctor advised.

"I can rest when the mission is complete," Chris scoffed.

"You'll likely bleed out in combat or end up septic by the time the team can get you to help, if they can get you to help," the doctor warned.

Jonas' booming voice joined the conversation, "Sounds like a no for battle readiness."

"Five by five and ready to go, Chief," Chris beamed, wincing again as he swung his legs over the side of the exam table.

Jonas grinned, "I love the Marine in you, Gunny. But we've got this next one. Stand down. The team will bring Hussein to you on a platter."

Chris grimaced and squared his gaze on Jonas', "Negative. That man called the order to attack the bridge my family traveled *because* my team was stationed there and because of the work and life that I chose. No, sir. I will be on the mission. I will look into that demon's eyes when we rip his soul away."

"Porter, talk some sense into this man. I have to meet in the situation room," Jonas said as a smiling face entered the room.

"He's right you, know," Porter said joining his friend's side. "We've got the next one. You heal."

Chris cast him a sideways glance, "Would you stand down if it were your family?"

"Let us do the heavy lifting, that's all I'm saying. We'll bring him to a black site and have you join us," Porter suggested.

"And if the op goes bad? Worse, that bastard dies in the assault before I get to him?" Chris growled.

"Then we bring his head back instead of his whole body," Porter quipped. "Seriously, you as well as anyone knows, justice is often served without those who are hurt getting a chance to square off. Justice is the end goal, right?"

"Yeah," Chris nodded sullenly, needing to look away as he sighed.

In the corner of his eye, he saw another body slip into the room. Cocking his head, he frowned in surprise, "The team let you come to one of their sites?"

Cait grinned as she stepped forward, "De facto team member. Not sure Fallon was thrilled, but Jonas made it clear."

"Welcome, I guess," Chris said. "You here to get me to sit out too?"

"Hell, no," Cait grinned, popping up on her heels. "Wanted to make sure you get off your arse and back into the game."

"I've got to check into the situation room," Porter said. With a hand on Chris' shoulder, he looked directly at his eyes, "Take it easy on yourself, okay?"

As Porter left the room, Chris looked at Cait. Realizing he hadn't finished fully pulling his shirt down, he completed the action and gingerly slipped off the exam table. Wincing slightly as he straightened himself up, he nodded towards the door, "Let's go for a walk, I need to move."

Cait wrapped an arm around his good side, to give him a little additional support. Looking up, she asked, "Do you mind?"

"No," Chris shook his head. He appreciated the friendship and bond they had created over the experiences since he helped her escape the camp in western Iraq. Having another woman close to him physically, even with the innocent intention, was uncomfortable for him. "I need to shake off the sedative the doc gave me."

"Well, he did just perform surgery and patched up a through and through," Cait said.

"A benefit of armor-piercing rounds, in this case," Chris shrugged. Wincing, he realized shrugging was off the table for a bit.

"We're almost there," Cait said softly.

Nodding, Chris agreed, "Yep."

Cait stopped and looked up, "But…"

"I don't know," Chris shook his head. "Feels right. We're taking some seriously bad people off the map and preventing them from carrying out terrible attacks. But they feel like any other mission."

Cait scoffed, "I've been chasing that heartwarming feeling of satisfaction in erasing bastards that had a hand in harming my family. It never comes. Just another evil face standing in my way."

"Feels like we're stuck in a purgatory. Hollow victories," Chris said.

"Not hollow, just not filling the holes we'd like them to fill. There is no magic endgame for us, not like what we'd like to think. This is our lives now. Our hurt and our willingness to stick our necks out where no one else of right mind or authority would or could. You are, what do they call you…Patriot X," Cait replied.

"Not much of a pep talk," Chris admitted.

"It's not a pep talk. It's reality," Cait said.

"You've been at this longer than me, how do you keep going?"

Cait danced a little with her feet as she breathed her reply, "Every mission target I take down is overlaid by the face of someone I lost. It makes pulling the trigger and tracking the next target easier. Even if there is just another target up next."

"Think it ever stops?"

Cait scoffed, "You were a Marine. Did you stop seeing evil in any corner of this world?"

"No, I suppose not," Chris admitted.

"Welcome to your new life, Patriot X," Cait whispered.

Their eyes locked for a moment. Cait's freckles seemed to dance along the bridge of her nose. There was symmetry in their pain and their support for one another. Chris felt like he was protecting a little sister…but not. It was something different.

"Let's get you into this mission," Cait urged.

"You aren't worried about me blowing a staple and bleeding out like the others?" he pressed.

"I am. I just know who you are. I know who I am. I'd rather die taking out the people who killed my family than sit on the sideline. I'm not afraid of dying. I'm afraid of no longer wanting to try," Cait said.

Chris nodded, "Yeah. That I get. I keep wondering what's left."

"After Hussein?"

Chris stopped suddenly, "Hussein's not the end. I've got a problem back at home."

"Don't we all," Cait grinned. "Let's get into that situation room and see what the plan is."

As they walked through the courtyard and in through the mansion to the room where the team had assembled, Chris left Cait's support and strode in on his own.

Jonas stopped and looked up. Pausing for a long moment, he considered the man who stood before him. Finally, he lifted a hand off the table he was leaning on and waved him in, "Well, are you going to join us?"

"Yes sir, Chief," Chris nodded and stood next to Porter as Cait filled in next to him.

"So, here's the situation we have. Hussein is set to present at the Peace Conference dinner in Paris. He'll use the opportunity to martyr General Naib as a soldier of peace who was viciously and wrongly targeted and killed by the West," Jonas began.

"He is going to have to reorganize without Naib. He'll likely go underground for a while. This will be our last chance for before he does," the team leader continued.

"Are we going to take him out in transit?" Fallon asked.

Jonas shook his head, "We need to infiltrate the conference itself. Our intel suggests he is not attending the rest of the conference, just participating as the keynote speaker. We'll have to hit him while he is on stage."

"We're going to take him out while he's on stage?" Cait gasped, admiring Jonas' audacity.

"No. He'd be martyred throughout the world," Jonas explained.

"Then what the hell are we going to do?" Fallon bristled.

"We are going to do the worst we possibly can to him. We are going to reveal to the world who he really is. We will discredit every word he has ever uttered, discredit every person who has ever supported him," Jonas declared.

Thirty Three

The Paris Convention Center was vibrant and festive. Dignitaries, politicians, royalty, and media personalities arrived in limousines escorted by personal security teams, French police, and a broad weave of secret service and intelligence officers.

Most of the team inserted days before the event. Holing up in forgotten crevices and dark, unpleasant utility wells scattered throughout the building. Eating engineered meals, rationing water packs, and bottling their natural excrements, they were able to infiltrate before the security teams began their lockdown procedures.

Using tech to cover their scents from search canines and even mask their thermal signatures, the team rode out the uncomfortable period in their own ways. Chris's body largely appreciated the time to heal. No stranger to similar op insertions, Chris was used to managing his team. Running the op in his head, rehearsing his role, imagining improvising if the op went bad.

When all but the scant night security was left in the building, the team would take liberty from their stations. Chris' location up in the catwalk of the large theater provided him a functional if dangerous workout tool. The scaffolding stretching across the stage and audience seats worked well for pull-ups, dips, and other exercises, even if meant hanging a hundred feet from the floor below to complete them.

Cait, on the opposite end of the ceiling, used the scaffolding like monkey bars and would hand over hand, make her way to visit.

Porter called home a nook used to channel cables and wires from the sound and lighting booth for his sniper perch. When the building was locked down, he had free reign in the locked room to stretch out and make it his own until the sun rose.

Kinza had the most room to move, but may have had the least enjoyable location. The subterranean utility space was dark, dank, and full of other creatures who called the space home. His spot was also set to be the most carefully searched and patrolled as the event neared.

Jonas and Fallon had the literal luxury to arrive as impeccably dressed dignitaries themselves. Each adopting a neutral nation with a well assembled cover to use as their identities. Each arrived separately and never communicated directly at the event. Largely following the crowd, they mixed into relative obscurity as they made their way to key locations in the auditorium.

Security teams, each having thoroughly searched and locked down the interior portions of the building focused their attention on the exterior as well as the large crowd that milled through the space. Metal detectors and scanners were mandatory, even for the highest dignitaries to move through.

Jonas and Fallon each replaced their event grab bags with an identical bag with definitively different goodies enclosed placed by Chris and Cait in discrete locations.

The rest of the team relished the added activity in the building to cover their noises as they moved to their assigned positions. Porter had used the prior evenings to cut out a small hole above the booth so that he could remove a small piece of wallboard as the center lights focused on the stage and darkened the remainder of the room. He had just enough room for a pair of muzzles to slip through. A fabric mimicking the wallboard covered another hole fashioned for his scope.

Kinza's work had largely been done earlier in the week. His devices were wired or backdoored into the convention center's systems. His initial role was to turn on the streams while the event was underway and less likely to be detected midstream.

Chris and Cait maneuvered to their positions directly above the stage. The most challenging part of their locations was to avoid being nicked by a light or creating movement that might be caught by a bored participant staring at the ceiling or an especially sharp guard.

Fallon pressed his Australian accent to mimic its British roots as he represented the Falklands. Flirting with a contingent of women from Sweden provided a solid cover and avoided speaking to anyone who might have more understanding of the small island.

Jonas adopted a small African country of Comoros and the little spoken Comorian Bantu language. He could smile, be cordial and fail to communicate with just about anybody at the event. Acting as a strong admirer of the keynote speaker, he selected a seat very close to the stage mirroring the location opposite the room that Fallon had escorted the Swedish delegation to.

"Next time, can I have Fallon's role?" Porter whispered into his earpiece as he used his scope to spy on his teammates as they secured their positions.

"Just sleeping in a hotel for the last few nights would be great, but I see what you mean," Chris whispered.

"I'd flirt with women from Sweden, too, if it meant not pissing in a bottle for days," Cait admitted.

"Alright team, our comms should be secure, but let's keep the chatter down to be on the safe side," Angel said over their earpieces. "All in position?"

"Affirmative," Porter called from his superior perch.

"Dragonfly is waiting for your clean exit after the finale," Angel said.

"Copy that. Going dark unless absolutely necessary," Porter said.

"Angel out."

Going dark for Chris was very literal and good thing. As the stage lights went on and the auditorium lights dimmed, his disappearance into the shadows was enhanced. Laying prone atop the scaffolding of the catwalk, he stared directly down on the podium.

He suffered through hours of speeches and grandstanding. As the Peace conference organizer concluded his speech, he lauded Barriq Hussein for his bravery and years of work promoting peace throughout the Middle East, Eastern Europe, and Africa.

"He leads the charge carrying the olive branch around the world, bridging Muslim ideals, removing the conflicts with other cultures and religions. He truly is the Harbinger of Peace, Barriq Hussein!" the speaker turned toward the side of the stage and applauded as the terrorist leader walked under the lights.

Smiling and waving, Hussein soaked in the adoration like a celebrity entering an evening talk show. Shaking the speaker's hand, Hussein nodded in appreciation and took the podium. Placing hands on either side of the lectern, he scanned the audience.

"Thank you, thank you. These are unprecedented times. I am honored to be here. I'd like to think peace was a light switch. Flip it and it's on, but it's not. Even when all sides agree that is the goal, it can be elusive. Lack of trust, lack of understanding, lack of acceptance, unwillingness to share resources are all competing with a world of peace," Hussein started.

"Just last week, we lost a great man. A man that I dubbed the 'Broker of Peace'. He was the elbow grease for my words and intention. Together, we led coalitions in Tunisia, Libya, Turkey, Syria, and Iraq, all areas plagued with violence, all worsened with imperialistic efforts of outsider countries.

The West does not understand our mission of peace. Resources and power are at stake, I understand that, but so are lives. When the region is destabilized, it creates a free for all to retrieve those resources. In doing so, the side effect is an attack on a boy's school. An attack on an embassy. The targeted execution of General Ravi Naib, the Broker of Peace.

These acts… these acts must stop!" Hussein stepped back from the podium for a moment, appearing to choke back his emotions. The audience was reeled into his message and his pleading affect.

"While General Naib was leading a humanitarian convoy en route to Syria, he was gunned down in a fiery attack that had all the fingerprints of a United States special forces attack. In all, we lost over a dozen humanitarian aid workers along with my good friend General Naib. Even the Jordanian emergency responders were attacked in this incident. These are the acts that derail peace," Hussein looked up at the giant screens behind him. Footage of the failed missile assault depicted a horrific scene, Cait's violent explosions lighting the room via the large monitors.

"Have you guys heard enough of this B.S.?" Kinza asked.

"Team, you are greenlighted. Execute! Execute!" Angel called into their earpieces.

Porter launched the first volley, a subtle 'thoomp' sent smoke grenades towards the stage, quickly filling the room and obscuring Hussein's position. Chris and Cait descended immediately from their high positions as the visibility reduced to near zero.

Rappelling on either side of the terrorist, they prevented him from exiting the stage. Using thermal goggles, they could see through the smoke. Chris delivered a quick punch to Hussein's throat, removing his ability to call for help. With a kick, Chris brought the target to his knees.

As the smoke reached the audience seats, Jonas and Fallon launched from their positions and donned their thermal goggles from their goodie bags. Taking either side of the stage, their roles were simple, prevent security from advancing towards Hussein's position. Using the advantage of being able to see human shapes clearly through the haze, they kept security at bay.

Porter switched to a sniper rifle fitted with a thermal scope. Instead of his usual munitions, he fired rubber bullets through his silenced rifle. He tried not to enjoy his task, but he couldn't help but to delight at dropping very confused guards and highly trained security detail. Knowing they would not be seriously harmed, it was the most fun he ever had with a sniper rifle.

Chris relished his role for an entirely different reason. As Hussein tried to struggle, Chris delivered a vicious blow to the base of the terror organization leaders' head triggering a shock wave down his spine and through his nervous system. The man slumped as his bladder emptied.

Wrapping the man in chains, Chris strung them through a loop welded to a plate. Working quickly, he bolted the plate to the stage floor, anchoring Hussein in place. Leaning into the beleaguered man, Chris cursed in his ear, "This is for every innocent life you stole. They were mothers, daughters, sons. They had names. Mine were Breanna and Macy. You'll rot in hell for eternity. Regardless of what god you claim to worship."

Chris stood up and tapped Cait on the shoulder. Having just delivered a kick launching a guard off the stage, she nodded and pressed into her earpiece. "Package is secure, time to head out boys."

"Copy that, Blaze. All head to exfil," Angel called.

Chris and Cait ascended the way they came, up the rappel lines to the catwalk. Jonas and Fallon collapsed their positions toward the podium and followed Chris and Cait. Porter held his position until they were clear of the stage. Quickly packing his gear, he headed for his exit.

Kinza flipped the remaining switches and executed the software he patched into the conference center's systems. Angel could run the entire sequence remotely after that. Eager to leave his dank dungeon, he moved towards his exit.

The smoke in the auditorium started to dissipate. Through a camera placed by Porter and patched by Kinza, Angel had a view of the room. Hitting a button, the lights from the sound booth shone a giant letter X that covered the entire stage. It had an eerie wisp to it as it filtered through the remaining smoke.

As the room slowly returned to normal, security details scrambled to recover. In the center of the stage, with a spotlight shining directly on him, Barriq Hussein, his arms lashed behind his back, kneeled in front of the crowd. He looked desperately around for help.

Security rushed towards the podium as the screens behind him were suddenly brought to life and the auditorium speakers filled with his voice. Footage of Hussein plotting attacks with General Naib played before them. Video of the results of his plotting shown on the screen before cutting to another plot, followed by another attack.

Images of Hussein shaking hands with known terrorists as well as certain dignitaries from around the world flashed on the screen, most followed by the horrific aftermath of a bombing, a mass shooting, or assault.

The audience froze as the screens continued to scroll piece after piece of evidence revealing the real life of Barriq Hussein. Account ledgers, emails, other tangible evidence were displayed on the screens.

Angel and the Cadre's tech team simultaneously pre-empted major news outlets around the world, broadcasting what the conference audience was seeing. Data drives filled with the compiled evidence were delivered to intelligence agencies in multiple countries.

Finally, the screens methodically flashed through images of all of Hussein's supporters worldwide. All of the people who touted him as the messiah of peace, who pushed programs in their countries supporting Hussein's agenda, who belittled their own countrymen who dared doubt or speak negatively about the man who they claimed deserved their utmost respect.

As the show ended, flickering, glitching digital X's filled the screens.

Chris helped Cait out of her gear and they each helped Jonas and Fallon up onto the catwalk. Racing along to their exit location, taking advantage of the failing smoke, they reached the crawl space that hung below the expanse of the roof.

Knowing the roof had been secured, they huddled against an outside wall as Porter joined them and a minute later, Kinza. "Execute," Jonas said.

Fallon nodded and pressed a trigger, launching a string of thermite against the exterior wall. Running alongside power cables, they had strung an innocuous looking line appearing like another utility cable from the conference center to a neighboring building. Launching themselves on hand-held trolleys, they slid from one building to the next.

"Dragonfly…," Jonas called.

"Already here, boss," Cara called as one of numerous news helicopters descended alongside the tall building.

Leaping the ten-foot expanse, the team rolled into the open helicopter door and slammed it shut. The news choppers were scattered around the scene as emergency responders and an army of French police blanketed the scene below.

Cara maneuvered the helicopter as though she were sweeping the scene with her infrared camera for footage as military helicopters swooped in and each hovering news reporter was being told to exit the airspace around the center.

"Sounds good to me," Cara said aloud, swinging the helicopter away from the scene as fighter jets screamed through the air, threatening any lagging reporters with a show of force.

Landing the helicopter at the airfield, they immediately raced towards a waiting plane. The entire country would be locked down as they sorted through the events at the conference center. The plane had been cleared for take-off prior to all flights being grounded from leaving Paris area airports.

"The France 247 news station pilot is going to be confused when his helicopter is already in his space at the airfield," Cara grinned.

"I think there are a lot of confused people in Paris… and around the world tonight," Porter added.

"Well executed, team," Fallon lauded, offering Chris an appreciative nod.

Chris nodded back, but he didn't feel like celebrating. He stared out the small plane window as the landscape screamed by. Hussein received better than he deserved. The humiliation and fall from grace paled in comparison to the pain he spread around the world. He knew there were thousands of broken hearts like his that couldn't quite take solace in his capture and fallen veil.

Jonas wasn't celebrating either, as he monitored air traffic on his laptop. "I'll feel better when we are out of France airspace."

"Having the pilot head straight for the English Channel and then wrap around the west into international waters. It's the fastest way out of French control," Cara assured. "At one thousand miles per hour, the Aireon is the fastest private jet in the world. Good thing we have talented friends with deep pockets, it's one of the most expensive, too."

"Can't outrun a fighter," Jonas grumbled.

Cara stared at her watch, "And we should be clear… now."

The jet swung left and headed for the open waters of the Atlantic Ocean before swinging south towards an airport where a helicopter waited to bring them to Camp Green.

THIRTY FOUR

The congresswoman squirmed opposite the reporter on the screen.

"In light of the evidence, what impression of your association with Barriq Hussein do you want to leave your constituents?" the reporter asked the congresswoman.

"Well," the politician stammered, "We are reviewing the discovery of the evidence and the odd manner in which it was presented."

"The facts are facts, regardless of the method in which they came to light," the reporter pressed.

Looking at the camera, the congresswoman gleamed, "This is why I am glad we live in a country that supports due process. Mr. Hussein was humiliated on a world stage with evidence that has yet to be verified."

The reporter looked perplexed, "There are videos of Hussein explicitly lining out the details of a terror attack days before that very attack happened corroborated with financial transactions and links from Hussein to Naib to other terror cell leaders."

"I can't speak to any of that. All I can stand by are the conversations I had with the man personally. A vision for a peaceful world softening the imperialistic views of the west with a more worldly status quo," the woman replied.

"I'm not sure I understand. Are you suggesting that you still stand by Barriq Hussein despite the preponderance of evidence pointing to his direct involvement in terror activity worldwide, including an attack on American soil which claimed the lives of a number of innocent civilians," the reporter raised an eyebrow.

"Well, clearly, I disavow any *deep* connection with Hussein. I continue to support the ideals we mutually shared," the congresswoman said.

"And what ideals are those?"

The congresswoman stammered, "A leveling of the world playing field. Western nations have been unwieldingly strong for the past century or more. This is harmful to other cultures that are comparatively disadvantaged."

"You mean cultures like those Hussein supported? Supporting mass violence not against another country with which it has dispute, but against her unarmed, innocent citizenry?" the reported asked.

"Well… no. Of course not," the congresswoman looked defeated as the reporter broke for commercial prior to his next segment.

The team huddled in the situation room as they watched a variety of news coverages from around the world. The overwhelming support had been overturned though some who had connections with Hussein struggled to come to terms with their outing.

"What happens to Hussein, now?" Porter asked.

"He is held in French custody. As you may imagine, countries are lining up to seek extradition. From the U.S., Jordan, Israel, Turkey…," Jonas replied.

Fallon scoffed, "The French rarely comply with such requests."

"True, but I think this is one that they will be happy to wipe their hands from. Hussein had not committed any crimes specifically against France. My hunch, is they'll turn him over to the Turkish government as a way to mend some issues between the two countries," Jonas replied.

"And of the people that helped him?" Cara asked.

"The evidence retrieved by Lanikov and Kinza is overwhelming. It will be sifted through. Indictments will be handed down, raids ordered, careers rightfully ruined," Jonas said.

"Chris?" Kinza cocked his head, noticing the ponderous look on his face.

"There are a couple of more strings I need to pull," Chris replied.

"The course has been set. Even for those strings," Jonas said. "Let the system take it from here."

"If there were people that sit in trusted roles complicit in Breanna and Macy's deaths, I'm not going to leave it up to the system to take care of them," Chris said.

"Let me take it to the group. See what we can do," Jonas said.

"I'm not asking for your help, Jonas," Chris snapped.

"I'll help," Cait stepped forward.

"I'm in," Kinza joined her.

"You're a brother, now," Porter nodded.

Their eyes fell on Drake Fallon, who shuffled a bit as he caught the team's eyes. Nodding, he added, "Yeah, I'm in."

Jonas surveyed the group as a whole, considering his next response.

"I appreciate that. I really do. But… I've got this. American politics is a different sort of danger that I don't want to drag the team into," Chris said.

"Just know we're for you, brother. We've got your back," Porter assured.

Chris nodded and excused himself. The team resumed analyzing the global responses to Hussein's exposure.

Cait slipped out and ran alongside Chris. "Hey," she called, but Chris kept his head down and kept walking.

Cait sped up. Yanking his arm, spinning him towards her, she snapped, "You aren't in this alone. Whether it is taking down a missile site in Jordan or a dirty politician in the U.S., we *are* in this together."

Chris didn't know how to respond to such a visceral response. The passion in Cait's eyes seared the seriousness of her plea into Chris' soul.

"I don't want you to get yourself into a situation you can't get out of and we… *I'm* not there to help you get out," Cait breathed. Without warning, she reached out. Grabbing a hold of Chris' collar, she yanked him forward. Staring into his eyes, she pushed her lips against his.

In shock, Chris absorbed the kiss for several long moments before Cait peeled back. Her eyes widened in horror, unsure herself of what she had done. As suddenly as she grabbed him, she struck again, this time slapping him across the face.

Chris reeled, looking bewildered, "What was *that* for?"

"*I don't know*!" Cait snapped, her freckled cheeks dusted with rouge. "Just be careful and accept my help, even if you don't want to bring the rest of the team into it."

Chris grinned, "So, you're part of the team, now, huh?"

Cait looked cross, "Maybe. Just don't tell them that."

Chris softened, "Look, I appreciate your help. If I need it, I will ask for it, okay?"

"Promise me."

"I promise," Chris acknowledged.

Cait danced a bit, "Sorry for… you know."

Chris nodded. A part of him kind of liked the kiss, even if was a shock. A big part of him, however, couldn't fathom kissing any woman other than Breanna.

A booming voice pulled them from the awkwardness of the moment. "Chris, do you have a moment?" Jonas called, casting a suspicious glance at the odd energy between the two.

"Yeah," Chris nodded. Excusing himself from Cait, he followed Jonas back into the main building at Camp Green. Walking towards the situation room, they reached the end of the hallway. Jonas opened door to a room Chris hadn't been in before. To his surprise, it revealed an elevator. Jonas waved him through.

"You're the first team member they had requested to see," Jonas informed.

Chris cast a puzzled glance, "Who?"

As the elevator doors began to open, Jonas said, "They're simply known as The Cadre."

Leading the way into a round room, several vertical screens formed a half circle. Jonas stepped onto a platform in the center of the room and beckoned Chris to join him.

Several silhouettes appeared on the screens. Each full size and apparently standing on similar platforms themselves.

"Gunnery Sergeant Chris Masters, it is a privilege to meet you. We apologize for the cloak and dagger veil from our side. It is a necessary precaution given our roles and the danger to the entire operation were we discovered," one of the silhouettes spoke, a slight distortion in their voice.

Chris took the whole scene in, for a moment feeling he was watching a sci-fi movie. "*Former* Gunnery Sergeant," he corrected.

"Yes, of course. Now, the famous Patriot X. A moniker we never figured would stick, but it seems to have added a certain validity to our actions," the silhouettes responded.

"Judiciously used, of course. Any linkage of operations has the potential for a forensic stringing of events, fighting styles, and motives to identify your team and perhaps, even the entire operation," another silhouette offered.

"We have been impressed with you and your addition to Jonas' team. We understand, as much as anyone not yourself can, the pain you must have gone through to this point and no doubt will continue to struggle with, we are deeply sorry for your loss," another silhouette added.

"Jonas has informed us that you do not believe your work to be done in relevance to the Hussein cell," one of the silhouettes shared. "We want to help, though we understand the subtleties needed in such a mission that it is best that you operate solo. We would like to provide you with travel and documents created by our intel team and any other assistance we may provide in advance of your objective."

Chris looked at the camera in front of him, "I appreciate your support and any assistance you can provide."

"We'll have our team set it up. Give us twenty-four hours, we will have documents delivered to Jonas," the silhouette said. "Good luck…Mr. Masters."

The screens went blank.

Chris looked at Jonas who shrugged, "That is as close as I have come to meeting them myself. There are rumors of politicians, billionaire tech moguls, no one on the teams is really sure."

"Teams?" Chris asked.

"There are several. We never work together or crossed paths. None other than Patriot X have received a moniker. Too dangerous for connecting events," Jonas answered. "It seems you have an evening to relax. You might want Doc to freshen your dressing, I noticed it has been seeping since Paris."

Chris shrugged, "The rappelling harness was a bit rough on it."

"Go get checked out. I'll assemble the team for dinner tonight. Bonding without bullets flying overhead can be a good thing. Even for a rogue group such as ours," Jonas declared.

Chris acknowledged the leader and headed for the infirmary.

Thirty Five

Chris headed to dinner in good spirits. The weight of action was off of his shoulders for a brief hiatus as he awaited the documents. He hadn't considered until The Cadre council offered to help, that he would be on watch lists if he tried to travel, especially being AWOL and entering the United States.

He had burned his identification when hunkered in the North Carolina mountains. He didn't even have any money to his name to try to acquire such things. He was so focused on completing each mission, these normal worldly tropes didn't even enter his mind. Instead of being concerned about passports and driver's licenses, he had only worried about which weapon load-out and ammunition he was carrying.

A voice broke Chris' rumination. "How're you doing, buddy? Doc get you re-patched?"

Chris turned to see Porter fall in step beside him. "Fit for duty," he replied.

"Glad to hear that. You're no good to a mission, even your own, if you aren't square," Porter said.

"Five by five, ready to go," Chris acknowledged, using his unit's terminology for good.

"Clear copy, Gunny," Porter grinned. He slowed his pace and Chris naturally followed suit. "Listen, since I ended up in this clandestine world, I haven't had many people I can connect with. I am glad you're part of the team. I hope when this is all done and you've clipped the last string, you find your way back."

Chris smiled a rare smile, "Thank you. Genuinely trusting me to have your six is irreplaceable. I can't promise where I'll land. Haven't been able to picture living when this is all over."

Porter adopted an equally rare look, with a serious frown, "Try to picture it because I can promise you this, while I didn't have the great fortune to know Breanna and Macy, I damn sure know they'd want you to live on. Never forgetting, but moving forward until God calls you to be with them."

Chris allowed the words to sink in, before responding, "Thanks. I know you're right. It's just not easy."

"I know," Porter acknowledged. "Come on, let's get you fed. You're going to need your strength more than ever if you're going to take on D.C."

Chris nodded silently as they continued towards the main building.

Dinner largely revolved around reflecting on the missions they had carried out since Chris and Cait's arrivals. The conversation actually became raucous and jovial when it slid to the results of their takedown of Hussein.

Social media erupted into a flurry of memes while newscasters who had previously sung his praises turned one hundred-and-eighty-degree pivots. Politicians who touted his peaceful mission scrambled over themselves to distance and disavow their connections.

Jonas called the table to order and toasted Patriot X. Returning home to turn Washington upside down. "We may not be there with you, but we will be there with you. We have approval to provide whatever remote support you need, including Angel. You just tell us what you need and it's yours."

"Thank you," Chris acknowledged. "It's been good to work with all of you."

"That sounds rather final," Fallon questioned.

Chris shook him off, "Not prophetic or anything, just to date."

"I look forward to having you back with the team," Fallon raised his glass of lager.

Chris studied his teammate who had scarcely uttered a positive word towards or about him since he arrived. A loss for words, Chris raised his glass.

"Wish I could go with you, there's a few people in Washington I'd like to knock upside the head," Cara blurted. "And a few I'd like to shake their hands, too."

Chris laughed, "Wouldn't mind you being there either. Your quick exfils while the path behind us is literally on fire has saved the day on multiple occasions."

"There is one other person that wanted to meet you," Jonas announced. "We don't typically break protocol…"

"Hello, Chris," a voice called as a young woman wrapped around the corner and entered the room. Chris had wondered about the empty place setting. He watched the petite figure enter the room. She offered a shy smile and a wave to the table.

"Angel!" Chris stood, as did the entire team. The response only made the woman more conscious of eyes on her.

With a curtsy, she nodded, "It is a pleasure to meet you, X. And you must be Blaze." Cait nodded.

"And you, Mr. Kinza. You have given me a scare on more than one occasion. It is a pleasure to finally meet you, and in one piece," Angel beamed.

Porter, Cara, and Fallon huddled to hug the typically virtual teammate.

"Chris, I present to you, Tamlyn. Otherwise known as Angel," Jonas announced from the end of the table.

"It's been quite the adventure over the last few months. I asked Jonas if it would be okay to join you following the take down of Hussein. That was one of the most interesting assignments and pleasantly bullet free, if you don't include the rubber kind," Tamlyn admitted.

"The Cadre prefers to compartmentalize, but Tamlyn convinced them after a blown mission Fallon, Porter, Cara, and I were on about a year ago, that running virtual overwatch was executed more strategically when the team members could put faces to the names they so closely relied on," Jonas shared.

"A faceless voice is just moving pawns around a board. I needed to know the humans on the other end of our comms," Angel said.

"Every life on the battlefield is worthy of trying to save if it can be helped. Whether my teammate's or the enemies'. If I put someone in harm's way or pulled the trigger, it wasn't taken lightly," Chris said.

"You could have killed Maher," Tamlyn blurted.

Chris paused, looking across the table, a bit pained. "*Not* pulling the trigger on Maher and Hussein may have been the hardest things I ever had to do outside of laying my wife and daughter to rest."

Tamlyn realized her impulsive comment may have triggered pain in Chris, "I'm sorry…I didn't mean…"

Chris waved her off, "It's okay. You were right and it was a good case in point. The choices we make on the battlefield, even if it is behind a computer screen, are never easy. What is the greater good? What lives are we saving or protecting by taking another life out? Is it ever worth it? Is there another way?"

"As a sniper, knowing I am killing someone defenseless against my bullet, those questions run through my mind each time. Defending innocents, my team, executing a terrorist who has taken the lives of non-combatants…those are the easy ones," Porter acknowledged.

"It is a tough life we live. Split-seconds to decide who lives and dies. Not pulling the trigger can be just as terrible, sometimes," Fallon added, his voice deeply sullen.

Chris looked into Fallon's eyes and began to understand part of the pain that plagued the man.

"We are all here because, fate, life, God…Allah," Jonas received an appreciative nod from Kinza, "Brought us together. Injustice made murky with politics and financial interests have carved pain into each and every one of us. We are here not for vengeance, but to make wrongs right. The Cadre might be secretive, but I can tell you, the missions they send us on have one thing in common. If we are successful, lives are made better. Whether liberating an oppressed village, freeing hostages, rescuing politically unreachable prisoners of war, or taking the life of a terrorist with hands soaked in blood, if we are sent out with our fingers on the trigger, we are saving a life somewhere."

"In the wake of scorched earth, new life rebounds," Kinza added.

"We may not be good at sowing new seeds, but scorched earth we are pretty good at," Fallon said.

The team raised their glasses, "To scorched earth!"

Thirty Five

Chris couldn't help but to walk away from the team dinner feeling a level above the numb that had been carrying for so long. He was heady about the work left to be done, but he was surprised by the support he was receiving from this band of strangers.

"Do you have a second?" Kinza's voice called as Chris started down the path towards the team bungalows.

Spinning, he nodded as Aban Kinza jogged after him.

"I won't keep you. I have no doubt you have a lot on your mind," Kinza stated. "I wanted to share with you before you left, words I need to express in the event…you choose to not return. We come from very different backgrounds – different countries, different religions. Yet, I see you as a brother."

Chris watched as the devout man carefully crafted his words, "Christians and Muslims share similar commandments, love of God and love of neighbor. The actions of a small minority fuel division, misunderstanding, mistrust, and even hate. There is no god but God. Our Muslim God and your God is one, so says the Qu'ran.

You fight beside me as though we've always fought for the same side. You rushed to the school in Turkey as though they were American children inside. I would do the same if we were across the Atlantic.

We may have many differences, but if we have love and respect for one another, together we can find peace. Together. It is a pleasure to fight by your side, brother," Kinza said, holding out his arm he added, "*As-sala 'alaykum*!".

"I trust you on my six anytime, Kinza," Chris replied. Shaking Kinza's hand, he said one of few Arabic praises that did not have to do with addressing an interdiction, "*Al-Hamdu lillahi*."

Kinza smiled, "Good luck to you."

"Take care, Kinza."

Chris turned and headed towards his bungalow. He sighed. War was hell, it is unfortunate when it is necessary.

As he turned the corner towards his bungalow, he rounded the cobblestone walk avoiding an overgrown flowering oleander.

In his weariness and false security of Camp Green, he didn't realize he was being stalked. His skillful assailant was an effective foe, utilizing the shadow of the foliage to extreme advantage.

Striking with sinewy speed, Chris was whirled around, his own body weight used against him as he was slammed against a wall. Through the dim light, he stared at the eyes staring back at him, almost shimmering with the reflection of the stars.

"Cait!" he gasped in an annoyed frown, "What the hell are you doing? That is a great way to get hurt…or worse."

Cait burst into a wicked grin, "I figured I'd take my chances."

Relaxing, Chris leaned against the wall. Cait did not let up on her grip. "I know you are mission focused. I wished you'd take me with you. You need someone watching your back, perhaps in Washington, D.C. more than anywhere."

"I can't. Besides, there's no way the people behind the screen will document you to get you there. I'm on my own. It's just something I need to do," Chris said. "Look, I appreciate your intent…"

Cait looked cross, "I'm not sure you do."

Launching onto her tiptoes, she pressed her lips into his. Despite the one-sided affection, she let it linger for a long moment before falling back to her heels. "I know what it is like to be hurt and angry. To have lost everything and everyone you loved. I also know it can make you dangerous and reckless. You don't need to come back here for me, but you *do* need to come back."

Letting go of her grip, she continued to stare into his eyes.

"The hardest thing I had to learn was to live again. To know how pissed my family would be at me if I didn't. So, I do. For them. Not for me," Cait said. Without waiting for a response, she spun away and disappeared into the night as silently as she appeared.

Thirty Six

Flying into Washington Dulles International Airport and stepping foot back on American soil was like returning to the home you moved out of for one more walk-through. Familiar yet foreign, yours but not.

Chris didn't have a home there anymore. He didn't have family or friends that he could visit, at least not without legal complications. It was his home, yet it wasn't.

Walking through the airport, he hailed a cab, unsure what facial recognition programs would identify him and what Homeland Security watchlists he had landed on in suspicion of his abduction of Mahaz Maher.

Focused on his mission, he directed the cabbie to a row of luxury apartments in McLean, Virginia. Stepping out, he took in the site. "Nice place for a reporter's salary. Treason must pay well," Chris muttered to himself.

Glancing around, he appreciated the late international flight. He didn't need to wander and wait to carry out his objective. He could arrive and make entry with few eyes falling on him.

Chris reviewed a number of access points to the building. Security was well monitored both electronically and by staffed patrol. He decided a direct approach was best. Ringing the videocom button, he stood askew of the camera so that only his chest was visible.

"Hello?" a sleepy voice called.

"Barriq Hussein sent me, we need to talk," Chris muttered in a guttural voice.

"What? I didn't receive any meeting requests," Clint Newsom stammered.

"This isn't the kind of meeting that would be managed in such a way. I have information on General Naib. It is imperative I deliver information to you. Tonight," Chris grumbled.

"Yeah…yes. Of course. I'll ring you in," Newsom agreed.

The door locks buzzed and the mechanism released, allowing Chris into the lobby. With a nod to the desk guard,

Chris walked confidently to the bank of elevators and pressed the button for the upper floors.

Hands in his pockets, his head swiveled from any direct camera angle Angel provided with the building schematics, he stepped forward, hitting the button for the penthouse suite.

As the doors slid open, Chris scampered to Newsom's door. With a soft rap, he beckoned.

Newsom slid the door open to the point it hit the security latch, his eye pressed to the gap to see who was standing in his hallway.

Chris struck out with his finger, jabbing Newsom in the eye, and leaned his shoulder into the door. Freeing it from the security mechanism, the heavy door smacked the reporter in the head as Chris marched through and closed it behind him.

Standing square in front of the reporter, he glared.

"You...," Newsom gasped.

"Me!" Chris growled.

As Newsom began to cry out, Chris delivered a severe punch that flipped Newsom over his living room sofa. Landing on all fours, holding his jaw, Newsom looked up in horror.

Chris strode forward, landing a vicious kick to the reporter, rolling him onto his back. With a foot on the man's throat so that he couldn't scream, Chris leaned over, resting his elbow on his knee as he leered towards Newsom. "You are not a nice man."

Chris paused, staring at the wide, frightened eyes looking back at him.

"I…I just share information. I report the news…," Newsom choked.

"You spread lies and mistruths that put other people in danger. You empower sick and evil zealots to strike against innocents. Your 'information', your 'news' killed my family," Chris pulled the photo he kept of Breanna and Macy out of his pocket and held it in front of Newsom.

"Your foolish, selfish, misplaced interests took the life of my wife and daughter…and so many more. Your trust in Barriq Hussein has cost the lives of innocent people around the world. You sit in your pious, self-righteous indignity without a clue of what *really* happens in this world. You turn against your own country as this evil entity, empowering terrorists to wage hate and violence in misplaced hatred," Chris spat, enraged. "You are a traitor. You are a pathetic tool of sleaze bag terrorists who are smarter than your Ivy League false virtues. You have killed so many, yet you'd never have the guts to fight yourself."

Chris lifted his foot and replaced its silencing effect with the muzzle of his pistol pointed directly between Newsom's eyes.

Angry tears welled in Chris' eyes as he thought of how the reporter's actions influenced the death of Breanna and Macy.

Newsom stared at Chris, seeing the real human pain he maliciously wrote about in favor of terrorists. He wrote and spoke about human atrocities, but he never experienced them. He never witnessed the true pain born by them. He witnessed that pain now.

With a sigh, Newsom looked away, his lips quivering, "I know. I know. I mean…I didn't, not at first. By the time I realized the man Hussein was, my whole reputation was exposed by him. It was better to continue to support him than to report the truth."

Chris glared in silence.

"I…I tried to tell the truth so many times. I tried to take my own life," Newsom's cheeks streaked with tears.

Chris looked on, unmoved.

"I tried jumping. I tried poison. I held a gun to my head and tried to shoot myself!" Newsom sniveled.

Chris stared at the man for several minutes, letting the reporter stew in his own anguish. Sighing, Chris let the pistol hang casually in his hand as his affect softened slightly, "My advice, don't try. If you're going to do it, do it."

Newsom's teary eyes widened, "Will you do it? Shoot me, please. Will you?"

Chris shook his head, "No. For once in your pathetic life, do something right. Do it yourself."

Chris pulled the slide to ensure a round was chambered. Spinning the gun so that he gripped the muzzle, he held it out for Newsom.

Reluctantly, the reporter took it, staring at the blued-metal firearm in his hand.

Chris lifted off of the reporter. Turning, he began his walk out of the reporter's apartment, not concerned for a moment whether he would be shot in the back or not. Calmly walking out of the apartment, he left Newsom holding the gun out in front of him, watching Chris close the door behind him.

Exiting the apartment building, Chris stepped out onto the sidewalk. Deep within the bowels of the structure, a gunshot interrupted the silence. Sending the pigeons roosting along its eaves scattering into the night sky.

Chris paused only for a moment. Instead of feeling bad about the sad loss of human life, he numbly crossed another name off of the list in his mind.

Thirty Seven

The Harry S. Truman Building was brimming with staffers, employees, and guests roaming through the lobby. As Chris stood in front of the security desk, he provided his credentials and prayed that Angel's team was successful at infiltrating the data logs and ensuring his photos did not match with any database.

After a long pause, the guard waved him through. Placing his things on a tray, they passed through the X-ray machine. Picking up his items on the other side, he strode with purpose towards the elevators.

Getting through lobby security was one thing, actually getting to the Secretary of State without an appointment was very much another. As the elevator doors began to close, a slender figure slipped inside. Pressing the 'Close Door' button, she held her hand out refusing another would-be passenger hoping to ride up.

The doors closed, Chris sighed, "What are you doing here?"

The woman spun and grinned, "How were you going to get through the Madam Secretary's staffers? Guards are easy."

"Okay, how did *you* get here?" Chris pressed.

"Anya," Cait grinned. "I told you someone had to have your back."

Turning back to face the doors as they opened on a middle floor, Cait literally pushed a startled staffer away from the elevator. With a crooked smile and wink, she offered, "Catch the next one, would you doll?"

"I assume you have a plan?" Chris asked.

"Do you? Because, I'd love to hear it," Cait teased.

Chris shrugged, "Intimidation?"

Cait laughed, "Secret Service would just shoot you."

"Okay, what do you have?"

"Anya sent me with a diplomatic package. Has to be delivered directly to the Secretary of State herself," Cait beamed.

Chris nodded, "Alright, that's better."

Arriving at the Secretary's floor, Cait turned back, "Did you hear about that reporter Newsom? Suicide. So sad."

The doors opened and she strode through like she owned the place. Chris tried to keep up, awkwardly trying to match her cover as armed security.

Standing in front of the Executive Secretary, Anya handed the young man a document. "Direct to Madam Secretary Green. She should be expecting it."

The executive secretary read the note, checked his computer terminal, and nodded. "Derek, please escort the envoy to Secretary Green's office."

As Chris strode forward in concert, the Diplomatic Security Service officer slashed his hand out into Chris' chest and directed a stern glare. Cait bounced behind him, "Uhh, he has to go where the pouch does until Secretary Green has it in her possession."

The DSS officer glanced at Cait and then back at Chris. "It's alright, Derek. It's not unusual for important items," the executive secretary acknowledged.

The officer grunted and removed his hand from Chris but walked in a manner that he could keep an eye on him.

As they reached the Secretary of State's door, another DSS officer stood by. With a nod from Derek, the officer opened the door. As Chris and Cait stepped through, Cait dropped the pouch just outside the door.

"Oops!" she exclaimed. Stepping back out into the hall, she bent over at the waist, her skirt hoisting in the air as she did.

For a moment both DSS officer's eyes were glued to Cait's posterior.

Chris recognized his moment and slammed the door shut behind him, securing the heavy deadbolts from the inside. Knowing it wouldn't take long for the doors to be opened, he strode directly to Secretary Green's desk.

Unflinching, Janice Green cast a raised eyebrow at the intruder, "What the hell is this?"

"I'm sorry for the method of introduction, but I thought you needed to see this," Chris announced.

"See what?" Secretary Green snapped.

"Look at your computer screen."

On cue, Angel infiltrated the Secretary's personal computer. Like Barriq Hussein at his conference, a barrage of clips, quotes, videos, and audio files scrolled on her screen.

The indignant look of Secretary Green turned to one of pale horror.

The guards burst through the door. Secretary Green held up her hand, freezing them in place. "Leave us!"

The DSS officers paused in confusion, seeing the Secretary's insistence, they relented. Stepping into the hall, they closed the doors but stood directly outside listening, ready to intercede.

Cait leaned against a hall table, studying the officers. "You got like, a snack bar around here or something?" The officers ignored her. "No? Okay," Cait shrugged.

Inside the office, Chris stood quietly as Secretary of State Green reviewed the flash display of the evidence scrolling across her screen. The most damning pieces drew direct links to her leading negotiations with Hussein which led to the transfer of U.S. weapons to General Naib and from Naib to terror cells throughout the Middle East.

"I, I've seen enough," Secretary Green looked ill as she turned away from the screen.

"It's tough to look at, imagine how difficult it is to live through," Chris snapped.

Secretary Green looked up at Chris, a glint of recognition in her eyes, "You're, you're the Marine they think captured Mahaz Maher from the Pakistani embassy."

"The man who detonated a bomb in North Carolina killing my family. The man was sent to North Carolina from your friends Barriq Hussein and General Ravi Naib. The man you worked so hard to free from Israeli custody so that he could return to his terror cell," Chris' glare burned through the Secretary.

Glancing at the screen, Chris scoffed, "Oh, *that's* a good one. Remember the attack on Ambassador Rogers in Tunisia? Again, ordered and carried out by friends of yours and get this, with weapons you helped supply. Oh, but wait, you knew about that, didn't you?"

Pointing to a string of intercepted emails, "Right there, the discussion you had with Hussein regarding Rogers predates the attack. The rest of the cake eaters in Washington might not be so moved by Breanna and Macy's blood on your hands, that's their *names* by the way…real people you helped destroy…I have to think your peers here in D.C. will find your complicit knowledge and instrumental assistance on an attack on a U.S. ambassador might pique their interest."

Secretary Green moved from shocked to cross, "What do you want, Mr…?"

"Gunnery Sergeant Chris Masters."

"Gunnery Sergeant, what do you propose? I can fund your new little group of vigilantes, what do they call you...Patriot X?" Green suggested.

"I don't need your blood money, Madame Secretary, I need you to leave your post and never hold any position of power in this country ever again," Chris growled.

Secretary Green looked away from Chris, her eyes falling onto the screen scrolling with overwhelming evidence against her. Finally, she sighed, "Alright. You win. I'll step down."

Chris was unmoved, "That's not enough. You need to confess to your sins...*all* of them. You'll go down as a misguided politician following ideals that in retrospect were not in the best interest of the country and admit to treason. You'll be hated, but you'll live out your life in whatever country club they stick demons like you. Personally, I'd put you in Gitmo with the other terrorists, the same ones you pitted against one another.

Or, we can force your hand. Drag you and your family through years of very public trials and maybe a sniper from some country you napalmed with your back-alley deals takes you out along the way. Either way, you're going down and your terrible legacy will be on display so the world knows exactly what you have done," Chris said.

"These aren't attractive terms," Secretary Green rubbed her face anxiously.

"There's always Clinton Newsom's route," Chris shrugged, his eye unremorseful.

Green's eyebrows danced in distress, "And if I refuse?"

"Then your more personal indiscretions become public. I mean, a woman of your stature, and which island was it you used to slip to for wanton debauchery when you were supposed to be overseas on official state business? What will your children think?" Chris spat.

The Secretary of State looked up at Chris. Her hardened visage fractured into defeat.

Nodding, she rasped, "Alright. Okay. I'll step down. I'll admit to working with Hussein and General Naib."

"And knowing about the attack on Ambassador Rogers," Chris added.

Secretary Green nodded weakly.

"You have seventy-two hours," Chris said. Without another glance or word, he strode to the door. As he pushed it forward, it bumped against one of the officers. "You need to move…out of the way," Chris shoved the officer further out of the way. Glaring at the officer who squared up at Chris before being summoned by Secretary Green to let them go.

"Bye boys!" Cait giggled as she fell into step with Chris.

Capitol Hill was buzzing with the request from Secretary of State Green to address the House Committee on Foreign Affairs in a public session. The abrupt event led to rampant rumors from Mid-East treaty talks to concerns over new conflicts.

Two days had passed with Chris fretting whatever political game the Secretary of State might try to employ. As she spoke, her message was brief, contrite, and to the point. With a stoic air, she announced that she always served with America in mind. In the global theater, intentions and implementation don't always mix and when they don't, they can have catastrophic results.

The Secretary defined her misplaced belief in Barriq Hussein and her program to topple regimes in the Middle East that she felt were contrary to world peace. She admitted knowing the collateral side effect of her work was the attack on Ambassador Rogers. She noted attacks like the one in North Carolina, while not her intent, were fueled by channels that she allowed to exist.

She admitted that she let herself, her family, and her country down. Resigning from her position, she awaited the Sergeant at Arms of the U.S. House of Representatives to escort her away from the podium and into custody.

For a brief moment, an image of a glitched letter X flashed over the scene, the podium perfectly intersected by the lines. Chris grinned, he had no idea how Angel and her team pulled that one off, but it was telling. Politicians and world leaders that support terrorists were put on notice. Supporting and allowing the killing of innocents would not be tolerated and their hallowed halls could not protect them.

From the moment Chris breached the Pakistani embassy, there were no walls he was afraid to scale for justice. He knew the danger in that ideal of vigilantism. Who decides justice? For him, it was simple. The line between right and wrong was not as blurry as some make it out to be. The taking of innocent lives, rape, and oppression were on one side of the line. He stood firmly on the other.

His thoughts were broken by the news reporter on the hotel television screen, "One of Secretary of State Green's final acts was negotiating the release of suspected terrorist Mahaz Maher into Pakistani custody. Maher was ripped from the sovereignty of the Pakistan Embassy following the bombing in Stone Bay, North Carolina. His connection with the incident was never confirmed and his abduction from the compound remains a mystery."

Chris glared at the screen. There was one final mission he had to carry out.

"Are you okay?" Cait asked softly over his shoulder. She sat quietly through the broadcast of Secretary Green's news conference. She could only imagine the thoughts and feelings that coursed through him.

Chris turned, taking in the friendly face. He had mixed feelings about her presence. He appreciated the support and the growing bond between them, but he was consumed with closing the chapters of his horror story.

Nodding unconvincingly, he shared, "Yeah. Just a few more things I need to take care of."

"Anything I can help you with?" Cait asked, placing a hand on his arm.

"No, there are some things I need to do alone," Chris said. As he turned to pull away, his eyes lightened, "There is one thing. I need you to fly out ahead of me, prep Jonas and the team. I am going after Mahaz Maher. But first, there a few things I need to wrap up here."

Cait tried to peer past Chris' eyes into the head of his, but was met with an unyielding veil. "I will."

"Thank you," Chris nodded.

With a final look and a soft smile, Cait disappeared into the hall.

THIRTY EIGHT

Chris traveled south, largely avoiding I-95. The last thing he needed was a traffic stop and the chance that his face was on a watch list somewhere that Angel's team may have missed.

Traveling the backroads that unite Virginia and North Carolina was cathartic. The breeze from the open windows, the trees flying by in a blur, the focus on the curves in the road took him away for a brief moment, the conflict that had overwhelmed his life.

His throat tightened and his stomach felt hollow as he brought the rental car into Stone Bay. He was excited, pained, saddened with a touch of warmth as he neared his destination. He timed his arrival for peak privacy.

Finding a hidden spot to park the car, he got out, closing the door quietly. Checking the fence, he found it locked for the night. With a quick glance, he leapt over and onto the lawn on the other side. He could have walked the next stretch with his eyes closed. He had worn a path prior to his life in self-afflicted exile.

Finding the spot he was looking for, he dropped to his knees. At first, he was pragmatic, noting the care and appreciating the fresh flowers that rested at each marker. As his eyes landed on the words etched in each slab of granite, Chris melted. Hands in his face, he buried his head to the ground in between the pair of graves. Gone was the numb that had encapsulated him, releasing him into an unfettered torrent of grief.

Despite burrowing into the grass, his eyes closed in the dark of night, he could see them. Breanna and Macy standing hand in hand, waiting for him. Waiting for him to come home to them. His broken heart shattered all over again. He would never talk to them, hold them, let them know with all of his earthly being how much he loved them. Never on earth, at least.

Chris had no idea how long he had been there. He didn't care. Dawn could have come. Police could have arrested him. General Naib could have risen from the grave and murdered him, he wouldn't have cared.

The hand on his shoulder was a surprise, the touch conveyed warmth and kindness. Looking up from his hands resting on the ground, he saw through the starry sky, barely lit by a pale moon, the face of Staff Sergeant Grady stood over him. Not saying a word, just calmly looking at his friend.

"Grady, what… what are you doing here?" Chris asked, collecting himself.

"I had the groundskeeper notify me if a stranger, especially one after closing, came to pay a visit," Grady admitted. "I didn't mean to disturb you."

"No, it's okay. I might have been stuck there forever if you hadn't," Chris said. "Not exactly safe for either of us to be here together."

"It's okay. We're away from view from any of the roads. The groundskeeper will alert me if anyone else pokes around. Satellite would be indefinitive, though surely raise suspicion," Grady said.

"This you?" Chris asked, pointing at the flowers.

"Vivian, mostly. I come by every evening I'm in town. The second family I visit when I return from a mission," Grady shrugged.

"Thank you," Chris said.

"They're family," Grady assured. "What are you doing here? You must have more than your share of targets on your back."

Chris nodded, "I do. I had to come. It may be my last opportunity."

"What do you mean? What's going on?"

Chris looked away and sighed, "One last mission. Gonna be a cluster."

Grady cocked his head, "These other missions... what's gone on in Jordan and Hussein at the Peace Conference... that you?"

"Among others."

"What brought you back stateside? Has to almost be more dangerous for you here than in chaotic countries that are easier to disappear in," Grady asked. His eyes widened, "Secretary of State Green didn't come clean with a sudden burst of conscience, she got a little nudge from a Marine."

"Former Marine," Chris muttered.

"Always a Marine brother to me, Gunny," Grady grinned.

"Semper fi, brother," Chris stood and placed a hand on his friend's shoulder.

"Can you tell me about this last mission?"

Chris paused and then shrugged, "I'm going after Mahaz Maher."

"Isn't he in Pakistani custody?" Grady asked and then laughed, "Not that that has stopped you before."

"I don't care where he is. I'm going to find him. See to it that justice is finally served," Chris said, his voice even.

"Yeah, probably gonna be a cluster," Grady nodded. "I wish the team was alongside you."

Chris looked at Grady, "Part of me does too. Part of me is grateful you're not. My job was to keep the team *out* of FUBAR situations."

"Then you shouldn't go yourself," Grady warned.

"It's not a should or shouldn't sort of thing," Chris glanced at the grave markers. "It's a have to sort of thing."

Grady nodded silently, and then said softly, "I get it, brother. You watch your six, just the same."

"Oorah," Chris said.

"Oorah," Grady repeated, his voice trailing. He couldn't help but think this would be the last time that he ever saw his friend.

Thirty Nine

Knowing that he was flying away from Breanna and Macy, from his country, for perhaps the last time, was hard for Chris. He couldn't imagine not calling America home, as much as he couldn't imagine not being with his wife and daughter.

The moment his feet hit Camp Green, he was pure focus, intent on the next mission. Porter greeted him as he entered the main building.

"Good to see you, Chris. Nice work with Secretary Green. Actions have consequences, leadership isn't exempt to that rule," Porter said as they walked toward the situation room.

"No, they're not, Porter. Good to see you, too," Chris said. He was glad to see Cait's smiling face, leaning over the table, pouring over a map with Jonas.

"Hey stranger!" Cait quipped.

"Cait, Jonas… good to see you both," Chris said as he entered the room. A glance at the map told him what they were working so hard on. He had reviewed those maps multiple times as a Raider. With a sigh, he slumped a bit, "Maher is in Afghanistan."

"Our intel team tracked him from the moment he left the Israeli holding facility. He landed in Pakistan, stayed two nights, and was shipped out in the dark of night on a black flight to Jalalabad. From there, a convoy moved through Kabul into no man's land. We were able to isolate the vehicles north of Mitarlam," Jonas replied.

Chris nodded, "I'm familiar with the area. Mountain, caves, deep bunkers…"

"Once in the underground system, he could be anywhere," Jonas looked concerned.

"But he won't be anywhere. He will be here," Chris pointed to the map.

Jonas looked confused, "How do you know?"

"Because my team looked for a bunker in that area. Based on what the intel team is showing, we were likely off by a click," Chris said. "This particular cell is known for its multi-regional connections, which is how Hussein and Naib worked. If Maher is their man, this would be the group he would be working with."

"Let's say you're right, there's no clean way in there, not without major air support and an entire army," Jonas frowned.

"A small or mid-sized group would struggle. A very small, highly effective team could get through," Chris suggested.

Jonas studied the map and considered the proposition while Fallon, Kinza, and Cara joined the group. "Based on the size of the convoy and their well-fortified location, they'll have both manpower and positional advantage. It's a suicide mission," Jonas concluded.

"I'll do it," Fallon raised his hand. "A two-man team dropped in from the north, not from the south as they'd expect would avoid preliminary exposure and conflict."

"I'm in," Kinza added.

"I'm in. Overwatch would provide a layer of support thwarting reinforcements and allow an opportunity for exfil," Porter agreed.

Cara scoffed, "What? You *know* I'm in. Can I have guns…no, missiles on the chopper?" Cara's eyes gleamed.

"I was *already* going," Cait shrugged.

Jonas stared at the map and then at the team. He couldn't risk the team on such a low probability mission. Chris could see it in his eyes.

Waving them off, Chris countered, "It's okay. He's right. It is a suicide mission. I can't put the team at risk."

The team pondered, each searching for a solution.

"Intel will pop up, we'll catch him outside the bunker," Cara suggested.

"Yeah, I mean, they didn't go through the trouble of dealing for him for nothing. They'll put him back in action and we'll get him then," Porter suggested.

Chris shuffled, "*I'm* still going. It's a solo mission. I just can't risk the team."

The team gawked at Chris.

"Chris…," Jonas started.

"I would love your help from a support status, but on the ground, in the bunker… the only chance is to slip inside discretely. It's easier for one man than a team," Chris suggested.

"Sure, maybe you get in, but getting out again…" Fallon shook his head. "It's impossible. Not without fighting your way out."

"If we could fight our way out, couldn't we fight our way in?" Cait asked.

Chris shook his head, "No. They would push deeper into their system of tunnels and disappear."

"Then wait!" Cait pleaded.

"My wife and baby girl's killer got away once. I can't let that happen again," Chris pressed.

"What do you need?" Jonas spoke up, long deliberating as the team chimed.

"Realtime satellite thermal scans of the area. If I miss someone on infil, I'm done. Maybe some gear, an air drop?" Chris shrugged.

Cara nodded.

Jonas agreed, "The moment you are in the bunker, your comms will be cut. You'll be on your own."

"I know," Chris acknowledged.

"What about exfil?" Porter asked.

"I'll try to get out, move higher into the mountains, call in for exfil by helo. If not, I'd wander towards the border, try and get into Pakistani airspace," Chris suggested.

Jonas recognized the exfil plan as hollow. Looking away for a moment, he exorcised his fondness for the man and looked instead at what he himself might do in the same situation. With a sigh, he relented, "Alright. We'll give you all the support we can and have Dragonfly standing by for exfil."

Porter started to protest and Cait's eyes widened, but Chris cut them off. "Thank you, Jonas. Everyone," Chris offered. "This needs to happen tomorrow. The longer we wait, the more likely I miss Maher moving out. I'll run over final plans with Jonas and Cara and I'll gear up."

Looking at the rest of the team, his affect was flat and telling. They were excused from the room. Each member passed by with a hand on Chris' shoulder, except for Cait. She glared at Chris from across the room and went around the table to avoid him on her way out.

Chris, Cara, and Jonas mapped out the infiltration plan with input from Angel and the intelligence team. When he was satisfied that he could at least make it to the bunker, Chris retreated to the supply room where he meticulously selected his gear for the mission.

Something was bothering him about the mission. He trudged his way through each detail of prep. He was driven to complete it, but he couldn't determine what was nagging at him.

He wasn't afraid of running a solo op. He wasn't afraid of dying, a dark part of him longed for an accelerated reunion with Breanna and Macy. There was something else.

In a similar way that he used to feel when he was doing what he needed to before a team mission, a vision popped into his head. Usually reserved for Breanna's indignant glare, Cait's exit from the situation room bore into him.

He understood the resistance to him running this op and running it on his own. The fact that these people cared about him and even more so, he for them, was a surprising byproduct of his being pulled into the rogue group.

Sighing, he hauled his gear over his shoulder and left the supply room. Heading to his bungalow, he knew he had just a few hours before he and Cara would take off for the Pakistani/Afghan border.

Passing Cait's bungalow, he paused. Looking past his own numbness, he recognized that Cait was sore with his insistence on the mission the way it was laid out. Dropping his gear at the foot of the stone path, he walked to her door. After a brief pause, he rapped his knuckles against the frame.

The sound of shuffling and an Irish accented mumbling was followed by an angry redhead staring through the head-sized crack she made in the door. "If you haven't come to tell me you changed your mind about a one-way mission, you best be gettin' on," Cait snapped.

"Can I come in?" Chris asked patiently.

Cait studied him for a minute, "Sure. Save me from waiting to cuss out your ghost."

Chris followed her in as the door closed behind them.

"Pour you a glass of whiskey? I understand the flight to Afghanistan is hell," Cait offered, waving her own glass in the air.

"Sure," Chris shrugged.

Cait poured a healthy splash into a glass and topped her own off. Handing it to Chris, she quipped, "I've been to many a wake, none where I could share a toast with the actual dead guy, though."

Chris set the glass down and addressed Cait squarely, "Look, I get it okay. And I'm not going to lie, I'm not afraid of death. I've welcomed a bullet from any one of the terror squads we faced if they were good enough. Take me out of this world without Breanna and Macy in it. Bring me back to them."

"You came here to tell me that? I already know you're running headfirst into a bullet," Cait scoffed.

"That's just it. I was. Something has been nagging me about this mission. I couldn't put my finger on it. Until you glared at me as you walked away," Chris said. His head dipped for a moment, "It's the same way I felt when I left Breanna when I was absorbed in prepping for a mission."

The room fell silent and still.

"I *am* okay with dying," Chris admitted. "But I *want* to come back."

Chris and Cait stood in front of one another. They were close enough that they could feel each other's breath. The spice of Cait's whiskey tickling Chris' nose. Their chests began to rise and fall at the same pace.

Chris licked his lips, slamming the entire three-fingered pour down his throat, he centered on Cait's eyes, "I can't promise I'll make it back. I can't. And I can't tell you what *this* is… I can't do that either."

Chris laughed in a whisper, "I know I'm not ready…for whatever…"

Focusing his eyes on Cait's her lips parting as she deciphered his message. Chris continued, "I am grateful to have met you and to have looked after one another…"

Cait's eyes grew cross, "Oh, shut the f…"

Chris' lips met hers before she could complete her curse. Cait dropped her glass to the floor, wrapping her arms around him, forcing his kiss to last longer. She wanted more. She also knew there was only so much that he could give her. Closing her eyes, she relished the closeness for a moment longer before pulling away.

"You make it back here, and we'll finish this conversation," Cait spat. Licking her lips, she softened, "I know this isn't easy. Just know… just know there are people that care for you."

Chris drank her words and nodded, "I don't have much heart left, if any. Whatever there is, it's… I care about you too."

"So, come back and not in a box," Cait snapped.

"I'll do what I can," Chris acknowledged. "Good night, Cait."

Cait watched Chris spin and walk away, pausing at the door, but continuing on without a second turn. She watched him grab his gear from the little stone walk outside of her bungalow and disappear into the night.

FORTY

The Titindare Ghar ridge rose above the road's end into the deep Afghani wilderness. A worn trail slipped under the trees, blocking most activity from image hungry satellites hovering above.

"X, the convoy vehicles are accounted for at the end of the road," Angel spoke into Chris' earpiece.

"Copy that. Good news, they are all still there," Chris said.

"Bad news, they are still *all* there," Angel emphasized.

"It was a nice quiet walk from the north," Chris said of the ruck he had taken from north of the suspected bunker.

"Thermal scans are clear in front of you until a hundred yards up slope. There I count a half dozen sentries forming a circle around the target area," Angel noted.

"We'll see if the front door is the only way in," Chris mumbled as he approached the area. Following a map of geological lines, the intel team had provided a rough idea of the structure of the tunnels leading to the bunker.

Chris looked for a natural skylight or vent leading into the bunker. Manmade vents with their anti-blast valves would be too small to slip through. Stopping two hundred yards out, he scanned the area. He couldn't recognize any formation in the terra that would indicate an opening.

"Front door it is," Chris muttered, pulling out his modified M14 Enhanced Battle Rifle. He chose the weapon for its all-around usefulness. He could mod it for close-quarters assault, use it as a carbine or modest sniping.

Slipping in the 22-inch barrel in favor of the 14, he attached his sniper scope. He considered the order of his targets. He knew once he initiated, it was game on. The entire bunker would know he was coming. He would have minutes to locate Mahaz Maher, assuming he could and assuming he wasn't killed early on in the search.

The other risk was, even if Chris wasn't shot, Maher might just slip deeper into the network of tunnels further out of

Chris' grasp. Screwing a suppressor to the end of the barrel, Chris readied. He might still be heard, but the sentinels would have a harder time pinpointing his location without muzzle flash.

As Chris set up his shots, he chuckled. The sentries were stationed in a pattern where each was relatively hidden in the terrain, but visible to one another. While they might see their comrade fall, making Chris work in greater haste, the advantage of finding a position where he could visibly sight each shooter was too good to be true.

"Angel," he whispered. "Please confirm the thermal scan."

"Copy, X. Hold," Angel called. "Thermal scan confirmed. There is a margin for error with the terrain, but that is all I see."

"Good copy, Angel. X engaging," Chris said.

Chris crept down the hill to the first sentry, paying more mind to avoid snapping twigs and crunching leaves than his target. Reaching the boulder the sentry used as his platform, Chris leapt. Wrapping a hand around the man's mouth, Chris fell backward, bringing the sentry with him. Chris slid his blade across the man's throat, killing him before they landed, but more importantly, preventing the slightest gasp from escaping his lungs. Rolling away, Chris wiped the blood off his blade on the fallen combatant's uniform and replaced it in its sheath.

Moving carefully to the boulder, Chris found an angle where two more sentries were visible. Resting his forearm on a rock to steady himself, Chris sighted on both combatants, calculating the shots. With a breath, he fired, dropping one, spinning, dropping the second.

Without pause, Chris rolled to the other side of the boulder. Again, he dove into a firing position. Sighting the furthest sentry and taking the shot. Swiveling his aim, he spied a second from that vantage, scrambling as the sentry saw his comrade fall. Before he could raise his arms, Chris dropped him.

Leaping on top of the boulder, Chris saved the most direct shot for last. Surprising the man by taking a direct line across the canyon, Chris sighted the sentry from a standing position just as the man's muzzle swung at Chris.

Firing twice, Chris dropped him before a trigger could be squeezed. Dropping to a knee, he spun in an arch around the area surrounding the cave entrance. "Angel, sentries down. I'm heading to the tunnel."

"Good copy, X. Thermal scans are consistent. You are on your own out there. Unfortunately, once in the cave, you're on your own. Godspeed, X. Angel out."

Chris slid down the slope to the cave entrance. A large supply door guarded the front while a smaller man-door provided easy entry for terror cell members. Chris leaned against the door, listening for movement.

His heart beat out of sequence for just a moment as the door pushed out and a man walked through, an unlit cigarette in his mouth. Chris grabbed a fist full of the man's shirt, yanking him completely free of the doorway. With his right, Chris plunged his combat blade into the man's throat.

The slightest gurgle left the man's lips before the cigarette dropped, the man following. Chris hauled the man to a bush, irreverently casting him aside. "So much for the fatwa, they were right, smoking *was* bad for you," Chris muttered.

Having already swapped out the smaller 14-inch barrel onto his assault rifle and eschewed the sniper scope for the faster target acquiring EOTech sight offering lowlight advantage, Chris slipped into the tunnel.

Closing the man-door behind him, Chris ducked into the deep shadows afforded by the wide spacing of poor lighting strung throughout the crude bunker. The mouth of the tunnel was filled with supply cases, providing Chris with ample cover. He preferred to use stealth as opposed to engaging in a gun battle for as long as he could.

Clad in black, his wrists, neck, and face covered in blackout face paint, Chris was very much a shadow himself. Slinking through the cave, he was able to push to the uncomfortable position of insertion where he was deeply positioned between armed combatants. Once a fight broke out, he would have to dodge bullets from both sides, a solo-op game ender.

Scanning further down the tunnel, as he squatted low in a shadow, he found the main interior access to the bunker. A pair of guards stood out front. Fighters and servants walking through the doors provided Chris a glimpse of what was inside. He counted at least half a dozen armed men lounging in that initial room, twice that in a procession walking past, among them, Mahaz Maher.

Out of emotion, Chris' heart pounded out another beat before his Raider Team training kicked in, leveling him to a calm state - as calm as one can get when they are about to engage in grossly lopsided firefight.

With a breath, Chris pushed forward. He wanted to enter that first room with as little notice as possible, which meant taking out the first two guards up close and personal without them shouting or firing at him.

As an unarmed worker passed by his scant cover, Chris struck. A hand around the man's mouth, his free arm wrapped around his throat. Pulling him back into the shadows, Chris squeezed hard and held the pressure until the man fell limp. Wasting no time, Chris slipped the loose *Perahan tunban* robe-like attire off of the worker and slipped it as best he could over his tactical gear.

Approaching forward, he hoped the poor lighting would obscure his dark painted face until he was within reach. Head bowed slightly, his eyes targeting both guards, Chris shuffled forward. With a Ka-bar in one hand and Strider folding knife in his other, Chris lashed out laterally, in a simultaneous attack on both guards. Catching one guard squarely in the throat, with a yank of his right hand, he severed the man's artery crumpling him to the floor holding his throat in suppressed gurgles.

Chris swung his focus to the second guard who was startled and distraught, but responsive. Chris didn't have to look up to know he had just missed. Pressing directly into the man, he slammed him into the wall, knocking the air out of him, giving him an opportunity to finish the task before an alarm could escape the man's lungs.

Peeling off the *tunban,* Chris took a large breath before hurling the door open. Using the brief glimpse he had of the men lounging, Chris cheated on his targeting. Moving left to right, he hit the man leaning against the wall sipping out of a cup. Two men on a sofa next to him fell next, in the center, a man pulled back the charging handle on his AK-47, Chris fired first. Swinging right, two men dove to opposite corners, fumbling with their rifles. Chris walked up and placed shots into each before they could target him.

Chris' mind spun. He had successfully breached the main bunker, now that shots were fired, it was game on.

FORTY ONE

The alarm and overwhelming commotion were immediate throughout the bunker. Shouts and commands in Arabic were heard preceding the familiar metallic clicks of weapons being chambered and magazines locked into place.

Chris set up an intentionally obvious trap at the interior bunker door with a pair of claymores staring at anyone eying entry. If the door was opened, they would detonate. Only a kamikaze run at the bunker would allow access behind Chris' back.

Feeling positive about his flank being largely covered, he did not feel exceptional about the unknown number of armed combatants between him and Maher or his now well-declared arrival.

Inserting a fresh magazine, he rolled his back to the first hall. A glance downrange was instantly met with AK fire towards his position, chafing at the concrete walls. Detecting three shooters, Chris dove to the floor to adjust his position, as he did, he lunged across the hallway not firing until he located a target, with a quick double-pull, he reduced his initial attackers to two.

Flipping up his thermal scope, he tossed a smoke grenade down the hall. Advancing, he pressed against a wall as blind fire filled the center of the corridor. Chris was able to calmly line up shots and walk past the first group of shooters.

Arriving at another door preceded by a gunner's nest, a barrage of bullets seared towards him the moment his shadow crested the hall. Hot steel found his right deltoid, tearing a bloody line across his arm.

Rolling out of the line of fire, Chris contemplated his plan of attack. The shooter and the pair he counted behind had an overwhelming positional coverage with solid cover, while Chris had a death tunnel with no cover to traverse.

The only idea Chris had was, he admitted to himself, one of the worst he had ever had. Placing a series of charges against the wall he was using for cover, he retreated down the hall. Ducking down, he detonated the blast. In the same motion, he launched himself back down the hallway, ignoring baseball-sized chunks of concrete shrapnel raining hail on him.

Unsure what his plan would provide, he dove to the ground, sliding next to a pile of concrete in the middle of the hallway. The explosion temporarily halted the barrage from downrange. Chris took the opportunity from his newly created, though scant, cover to take a single well-placed shot, hitting the machine gunner in the forehead before the remaining men fired shots peppering the pile of concrete rubble protecting Chris.

As one shooter took over the machine gunner duties, the other stalked Chris, waiting for his head to pop up to take an aimed shot. Freeing a flashbang from his vest, Chris launched it overhead. The blast rang through the tunnel, shaking even Chris who was prepared for it. Ignoring the pain and disorientation, Chris took a shot downrange, taking out the man with the assault rifle.

To Chris' dismay, the man on the heavy gun sprayed blind shots down the tunnel. Chris pressed flat to the floor as the barrage was incessant. "I think I might have made him mad," Chris muttered to himself, trying to keep himself pancaked to the ground.

The angry, non-stop spray of the heavy gun hit its limit. The gun stopped firing as the carbine continued to spin harmlessly. The moment Chris recognized the sound, he was leaping over the rubble and sprinting down the hall.

The man behind the gun finally realizing he was empty first moved towards adding a new feed. Recognizing that he did not have adequate time to reload, he drew his pistol. As he raised it, Chris unloaded two double-shot squeezes of his own trigger into the man.

Battered, bleeding, partially deaf and blind, Chris arrived at the door at the end of the hall. Pressing his ear, he couldn't hear anything. He couldn't detect any triggers around the door, though they may, and likely were, discrete on the other side for just this occasion.

Yanking the door open could immediately put an end to the mission and Maher would be free to roam the earth and levy harm against innocents. If Chris didn't open the door, Maher still got to walk. His choice was made for him, the consequences yet a mystery.

Stringing a pair of shape charges to either side of the door, Chris used the ballistic shield of the heavy machine gun for cover. Detonating the blast, Chris was up and over the barrier and through the door before it was entirely free from its hinges, the chunk of steel hitting the floor.

In his peripheral vision, Chris spied a pair of muzzles on either side of the doorway. Assault rifle pressed against his side for stability and pistol in his left hand, he fired simultaneous one-handed shots at the guards recovering from the explosion.

Stepping forward, Chris' scan shocked him. There were no other gunmen pointing muzzles at his face, just one man in the center of the room. Lounging casually in the middle of the bunker, Mahaz Maher sat, one arm over the back of a sofa, his legs crossed comfortably.

"Hello, my old friend. You are quite the resilient one. Well, here I am," Maher waved his hand in the air. Placing both arms in front of him, he held his wrists out for Chris. "Take me away. We'll see how long this incarceration lasts. I hope I get to go to Gitmo this time, The Israelis were… quite unkind to me." Maher wrinkled his nose as he recalled the information gathering techniques employed by the Israeli Mossad.

"Come on now, there is another platoon that is likely to engage from the bowels of the tunnel system at any moment. Things will get ugly when they arrive," Maher spat.

Chris stared at the terrorist assassin. The man's wicked smile tore at Chris' heart. He could picture Breanna in the driver's seat, glancing at Macy as they drove across the Stone Bay bridge. Maher's nasty grin in the backdrop.

"Yeah, that's not happening this time, *friend*," Chris snarled, snapping his pistol in position, firing a shot to the perfect center of Maher's forehead. Chris' glare continued to burrow into the terrorist. Stepping closer, Chris squeezed the trigger, keeping it pressed until the entire magazine emptied and the slide locked open, waiting for a new mag to be inserted.

Chris subconsciously locked a new mag into place, doing the same for his assault rifle. The sound of a pair of claymores detonating at the interior bunker door told him the fight was only just beginning.

Forty Two

Moving quickly, Chris knew his only shot, though razor thin, at making it out alive was to get to the exterior tunnel intersection before the platoon Maher threatened made their full arrival. If it was members of the platoon at the door detonating the claymores, it was already game over.

Chris sprinted down the hall. Seeing two armed men haul a man in a *tunban* out of the way, he understood. The terror cell soldiers forced one of the servant workers to open the door.

Turning over their shoulders, the faces of the men moving the body fell in horror as Chris sped towards them, his assault rifle at the ready. With a double squeeze each, Chris brushed by with scarcely a second glance.

Hearing the sound of the impending platoon down the intersecting hallway, Chris disregarded cover for speed. Facing the insurgents he had snuck by in the beginning of the assault head on, Chris sighted as he ran.

For every man that Chris hit, another gunman had opportunity to take aim. Chris felt the first bullet hit the ceramic plate, cracking a rib. Dropping another, Chris reeled from a second shot to his side. "Well, there's another rib," he gasped, ignoring the pain and challenge breathing.

Targeting another gunman left Chris vulnerable from the opposite side of the tunnel, a round from an AK burrowing just under his clavicle. Spinning him, Chris took desperate aim at another insurgent as a shot ripped through his thigh and another his opposite hip, yet another shattering another layer of ceramic in his vest, punishing his already painful chest and lungs.

Dropping to the ground, Chris kicked his boots into the floor of the cave, shoving him against a row of supply crates. Blood was seeping through his shirt, the shot above his vest leaving his left arm nearly useless. The shots to his leg and hip left him immobile.

Chris could hear a number of boots echoing down the tunnel and shouts announcing their presence as commands were levied as they merged with Maher's bunker system. Shooters lined up en masse to cue on Chris.

Surrounding him from the flank while the gunman at the entrance of the tunnel hunkered in wait, the foretold platoon took cover positions. Gunfire ripped through the cave, shattering supply boxes all around Chris. Shrapnel and bullet fragments showered onto his position.

As the combatants grew braver, a contingent pressed forward. Chris made the first few men pay for their boldness, but a second layer was able to advance their position with better angles to refute his cover. A shot ripped through Chris' right arm. Flattening to the floor, Chris dragged his barely operational body to a corner.

The move bought him a bit of fresh cover as well as opened up a firing lane for him. The advanced gunman exposed, Chris systematically took them out and forced their comrade's positional retreat. Orders in Arabic bellowed throughout the cave and Chris quickly understood. They were to push forward until he was dead, even at their own peril.

Chris pressed against his corner, half-conscious, loss of blood and overwhelming pain sending him into shock. His eyes flickered from inky blackness to flashes of the tunnel and the movement of the gunmen advancing towards him and their subsequent muzzle flashes to the faces of Breanna and Macy. His wife and daughter seemed to be calling to him. Waving for him to follow. He wanted to. He wanted to slip into sublime peace, put the world of chaos and violence behind him. Breanna seemed to turn with a warning, waving him back. In semi-lucidness, Chris turned. The first wave of advancing combatants was in front of him.

Chris nodded to the image of Breanna and fired. The first three men tumbled but were immediately replaced by three more. He fired. Exhausted. On fire and in pain. Wanting desperately to join Breanna and Macy.

Shots peppered his vest as the terrorists shot wildly as they ran towards him. Chris tried to raise his gun. It was so heavy. Firing once, he dropped a man. Firing again, he was rewarded with a hollow click. His mag was empty. Instinctively, he released the mag and patted his vest for a spare.

Before Chris could produce a fresh magazine, he listed to his side, spitting blood from his mouth. He lay there watching a series of boots rapidly approaching. He blinked. When his eyes reopened, he saw Macy's face. She was on the ground with him, grinning, encouraging him to come with her. Her tiny hand tugged at Chris' shirt for him to follow her.

Breanna strode forward, her calm presence such a stark contrast to everything in Chris' world since she passed, placed her hand on Macy's shoulder. Shaking her head softly, she beckoned her daughter.

Breanna kneeled next to her husband. The cave had gone silent. Only Breanna's words pierced his ears. They were not the words he expected to hear. "You're not done, baby. We'll wait for you. You need to go back."

Chris reached his hand out. He didn't understand. Breanna rose as she took Macy's hand. They began to make their way down the tunnel without him. Macy smiled and waved at her daddy and blew him a kiss while Breanna gave him a warm, reassuring smile. They disappeared into the abyss of the dark tunnel.

Chris blinked again. The boots in the tunnel were closer. He didn't know how he could fight. He could hardly move. He could barely remain conscious. He didn't understand why he was still there.

To his shock, the boots abruptly changed position. Flying horizontal to the ground, they were replaced with bodies and lifeless faces staring at him. From Chris' vantage, his weary face pressed down on the floor of the cave, it was a horror show as the bodies piled up.

His hearing ebbed in and out as his brain barely clung to functioning. Gunfire erupted from everywhere.

Immobile, Chris could only hear the chaos and see the body count grow. He was startled as a face slid into view and a hand laid on him. Cait's freckled face streamed with tears as she screamed for help.

Kinza slid into position on his knees and began assessing Chris, a med kit ripped open.

Porter, Fallon, and Jonas made a semi-circle around Chris as Kinza worked and Cait looked on. Kinza plunged a needle into Chris and as the plunger was pressed, Chris' mind went dark.

The team worked efficiently as Chris was prepped for extraction. Fallon led the charge, cutting through the ranks. Cait, satisfied there was nothing more they could do for Chris at that moment, inserted herself into the firing line, using her rage to rain hell on any insurgent who dared to approach the mouth of the cave.

Porter ran sentry as Jonas and Kinza lifted Chris and began the retreat out of the tunnel. Cait and Fallon walked backward as they eyed targets downrange. When Jonas and Kinza had Chris clear of the cave, Fallon nodded to Cait. Together, they turned and ran in pursuit of their teammates. When they reached within steps of the open exit door, Cait pressed the detonator she had strapped to her vest. The entire cave leading to the bunker erupted into a violent blast, a wall of flame and a concussive blast rocked the tunnel. The walls and ceiling trembled until the hillside collapsed on itself, strangling the cave and anyone in it.

Outside, Cara's approach was perfectly timed as she hurtled the helicopter between the ridges of the Afghan mountains. Halting the helo feet off of the ground, Jonas and Kinza wrestled Chris on board while the rest of the team leapt into the space around him.

Pulling back on the stick, Cara rocketed the helicopter away from the scene and made a full-speed sprint out of Afghanistan.

Forty Three

Chris blinked his eyes slowly. The light grew until it was so bright that he winced. The world began to take shape around him as his vision came into focus.

A pair of green eyes surrounded by freckles lay next to him. Staring at him. Eyes wet from anxious tears, blinked the salty liquid away.

"I saw you. I saw you before I…" Chris grimaced as he moved.

"Before you went unconscious," Cait said.

"What the hell happened?" Chris asked.

"Well, you were clearly getting your arse kicked," Cait started.

Chris swallowed, "No, how did you happen to be there?"

A voice boomed from the door to Chris' room, making Cait sit back from Chris' side.

"Looks like our hero is back in one piece," Jonas stood, smiling alongside Chris' bed, more faces popping up beside him.

"How did you guys happen to be there?" Chris choked, readily accepting a bottle of water handed to him.

"The entire team made it happen. After you left, Cait burst in like a hurricane, and frankly, the entire team backed her. They all threatened to leave if they weren't greenlit for the operation," Jonas explained.

"Even Fallon?" Chris winced as even the slightest movement sent a shock wave of pain through his body.

"Even me, sport. Not a fan of suicide missions," Drake Fallon admitted. "But I am even less a fan of leaving a teammate out there on their own. We had to bring you home."

"You were inches from death, my friend," Kinza sighed.

"He saved your life," Porter added.

"You all did," Chris said.

"I got to use rockets!" Cara gleamed, leaning in past Porter's shoulder.

"You did?" Chris smiled.

"Yes, while I made a loop waiting for exfil, I located the entrance to the other bunker that linked to your tunnel. I lit it up almost as well as Cait's work," Cara nodded joyously.

"The Afghan government is taking credit for 'shutting down a terror cell' in the eastern mountains," Jonas declared.

"Did you get him?" Cait asked impatiently.

Chris nodded, "I got him."

"So, what now? Your mission is over," Porter said, his voice revealing his trepidation.

"I don't know. I think we completed what I signed up for," Chris said. "I honestly never pictured being alive after it was all done."

Jonas leaned in with keen interest, "If it's any interest to you, Anya called. She's gotten into a spot of trouble with a… *sensitive* shipment missing off of the coast of Somalia."

Chris grimaced.

The team doctor strode into the room to check Chris' monitors, "Perhaps once he heals from the broken ribs, punctured lung, multiple surgeries to remove bullet fragments, repaired ligaments and sutured arteries, you can discuss his ability to chase after Somali pirates."

"Perhaps," Jonas nodded. Corralling the team, he prodded them out of the room. "Let's let him heal, *then* we can pepper him with reasons to stay on the team."

As they left, with the doctor and his notes in tow, only Cait remained.

"How about you?" Chris asked.

"How about me, what?" Cait cocked her head.

"Are you remaining on the team?"

She squinted before answering, "Depends. They're nice and all, but there is only man that I trust to have my back."

"Thanks for having mine."

Cait looked cross, her celestial green eyes stinging with tears, "I thought you were going to die. I've done some crazy things, but that was a foolish mission. "

"I had to," Chris didn't apologize.

Cait spun as fear, pain, and frustration surpassed the capacity of her emotional dam, exploding into a rare torrent of tears from the diamond-strong woman.

Lashing out, Chris grabbed her arm. Ignoring the pain, he lifted himself upright on the edge of the recovery room bed and pulled her close so that they were eye level.

Cait angrily swiped at her tears, embarrassed by their uncharacteristic appearance.

"I had to take Maher down. I had to close that door. It was a pit to my soul. It was a chapter of my life I had to put to rest, one way or another. It was a bit against the odds, but I told you had I *wanted* to make it back," Chris looked directly into the emerald pools that tried to dart away from his eyes but were drawn in.

"I saw them. I saw Breanna and Macy while I laid on the floor of that cave. I thought I was going to die. I thought they had come to take me with them," Chris said, his own eyes welling with moisture.

"Breanna, she wanted me to go on," Chris said, his voice shaking.

"Most women would," Cait said.

"I'm not sure it meant with another woman," Chris wavered.

Cait grinned, "*Every* woman knows a man needs help and can't survive on their own. I know I would want *my* man taken care of in my absence."

Cait looked deeply into Chris' eyes, "And every woman will also be clear, 'Oh, I'm taking him back when the time comes,' but I'd feel good that he was as whole as he could be until we were together again."

Leaning forward, Chris gently wrapped his hand softly around the back of her head and pulled her forward until her lips met his.

They didn't know how long they were locked in their emotional embrace, when the sound of a hand clapping against the doorjamb caught their attention. Peeling back from one another, they found a grinning Porter leaning into the room. "This mean you're staying on as part of the team?"

Cait and Chris looked at each other before looking back at Porter. In unison, they declared, "Perhaps!"

Made in the USA
Columbia, SC
09 June 2024

36394834R00297